Marriage Arrangements

**For better, for worse,
for convenience...or for love?**

By Request™

Marriages by Arrangement

A MARRIAGE HAS BEEN ARRANGED
by
Anne Weale

TO TAME A PROUD HEART
by
Cathy Williams

NEVER A BRIDE
by
Diana Hamilton

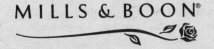

MILLS & BOON®

MILLS & BOON and MILLS & BOON with the Rose Device are registered trademarks of the publisher. Harlequin Mills & Boon Limited, Eton House, 18-24 Paradise Road, Richmond, Surrey, TW9 1SR

MARRIAGES BY ARRANGEMENT
© by Harlequin Enterprises II B.V., 2000

A Marriage Has Been Arranged, To Tame a Proud Heart and *Never a Bride* were first published in Great Britain by Harlequin Mills & Boon Limited in separate, single volumes.

A Marriage Has Been Arranged © Anne Weale 1997
To Tame a Proud Heart © Cathy Williams 1996
Never a Bride © Diana Hamilton 1995

ISBN 0 263 82417 9

06-0007

Printed and bound in Spain by Litografia Rosés S.A., Barcelona

Anne Weale was still at school when a women's magazine published some of her stories. At twenty-five she had her first novel accepted by Mills & Boon®. Now, with a grown-up son and still happily married to her first love, Anne divides her life between her winter home, a Spanish village ringed by mountains and vineyards, and a summer place in Guernsey, one of the many islands around the world she has used as backgrounds for her books.

A MARRIAGE HAS
BEEN ARRANGED
by
ANNE WEALE

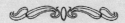

CHAPTER ONE

THE last place Holly would have expected to meet Pierce Sutherland again was at half past six on a dark, chilly autumn morning outside New Covent Garden Flower Market, long since moved from its original *My Fair Lady* location near the famous opera house to an ugly modern building on the south side of the Thames.

Holly, obsessively punctual and usually too early for everything, had been the first person to join the organiser at the rendezvous outside Gate Four.

Now about twenty people, including several shyly smiling Japanese ladies who didn't appear to speak English, were drinking hot coffee provided by the friendly young woman organiser with a clipboard and list of everyone who had booked for 'A Guided Tour of Covent Garden with a Champagne Breakfast and Flower Demonstration'.

A luxurious, chauffeur-driven car glided to a halt a few yards away. A tall man stepped out on the offside, surveying the group of coffee-drinking women with the same arrogant stare that Holly remembered from the last time she had seen him, five years ago.

What in the world was *he* doing? she wondered. Her heart gave an involuntary lurch in case he recognised her. Not that it was very likely. He hadn't changed, but she had. She was a different person from the nineteen-year-old who had deliberately tested his sense of humour and found him totally lacking in the all-important aspect of a man's character.

'Never lose your heart to anyone unless they have a good sense of humour,' her father had warned her, in one of their last discussions about life and love. 'Watch out you don't get involved with a pompous ass. There are a lot of them about.'

Professor Nicholson had smiled as he'd said it, but his warning had been a serious one. He himself, after losing his first wife when Holly was three, had made a bad error of judgement in marrying her stepmother, the female equivalent of a pompous ass.

He knew it. His daughter knew it. His colleagues and friends knew it. Only the second Mrs Nicholson was unaware of it. Their relationship was not unlike that of Mr and Mrs Bennet in *Pride and Prejudice*: an erudite man bound to a pea-brained woman whose younger daughters were as silly as she.

But Chiara, the eldest of Holly's stepsisters, although not a clever girl, was both beautiful and sweet-natured. Together from early childhood, she and Holly had grown as close as real sisters. Holly saw herself in the role of Elizabeth Bennet with Chiara as the lovely Jane Bennet.

So far their lives had not reached the happy conclusion of Jane Austen's famous novel. Holly had yet to meet anyone as compellingly attractive as Mr Darcy and Chiara was in a relationship unlikely to lead to permanent happiness. Their lives, so much freer and fuller than the stiflingly restricted lives of Jane Austen and her contemporaries, were still beset by the same basic problem: how to find Mr Right in a world full of Mr Wrongs.

Five years ago, Chiara had thought Pierce Sutherland was her Mr Right. Holly had always had reservations about him, and her fears had proved correct. Three months after taking Chiara to bed, Pierce had replaced her with another beautiful girl. The end of the affair had left Chiara with many generous mementoes of his transient passion for her, and it was an exaggeration to say that he left her heartbroken. Not long after their breakup she had been involved in another affair.

But that didn't alter the fact that Pierce had behaved like a rat, confirming Holly's instinctive distrust for him.

The other passenger in the stately Rolls-Royce was an elegant Japanese lady who seemed to be someone of importance, judging by the excited twittering among her compatriots. She waited for Pierce to come round the back of the car to join her.

When he did, the top of her sleekly coiffed hair was barely level with his chest and her pale, exquisite complexion and delicate features were a striking contrast to his tanned skin and rugged bone structure. Yet they did have something in common. She was dressed in a reversible cashmere shawl draped over a soft wool suit which undoubtedly had a top designer's label stitched inside it. Her leather boots and her bag were of the finest quality. She had style, and so did Pierce. Even Holly couldn't deny him that. Today he was wearing black trousers and a black cashmere turtle-neck sweater under a pale grey jacket that matched his cold light grey eyes, which were in striking contrast to his black hair and eyebrows.

By birth an American, by inclination an Anglophile, Pierce had come to England as a Rhodes scholar at Oxford University. He had never returned to his own country, preferring to have his main base in London and two or three *pieds-à-terre* in other parts of Europe.

Unlike Holly's father, who had spent his life on research projects of benefit to humanity, Pierce was a selfish man who used his brains for his own ends. When Chiara had met him, he had already been rich. By now he must be rolling. Whether he did a whit of good with his money, apart from giving lavish presents to his popsies, Holly was inclined to doubt.

Now, his hand under his companion's elbow, he steered her towards the organiser. While she exchanged gracious bows with her compatriots and the Englishwomen, he had a low-voiced conversation with the girl in charge of the tour.

Holly was too far away to hear what was said but, while his attention was focused on the organiser, she was able to study his face, looking for evidence that his sybaritic life-style was beginning to tell on him. Surprisingly, she could see none of the usual signs of high living. His jawline was still clear-cut, his waistline as lean and taut as it had been the first time she'd met him. He must be thirty-five now, but looked as fit and tough as men ten years his junior whose lives were extremely active, not spent, as his was, behind a desk doing deals. The expression 'fat cat' had been coined for men like Pierce Sutherland. Yet he didn't fit the image it conjured up. Physically, there was nothing soft, sleek or visibly decadent about him.

After he had dumped Chiara, Holly had forced herself to forget about him. It had been surprisingly difficult. He was one of those people of whom it could truly be said once seen, never forgotten. But she hadn't thought about him recently and the last thing she wanted was to renew their acquaintance. She was still eyeing him with disfavour when the demonstrator arrived.

'Good morning, ladies,' she said loudly, ignoring Pierce's presence. 'As there are thirty of you, we're going to split you into two groups. While I'm showing one group round, Lucinda will take the rest of you to the shops selling accessories. Then we'll change over.' She began to count heads.

To Holly's relief, the outcome of this exercise was that she was in Lucinda's group and Pierce and his companion were in Mrs Challoner's group.

Inside Gate Four, the market was revealed as a huge hangar-like space divided into blocks by a grid arrangement of wide aisles. Suspended from the centre of the roof was a big blue clock with a bell above it. Mrs Challoner's group went in one direction, Lucinda's in another.

Her circuit of the shops selling many kinds of baskets and vases, reels of plastic ribbon, florists' wire and Christmas garlands and decorations was over some time before Mrs Challoner had concluded her tour of the flower and plant stands.

While Lucinda's group were wandering about, waiting their turn to go with her, a woman in a red jacket said to Holly, 'I wonder who the tall guy is? Do you suppose he's a bodyguard? The Japanese person with him looks as if she might be Mrs Mitsubishi or Mrs Toyota…one of their multimillionaires' wives. Whoever she is, the guy with her speaks fluent Japanese.'

'How do you know that?' asked Holly.

'I passed them just now,' said Red Jacket, with a gesture at the aisle intersecting the one where they were standing. 'I heard him translating for her…with the other Japanese listening in. I'm surprised they come to a thing like this if they can't speak English.'

'Perhaps they can understand it better than they speak it,' said Holly. 'They may be married to businessmen and have time on their hands while their husbands are attending meetings.'

When it was time for the groups to change leaders, this took place without Holly being noticed by Pierce.

Considering that he was notorious for his roving eye, and that, apart from Lucinda, she was the only young woman in either group, she found it a tad deflating that he hadn't even given her a glance. But the parts of her which might have caught his eye—her legs and her figure—weren't shown to best advantage by the warm clothing they had been advised to wear. In navy blue trousers and a yellow foul-weather jacket over a bulky sweater over a long-sleeved T-shirt, she had no visible shape, and her face had never been her fortune. There was nothing really wrong with it. Her skin was clear, her eyes large, her good teeth the result of a healthy diet and good dentistry. But even when she was made-up and dressed to kill she wasn't a knockout like Chiara.

'Pleasant' and, possibly, 'nice' were the words she felt people would use if asked to describe her. She didn't merit the superlatives applied to her stepsister, nor did it bother her. Holly had never longed to be beautiful. She was comfortable with the way she was. Her mother hadn't been a beauty but her father had fallen in love the first time he'd seen her, and been desolated by her death. Someday, Holly hoped, someone would feel that way about her. Someone good, with decent moral values—not a womanising beast like Pierce.

The room where they were to have breakfast was up a staircase leading to the first-floor gallery.

It was an L-shaped room with a circular table in the angle of the L and several long tables filling the rest of the space. As soon as everyone was seated, staff began going round with bottles of champagne and jugs of chilled orange juice for those who wanted the wine in the form of Buck's Fizz or what two Americans present called 'mimosas'.

Holly preferred her champagne neat. As she had come

by taxi, having stayed overnight at Chiara's flat, to which she would return for lunch before catching a train back to Norfolk where she was living and working, she didn't have to restrict herself to one glass like those who had come here by car.

Pierce was seated with his back to her at a table which, apart from him, was exclusively Japanese. He was holding forth in that language and evidently telling a joke for suddenly there was an outburst of laughter, not the sound made by Europeans but a gentle tinkle of titters as all the dark eyes gleamed with merriment and ivory hands covered their owners' mouths.

After her first surprise that Pierce should speak their language, Holly realised it was probably not because he was drawn to Japan by its culture but because of its power as a trading nation. The making of money was his principal interest. Very soon, so she had heard, Japan would be in control of all the world's biggest and best electronics industries. No wonder he wanted the advantage of being fluent in that language.

As she ate croissants and crumpets and took a minor part in the conversation at her table, her gaze was repeatedly drawn to the broad shoulders and tanned quarter profile of the only male in the room, apart from a waiter serving coffee.

When most people had finished eating, Marisa Challoner rose to begin her demonstration.

'I suggest that those of you sitting with your backs to me should turn your chairs round rather than craning over your shoulders,' she began.

Holly had no need to move because from where she was sitting she had a good view of the demonstration table. But to her slight alarm she saw Pierce changing his position. From now on he would only have to turn his head a little to the left to be looking directly at her. She could only hope his role as an interpreter would keep his attention fixed on Mrs Challoner.

As she opened a small exercise book and prepared to make notes, Holly debated resting one elbow on the table and shielding her face with her hand. Then she chided herself for being stupid. Of course he wouldn't recognise her. They had met only once, at that deadly stuffy dinner party when, according to her stepmother, she had behaved disgracefully, proving herself to be both bad-mannered and childish.

Actually, apart from Mrs Nicholson, Chiara and Pierce, everyone had either roared with laughter or been convulsed with giggles. But he hadn't seen the joke. She could still remember the icy look in his eyes and the unamused set of his mouth.

The demonstration held everyone mesmerised by the clever way in which, with unpromising materials, Marisa Challoner created an arrangement worthy of a luxurious drawing room. As she worked, she chatted about her most exciting commissions. The five-hundred-pound bouquet to be sent to a film star. The recording star's lavish wedding for which, out of a million-dollar budget, a hundred thousand dollars had been allocated for flowers. The summer cruise in a millionaire's private yacht which she had been asked to decorate with flowers worthy of the haute couture clothes worn by the guests for dinner.

It was when, at the end of her talk, Mrs Challoner looked round the room and asked, 'Any questions?' that Holly forgot about keeping a low profile and was one of the people to raise a hand.

Before she had time to reconsider this rash act, she had caught Mrs Challoner's eye.

'Yes, what's your question?'

Stating it, Holly knew she was now engaging the attention of the one person in the room whose notice she had wanted to avoid. Increasingly aware of a pair of ice-chip grey eyes focused on her face, she scarcely heard a word of Mrs Challoner's answer to her query.

When, during the next question, she sneaked a quick glance at Pierce, he was still watching her. As their eyes met, he inclined his head, a clear signal that he had recognised her and would come over when the proceedings finished.

A succession of eager questions gave her ten minutes to brace herself for the encounter. She wondered what he would say. Perhaps he would ask about Chiara. As photographs of her stepsister were often in the gossip sections of the glossies and the tabloids, he could hardly fail to know that his affair with her had led on to other relationships of an equally ephemeral nature. In Holly's opinion he had set Chiara on the road to her present life of reckless pleasure-seeking with other people picking up the bills. Most of them older men. Some of them married.

Holly was repelled by her stepsister's way of life. It caused her almost as much pain as if Chiara were hooked on drugs. They had argued abut it endlessly, Chiara refusing to see why she shouldn't make the most of her one asset, her looks.

Around her, people were putting on coats and agreeing it had been a fascinating experience, well worth the cost.

'It's been a long time,' said Pierce, looming over her. 'How are you, Holly?'

She was astonished that he remembered her name, even if it was an unusual one. 'I'm well... And you?' she responded, with frigid politeness.

'Very well, thanks. Are you living in London now?'

'I came up specially for this. I'm based in Norfolk.'

'Are you married?'

She shook her head.

'Working?' he asked.

'I'm a garden designer.'

'It must be a satisfying job…providing you can get enough commissions to keep you going. Has the economic downturn been hard on you? Or do you work for a firm sufficiently well-established to survive the hard times?'

'I work for myself. I'm surviving. How about you? Still wheeling and dealing?' She couldn't disguise her contempt for a life spent manipulating the profits of other people's hard work.

'You could say that. Not quite in the same way as when Chiara and I were together. How is she? Still a playgirl, or has she settled down now?'

'It was you who made her a playgirl.' Holly hadn't meant to start a row with him here, but his casual enquiry riled her, reviving the impotent animosity she had felt towards him before.

'I wouldn't say that,' Pierce said equably. 'Chiara had several amorous adventures before I came on the scene. A girl with her looks was bound to attract a lot of men. She knew the score. You were the one with romantic illusions about life.'

There being no one close to them, she said in a low, angry voice, 'Considering we hardly spoke to each other, I consider that statement a bloody impertinence.'

It was rare for her to use swear words, but the bold way he had confronted her, as if expecting a welcome, made her furious. She longed to cut him down to size.

He said, 'Chiara often talked about you. She was worried that you would be hurt…that you weren't equipped to cope with people who didn't share your ideals. She felt losing your mother very young, and then your father, had made you vulnerable. I didn't agree. I thought you sounded tougher than you looked.'

'Streetwise enough to see through you,' she retorted. 'I knew you would ditch Chiara as soon as she began to bore you. I didn't like you then, Mr Sutherland, and I don't want to know you now. I'm amazed you have the gall to approach me. If you had a shred of conscience, you would have slunk out of here with your tail between your legs.'

Then, as she was about to add a frosty 'Excuse me' his Japanese friend appeared at his elbow. Speaking perfect English with hardly any accent, she said, 'I am ready to leave when you are, Pierce. Perhaps we can give a lift to your friend. They say it is raining outside now.'

When Pierce introduced them, politeness forced her to mask her annoyance with him while she spoke to Mrs Shintaro.

'Did you come here by car or taxi, Miss Nicholson?' the older woman enquired.

Holly was tempted to lie. But if it was raining heavily she didn't want to get soaked looking for a cruising taxi in an area where there might not be many, if any, for hire.

The previous afternoon she had been to the Bankside Gallery to see an exhibition of paintings of gardens. It, too, was south of the river, on the far side of Blackfriars Bridge. Afterwards, outside the gallery, an elderly lady walking with the aid of sticks had been almost in tears because of the dearth of taxis to take her back to the West End. Afraid of being mugged, she had begged Holly to stay with her. When, after a long wait, a taxi had finally appeared, she had insisted on giving Holly a lift in it. Now, in spite of her reluctance to prolong the encounter with Pierce, perhaps it made sense to accept a lift in Mrs Shintaro's limousine.

Five minutes later, sharing the back seat of the limousine with Mrs Shintaro while Pierce sat beside the driver, Holly was glad she had. The rain was bucketing down, and as they crossed Vauxhall Bridge she saw a pedestrian's umbrella blown inside out by the wind gusting down the river.

'It was kind of Pierce to come with me for, although I speak English well, with any technical subject there are always unfamiliar terms,' said Mrs Shintaro. 'He is a brilliant linguist and, as you may have noticed, was a great help to my compatriots whose English was not very good.'

'I thought it brave of them to come. What did think of the demonstration?' Holly asked. 'Mrs Challoner's way of doing flowers is so different from ikebana.'

'You know about ikebana?' Mrs Shintaro looked surprised.

'I don't know much,' said Holly. 'Only what I read in a book by Shusui Komoda.'

Pierce turned to join the conversation. 'Holly tells me she's now a garden designer, Fujiko. The last time we met, five years ago, she was at college and I was dating her sister who is two years older.'

'You make it sound like a boy-and-girl romance,' Holly said coldly. 'It wasn't like that and you know it. You were thirty to her twenty-one, and you seduced her.'

She hadn't meant to revile him in front of Mrs Shintaro and the driver, but the angry accusation came out before she could stop it.

'I didn't seduce her,' Pierce said calmly. 'That was done in the back of a car by some upstanding young guy called Matt, or it may have been Mike. He enjoyed it. She didn't…and for a fortnight afterwards she went through hell, thinking she might be pregnant. With me she knew where she stood, she had a good time and she ran no risk of pregnancy.' Smiling slightly, he turned to the older woman. 'I hope these intimate details don't shock you, Fujiko, but this may be my only chance to correct Holly's misapprehensions.'

'I have lived in the West too long to be shocked or surprised by anything,' she said mildly. 'Is it true you treated your girlfriends unkindly when you were younger?'

'On the contrary, I was exceptionally nice to them. If you were to ask Chiara, I'm sure she'd tell you she had a very good time with me. We went to the Seychelles together. I gave her a Cappuchino sports car. We attended a lot of parties where she could show off the clothes charged to my account. Just before we called it a day, I bought her a ring she wanted.

'Chiara never gave me any presents,' he added drily. 'Except herself, of course. But apart from her face and her body she didn't have much to offer. Her general knowledge was limited. She had very few opinions. It was like making conversation with a rather dim fifteen-year-old. She may have improved since then, but five years ago I found her seriously boring.'

'That's vile of you,' Holly exploded. 'I've never heard a more disgusting example of blatant MCPiggery.' She turned to the woman beside her. 'You may not know the expression. MCP means male chauvinist pig and Pierce has to be the king of them. Would you please ask your driver to stop and let me get out? Another minute in this car and I'm liable to lose my temper.'

'No, no, it's raining too hard. You will be soaked to the skin,' said Mrs Shintaro. 'I have a better idea. We will all go to my apartment where you two can quarrel in private and get to the bottom of this matter. For I have to tell you, Miss Nicholson, your description of Pierce does not match *my* knowledge of him. My late husband, who was a good judge of character, thought very highly of Pierce. He has qualities not often found in Americans and Europeans.

Whatever happened with your sister was some time ago. He would not treat her badly now. Of that I am certain.'

Ignoring Pierce and forcing herself to speak quietly, Holly said, 'I'm sorry you've been involved in this clash between us. It was bad luck our paths crossed again. But I'm sure Pierce couldn't care less what I think of him. I don't like him and never shall. If your husband did and you do, then I hope he won't ever let you down.'

Diplomatically changing the subject, Mrs Shintaro said, 'I'm interested to hear you are a garden designer. England and Japan are both famous for their gardens, although, of course, they are very different in style. Where did you train for your profession?'

It was difficult to resist the warmth of her interest. She fixed her liquid dark eyes on Holly's face as if she were genuinely eager to have her question answered.

'I took a course at Denman's,' said Holly. 'It's a beautiful garden in Sussex where a well-known gardening writer has set up a school of garden design. After I'd got my diploma, I won a national competition for garden design and that led to two commissions. In the early stages, there's a lot of luck involved. But I had secretarial skills to fall back on if things went badly. I could always earn my living as a temp. That's someone who does office work on a temporary basis,' she explained.

'You sound very practical and sensible, but you must also be artistic. All the great gardeners are artists. Who has inspired you? Whose work do you most admire?' asked Mrs Shintaro.

This was a difficult question to answer without knowing how much, if anything, the Japanese woman knew of the history of English gardening and its most famous practitioners. But it sooned emerged that Fujiko Shintaro was far more knowledgeable than a great many English people and had visited many of the finest gardens in Europe.

Their conversation flowed with unexpected smoothness. Had it not been for Pierce's presence, Holly would have relaxed and enjoyed talking to one of the most interesting people she had ever encountered. She had always been drawn to the Japanese and sensed that in Mrs Shintaro she was privileged to meet someone special from whom, in other circumstances, she could have learnt much of value to her.

It seemed the liking was mutual, for, when the car drew up outside a canopied doorway in an elegant street not far from Grosvenor Square, Mrs Shintaro said, 'If you are not in a hurry, I would like you to see some paintings in my apartment. My driver will take Pierce home now and when we have finished talking he will take you wherever you wish to go.' To Pierce she added, 'We shall see each other at Catrina's opening on Friday. Thank you for coming with me this morning.'

He turned to her, smiling. 'It's always a pleasure to be with you, Fujiko.' His smile disappeared as he focused on Holly. 'Give my regards to Chiara when next you see her. I should be surprised if she shares your feelings about me. Try to be less judgemental, Holly. The first time we met, I liked you very much. Now you seem rather priggish...not an attractive characteristic.'

His sardonic tone made her livid. For the first time in her life, she experienced a powerful impulse to apply her fist to someone's face with all the force she could muster.

But Mrs Shintaro was already alighting from the car. Repressing her anger, Holly moved along the seat to be ready to step out after her.

When Pierce said, 'Goodbye,' she ignored him.

*   *   *

Fujiko Shintaro's penthouse apartment was the most luxurious place Holly had ever seen.

'Before I take you on a tour of my pictures, let's have some coffee, shall we?' her hostess suggested. 'But first you may like to wash your hands.'

She took Holly to a beautifully appointed cloakroom and left her to take off several layers of clothing made unnecessary by the central heating.

Among the many works of art which Holly saw during her time at the flat, one she particularly liked was a large bronze hand embellished with an elaborate bracelet or cuff and having a strange design engraved on the palm.

'Is this Japanese?' she asked, admiring it where it stood, the palm upturned, on a tabletop of thick glass.

'No, that was found in Nepal by my grandson,' said Mrs Shintaro, smiling. 'He has fallen in love with the mountains of the Himalaya. He noticed the hand in a Nepalese market. It was being used as a container for screws. He thought I would like it and bought it for me. It is one of my dearest possessions because he and I are very close. His mother was my youngest daughter. She married an American. They both were killed in a tragic accident when Ben was only eight years old. I did my best to comfort him and later, when I lost my husband, he did the same for me. It was through him that we met Pierce, who has a similar hand he also found in Nepal.'

When Holly made no comment, she went on, 'Pierce is also mad about mountains. With some men, they are a passion as powerful as love or religion.' She paused. 'If your sister doesn't feel any anger towards Pierce, why must you dislike him so strongly, Holly? Anger is a corrosive emotion. To hate someone for a long time is not good for the soul.'

'I haven't done that,' said Holly. 'Until today I had almost forgotten his existence. I *was* angry years ago, but you can't boil with rage indefinitely. The fact remains that even if he wasn't the first, it was Pierce who made Chiara realise her beauty was…well, to put it bluntly, a marketable commodity. Since her affair with him, her life has been a succession of liaisons with rich men. She doesn't love them. She uses them, the way Pierce used her. Wouldn't you feel as I do if he had done that to your daughter?'

Mrs Shintaro nodded. 'I'm sure I should feel very angry. How did your parents react?'

Holly explained that Chiara had only one parent—a mother not noted for her wisdom. When she had filled in their background, she said, 'Perhaps Pierce is a split personality who lives the way bigamists do, keeping different aspects of himself in separate compartments. He may not parade his girlfriends in front of his other friends.'

'It's possible, but I doubt it. He appears to have an unusually open nature. He often says things other people find shocking…as he did this morning. He was very frank about his relationship with your sister.'

'Egotistically frank!' said Holly. 'He sounded proud of himself…as if giving Chiara a car and taking her to the Seychelles made everything all right. The man has no morals at all. To him, women are commodities, not equals.'

'My views on equality are naturally different from yours,' said Mrs Shintaro. 'We are of different generations and cultures. All I can say is that to earn Pierce's respect a young woman would have to have exceptional qualities, because he—' She broke off as her Japanese manservant entered the room. He bowed before delivering a message.

Mrs Shintaro answered him in Japanese before turning back to Holly. 'My butler has reminded me that I have a luncheon engagement, which will be a great deal less enjoyable than lunching with you. However, I hope there'll be other opportunities. Do you come to London often?'

'I sometimes stay with my sister when she's at a loose end. She could come and stay with me, but she isn't keen on the country,' said Holly as they crossed the room.

'I should like to meet you again,' said her hostess. 'I'm interested in young people and especially in those, like yourself, who have chosen unusual careers. If you'll write your address in my visitors' book, we can keep in touch.'

On the train back to Norfolk, Holly wondered what Fujiko Shintaro would have said about Pierce had her butler not intervened.

She spent most of the journey thinking about him and about the old saying that a leopard never changed its spots. Anyway, just because their paths had crossed this morning, it didn't mean they would do so again. His world and hers were poles apart. Nor did she think it likely that Mrs Shintaro would keep in touch with her.

Remembering her mention of her grandson, Holly wondered what Ben was like. Often people with mixed blood were exceptionally good-looking, combining the most attractive features of both the races in their genetic make-up. Having American blood in him, he would probably be much taller than his mother and his grandparents, but perhaps retain the subtle ebony-ivory colouring that Holly had always found attractive, especially in babies—dear little solemn-faced bundles who, when sometimes she passed one in a pushchair, she felt an impulse to scoop up and cuddle.

Nowadays, merely tickling a stranger's baby under the chin was liable to be misinterpreted. But at least one could still make friendly overtures to other people's cats and dogs without being eyed with suspicion by their protective owners.

Holly had grown up with her father's black Labrador, Tom, but he, the most angelic dog one could ever have hoped to meet, had died of old age when she'd been ten. Now she had Parson, her cat, to lavish with love. Unlike many cats, who were affectionate only when they were hungry, Parson was always nice to her. Nobody had told him that cats were supposed to be aloof and capricious. He seemed to know she had rescued him from death by starvation when he was a kitten. Sometimes she wondered what would happen if and when she fell seriously in love. How would Parson react to sharing the bed he regarded as his and her territory with a third party?

So far neither of her two unsuccessful relationships had involved making love in her bed. What had happened—nothing ecstatic!—had taken place out of doors, in summer.

Perhaps, like the legendary Gertrude Jekyll, whose gardens and thoughts on gardening were still an inspiration to the garden gurus of today, she was destined to remain unmarried. In thirty years' time she too might be a guru, her name synonymous with some of the loveliest gardens in England.

In some ways it was a nice prospect. But it would have been even nicer if she could have been sure that in the years to come, on winter evenings, when she was browsing through nurserymen's catalogues and planning new plantings, there would be someone on the other side of the fire—someone who would look up from his book and say, 'Time for bed, darling, don't you think?' with a special warm glint in his eye to signal that it wasn't only sleep he was thinking about.

CHAPTER TWO

Two weeks later, on a bright, blowy morning in November when the leafless trees on the skyline gave the landscape the look of a Rowland Hilder watercolour, Holly stopped work at noon after an energetic morning's digging.

Having discarded her sweater a couple of hours earlier, she now slung it over her shoulders and was tying the sleeves in a loose knot when someone came through the arch in the old yew hedge and made her whole body quiver with consternation.

'Good morning,' said Pierce Sutherland, strolling towards her, taking in the evidence of her morning's endeavours. 'I was told I should find you here. Your cheeks are glowing like *Felicia* roses. Are you ready for lunch?'

'What are you doing here?' she demanded apprehensively.

'I felt like a drive in the country and I wanted to see you again so I twisted Fujiko's arm until she revealed where I'd find you.'

'I can't think why you should want to see me again when you know how much I dislike you...and always shall,' Holly said crossly.

'Always is a long time. You know what they say: Never say never. To predict that you'll always feel the way you do at this moment is a little rash, don't you think?'

'I can't see why it matters to you. You've already got

ninety-five percent of the female sex ready to dance to your tune. Why do you need me to succumb to your charm?'

'I'm attracted to you, Holly. I was the first time we met. But you were only nineteen, hardly out of the egg. I was thirty and involved with your stepsister. I thought what you did after dinner that night was the funniest thing I'd seen in years. I liked your sense of humour. You were the first girl I'd met who would dream up a gag like that.'

Taken aback, she was unable to hide it. All these years she had held it against him that he'd failed to see anything amusing in what she had done. Now he was telling her that, behind the mask of disapproval, he had been breaking up. Could she believe him?

'I'm told there's a very good pub a couple of miles from here. In the hope of persuading you to lunch with me, I booked a table before I left London. Will you lunch with me, Holly? Will you give me a chance to prove that, whatever I've done in the past, I'm not such a bad guy now?'

It was hard to refuse such a persuasive invitation, especially when it came from a man whose attractions could not be denied even by his worst enemy. This morning he was wearing pale blue jeans with a matching blue denim shirt under a darker blue canvas field coat with a yellow corduroy collar and corduroy linings turned back above his shirt cuffs.

In the sunlight, his thick black hair had the sheen of health and vitality. Like his brown skin and the clear whites of his eyes, it signalled a body in perfect physical condition.

'All right...but I still don't see why my good opinion matters to you.'

She picked up the worn canvas bumbag in which she kept her few necessities and slung it over her shoulder. Hopefully there would be a chance to comb her hair and put on lipstick when they arrived at the pub.

As they left the part of the garden where she had been digging to walk in the direction of the house being built for the couple she was working for, Pierce said, 'Tell me about this set-up. The house is new but the garden looks old.'

'The owner first noticed the place from the cockpit of his private aeroplane. Do you have a plane?'

'I do, but I didn't use it to get here this morning. Within easy reach of London I prefer to drive. The owner saw marks similar to crop marks, I presume?'

'Yes, the outlines of a large garden. But he found out the house that went with it had been demolished forty years ago. So he bought the site and had a new house designed which is smaller and more labour-saving than the original mansion. But the garden will be largely a re-creation of the one designed by Harold Peto at the beginning of the century. The yews were planted by him and a lot of other things are emerging from what seemed at first to be just tangled thickets.'

Surprising her with his grasp of the task involved, he said, 'Who's been responsible for the detective work? The owner or you?'

'Me mostly, and I've enjoyed it. I like digging up facts and following clues.'

'When will the job be finished?'

'The house is due for completion in the spring and the garden will be in place then, ready to hand over to the permanent gardener when they've appointed him or her.'

'What's next on your agenda?'

'Nothing definite. I've got various gardens I'm keeping an eye on. There's going to be a feature on one of them in the January issue of *House & Garden*. That may lead to some new commissions. How come you've heard of *Felicia* roses?'

'I noticed them at someone's house and asked what they were. I like to know what I'm looking at. The texture and colour of your cheeks reminded me of their petals. You were still in bud when we met before. Now, if you were a rose, you'd be ready to pick for the house or to be the focal flower in a painting by Fantin-Latour.' He slanted a quizzical smile at her. 'Yes, I've heard of him. Surprising, isn't it? You had me tagged as a total philistine, didn't you?'

'I wouldn't have thought nineteenth-century French flower painters would be of much interest to you,' she conceded.

'Everything's of interest to me. Life is like a vast warehouse, crammed with goodies from every corner of the globe and every century since the beginning of time. You have to rummage around and see what's on offer before you can make a choice of the things you want to select for your own treasure store. Some people never go beyond the section containing flashy ghetto-blasters, expensive cars, designer clothes and that sort of stuff. But I'm beginning to discover the things in the distant corners of the warehouse—things tucked away in cupboards or hidden under dust sheets, things you have to unearth. For example, Fantin-Latour.'

Holly was silent, stunned by the realisation that if this was how he looked at life he would have got on with her father. He, too, had seen the world as a place of wonder and delight, but had vacillated between anger and despair because most people's aspirations were so low, their horizons so narrow.

'When did you find your way into the gardening section of our metaphorical warehouse?' Pierce asked.

'My grandmother let me help in her garden. She gave me a plot of earth and some child-sized tools and a whole lot of seeds. It started from there.'

'Where do you live while you're working on this project?'

'I'm renting a summer holiday cottage. It doesn't have central heating but there's a closed stove which keeps the living room cosy. I've bought a trailer-load of logs and an electric blanket to keep me warm in bed.'

She spoke without thinking and instantly regretted it, feeling the glance he bent on her but determinedly ignoring it.

'Do you sleep alone all the time...even at weekends?'

'I never sleep alone. I share my bed with a very nice cat. He's been doctored to stop him prowling and yowling at night. It's a pity human tom-cats can't be neutered. It would save everyone a lot of trouble.'

Pierce laughed. 'No one would guess to look at you that you held such Draconian views. You look rather gentle, but clearly that's a false impression. Perhaps in an earlier life you were the high priestess of a matriarchal society in which most of the males were castrated at puberty apart from a few kept for breeding purposes. And even those wouldn't have been allowed to enjoy their masculinity for long.'

'I'm not a hater of men as a sex. I just object to those who have sex on the brain,' she retorted. 'I'm not flattered by being treated as a sex object. I dislike it intensely.'

'You could try wearing a burka, that long black garment that some Muslim women wear to avoid being admired by men. But I suppose it wouldn't be practical for the kind of garden designer who gets earth on her hands. Is that usual, a designer digging? I thought they spent more time using a slide rule than a spade.'

'I guess it depends on the designer. I find that work like digging helps me to sort out problems on the aesthetic side.'

'I find that too, but when I have a problem I go to my

club and swim. It's the same solution: repetitive physical activity makes the brain work better than it would if you sat staring into space.'

They had come to where the workmen had parked their cars. In the line-up of serviceable family cars, the instantly recognisable elegance of an old but well-kept Jaguar immediately drew the eye. She had expected him to have something ostentatiously and insanely expensive, but it seemed he didn't need the ego-boost of being envied by all the men for whom cars were a major status symbol. He had said as much earlier, but she hadn't quite believed him.

She was impressed by his manners. He opened the front passenger door for her and even pulled the seat belt out of its reel and handed it to her before closing the door. Most of the men she mixed with didn't do all that stuff. Some of them didn't even know it had once been standard behaviour. But she did because her father had had beautiful manners. She measured all men by him and found most of them wanting.

As he started the engine, Pierce said, 'Tell me about this very privileged cat of yours. I have a cat myself...a Maine Coon, if you know what that is. But we don't sleep together. She has a basket in the kitchen.'

'Maine Coons are large, with fluffy breeches, aren't they?'

'That's right. Breeches and ruffs and big personalities. My father's eldest sister was a leading light in the International Society for the Preservation of the Maine Coon. She was a strong-minded lady who didn't approve of Britain's archaic quarantine regulations. When she came on a visit, she smuggled Louisa, then a kitten, through Customs. Within five minutes of her arrival at my place, the household had expanded to include an illegal immigrant. Does that shock you?'

'It surprises me. Being, as you pointed out, very priggish, I wouldn't ever deliberately break the law.'

'Maybe not, but would you report someone who had?' he asked. 'Would you turn in your favourite aunt?'

'No, I wouldn't,' she conceded. 'And if the cat had had all the necessary shots I don't suppose there was much danger of it bringing in any diseases, certainly not rabies. One of my grandmothers who was a great traveller thought the British were totally paranoid about rabies.'

'The British are either some of the world's greatest adventurers or they're extremely insular and can't get their minds round the idea that there are other ways of life that might be better than theirs. But, having said that, I've chosen to live here in preference to where I was born and all the other places I could have settled. Getting back to cats…what breed is yours?'

'A common tabby, but he does have nice markings and a little white clerical collar, which is why he's called Parson. Sometimes he comes to work with me, but today he had gone through the cat flap before I got up. Luckily the people who own the cottage also have a cat, so Parson can come and go as he chooses. The downside of that is that often, when I get home, he's left something dead on the floor. Who looks after your cat when you're away?'

'I have a man and a daily. Hooper doesn't live in but he's around long enough for Louisa not to get lonely.' He took his eyes off the road for a moment to glance at her. 'Who would have thought, after the spat we had last time, that we'd be comparing cat notes in this companionable way? I suppose you realise that, if you had flared up at me in front of most Japanese, they would have been profoundly shocked. They go to extreme lengths to avoid confrontation. Politeness is deeply engrained in their character. They never have altercations or behave aggressively in public. To be impolite causes huge loss of face.'

'Mrs Shintaro seemed to take it in her stride. Afterwards she was very nice to me.'

'She's extremely broad-minded. Her whole married life has been spent adapting to other cultures and smoothing over situations which would never have arisen in her own country. When she was in her twenties, she must have been every man's dream of the perfect woman…beautiful, intelligent, loving and totally supportive.'

'Totally submissive is what you really mean, I suppose. But not *all* men want a woman to be a doormat. My mother was making her name as a radio producer. My father insisted on her keeping up her career. If she hadn't died, he would have gone on encouraging her to make the most of her gifts. He would have despised your attitude to women.'

'Perhaps his own was different before he met your mother,' said Pierce. 'My attitude to women depends on their attitude to themselves. If all they want is a good time, I'm happy to oblige them. You accuse me of leading Chiara down the primrose path, but I couldn't steer you in that direction, could I?'

'You wouldn't have succeeded with Chiara if she'd had a sensible mother,' Holly said shortly. 'My stepmother was fool enough to think you might marry Chiara. Instead of discouraging the relationship with you, she egged her on. I knew it would end in tears. That was obvious from the beginning.'

'But it didn't end in tears,' he said equably. 'Chiara wasn't heartbroken. She was never in love with me. You credited her with the feelings you would have experienced if a man you were involved with had called an end to the affair. At nineteen, you would only have done what your stepsister did if you had been in love...or imagined you were.'

Reluctant as she was to agree with him, inwardly Holly had to admit there was a good deal of force in his argument. Chiara had been upset, but it had been mainly wounded pride rather than real heartache which had been the cause of her tears.

'That doesn't alter the fact that you gave her a taste for high life and luxuries she couldn't afford except by...by selling herself to other men like you. You got her hooked on rich living in exactly the same way that other girls get hooked on drugs. And if you'd done that to her, I would have made you pay for it if...if I'd had to kill you myself,' Holly said quietly.

'Got hold of a gun and shot me?' He gave a soft laugh. 'Yes, I believe you would. But the fact is that Chiara had nothing more damaging than champagne while she was under my aegis. I smoked some pot in my teens but I drew the line at the rest of it. I don't need that kind of high. I've always found wine and women adequate stimulants. How about you? How do you get your kicks?'

'From my work mainly. But it's more a case of quiet satisfaction than kicks. Gardening might seem dull to some people, but in fact it's very fulfilling. There's always something to look forward to. I can't wait to see how this garden I'm working on now looks in two, three and four years' time. I suppose it's the same sort of gratification that people get from watching their children grow up.'

'It sounds a little tame for someone of your age. Don't you want excitement...adventure...nights of passion... mornings when someone rings up and persuades you to do something crazy?'

'I think you're taking the mickey. You can't charm me, so you mock me. There's something about women like me—women who aren't flattered by your attention—that irritates your ego.'

'Perhaps. But who knows? Like the grain of sand the oyster deals with by creating a pearl, our mutual irritation may eventually be transformed into an enjoyable friendship. Are you prepared to give it a try?'

'Not really,' Holly said coolly. 'I don't believe you're capable of friendship with a woman, any more than a leopard can be friends with a gazelle.'

Pierce made no comment on this, perhaps because they had reached the junction with a busy main road where he needed to give more attention to the traffic. Even after they had joined the stream of vehicles and were heading in the direction of the nearest market town, he didn't pick up her barb and toss it expertly back at her.

She wondered what he was thinking. Perhaps she had made a mistake in not accepting the proffered olive branch with outward grace and inward scepticism.

The pub which was their destination was two or three miles outside town, a little way off the main road. A large car park was an indication of its popularity but perhaps its main trade was at weekends, for today there were not many cars there.

The interior was 'ye olde worlde' but not off-puttingly kitsch.

'If you want to go and tidy up, the Ladies' is over there,' said Pierce, spotting the discreet sign before she did. 'What would you like to drink before lunch?'

Holly felt that his manner had suddenly changed to the avuncular attitude of a worldly man finding himself in charge of an exceptionally gauche teenager, like a long-suffering godfather taking an awkward sixth-former out to lunch in the absence of her parents.

She said, 'A vodka and tonic with ice but no lemon, please,' and headed in the direction of the loos.

There she discovered she didn't have a lipstick with her, only some colourless salve and a tube of cream, protections against chapped lips and hands. There wasn't much she could do to boost her self-confidence other than release her hair from the band tying it back at her nape. Swinging in a loose bob just above shoulder-level, it made her look slightly more sophisticated. But she would have given a lot to have some eye make-up, scent and a pair of earrings with her. Not because she wanted to look more attractive, but simply as boosts to morale.

Why did I let myself in for this? she asked her reflection in the mirror. Why didn't I say no?

With a thrust of annoyance she faced the vexatious answer to both those questions. In spite of what he had done to Chiara, in spite of her own strong dislike of him, she had come because Pierce intrigued her. She was drawn to him in spite of herself. Moths didn't know they would burn their wings by being lured by the light inside a lampshade. She *knew* Pierce was dangerous, and yet she couldn't resist this closer contact with him.

Chiara had been attracted by his wealth and his lavish lifestyle as much as by his looks and his powerful sex appeal. But Holly was drawn by the man behind the public mask. She wanted to know what made him tick and if, behind his appearance of total self-confidence, there were hidden weaknesses, parts of him which could be hurt.

Not normally cruel and revengeful, she found herself wanting to wound him, to exert the same sort of power he exerted on the women he made his playthings. She knew it was completely mad, but she wanted to have Pierce Sutherland in *her* power and make him know what it felt like to be treated the way he had treated Chiara. At the same time she knew she had none of the weapons she needed to achieve that objective: not beauty, not a brain to match his, not irresistible sex appeal…none of the things she needed to be able to play him at his own game.

Her only resource in dealing with him, the one thing which set her apart from all the other women he had known was her resistance to him. And how long would that be a safeguard if he decided to undermine it? She would be like the commander of a city under siege. She would have only two options, one of them to surrender.

Pierce was not at the bar when she rejoined him. He was sitting at a corner table, glancing at a copy of *The Times* which he had taken from a selection of newspapers and magazines on a table in the centre of the room. When he sensed her approaching, he tossed it aside and stood up, taking in her loose hair.

'I've already made my choice,' he said, indicating a menu lying on the table next to her drink.

After sating herself, Holly picked up the glass. She didn't say 'cheers' or anything similarly friendly before she took her first sip.

'I've a casserole ready for my supper so I won't have much lunch. I'm used to a sandwich and an apple at this time of day.'

'Do you like cooking?' he asked.

'I like eating. Where I'm living at the moment, it's cook or go without. The nearest take-away place is six miles away. Anyway, I'm not into junk food.'

'I can see that. You glow with health. I should think your breath is like sea air, even first thing in the morning.' As he said it, he smiled into her eyes.

The effect on Holly was catastrophic. Immediately, she had a vision of lying in a half-acre bed, under the lightest and most luxurious swan's-down duvet, with Pierce stretched out close behind her, propped on one elbow, both of them naked. And what she saw in her mind's eye caused such a strong reaction that she gave an audible gasp as sensations she wasn't prepared for shot through her insides like an electric charge.

To make matters worse she was almost certain he knew what was happening to her, had set out to have this effect and was amused and pleased at having achieved it.

'It's not difficult to stay fit when you're leading a natural life,' she said, trying to sound composed. 'If I worked in a city office, I would never feel well. I don't know how people survive that sort of environment, especially offices with no natural ventilation.'

'I agree.' Pierce picked up his glass and drank some lager. 'Given no other options, I would rather sweep leaves in the park than be a commodities broker. The lives those guys lead is inhuman. At the end of a twelve-hour day, all they're fit for is propping up a bar or snorting cocaine. And for what? Only money. No job satisfaction. No security. No esteem worth mentioning.'

'"Only money" is easy to say when you have plenty of it,' said Holly. 'I can't see you as a park sweeper; I really can't.'

'Neither can I,' he said, smiling. 'But luckily I was born with more than two options…almost unlimited options. All you need in this world is some brains and a lot of ambition and you can't go wrong. Whatever you want you can have, but you have to work for it. Look at you. You wanted to be a garden designer and you are. But I doubt if what you've achieved fell into your lap. You had to strive for it.'

'I haven't achieved much so far. I'm only at the beginning. But I think it's the kind of career which will mesh with the other things I want.'

'Which are?'

She gave him a level look. 'A husband and children. That old-fashioned thing called marriage which people like you despise.'

'Where did you get that idea? Because I didn't marry Chiara, it doesn't mean I don't want a wife when the right woman comes along.'

'And will you be faithful to her?' she asked. 'Or will you continue to have affairs on the side?'

He didn't reply immediately but gave her a long, thoughtful look which she found quite hard to hold.

'On the basis of very little evidence, you've jumped to a lot of conclusions which are about as accurate as the stories in the tabloid press,' he said. 'Tell me, are you exactly the same as you were five years ago?'

'Of course not, but five years ago I was still in my teens.'

'Yes, I remember you well,' he said, smiling faintly. 'You were wearing a dress that didn't suit you and your hair was badly cut, but even so you had something about you…the promise of how you are now.'

The caressing tone of his voice and the look in his eyes, which were not as cold as she had thought—or, at least, not when he chose to soften the expression in them—made Holly lower her gaze in the hope of masking her response.

Did he really remember her as clearly as he made out?

'The whole evening was an exercise in over-the-top pretentiousness,' he went on reminiscently. 'If there were a prize for bad taste, your stepmother would certainly be on the short list.'

'And you would be on the short list of guests who have no compunction about running down their hostess,' Holly said frostily.

'Oh, come on, Holly; I'm only speaking the truth. It was

making you cringe. I watched you. You wanted to sink through the floor.'

She couldn't deny it. She *had* cringed. But her father never had. Unlike Mr Bennet in *Pride and Prejudice*, Professor Nicholson had never by the flicker of an eyelid revealed the embarrassment his second wife's affected, snobbish behaviour had caused him. Only sometimes, alone with his daughter, had he permitted himself some wry comment which he knew he could trust her not to repeat to anyone. But, of course, by the time of the party under discussion, he had already died of a massive heart attack.

'I was having a bet with myself,' Pierce went on, 'that when all those piddling courses of second-rate food finally came to an end Mrs Nicholson would rise to her feet and sweep you all off to do whatever women do when they leave the men to drink port and "put the world to rights".'

The accuracy of his memory and the exactness with which he mimicked the arch inflection of her stepmother's voice when she'd made this remark made Holly smile in spite of herself.

'You are very unkind.'

He shrugged. 'I was massively bored by it all. You can't expect me to be kind about someone who put me through several hours of acute boredom. I was tempted to get up and walk out. Life is too short to sit through that sort of nonsense. It was only when we joined you in the drawing room that the whole thing was made worthwhile.'

Suddenly his face was alight with warmth and humour, his grin revealing the fine teeth she had only glimpsed while he'd talked.

'You were sitting by yourself on an uncomfortable chair, looking as if butter wouldn't melt in your mouth. And then, when the coffee had been passed round and the woman with the double-barrelled surname was holding forth in that falsely plummy accent, you suddenly crossed your legs and lifted your long skirt a little…revealing those huge hairy feet with claw-like toenails.'

He gave a deep bay of laughter, clapping his hand against the hard length of his thigh. 'I should think they could hear her shriek at the other end of the street. For a minute she thought those appalling great feet were real. Her eyes were on stalks. It's a wonder she didn't have hysterics.'

Remembering the expression on the face of the woman he was talking about, Holly began to smile and then to dissolve into laughter.

'But you weren't amused then,' she reminded him. 'You couldn't have looked more po-faced.'

'I was clenching my back teeth so hard, it's a wonder they didn't fuse. Inside I was breaking up. When I laughed about it later, Chiara was very annoyed with me. She didn't share your sense of humour. In fact I don't ever remember her belly-laughing at anything. The best she'd manage was a breathy little giggle. Now don't flare up and bite my head off. If we can't speak frankly to each other, we're never going to get anywhere. The bedrock of friendship is truth.'

'If that involves running down my sister, we're never going to be friends,' Holly informed him.

'I'm not running her down. I'm being honest. She's a beautiful girl but she has no sense of humour. Never in a million years would she have worn those feet in those circumstances. Where did you get them, anyway?'

'They were a present I'd bought for my best friend's younger brother's birthday. I'd always wanted a brother and Dan was the next best thing. When the others went up to my stepmother's bedroom, I went to mine, where the feet were waiting to be wrapped up. The reason I put them on was to test whether *you* had a sense of humour. I didn't think you were going to ask Chiara to marry you, but in case you did I wanted to run through the checks my father advised me to make on anyone I thought I was in love with.'

'And what were they?' Pierce enquired.

'The first was a good sense of humour. The others...I don't want to discuss.'

'Which means, I suppose, that they have to do with sex... a subject you aren't comfortable with...or, at least, not with me...not yet,' Pierce remarked drily.

His shrewdness was disconcerting. He made her feel he could see inside her head and read her thoughts, like someone illicitly accessing the files stored on another person's computer.

It was a relief when he said it was time they ate, if she had decided what she wanted.

Holly had half expected that his lunch would be the T-bone steak with French fries and grilled tomatoes and mushrooms. But when one of the barmaids had come to take their orders and Pierce had told her that his guest would have the cottage cheese salad with pineapple, his own order turned out to be stuffed peppers with a baked potato and a side salad.

To drink, he ordered spring water, asking Holly if she preferred it still or sparkling.

'Still, please.'

When the waitress had left them, he said, 'If I weren't driving, we could share a bottle of wine. But if you're working this afternoon you probably don't want to drink much either. By the way, I bring a message from Fujiko. If I succeed in healing the breach between us, she would like me to bring you to a party she's giving on the twenty-fourth. Her parties are always first-rate. I know you'd enjoy it. Will you let me be your escort?'

'Do I need an escort? Wouldn't I be acceptable on my own?'

'Of course, but rather than putting you to the trouble and expense of going to London by train Fujiko felt it would be easier if I fetched you in my chopper. The invitation includes a bed for the night…a bed in Fujiko's apartment. I can imagine your reaction if I offered you one at my place. Although if I did you would have nothing to fear,' he added quizzically. 'I never make passes unless I'm sure they'll be welcome.'

Holly ignored this sally. Did she want to go to a party under Pierce's aegis? What did her wardrobe include that would do for a smart London party which might be black tie? Nothing. Not even a little black dress, because she had never had that sort of social life.

'The reason she's giving the party is because her grandson's coming over,' Pierce went on. 'Did she tell you about Ben? He's the apple of her eye, and deservedly so. He's a sweet guy. You'll like him. He's the antithesis of me,' he added drily. 'Kind, gentle, deeply chivalrous towards women. Ben is a combination of all that's good in two very different cultures. People like him are our best hope for the future. So…will you come?'

Holly took a deep breath, knowing instinctively that she could be about to make the worst mistake of her life.

'All right…yes…yes, I will.'

CHAPTER THREE

THE day before Mrs Shintaro's party, Holly went to London by train, intending to spend the next two nights with Chiara.

Two days after lunching with Pierce, she had telephoned him to say it wouldn't be necessary for him to fetch her in his helicopter. She had made other arrangements.

He accepted this decision without argument. Nor did he quibble when she added that she would also get to the party under her own steam and meet him there.

Perhaps he suspected she might be staying with her stepsister and preferred to avoid an encounter with his ex-girlfriend.

Chiara, when she opened the door of her Chelsea flat, was sporting a golden tan acquired on a recent visit to southern Spain where Eric, her current 'close friend', kept a yacht berthed at Sotogrande, a glitzy resort at the Gibraltar end of the Costa del Sol, or the Costa del Golf as it was sometimes known.

'*Darling*...lovely to see you.' She embraced Holly warmly. 'You look a bit peaky. Are you all right?'

'Couldn't be better,' said Holly. 'Just not as suntanned as you are. How was Spain?'

'Oh...not bad,' said Chiara, shrugging. 'I got a bit bored with the wall-to-wall wrinklies. The average age on the Costa has to be seventy at least. You hardly ever see a woman who isn't on her fifth or sixth face-lift...apart from a scattering of bimbos.'

It didn't seem to occur to her that many people would regard Chiara herself as a bimbo, Holly thought, with a pang.

Since her stepsister had been with Eric, she had taken to having her hair done an even lighter shade of blonde and to wearing increasingly *outré* clothes. Obviously Eric liked her to attract attention, but it wasn't the kind of notice which would have pleased Pierce when she had been with him. Under his aegis, Chiara had worn clothes by Armani and Calvin Klein, clothes in subtle good taste which Holly had had to admire even if she hadn't approved of Pierce paying for them.

But now Chiara was buying creations by the wilder, most way-out designers, and although they cost a lot of money somehow they made her look cheap.

'I didn't expect you to come up again so soon after using the flat while I was away,' she remarked on the way to the living room. 'What brings you here this time? More research work?'

'I want to do some Christmas shopping…and I need to find something to wear for a party tomorrow night.'

'A party in London? How come?'

While Chiara made coffee, Holly explained about meeting Mrs Shintaro at New Covent Garden and being given a lift because it was raining heavily. For the time being she left Pierce out of it.

'How exciting!' Chiara's pansy-dark eyes glistened with interest. Parties, and planning what to wear to them, were the breath of life to her. 'But you don't need to buy anything, silly. Have a look through what I've got. There's bound to be something you'll like.'

Although it was seldom apparent to other people, because they presented themselves in totally different ways, Chiara and Holly had almost identical vital statistics.

Later, after coffee and when Holly had unpacked in the spare bedroom, Chiara took her to her own bedroom where a long bank of built-in closets housed her extensive wardrobe.

One of Chiara's most likeable characteristics was her generosity. She had always been happy to share her things with her sisters and stepsister.

Now, for Holly's delectation, she showed all her most recent buys, including a selection of what she called 'LBDs', meaning little black dresses, but not of the discreet, undating standby variety. The ones she had picked out all made strong, sexy statements which Holly lacked the panache to carry off.

For a moment, as Chiara held against herself a barely-there sheath of clingy crushed velvet which would mould to every curve of her body in explicit detail, Holly wondered how Pierce would react if she went to the party showing maximum cleavage and leg.

But it wasn't her style. Never had been and never would be. She didn't want men's eyes crawling all over her as they mentally stripped off the little she was wearing. She wanted to look alluring, but not to flaunt her sexuality.

The telephone rang and Chiara answered it. 'It's Eric. I'll talk to him in the living room. Have a look through. Try things on,' she said, indicating the other cupboards. 'Hang on a minute, sweetie. I'll be right with you. I've got Holly here. She's just arrived. We're going to spend the afternoon shopping…unless you have other plans for me,' she added, with a meaningful giggle.

Holly had never met Eric. She had only seen photographs of him posing on board his yacht in a peaked cap. He was in his late forties, had two divorces behind him, and Chiara said vaguely that his wealth came from pharmaceuticals. He looked to Holly as if he might be involved in something shady. Of all Chiara's men-friends, from what little she knew of him, she liked him the least and hated the thought of his picking up the bills which her sister had no means of paying herself, except by selling some of the jewels she had acquired.

Crushed tightly together in the other cupboards were garments which sooner or later would be given to a charity shop to make room for new things. Had they belonged to Holly, she would have taken them to a dress agency in order to recoup a little of what they had cost. But thrift was a concept beyond Chiara's grasp.

As her gaze coasted over the rainbow of vivid colours, looking for something more subtle, Holly's eye was caught by a sky-blue shoelace peeping out from between something made of yellow satin and its black lace neighbour. Investigating, she found that the shoelace with its matching metal tag was stitched to the sleeve of a lime-green jacket. Extracting it from the crush, she found there were other laces in other colours, stitched on like stripes with their ends left free. The colours were those found in a box of fondants: pink, lemon-yellow, lilac. The effect was charming.

Holly tried the jacket on. It wasn't her usual style, but it suited her. The statement it made was spring-like and carefree. It spoke of April in Paris, bunches of bright balloons, ice creams in many flavours. When she looked, the label said Moschino.

'Oh, heavens, that's ages old. I saw it on a display model when I was on the escalator at Harvey Nicks and I couldn't resist it,' said Chiara, returning. 'It's fun, but somehow not me. I've hardly worn it. It's lovely on you, though.'

'Did Pierce buy you this?' asked Holly.

'God, no! It's not *that* old,' Chiara said, amused. 'What ever made you think of him? Pierce was a *long* time ago.

All the stuff I wore when I knew him would look really draggy by now.'

'I ran into Pierce,' said Holly. 'He was at New Covent Garden with Mrs Shintaro. He's a friend of her grandson.'

'Did he recognize you?'

'Surprisingly, yes, he did.'

'He always had a fantastic memory. I could never get away with fibbing to him. He'd catch me out straight away.'

'Why did you need to fib to him?'

'Oh, I don't know…one just does,' Chiara said airily. 'Men are such tricky creatures. You have to learn to manage them. I didn't know that then and I handled him awfully badly. It was always he who called the shots.'

'Doesn't Eric?'

'Definitely not! I've got him eating out of the palm of my hand. The fact is, darling, that the entire male sex is so hooked on sex that when they're in need of a fix you can make them do anything you want. For women who understand that, anything is possible.'

Holly frowned. 'It sounds horrible…like pushing drugs.'

'I suppose it is in a way, except that it doesn't do them any harm or kill them. Well, it might if they were quite old and they overdid it, I suppose. But normally it just puts them in a good mood—the kind of mood when they'll give you the moon if you ask for it. I sometimes think I could write a best-seller—*How to Manage Men*. But really it's so dead simple that it wouldn't cover more than a couple of pages.'

On impulse, Holly said, 'Do you really enjoy having sex with Eric?'

Chiara gave a peal of laughter. 'No, but he does, and that's what counts.'

Holly said nothing. Her own view of sex had been

formed by her father who, long before she had started menstruating, had given her a book which explained the workings of her body and the reproductive process. Then, later, at some appropriate moment, he had mentioned that physical love was one of life's most glorious experiences and, for that reason, not to be undertaken casually, like lesser pleasures.

'Any fool can jump into bed and they do…in droves,' he had told her. 'If you can, hang on a bit, Holly. Wait till you're seriously in love, because it makes all the difference.'

But of course she hadn't listened to him. Curiosity and attraction had been the reasons for her first experience, and loneliness and attraction had propelled her into the second.

Chiara said, 'Let's have a look for a skirt you could wear with that jacket. Not black—that would be too heavy for it. Something to pick up the colour of one of those sneaker-laces.'

As Chiara had a date with Eric that evening—they were going dining and dancing with another couple—Holly took herself to the theatre. The others were still on the town when she returned.

The last time she had been to the theatre in London, she had gone to sleep thinking about the play. Tonight it was Pierce who filled her thoughts. Reluctant as she was to admit it, she knew she was looking forward to seeing him tomorrow night. On her way to the theatre she had wondered if he might be there, his height and his thick dark hair making him easy to spot even in a crowded auditorium. But although she had scanned the front stalls and the boxes from her seat in the dress circle, he hadn't seemed to be there. She had felt absurdly relieved. Somehow, to see him escorting some glamorous woman would have dimmed her anticipatory excitement about the party tomorrow.

As Chiara had always been able to burn the candle at both ends, she appeared in the kitchen while Holly was having breakfast the next morning.

'Pour me a tall glass of orange juice, would you? I didn't get to bed till three. But a hot shower will put me right. Then we'll go out and shop till we drop.'

It was while they were having a light lunch at a restaurant where the daytime clientele were women laden with shiny paper carriers bearing names familiar to all readers of *Vogue* that Chiara asked, 'When you met Pierce, did he mention me?'

'Yes. He asked how you were and if you were still single or settled down.'

'That's what he told me I should do. He said I wasn't cut out to be a playgirl. Actually he was very rude. He said that to get to the top as a rich man's darling you had to have brains as well as beauty, and I wasn't clever enough. Well, he was wrong actually. Because while we were down on the Costa, I met someone *really* rich...far richer than Pierce or Eric.'

Holly was appalled. 'Oh, for goodness' sake, Chiara, you're not going to ditch Eric and start yet another of these awful affairs, are you? Pierce was right. What you need is a loving husband and babies. They would make you so much happier than all these horrible older men whose only attraction is their money.'

'Settle down in suburbia with a mortgage and a grizzling toddler in a pushchair? Not likely!' Chiara exclaimed. 'I'm not going to look the way I do now for ever. While I do, I'm making the most of it. And you ain't seen nothing yet, baby, because this guy who gave me the eye on the waterfront at Sotogrande is one of the big-league players. If he fancies me as much as I think he does, I'll have diamonds in every orifice, not just my navel.'

'Lots of men give you the eye. What makes you think he's going to follow it up?'

'Because he sent me a note. It was delivered by hand by one of the stewards on his yacht and it came with a box of chocolates. One of the chocolates was missing. In its place was a huge chunk of aquamarine. I've had it valued. It's worth two thousand pounds. I can't show it to you. It's in a safety-deposit box at the bank. Don't you think that's the most romantic gesture you've ever heard of?'

'What did the note say?'

'Just that he thought I was the most beautiful woman he had ever laid eyes on and he felt sure our paths would cross in the near future.'

In the taxi taking her to the party, Holly knew that she had never looked better. Chiara had done her hair for her, using a styling mousse which added an extra sheen and would hold the ends firmly flipped up.

To go with the Moschino jacket, her stepsister had produced a soft, swingy skirt made of several layers of violet chiffon to tone with the lilac laces. Luckily they both wore size six shoes and Chiara's extensive selection included a pair bought to go with the chiffon skirt, and she even had a pair of lace-topped sheer violet stay-ups.

Holly had never worn stay-ups before and when she was trying them on, wearing rubber gloves to avoid the risk of snagging them, Chiara had said, 'They won't sneak down your legs, I promise you. I wear them all the time. They're much sexier than pantyhose. It gives a guy a real buzz suddenly to feel bare flesh where he thought he was going to feel Lycra.'

'Maybe so, but nobody's going to be putting their hand up *my* skirt tonight,' Holly had said. 'Honestly, Chiara, your relations with men seem to revolve round sex. Don't you ever wish they would grope round your mind for a change?'

'I haven't got that sort of mind. All the things that interest me, men don't want to know about it, and the stuff they drone on about—cars and golf and investments—bore me to death.'

As the taxi sped in the direction of Grosvenor Square, Holly gave a long sigh. She was deeply worried about Chiara. This new affair that she had in prospect with the donor of the aquamarine sounded much deeper water than she had swum in before. But there seemed to be no way of stopping her getting involved if the man concerned wanted her.

Outside Mrs Shintaro's apartment block, a liveried doorman opened the door of the taxi, touching the brim of his cockaded top hat as he said, 'Good evening, miss.'

Holly stepped out and paid the fare with notes taken from a clutch purse of soft glacé kid to match her evening shoes. She would not have bought such high heels for herself and felt slightly awkward in them, but they did flatter her legs, which had never looked longer or more shapely than they did tonight.

As she was about to walk into the building, along the stretch of carpet which led from the kerb to the entrance, protected from rain by an awning, someone pipped the horn of a car.

Turning, she saw Pierce's Jaguar waiting to take the space occupied by her taxi. As she looked through the windscreen he waved to her.

A few minutes later, having handed over his keys to the valet who would park the car for him, Pierce turned to her and said, 'You look wonderful, Holly. I thought you were strictly an open-air, outdoor girl, but tonight you epitomise glamour. What an amusing jacket.'

'Thank you.' She decided not to tell him it was borrowed finery. 'You look very nice yourself.'

He was wearing a pale grey suit with an apricot shirt and tie, all of recognisably superb quality.

He acknowledged her compliment with a slight inclination of his head and then, taking a step back and looking down, said, 'It's a crime to hide those legs in trousers. This is the first time I've seen them.'

Knowing she was starting to blush, she said, 'Skirts aren't practical for gardening.'

Taking her lightly by the elbow, Pierce steered her into the lobby with its luxurious carpet, sofas, silk-shaded lamps and lavish flower arrangements.

There were two lifts, one of them open. In its mirror-lined walls, she caught an unexpected glimpse of him looking down at someone she scarcely recognised as her everyday self.

She had thought he was out of her class, a godlike being she could never hope to ensnare, even though he had claimed to be attracted to her. But now, suddenly, catching sight of their reflections, for the first time she felt it was possible for her to make a small dent in his well-armoured heart. Not for long. Certainly not for ever. But for long enough to make some memories she would always be glad she hadn't missed.

'Although you insisted on coming here by yourself, I refuse to allow you to leave under your own steam,' said Pierce as the lift doors closed. 'Where are you staying?'

'Chiara has a place in Chelsea. I'm spending two nights with her. We're still close. I don't have any contact with her mother and sisters now. Her mother has married again. She's living in Scotland.'

'An obnoxious woman. When Chiara told me who your father was, it was hard to fathom what had possessed him to marry her. But I suppose he thought it was the best thing for you.'

'Yes, and I think she put on an act for him.'

'People of both sexes do that. It's the reason for so many breakups,' Pierce answered drily. 'Whether they're married or only shacked up together, couples suddenly wake up to the fact that the person they're with is someone different from the person they were before the decision to merge. Let's make a pact never to be on our best behaviour with each other.' He smiled. 'That way we'll know where we stand.'

She looked up at him. 'I already know where I stand with you. I'm the Thompson gazelle and you're the leopard. If I don't watch out, you'll have me for dinner.'

Before Pierce had time to reply, the lift doors opened, revealing the landing outside the entrance to the penthouse which tonight stood open, giving a view through the wide hall into Mrs Shintaro's beautiful drawing room.

When she realised what a glittering throng Mrs Shintaro had assembled to meet her grandson, Holly was glad she had Pierce beside her and didn't have to brave the throng of elegant women and distinguished-looking men on her own.

Although she had never been shy, it was nice to feel his hand on the small of her back as they crossed the space between the lift and the wide flight of shallow stairs leading down into the huge room, tonight lit by glittering crystal sconces as well as enormous table lamps making pools of flattering light.

Some people were already relaxing in the groups of sofas and chairs in different parts of the room. Others were standing in groups. Everyone was drinking champagne being served by Japanese waiters in starched white tunics and white gloves.

'Pierce…Holly…' Their hostess had seen them and came hurrying towards them, wearing an exquisite robe of diaphanous dark brown *dévoré* velvet and pearls which could only be real, so beautiful was their soft lustre.

'My dear, you look simply lovely. I knew you would.' Mrs Shintaro embraced her, pressing her cheek to Holly's in a gesture which was as soft as the brush of a moth's wing but far more affectionate than the conventional 'mwah-mwah' kiss.

Lifting her face to receive Pierce's salutation, she said, with a twinkle in her eyes, 'So…there is a détente, as diplomats say when there's an easing of tension between nations which seemed on the brink of strife. I am delighted to see it. Now I want you to meet my treasured grandson, Holly. I have told him how much you liked the Nepalese hand. He's looking forward to meeting a girl with such discriminating taste. Where has he gone to?'

As she started to look round the room, from the opposite direction a young man came through the crowd, making a beeline for Pierce.

Slightly to Holly's surprise, the two men not only clasped hands but gave each other a hug—the kind of embrace which might be exchanged by brothers who had been apart a long time.

She found herself oddly touched by the open affection between them. It threw a new light on Pierce's character. A man who could feel and inspire deep, close friendship must surely be capable of loving? Why his ability to love should be important was something she didn't have time to examine.

As they drew back, the young man turned his attention to Holly. Before his grandmother could present him to her, he said, 'The garden designer, right? I'm Ben Rockland. How do you do, Miss Nicholson.'

'Hello, Ben... Please call me Holly.' As they shook hands, she remembered wondering if he would be good-looking.

He was. She had never seen such a superb example of the mingling of two races. From his American father he had inherited a tall, well-built physique, from his mother, the liquid dark eyes, finely marked brows and jet-black hair of his Japanese ancestors. If she hadn't already met Pierce, she would have thought him the most gorgeous male she had ever seen.

It wasn't until later in the evening that she had a chance to talk to Ben one-to-one. Supper was served in the other parts of the apartment, in a room lined with books and on a glassed-in terrace overlooking some of the city's land-marks, which were picked out by beams of light. Everyone had been given a place at one of the large round tables each seating eight guests.

Holly found herself placed between Ben and an elderly man who introduced himself as an archaeologist. Through the first course she talked to him, and then he turned to his other neighbour and the same thing happened to Ben, leaving them free to concentrate on each other.

He opened the conversation by saying, 'My grandmother has been telling me how she met you. But she said you and Pierce had met before the visit to New Covent Garden.'

'Briefly...a long time ago. You know him much better than I do. You share a passion for mountains, I hear.'

'That's right, and now we're discussing doing an expedition together. Does the name Aconcagua mean anything to you?'

Holly shook her head.

'It's a mountain in Argentina, the highest peak in the Americas. We're going to tackle it in February.'

'Will it be dangerous?'

'Crossing the road can be dangerous,' he answered, smiling. 'It's a difficult summit because of the weather conditions, but it's a mountain you can walk up. There's no serious climbing involved.'

'How long will you be away?'

'Five weeks.'

'It will be an anxious time for your grandmother. She's bound to worry about you.'

'I know. I'm trying to convince her that nothing bad can happen to me while I'm with Pierce, but she still doesn't like the idea. I guess women never do want people they love to take risks, even small ones. But men need a sniff of adventure every so often. Our everyday lives are so tame. We need to live rough for a while, to pit ourselves against the elements.'

'Tell me how you met Pierce.'

'We were both in Nepal, trekking. One day I met up with a small group who weren't experienced trekkers. One of them was showing signs of altitude sickness. I couldn't persuade him he was risking death by pressing on. Then Pierce came by. He has the sort of authority nobody argues with. When the crisis was over, we decided we liked each other. As we were going the same route, we went on together. Not walking together all day, but meeting at each day's end and sleeping in the same lodge. We've been friends ever since. I admire him more than anyone I've ever met.'

'He speaks highly of you,' said Holly. 'Why do you admire him so much? From where I stand he's not especially admirable.'

Yet even as she said it she knew her perspective had altered. She no longer felt hostile towards him. Somehow her feelings had altered. Not at any particular moment. It had happened gradually, subtly.

'Really? But then you don't know him as well as I do.'

'What I do know isn't to his credit.' As soon as the words were out, she wished she had left them unsaid. When Ben looked surprised, she added, 'He had an affair with my stepsister. Then he dropped her.'

She knew as she spoke that she no longer blamed him. There were two sides to every story and perhaps if she knew his side…

'Yes, I've heard he treats women in a way they don't like. But maybe they ask for it. If they're mainly after his money, why should he be nice to them? Did your stepsister love him?'

'No, I don't think she did,' Holly admitted.

'Then she doesn't have much to complain about, does she?' said Ben. 'I don't think he'd hurt anyone who loved him. He's tough, but he isn't cruel. He cares about people more than any man I know.'

'He does?' she said, puzzled. 'In what way?'

Before Ben could answer, the woman on his other side addressed a remark to him. He was obliged to reply. For the rest of the meal they had no further chance to discuss Pierce's character.

When dinner was over, Holly found herself talking to a variety of people, all of them interesting but none of them the person she wanted to be with.

From time to time she saw him talking to other people and she wished she could feel him watching her across the crowded room…like the man and the girl in the song from her parents' favourite musical, the one they had seen on their honeymoon. But Pierce seemed to have forgotten her existence. He never once looked her way.

It was after midnight when the party began to break up. Suddenly Pierce was beside her.

'Are you ready to go?'

'Whenever you are.'

'Let's find Fujiko.'

There were too many guests departing for them to spend long with their hostess. She had her tall grandson beside her.

To Holly's surprise, Ben kissed her goodbye. 'See you soon, I hope.'

Going down in the lift with two other couples. Pierce's replies to her small talk were noticeably monosyllabic. In the lobby they had to wait a few minutes for his car to be brought round.

It was he, not the doorman, who opened the passenger door and watched her tuck the folds of her skirt round her legs.

When the car was in motion, he said, 'I gather you and Ben took to each other.'

'I liked him very much. He told me about your expedition in February and the way you met each other. What does he do for a living? We didn't get to that.'

'By training he's a lawyer, like his father and grandfather. But he doesn't want to practise law. Having an income from a substantial trust fund, he doesn't need to work at all. But he wants to do something useful. The question is— what?'

'Does he have a girlfriend?'

'Not that I know of. I expect he's had lots of girls. He's a good-looking guy. But I don't think there's anyone special. Don't lose your heart to him, Holly.'

'I wasn't planning to, but why the warning?'

'Ben hasn't found his way yet. He's still looking for the right direction. People have to know who they are before they can make important decisions like marriage.'

'You don't believe in love, then? In meeting one's soul mate?'

'I wouldn't say that, but I think it's a pretty rare thing, not something to wait around for, because it may never happen. In general, being happy is something people achieve on their own, not through someone else.'

'Some people say it's because women have careers that so many marriages break down.'

'It's not the career that's the problem. It's the way it's handled,' said Pierce. 'Life is all a question of priorities. But I think I'll expound my theories on that some other time. If you normally get up at six, you must be ready for bed.'

'Strangely, I'm not tired tonight. Usually my light goes out soon after ten. Do you have a lot of late nights?'

'I don't go to many parties. I do tend to read late.'

By now they had reached the street where Chiara lived.

Holly said, 'The flats have their own underground park but it's only accessible to card-holders. As you can see, the street is always fully parked. If you'll drop me off halfway along—'

'I'll double park for a few minutes while I see you safely inside,' he said, in a tone which forbade any argument. 'Street robberies happen all over London these days, not just in seedy areas.'

As he stopped the car, Holly finally nerved herself to say what had been in her mind since they'd left the party.

'Pierce, are you very busy tomorrow? Could you possibly spare half an hour to advise me on something I'm worried about?'

'Of course. What train are you catching?'

'Any train will do. I'm my own boss. I fix my own timetable.'

'To fit you in tomorrow morning would mean reshuffling

a lot of appointments. But I'm not tied up for lunch. Why not come to my place and meet Louisa?'

'Louisa? Oh, yes…your cat. OK, that would be fine.'

He produced a card and wrote his private address on the back of it. Then he walked her to the door of Chiara's flat which had its own entrance along a landscaped walkway under perpetual surveillance by discreetly sited cameras.

Holly wondered if he would kiss her goodnight. Part of her hoped he wouldn't. A kiss from Pierce, even if only on the cheek, the way Ben had kissed her, would be far more disturbing than other men's social kisses.

Another part longed to know what being in his arms would be like.

As she tried to lessen the sound of her heels on the paving, in order not to disturb people who were sleeping, her heart began to beat in slow, suffocating thumps.

CHAPTER FOUR

HAD Holly been on her own, she would have had the key in her hand long before she reached the door. But tonight, protected by the presence of a man whose tall, powerful build would make most muggers think twice, she didn't open her purse until the last moment.

Pierce took the latchkey from her and inserted it quietly in the lock, pushing open the door. Chiara had left the hall light on. Whether she herself was still out there was no way of telling.

'Till tomorrow,' said Pierce, in an undertone. He held out his hand, a slight smile flickering round his mouth.

His fingers and palm were warm, and although his clasp was firm she knew it was nothing like the grip he had exchanged with Ben.

'Thank you for bringing me home. Till tomorrow,' she echoed, looking up at him.

There was a moment when she thought he might be debating whether to kiss her. But perhaps it didn't cross his mind.

Seconds later, he had released her hand and gestured for her to step inside and close the door.

Next morning she overslept. Troubled thoughts had kept her awake for a long time. Chiara was eating muesli and flipping through *The Tatler*, an upmarket glossy aimed at people in the social swim, or those who admired and envied them.

'I'm in for the third month running,' she announced on a note of triumph, showing Holly a picture of herself revealing more cleavage than anyone else on the same page.

'Congratulations.' Holly opened the fridge and took out a carton of orange juice.

'How was the party?' asked Chiara.

'Good...very good.'

'Who brought you home?'

'Pierce.'

'Did he know you were staying with me?'

'Yes.'

'Did you ask him in for a nightcap?'

'No.'

'Why not? Were you afraid he'd make a pass?'

'Not asking him in avoided that possibility.'

'Maybe he's between girlfriends and wouldn't mind seeing me again,' said Chiara.

'Would you like the satisfaction of telling him to get lost?'

'I might...or I might let him pick up where we left off.'

'I don't understand you, Chiara. Don't you have *any* scruples? Yesterday you were talking about ditching Eric for this man who gave you the aquamarine, and now you're interested in Pierce. How can this sort of life possibly lead to happiness?'

'I'm not like you, Holly. You're a fanatical idealist. You want life to be like a fairy story. It isn't and never was. Who do you know who's living happily ever after? Nobody. OK, your parents might have done, but only *might*. You can't say for certain because your mother died before the gloss had worn off.'

Holly sighed. It was no use arguing. They saw life from different perspectives, hers perhaps as extreme as Chiara's.

When Pierce himself opened his door to her, he was still in the dark blue suit of the kind she associated with board-rooms and the corridors of power.

'Come in. It's Hooper's day off so I'm having something sent round from a restaurant.'

'Oh, dear…I hope I'm not putting you to a lot of trouble. It's just that you're the only person who has the know-how to advise on the situation I'm bothered about.'

'I'm flattered to be asked,' he said, standing by to take her raincoat. 'It shows how far we've advanced since that morning at New Covent Garden.'

After hanging her coat in a cupboard, he led the way to a huge double-cube room with an enormous north window.

'Was this an artist's studio?' Holly asked, gazing round.

'You've got it in one. Nearly a hundred years ago, this was the studio of a very distinguished artist who specialised in paintings of domestic life in Ancient Rome. That way he gave an air of respectability to pictures which, by the standards of the day, were extremely erotic. Scantily dressed Roman maidens, attended by semi-nude slaves, lolling around on the steps of marble bathing pools…that sort of thing. What will you drink? Vodka and tonic?'

'Yes, please.'

While Pierce went to a side table set with rows of bottles and glasses, Holly wandered around, admiring the profusion of Oriental rugs laid almost edge-to-edge on the parquet floor and the massive expanses of books lining sections of the walls.

Suddenly she became aware of a pair of large golden-green eyes, black-rimmed as if with kohl, watching her from the depths of a large armchair.

'Oh…you must be Louisa,' Holly said, smiling.

The cat twitched large tufted ears, her expression enigmatic. With slow deliberation, she uncurled from her resting position, stretching each leg in turn. Then she leapt lightly to the floor where she sat down on her hind legs and gave a desultory lick to one upraised front paw.

Holly went down on her haunches, making small pursed-lip noises and rubbing her fingers together in a gesture of invitation.

After some thought, Louisa walked slowly towards her. In colour, her coat was not dissimilar from Parson's, but much shaggier, with a thick pale grey ruff and a long tapered tail covered with flowing hair.

Two yards from Holly's outstretched hand, she veered in a different direction.

'Your cat has just cut me dead,' said Holly, rising to her feet. Pierce was still fixing their drinks and hadn't witnessed the snub.

'She takes time to make up her mind about people,' he said as he brought the drinks to where she was standing. 'Some of my oldest friends are still trying to ingratiate themselves with Louisa. She's a very discriminating pussy-cat. Perhaps she senses that you have reservations about me.'

'Not as many as I had or I shouldn't be here.' Holly took the glass he offered. 'Thank you. Happy landings!'

'Is that what your father used to say?'

'Yes. How did you guess?'

'Male intuition. We have it too, you know. Not as finely tuned as female intuition, perhaps. But we do have it.'

'I'm sure you do. Sometimes I feel you can see straight through me,' Holly said, with impulsive candour.

'On the contrary, I spent a long time pondering this problem you want my advice on, but I've no idea what it is.

Let's make ourselves comfortable and you can tell me all about it.'

He led the way to a sofa designed for the comfort of people his size. Before sitting down, he moved some cushions from the centre to the end where she would be sitting to make it more comfortable for her.

Holly took a swig of her drink. She had been rehearsing what to say all the way here, but still found it difficult to know where to start.

'If a man and a girl exchanged looks in a public place, and shortly afterwards the girl received a very expensive jewel from him, what would your reaction be?' she asked.

For the first time since they had renewed their acquaintance, Pierce's grey eyes took on the cold look she remembered from their first meeting five years ago. His whole face seemed to harden. As he had no superfluous flesh on his cheeks and neck, it was easy to see the movements of the muscles under the closely shaven brown skin. Right now he was clenching his teeth, causing knots of sinew to form at the angles of his jaw.

'Have you ever done that yourself...wooed a woman you wanted with a fabulous gift?' she asked.

'Certainly not!' he said curtly. 'My only extravagant gestures have been for services rendered.'

The statement made Holly wince. She realised suddenly that Pierce's attitude to sex was as deeply distasteful to her as Chiara's. He looked a superior being. Why couldn't he act like one?

'What was this expensive jewel?' Pierce asked.

'A two-thousand-pound aquamarine. It came in a box of chocolates. It was the size of a chocolate...huge. Like a chunk of crystallised sea-water.'

'How do you know what it cost? Did it have the receipt with it?'

'Chiara took it to a jeweller. She couldn't believe it was real. But he said it was...a stone of the finest quality.'

Pierce's expression changed. 'It was sent to Chiara...not you?'

'Well, of course. Nobody would send *me* something like that,' Holly said, with a wry smile. 'I'd be lucky even to get the handmade chocolates.'

'You underestimate yourself,' Pierce said brusquely. 'When and where did this happen, and what do you know about the man who gave Chiara the aquamarine?'

Holly told him all she knew. 'What terrifies me is that he may be a criminal,' she said, frowning. 'It's a well-known fact that there are some very shady people living on the Costa del Sol. People involved with the Mafia and all kinds of sinister rackets.'

'Does she know the name of his yacht?' Pierce asked.

'No. I asked her that. My first thought was that the only person able to afford such an extravagant gesture would be an Arab prince. A lot of them do have villas and luxury yachts on the Costa del Sol, I believe.'

'Yes, they do,' Pierce agreed. 'I've been there and seen them playing for high stakes in casinos and at private parties. Did this guy look like an Arab?'

'He had black hair and eyes and an olive skin, but so do Spaniards and South Americans.'

'Did you ask her if he had a beard?'

'No, I didn't think of that. Do most Arabs have beards?'

'A lot of them do...not all. It's a pity she didn't notice the name of the boat. With that, we could have run an extensive check on him. Without anything to go on, we're stymied. We can only wait to see if he follows it up and then hope to get some kind of lead on him.'

He shifted his position, moving along the sofa until he was close enough to put his hand over her free hand. 'Don't fret about it, Holly. I don't think it's very likely that Chiara is going to wind up a prisoner in a harem or the mistress of a Mafia boss. You're looking at the worst scenario.' He gave her a long thoughtful look. 'It's not impossible this guy took one look at Chiara and fell in love with her. It can happen like that…so they say.'

'I can't believe that you, of all people, attach much weight to *that* scenario.'

'Why d'you say "you, of all people"? If you prick me, do I not bleed? If you tickle me, do I not laugh? If you poison me, do I not die?'

He was misquoting Shylock in Shakespeare's *The Merchant of Venice*, and it pleased her that he assumed she was as well read as he.

'Of course…but how many men experience love at first sight? One in a thousand, I should think. It seems to happen to women more often than it does to men, and even then often it's only an infatuation…not the real thing.'

Pierce took his hand from hers but didn't move back to the other end of the sofa. 'Perhaps. One thing is certain; it wasn't a *coup de foudre* on Chiara's side,' he said sardonically. 'Your stepsister would never give up everything for love. I sometimes wonder if any of your generation of women would. You're a new breed. Love is no longer your whole existence the way it used to be. Now you think about love the way men do, as a thing apart, to be weighed and measured against life's other prizes.'

'Perhaps some of us do,' said Holly. 'But not all of us. A lot of life's prizes are still out of reach for most women. If you added up all the successful career women and other female achievers, they'd still be a tiny fraction of the entire sex. There are thousands of women in the world who are literally slaves, for heaven's sake.'

'Men too…slaves of poverty. Save your feminist polemics for someone else, Holly. I know more about the world's underclasses than you might imagine.' His dark eyebrows drew together. 'Too damn much,' he said, in a harsh voice.

Holly wondered what he meant. Before she could ask, a bell rang.

'That'll be our food arriving. Stay and finish your drink. I'll call you when lunch is served.'

He sprang up and strode off towards a door in the far corner of the room.

When he had gone, she rose from the sofa and wandered about, looking at his pictures and possessions. Had she been shown this room before meeting its owner, she would have formed a very different impression from the one fixed in her mind by their first encounter at her stepmother's party.

Everything here indicated a man whose inclinations were intellectual and artistic rather than solely sybaritic. His library was as wide-ranging as her father's had been, with many books on philosophy and history that she had seen before on Professor Nicholson's shelves.

After his death, his second wife had lost no time in clearing his study and having the room redecorated. Holly had come home from secretarial college to find his books had been sold to a second-hand dealer. It had been a betrayal of trust she still couldn't bear to think about. After that, as soon as she'd been able to she had left the house which was no longer home to her, to stand on her own feet.

Taking a well-worn leather-bound copy of *An Introduction to Kant's Ethics* from the shelf, she opened it, expecting to see Pierce's signature on the flyleaf. Instead, to her amazement, she found herself looking at her father's book-plate with his name written in ink under the printed *'Ex Libris'*.

Overcome with excitement, she ran to the door in the corner, calling, 'Pierce…Pierce…where are you?'

He appeared in another doorway at the end of a passage. 'Here I am. What's the matter?'

'Where did you get this book?'

'What is it?'

'*Kant's Ethics.*'

Like her father, he obviously knew every book in his possession. 'A dealer I know rang up and said he'd bought a collection of books which might interest me. That was one of them. Why?'

'Because it belonged to my father. Look, here's his book-plate.' She thrust the book at him. 'All these years I've been wondering where his books were…imagining them scattered in houses all over the country. I never go past a second-hand bookshop without hoping to find one and buy it back. And the first time I've ever seen one is here, in your house. It's incredible.'

'P.J. Nicholson… Good Lord, was he your father? I didn't make the connection. I suppose, never having met him, it didn't occur to me that the previous owner of this book could be Chiara's stepfather, even though she had mentioned he was ''boringly brainy'', as she put it.'

'Can you remember how many of his books you bought? Several…a dozen…more than that?'

'About a hundred, as far as I can remember. Tell you what, after lunch why don't you pick out as many as you can carry and take them back with you?'

'Oh, no, I couldn't do that. They belong to you now. It's just so lovely to know where they are…that they've found a good home.'

'That's a change of tune,' he said drily. 'You didn't feel that way the second time we met.'

'Well, I do now. I'm beginning to think I misjudged you.

I'm not saying I think it was right to make Chiara your mistress, but it wasn't as bad as it seemed to me at the time.'

They ate lunch at a small fruitwood table in a corner of the studio, with Louisa watching from the arm of a nearby sofa.

Pierce did not feed her titbits but occasionally glanced in her direction with an affectionate look which she returned with a blink of her beautiful eyes. Holly wondered if, on evenings when he wasn't out, she lay on his lap, being gently caressed by one of his long, tanned hands while the other turned the pages of a book.

'How did you spend this morning?' he asked.

'I didn't do very much. I was up later than usual. I packed my things and then I went out and found a nice card for my thank-you note to Mrs Shintaro. Then I roughed out my note and rewrote it in my best handwriting. Then I posted it, and then I came here.'

'She'll be pleased you took the trouble to write. Most people only ring up. Some don't bother to do that. Being punctilious herself, Fujiko sets store in the traditional forms of politeness. In the past, some of Ben's girlfriends have upset her with their offhand manners. Her own marriage was *o miai* which means arranged by her parents. An *o miai* marriage isn't a matter of compulsion. It's a bringing together of people who seem to their parents or friends to have plenty in common. Fujiko and her husband were so compatible that not long after their marriage they were as much in love as any Western couple.'

'Does she want to arrange Ben's marriage?'

'She'd like to see him marry a Japanese girl. But as Fujiko herself is now very westernised and spends more time in London and New York than in her own country, I think it's unlikely Ben will ever return to his ancestral roots.'

After a pause he added, 'One of the books which was your father's is a history of the Second World War and its aftermath. That war left hundreds of thousands of what were called "displaced persons". They could never go back to where they had lived before, but they were never really at home where they ended up when it was over. Unlike the DPs, Fujiko and Ben have money and status. But in a sense they are both displaced persons, suspended between two cultures and not quite at home in either.'

'Will you always live in England?' she asked. 'Have you transplanted completely?'

'I think so, but always is a long time. Who knows? When I'm an old man, my wife and I might decide we would rather spend this time of year in a warmer climate. I shouldn't want to retire to the Costa del Sol, but I have friends who live in the mountains behind that coast. They're not far from an international airport but the way of life in their village dates back to a time long before flight was dreamed possible. It's a lovely place…very peaceful. I can visualise living there.'

'You are going to marry one day, then?'

'That was never in doubt.' Today they were drinking wine and he broke off to top up their glasses. 'But until my own life was properly organised, it would have been premature to look for a wife.'

'You make a wife sound like something that can be shopped for. I thought, like husbands, they cropped up when least expected.'

'So they may, but the circumstances have to be propitious. For instance, the first time we met neither of us was ready for marriage. You were too young and I had problems with my working life. Let's assume I had never met Chiara but had come to the party as somebody's house guest. On the premise that we had taken one look at each other and thought, This is it, do you think it would have worked out?'

It was such a strange thing to say that Holly was momentarily nonplussed.

As she floundered for a reply, Pierce answered for her. 'It wouldn't have got off the ground. But now the situation is different. We both of us know who we are and where we're heading. If I were to suggest that we pooled our resources, and if you were to agree, we'd stand a good chance of becoming one of those ideal couples whom everyone wants to emulate but very few do.'

Unable to meet the teasing gleam in his eyes, Holly looked down at her plate, at what remained of a salmon steak which had followed a first course of Chinese prawns on a bed of green tagliatelle.

'Without being in love to begin with?' Her mouth felt curiously dry.

'What does "being in love" mean to you? Define it for me.'

'Being very strongly attracted…liking a person's mind as well as their physical looks…trusting them…wanting to be with them always…feeling that life without them would be an endless desert…' With a gesture expressing the impossibility of putting such a complex emotion into words, she gave up.

'I would disagree with that last bit,' said Pierce. 'Life is never or rarely a desert. Happiness shouldn't depend on being with another person. I'd go as far as to say you can only love someone else if you love and are satisfied with the life you're leading before they show up. It's all right to feel something's missing…that there's another dimension that will make it all even better. But I'd only marry a girl who had got her own act together…as, for example, you have.'

'Well, yes, that makes sense,' said Holly. 'The only thing is, you can't always go by appearances. When you came to that party with Chiara, you seemed to have life on a string. Now you say that was not so.'

'I was making a lot of money, but I didn't feel what I was doing served any useful purpose other than making me richer. I needed a greater challenge and certain intangible rewards. Now, by redirecting my energies, I have both.'

At this point the telephone rang. Pierce excused himself to answer it.

Holly, whose mobile phone had revolutionised her life, was a little surprised that he didn't keep one within arm's reach but went to a jacked-in set at the far end of the room.

She was wondering what form the redirection of his career had taken, and intending to ask him, when after a very brief chat with the person on the line he came back.

'I'm sorry, Holly. I'm going to have to cut this short. I need to get back to my office. I was hoping to take you to the station, but you'll have to call a taxi. This is the number to ring.' He had already written it down on a page from a pad by the telephone. 'But stay and finish your lunch. There's no need for you to rush off because I have to. Maybe if I'm not around, Louisa will unbend and make friends with you.'

'But what about locking up?' she said anxiously. 'Are there complicated burglar alarms which need to be set?'

'No, it's all completely automatic. You don't have to worry about a thing…except the calories in the pudding,' he said, with a smile. 'Which, judging by the shape you revealed last night, isn't a problem for you anyway.'

As she rose from her chair, he added, 'About the problem

with Chiara— I'll give it some thought and call you...
possibly tonight.'

'Thank you for lunch, Pierce—' she began.

'My pleasure. I only wish I didn't have to dash off. We
must do it again...very soon.'

He put his hands on her shoulders and bent to kiss her
on both cheeks.

Seconds later, while she was still in a whirl from the
touch of his lips on her face, he was on his way to the front
door.

Holly's train journey back to Norfolk seemed to pass in a
flash, her thoughts being in such a flurry of astonishment,
joy and apprehension.

How could she be in love with a man who, only a short
time ago, had been the one person on earth she heartily
detested? Could it be, could it *possibly* be that his conversation at lunch meant that he was beginning to feel she was
someone special, someone different from all his girlfriends—someone he could come to love?

Suddenly, to be loved by Pierce was more important than
anything she had ever set her heart on since she'd been a
little girl longing to find that one of the parcels under the
Christmas tree had a camera in it.

Since then there had been many other things she had
wanted, including the prize which had given her career such
a boost. But none had been even fractionally as important
as this. On this her whole life depended. For, if he didn't
want her, how could she ever make do with anyone else?
It had to be Pierce or no one.

The instant his hard male cheek had brushed hers and
she'd felt the slight movement of his lips in what, outwardly, had had no more significance than Ben's kiss the
night before, or a thousand other social kisses, her mind

had at last acknowledged what her heart had known for a long time.

She had been in love with Pierce Sutherland since he'd first walked into her life. That was the real reason she had been so upset when he'd ditched Chiara: the man she had wanted to idolise had proved to have feet of clay and her nineteen-year-old heart, unable to come to terms with that, had taken refuge in pretending to loathe him.

After making herself a light supper and giving Parson his favourite evening meal—sardines in tomato sauce—she went to bed early.

She was reading the current issue of *The Garden*, with Parson curled on the outside of the old patchwork quilt she had found in a junk shop, when the telephone rang.

'Hello?'

'It's Pierce. I'm sorry I had to desert you.'

'It didn't matter. It was good of you to see me in the first place.'

'Nonsense. I wanted to see you. Lunching with you was a lot more enjoyable than having a sandwich at my desk. Listen, tomorrow I have to go overseas for a few days. I'm not sure when I'll be back, but as soon as I am I'll call you and we'll pick up where we left off. Also something came up this afternoon which I need to consult you about. I won't go into it now, except to say that it's right up your alley.'

'Something to do with gardens?'

'It's too complicated to explain on the telephone. Take care of yourself, Green Fingers.'

'You too. Where are you going?'

'Africa. I have to say goodnight now.'

'Goodnight, Pierce…' she waited until he had cut the connection before adding softly, 'Darling.'

*   *   *

The day after Pierce's departure two nice things happened, followed by something upsetting.

Holly was having her breakfast when Mrs Shintaro called to say she had a long-standing invitation to a golden-wedding lunch party at the country home of some old friends she had met when they and her husband, then a young diplomat, had been *en poste* in Rio de Janeiro many years ago. As their house was only ten miles from where Holly was living, and Ben was taking the place of her usual driver, she wondered if Holly would take him under her wing for a few hours until it was time for him to collect her for the journey back to London.

Holly agreed with alacrity, feeling sure that Ben would be able to explain many things she wanted to know about Pierce, as well as clarifying the remark he had made during supper at his grandmother's party.

Unfortunately it was a horrible day for their drive, with rain sloshing down and no sign of a break in the clouds. As she wasn't able to work outside, she spent the morning preparing a hot lunch. While she was cooking, the postman delivered a large padded bag which proved to contain half a dozen of her father's books.

Pierce had written in handwriting as bold and incisive as his personality:

I've always believed that we make our own destinies, but now I'm beginning to wonder if there's something in fate after all. The African trip is a nuisance just now but can't be avoided. Keep a space for me in your diary in the early part of next week. It will be a professional assignment with personal intervals.

She was still pondering what the last sentence might mean when Ben arrived, wearing a leather aviator's jacket over a coral sweater which set off his colouring.

'This is very kind of you, Holly. I hope I'm not disrupting your life too much by descending on you this way. The people my grandmother's lunching with would have fitted me in, but I would have felt like an interloper. They're all around sixty or seventy. Lunching with you will be a lot more fun.'

'You're not disrupting anything,' Holly assured him. 'Because of the heavy rain I'd switched my schedule around to make this my day for house-cleaning. Now the chores are done, the rest of the day is free. If it should clear up later I'll take you to see the garden I'm working on, but I've just heard a radio forecast and I think we're going to be house-bound.'

Ben had run down the garden path with a yachtsman's bright yellow waterproof worn like a cloak over his sheepskin-lined leather jacket. Now, from its capacious pockets, he began to take various packages.

'In Japan it's the custom to take one's hostess a present,' he said. 'As I didn't know I was coming until this morning, I had to shop in a hurry. These are not what, given more time, I would have chosen for you, but they may come in useful.'

As she unwrapped his offerings, Holly found he had paid a flying visit to the grocery department of Fortnum & Mason, one of London's most famous stores, and selected a range of their special delicacies.

'They all look delicious…thank you. Let me hang up your coats… Oh, this is Parson, my cat,' she added as he, hearing an unfamiliar voice, came through from the kitchen to inspect the visitor.

Ben went down on his haunches. 'Hi, Parson. You're a fine fellow.' He stroked the tabby's broad head and tickled him under one ear, setting off Parson's deepest, most friendly purr.

'I wish I'd had that effect on Louisa, Pierce's cat,' said Holly, watching them making friends. 'She was very uppity with me. Have you managed to win her over?'

'She's OK with guys but jealous of women,' said Ben, standing up. 'A long time ago, Pierce had a girlfriend who was allergic to cats and Louisa had to be shut in the kitchen whenever she was around. I think she was deeply offended and has never got over it. Forgive me if I'm being too nosy, but are you and Pierce starting something?'

Holly was disconcerted. 'What makes you think we might be?'

'My grandmother told me that when she gave you a ride back from New Covent Garden you were reacting to each other so strongly that she thought the atmosphere was about to ignite.'

'That was because he was then at the top of my hate list,' said Holly. 'I don't feel that way about him now, but our friendship is still very new. What did you mean when you said he cared about people more than anyone you knew?'

'Pierce has been fighting a battle against corruption in the developing countries,' said Ben. 'He realised how much aid from taxpayers in the rich countries was never reaching the people it was intended to help and began a campaign to change that. Now he's set up an organisation, of which he is the dynamo, that's already made a big difference to the situation worldwide. Of course it's also made him a lot of powerful enemies among the people who were making fortunes for themselves by siphoning off money and relief supplies. But I don't think he's as much at risk now as he was in the early days. If they could have got rid of him then, the whole project might have foundered.'

'You mean they might have killed him?' Holly asked, shaken.

'Oh, sure. If you were lining your pockets from the bottomless pit of international aid, how would you feel about a guy who was trying to stop you? They hated his guts and they were the kind of people whose enemies wind up feeding the crocodiles or worse.'

'Is he in danger now…on this trip to Africa?' she asked.

'Probably not. The organisation he founded is too solidly based to fall apart at this stage. There would be no point in wiping him out. Don't worry: he can look after himself. He's not a guy who ever takes stupid risks. He might take a calculated chance sometimes, but he doesn't make careless mistakes. You don't need to lose any sleep about him.'

'At the moment Pierce and I are just friends,' Holly said pointedly. 'The only thing that keeps me awake at night is wondering where my next commission is coming from.'

But, later, after Ben had left to pick up his grandmother, she knew that what she had told him wasn't true. She *would* be anxious about Pierce until she knew he was safely back in London.

She had put some more logs on the fire and was sitting, with Parson curled on her lap, listening to his rhythmic purr and the sound of the rising wind and rain beating on the curtained windows, when the telephone rang.

Irrationally hoping it might be a call from somewhere in Africa, Holly was surprised to hear her stepsister saying angrily, 'What the hell do you mean by telling Pierce what I told you? It's none of his damn business…or yours, come to that. You've no right to go shooting your mouth off about my private affairs. And he's got no bloody right to come roaring round here, telling me how to run my life.'

'When did he come to see you?' Holly asked, bewildered and shocked by the rage in her stepsister's voice.

'Last night. Barged in here as if he owned the place and read me the Riot Act about behaving recklessly and being a worry to you. I tried to keep him out, but anyone would have thought it was a police raid the way he stormed in and started hectoring me. The worst of it was that Eric was in the bedroom. Naturally he wanted to know what the hell was going on.'

'Did Pierce tell him?'

'He didn't need to. He'd already said enough for Eric to guess that something was up. By the time Pierce had gone, he was spoiling for a row. I lost my temper and shouted back at him. Eventually he slammed out. The chances are, I'll never see him again...and all because you blabbed to Pierce about something that doesn't concern either one of you.'

In the moment before she slammed the phone down, Holly heard her bursting into noisy tears.

CHAPTER FIVE

THIRTY seconds later Holly rang Chiara's number, only to hear a recorded answering-machine message.

After the tone, she said, 'Chiara, I had no idea Pierce intended to deal with this business as he did. Truly I didn't. But I can't deny that I did consult him. He seemed the only person I could turn to for advice. I was worried about you… seriously worried. Bad things can happen to girls who get involved with men they know nothing about. I'm sorry if the way Pierce handled it has made things difficult with Eric, but I have to say this isn't Pierce's fault or mine. It's yours…for two-timing Eric…or at least being prepared to ditch him if a better offer turns up.

'If I didn't love you, I wouldn't care what you did. But I can't bear to see you going down this dangerous road which could end in a sordid story in one of the tabloids. You've never been very good at facing unpleasant facts and you won't get any sensible advice from your mother. Pierce knows the world better than either of us. Please think over what he said to you. Please don't shut me out of your life. I'm not going to sleep a wink unless you call back.'

Chiara didn't call back, nor did Holly really expect her to. After the quarrels of their childhood and teen years, her stepsister had invariably sulked—a trait she had learned from her mother, who had used the same technique with her second husband if he'd made what she'd call 'a fuss' about her extravagance.

It had been an unhappy marriage on every level and eventually they had slept in separate rooms, not only, Holly suspected, because of her father's heart condition but because the intimacy of sharing a bed had become distasteful to them both.

She had never been able to understand how her father could have contemplated a sexual relationship with Nora in the first place. But, of course, she had seen her stepmother through the eyes of a child who would have resented anyone usurping her natural mother.

When she had been old enough to view the situation sensibly, she had realised that at the time of the marriage Nora must have been almost as lovely as Chiara was now. Was it surprising that her father, desperately lonely and needing someone to care for his motherless daughter, had been seduced by Nora's alluring looks and the winning ways she could adopt when it suited her?

Holly didn't stay awake all night, but her restless tossings and turnings caused Parson to remove himself from his preferred position against the small of her back and station himself near the footboard of the pine double bed, a reproduction of a French farmhouse bed.

It was Pierce's handling of the matter which had been on her mind during the night and still preoccupied her the next morning as she gave Parson his breakfast before attending to her own.

She wanted very much to believe that Pierce's impetuous action, so different from the cool-headed behaviour she would have expected of him, had been prompted by feelings warmer than mere friendship. Could it be—oh, please let it be!—that he was beginning to feel the same way about her as she did about him?

She had eaten her muesli and was peeling a couple of satsumas when the telephone rang.

'Hello?'

'It's me,' said Chiara. 'I've cooled down a bit since last night. I'm still furious with you, but I suppose you meant well.'

To Holly's amazement, she heard her stepsister giggle. 'I've just had a huge basket of flowers by special delivery. They're from Eric. The note says he's sorry he shouted and swore at me last night. He wants to come round this morning and take me shopping. Reading between the lines, he's going to buy me something bigger and better than an aquamarine. There's a bracelet in a shop in Bond Street I rather fancy. It'll cost him an arm and a leg, but why not? He can afford it.'

'Does that mean you're going to stay with him and give the aquamarine back when the other man makes contact with you?'

'Not likely! Why would I do that? Honestly, Hol, your ideas are so Victorian, it isn't true. I suppose it's because you only earn peanuts yourself and you and whoever you marry will never have any serious spending power. But the men I know are in a different league. A diamond bracelet to them is like a packet of seeds to you.'

Probably because she was tired, Holly was on a short fuse. She said crisply, 'Personally, I'd rather have an inexpensive engagement ring from a man who loved me and wanted to marry me than a million pounds' worth of jewels from a lot of randy older men to whom I was nothing more than a sex object. Excuse me, I have to go and earn another peanut.'

She rang off.

The days that followed seemed endless. Holly scoured the columns of *The Times*, fearful of finding a paragraph about the body of an unidentified European male being found in mysterious circumstances in some part of Africa. That she didn't even know which part of that vast continent he was in somehow increased her anxiety.

Every time the telephone rang, her heart seemed to stop beating until the caller identified himself.

In between times she went over every word Pierce had said to her, looking for nuances she might have missed the first time.

When, at last, he did ring it was after she had turned out the light and was lying awake, thinking about him.

Thinking it might be Chiara, with whom she hadn't spoken since the peanuts conversation, she let it ring several times before picking up the receiver.

'Hello?'

'It's Pierce. How are you?'

Holly shot into a sitting position, disturbing Parson, who stopped his drowsy purring and gave a mew of displeasure.

'Pierce! Where are you? Are you all right?'

'I got home five minutes ago. I'm fine. What about you?'

'Fine...great.' The fact that he had called her so soon after his arrival made her spirits soar. 'How was your trip?'

'Successful, but I'm glad it's over. How soon can you give me that day I asked you to keep free?'

'As soon as you wish.'

'Tomorrow?'

'Yes, if you like.'

'Tomorrow it is. I'll pick you up about nine.' He explained where the airfield was and then added, 'Tell that cat of yours he may have to fend for himself for twelve hours...possibly overnight.'

'Why overnight?'

'Because we'll be going to Devon and at this time of

year weather conditions can worsen quite rapidly. We might need to spend the night locally.'

'OK, I'll make some contingency arrangements.'

'Until tomorrow.' Pierce rang off.

The following morning, Holly had her first experience of flying in a helicopter. She had heard they were difficult to handle, but Pierce seemed to have no problem in keeping the machine smoothly on course for their destination.

England, seen from a much lower altitude than she had flown at before, presented a fascinating patchwork of fields, villages, woods, major and minor roads, grand and less grand country houses, private swimming pools, flooded quarries and what he told her were fish farms.

In a fraction of the time it would have taken to get there by road or rail, they arrived on the other side of England, landing at a small private airfield where Pierce had arranged for a car and a driver to be waiting. A basket containing coffee and sandwiches had also been laid on, and Holly began to realise how relaxed and enjoyable journeys could be when masterminded by a man with unlimited resources.

It was during this stage of the journey that he finally disclosed the purpose of the trip.

'For a couple of years I've had one of the best estate agencies looking for a country place for me,' he explained. 'I've visited dozens of houses all over England but none of them had that special something about them you want in a place you're hoping to live in for the rest of your life and hand on to your children. The house we're going to see this morning came on the market a month ago. I've already been over it twice. Now I'd like to have your opinion of it.'

'But Pierce, I don't know about houses. I only know

about gardens…and there are people far more expert than myself whom you could consult.'

'Perhaps, but experts tend to be older rather than younger and I want to know how the house strikes someone of your age. Is it a white elephant which ought to be left to moulder into a picturesque ruin, or is it a dream waiting to be realised?'

'Why has it come on the market?'

'The old man who owned it died. He was in his nineties and very short of money. The place has been badly neglected for a couple of decades. He did have descendants, but none of them wants it. Apparently his sons and daughters were all adventurous, as he was himself in his youth, and they settled in places like New Zealand and Costa Rica. They and their children have rooted in other countries and don't want to be transplanted. So the house is up for grabs; only, it's so far gone that most buyers don't bother to view it, or take one look and get back in their cars.'

By this time Holly had grasped why he had laid on a driver. Clearly the house was well off the beaten track, reached by a labyrinth of largely unsignposted lanes in which anyone unfamiliar with the area would easily lose their way.

'It's a long way from the nearest railway station and over an hour from the motorway. For anyone work-based in London the only practical transport is by air,' Pierce went on. 'However, at the moment the grounds are in such a shambles, there's nowhere to land. Anyway I wanted you to see it from the ground. We're nearly there now. The main gate is round the next corner.'

The iron gates which came into view a few moments later had, judging by their design, been beautifully wrought by a master craftsman at least two hundred years ago. Now, flanked by ornamental lodges not large enough to be called cottages, the gates were long overdue for a fresh coat of paint. Chained together and padlocked, they barred the way to a wide drive lined with ancient beeches, their massive branches now leafless.

As the driver got out to unlock and open the gates, Holly had a curious feeling that she had seen this gateway before. Yet she knew she couldn't have done so because she had never set foot in Devon.

The meadows on either side of the drive were being grazed by sheep, those near the fences raising their heads to stare impassively at the passing car.

Then, as it rounded a bend, the house came into view, and again she had an uncannily strong sensation of *déjà vu*.

'I wonder if it's been featured in *Country Life*?' she said, half to herself. 'It seems so familiar. What is it called, this house?'

'Not something you would expect in this part of the world,' said Pierce. 'It was built in 1815 by a colonel who'd been invalided out of Wellington's army. He'd been badly wounded in some of the fiercest fighting of the Peninsular campaign. Like many veterans of that war, he called his house after a battle he'd fought in. Talavera. It's an odd name to find in the wilds of Devon, isn't it?' Something in her expression made him ask, 'What's the matter?'

'Nothing. It's just that Talavera is a very familiar name to me.'

'How come? Did you do the Peninsular War in your history lessons at school?'

'No, it was reading novels set in the Regency, not history lessons, which taught me about that period. But that's not why the name Talavera strikes a chord. One of my favourite vases for very small flowers like primroses and violets is a little yellow pottery jar. On the bottom is written, in

Spanish, ''Made by hand—Talavera.'' I found it in a charity shop. I suppose the previous owner brought it back from Spain as a souvenir.'

By now the car had drawn up in front of the house and the driver was opening the rear door on Pierce's side. He sprang out, turning to offer his hand to Holly.

Even though most of her attention was focused on the house they had come to see, the contact with his palm and fingers sent a frisson of pleasure feathering along her nerves.

'The style is called Picturesque Gothic,' said Pierce as they stood side by side, looking at the façde of a substantial mansion which, in spite of its size, had a cosy, almost cottagey air about it. Perhaps this came from the windows with their pointed-arch glazing bars, or from the mock battlements along the roof-line and the ornamental turrets at each angle of the building.

'The central block was built first and then the wings added on as the family expanded,' said Pierce.

The driver, who was evidently under instructions from the Devon office of Pierce's estate agents, was unlocking the front door for them.

As she entered the hall, lit by sunlight streaming through French windows at the far end and through a large window at the turn of the graceful staircase, Holly was aware that the house was in dire disrepair. Yet instantly, in her mind's eye, she could see it as it had once been and could be again.

As Pierce showed her round, no one with eyes in their head could have ignored the evidence of galloping decay. In the small bathroom part of the sprung floor had collapsed. In the attics, a score of buckets were positioned to catch drips from holes in the roof.

'Have you worked out what it would cost to put it in order?' she asked him.

'Only roughly, but it's a daunting amount,' he said, his mouth wry. 'Don't tell me what you think of it until we've looked round the grounds.'

To Holly, neglected gardens had a beauty all their own. When they came to the walled kitchen garden, it evoked powerful memories of sitting in the circle of her father's arm while he read her the stories he had loved as a small boy, his first favourites being the little books by Beatrix Potter about families of rabbits, and mice who could do fine embroidery.

It was in a corner of the kitchen garden that Pierce turned to her and said, 'Do you think I'm mad even to contemplate taking it on?'

Above a serpentine wall of mellow old bricks could be seen the chimneypots of the house and the tops of many fine trees.

'I don't think I should say what I think,' she said slowly. 'It's a purely emotional reaction, completely divorced from common sense.'

'Are you saying that you like Talavera?'

'I feel the same way about it as I did about my yellow pot. That was love at first sight and so is this,' she admitted. 'If I had the money—which I haven't—I could spend the rest of my life putting Talavera to rights. It may be falling to bits, but for me it has everything a house should have. Atmosphere…charm…character…all those intangible factors which have nothing to do with practicality and everything to do with being happy in a place.'

Pierce turned away and took a few paces along the weedstrewn brick path. Then, returning to where she was standing, he said, 'I feel the same way. My head tells me I must be mad. My heart says otherwise. I *do* have the means to do it, but I wanted someone whose judgement I value to tip the balance for me.'

'I can't think why you should value my judgement. What I know about high finance would fit on the head of a pin,' she said.

'Very probably,' he answered drily. 'But you've managed to pick your way past all the disasters you could have fallen into since you left school. Dead-end jobs, rotten relationships and so forth. You have to have a good head on your shoulders to have done that. Also women have an instinct about houses. They see the potential more clearly than men do. On the whole, it's still women who turn a house into a home. They're visualising the furnishings while a man is still wondering if he can handle the mortgage.'

'Presumably a mortgage isn't something you have to worry about.'

'If I needed one, I'd be unlikely to raise it on a property as derelict as this one. My surveyor will probably discover that every known form of rot is rampant and it's thoroughly unsound structurally. But who cares? You've fallen for it. So have I. Between us, we'll restore it to the way it should be, with some discreet modernisations to make it more comfortable than was possible when it was built.'

Holly wasn't sure what he meant by 'between us'.

'Are you putting me in sole charge of the restoration of the garden?' she asked.

'That's the idea…if you're willing to take it on.'

'I'd adore to…but I do wonder if you wouldn't be better advised to get one of the big names in my field to do it. If you were a stranger, of course I'd grab it with both hands and fight off the competition for all I was worth. But you're not…you're a friend, so it's different. Am I the best possible garden designer for this project? I have to ask myself.'

'You're the one I happen to want…and you won't be as expensive as the big shots,' he added, with a teasing gleam.

'You can make your name on this, Holly. You can make Talavera as famous as the gardens at Sissinghurst and Hidcote and Great Dixter. Since I met you I've been doing some homework. I now know a lot more about garden design than I did a few weeks ago. I believe, under your tuition, I could become seriously interested. And perhaps there are things I can teach you.'

There was something in his eyes as he said this that made her breath catch in her throat.

She watched him take a step forward, narrowing the space between them, and she felt like a rabbit hypnotised by the headlamps of a car, unable to move.

Pierce put his hands on her shoulders as he had when he'd kissed her goodbye in his house in London. But this time she knew instinctively that it wasn't going to be an innocuous kiss on the cheek such as people exchanged all the time without altering the nature of their relationship.

Unable to meet the gleaming grey gaze focused on her, she closed her eyes.

When she felt his lips touching hers, her whole body seemed to melt. The pleasure was so intense that it seemed to consume her. She felt like a candle melting into a pool of wax.

By the time he'd stopped kissing her, Pierce had both arms round her. Without their support, she felt she might have fallen over.

Making a big effort to pull herself together, she said, 'I don't think we should be doing this. Business and pleasure don't mix.'

'Not as a general rule—no. But there are exceptions.'

She couldn't believe he could be so in control after reducing her to a quivering bundle of delicious sensations.

'I don't think this is one of them, Pierce. I really don't,' she said, trying to sound firmer than she felt.

She drew away and he let her.

'You're still nervous of me, aren't you?' he said, watching. 'What do you think I'm going to do to you? Make love to you and then walk away, as I did with Chiara?'

Holly felt herself flushing. She said, 'Soon after you'd gone to Africa, Chiara rang up in a rage because I'd told you about the aquamarine. What made you burst in on her like that?'

'It's no use treating Chiara with kid gloves,' he said calmly. 'She's like her mother: self-centred, acquisitive and flighty. She doesn't respond to kindness, which she interprets as weakness. She needs very firm handling. It wouldn't surprise me if your father was too nice a man to keep your stepmother in her place. Women like that can make life hell for their husbands and lovers. I don't think much of Chiara's current meal-ticket. He's a windbag: full of hot air but with no real guts.'

'You're right about that,' said Holly. 'The day after storming at her, he sent her a huge bouquet and offered to take her shopping. But I can't see that your tirade did any good. It hasn't put her off the other man.'

'I went off at half-cock,' he admitted. 'There were reasons for that but I won't go into them now. Let's go back to the car and have lunch. I asked them to put up a picnic. The driver can walk to the pub. It's only half a mile away.'

'I wish I'd brought my camera with me,' said Holly as they left the kitchen garden. 'It's a perfect day for taking snaps. I could have shot several rolls. It's hard to remember everything after only one visit.'

'Once the place is mine, you can come as often as you wish. The pub does B and B and is said to be comfortable. We can make it our field headquarters. If the house were yours, who would you choose to decorate it?'

'If it were mine, I'd do it myself, bit by bit.'

'That would take for ever. Not all professional decorators leave their signature loud and clear on every house they come near. I've heard of a man in Wiltshire who's said to be very good. He advised the Prince of Wales about High-grove. It's not my ambition to make Talavera a show-place. Let the garden be famous, by all means,' he said, smiling at her, 'but I want to keep the house private. A place for me and my family to escape from the turmoil of the world.'

When he spoke of his family, it gave her a curious pain in the region of her heart.

They had lunch in the sunny hall, beside the open French windows. The driver set up a folding table and two green canvas director's chairs. He spread the table with a green and white gingham cloth.

'We'll do the rest,' said Pierce as the man began to un-strap a large picnic basket. 'You get along to the pub.'

'Very good, sir. What time do you want me back here?'

'Half past two.'

When he had gone Pierce took over the unpacking of the lunch.

'When are you hoping to be able to live here?' Holly asked, standing by.

'Why don't you sit down and relax?' he suggested. 'I should think it will take two years to make the place hab-itable. Years of neglect can't be repaired in a hurry.'

She watched the deft movements of his fingers as he uncorked a bottle of white wine taken from a cool-bag.

'Was the last owner a direct descendant of the man who built the house?' she asked.

Pierce nodded. 'It's been passed down from father to son for getting on for two centuries. I'd like to think history will repeat itself and my descendants will be living here in the twenty-second century. Continuity is important. I be-lieve in people breaking out of the environment they were born in and having a look at what else the world has to offer. But I also believe in the importance of roots. I had a stable background when I was growing up. I want my sons and daughters to have the same advantage.'

'What if you fall in love with someone who doesn't want to have children?' Holly asked. 'A lot of people are opting out of automatic parenthood these days.'

He gave her a keen look. 'Are you one of them?'

The truthful answer would have been, No, I'm not. I can't think of anything I'd like better than having your babies.

Instead, she said, 'I'm open-minded. I don't think it's a decision one can make in advance. You may be able to plan your future but mine will depend on the man I marry. He might be committed to spending his life in a way which would rule out having children.'

'If he were, would you give up your career for him, just like that?'

'I would rather not, but I might have no option,' she said lightly. 'I think wherever I found myself I could always find something to occupy me, but love isn't something most people get a second shot at. Not what I mean by love anyway.'

'Ah, yes…the man who will make the desert bloom for you.' As he handed her a glass of wine and reminded her of her definition of love, his eyes held a glint of mockery.

'Aren't you having some wine?' she asked.

'I never drink when I'm flying.'

He went on unpacking the lunch, setting out china plates and stainless steel cutlery before starting to open the boxes containing the food.

Holly sipped her wine and wondered if he had any inkling that he was the man who could make the desert bloom for her. Somehow she didn't think so. He had said there were things he could teach her and she didn't doubt it. But what she wanted from him was more than a short course in the delights of physical love.

Remembering his kiss in the garden, she took advantage of his concentration on the lunch to look at the well-cut mouth which had stirred those wild feelings in her. She knew that if it was his intention to seduce her she had little hope of resisting.

She said, 'How did you come to speak Japanese fluently?'

'I enjoy learning languages. Japanese is particularly interesting. You have to adjust your style of speech to suit the person you're addressing and there are words which women use and others which men use. If a foreign man uses a lot of the words associated with women, there'll be jokes about him learning Japanese on the pillow. Which, in case you're wondering, I didn't,' he added drily. 'Fujiko has helped me to master the finer points, but mainly I learnt Japanese on long-haul flights and when there was nothing worth watching on TV.'

After a pause, he added, 'Chiara was a TV addict. Am I right in assuming you're not?'

Holly nodded. 'It was always a bone of contention between my father and stepmother. They didn't have rows about it. He would quietly withdraw to his study. Apart from a few programmes about archaeology and science, he found TV boring.'

'And you?'

'I feel the same way. As a child I watched the box sometimes, but mostly I was busy doing homework. I had to work terribly hard to get the results Dad expected. My stepmother thought him too exacting. But if he hadn't been I wouldn't have done half as well. Not that I was ever at the top of my class. But I did do my best. Children need to be put on their mettle…don't you think?'

'I couldn't agree more,' said Pierce. 'I don't have a lot of patience with any spectator activities. I don't want to watch someone else climbing a mountain. I want to do it myself.'

'Ben says this expedition you and he are doing in February isn't very dangerous. Is that true?'

'Would you mind if it weren't true?'

'Mrs Shintaro would worry if she knew Ben was at risk.'

'Naturally, but would you worry if I were risking my neck?'

She sidestepped the question by saying, 'From what Ben tells me, it sounds as if you often risk your neck…or have in the past.'

Pierce shrugged. 'Perhaps…in the early stages. Not any more. Now my theories have been proved, I have a lot of powerful backing. There would be nothing to gain by having me blown away.'

'When that risk existed, didn't it frighten you?'

'Not as much as getting my project off the ground excited me. Have you been involved in something which involved a degree of risk but an equal or greater degree of excitement and challenge?'

'I don't think so.'

'How about our relationship?'

'I don't see the connection.'

'I think you do,' he said drily. 'But you'd rather not discuss it. When I kissed you just now in the garden, what you felt was a mixture of pleasure and terror. When I asked you if you were afraid of being dumped like Chiara, you dodged the issue. *Is* that what worries you?'

'No, because I'm not going to put myself in a position where you could dump me,' she said levelly. 'Yes, I enjoyed it when you kissed me. But that's as far as it goes, Pierce. I'm not in the market for a casual affair based on sexual attraction. I've been there and done that and it was disappointing. Even you won't tempt me to repeat that mistake. You're very attractive...very charming...but you aren't offering what I want.'

'Which is?'

'An old-fashioned "closed" relationship between two people who don't want anyone but each other...ever.'

Pierce handed her a pair of salad servers. As she helped herself to a mixture of greenery which he had already dressed with vinaigrette, Holly wondered what he was thinking.

But he kept his thoughts to himself, steering the conversation into impersonal channels while they ate the marinated herring which went with the salad.

This was followed by a quiche with a red salad and for pudding there was an almond and honey ice cream from a cooler. Even the coffee, though vacuum-flasked, was unusually good.

'Wonderful food to find in the wilds of Devon,' said Holly.

'Devon isn't as wild as you might think. It's where a lot of downshifters come...people who've had enough of the rat race and want a more civilised life. The woman who put up this picnic is a downshifter. She used to organise lavish buffets and hampers for Glyndebourne and Ascot and the top end of the corporate hospitality market. Then her husband was summarily sacked by a company he'd served well for twenty years and they both decided to downshift. Luckily their children had just finished school. They're twins, a boy and a girl, and bright enough to have gone to university. But they've both decided there are too many graduates competing for too few jobs so they're taking another route.'

Holly was favourably impressed by his intimate knowledge of a family whose fortunes would have had little impact on most of the chief executives whose companies had used the wife's service while she was working in London.

She said, 'It's not only the competition for jobs that's a problem, it's the shortfall between grants and expenses so that by the time students graduate they're in massive debt to their banks. If my father hadn't left me some money, I could never have gone to secretarial college and then on the garden-design course without a bank loan. Being in debt's not a good way to start out.'

'What would you have done without his money?'

'I'd have worked my way through college and done garden design on a part-time, long-term basis. There are courses designed for people who have to do it that way. Which reminds me—the normal procedure at this stage is for us to discuss exactly what you want done here so that I can give you an estimate of how long it's likely to take and what it will cost. And I think, in fairness to both of us, you ought to consult at least two other designers. It's such a prize commission that I'd rather win it on merit than have it handed to me on a plate.'

Pierce drank some coffee, watching her over the rim of the elegant bone china demitasse.

'Is that because you suspect there are strings attached to it?'

'Certainly not! If I thought that, I wouldn't be here.'

He gave her a lazy smile. 'What a puritan front you present, Holly. Repelled by the thought of an overdraft. Repelled by Chiara's use of her only assets, her face and her body. But when I kissed you, you didn't react like a puritan, except for that prim little speech about not mixing business and pleasure. The way your lips felt under mine, and the way you relaxed in my arms while we were kissing wasn't strait-laced. You enjoyed it as much as I did.'

There was nothing she could say which wouldn't be an outright lie.

He read her mind. 'And lies stick in your throat too, don't they? You want to deny it, but you can't. You feel the attraction between us as strongly as I do. But your price is higher than Chiara's. You've just spelt it out for me. Not only marriage but also lifelong fidelity. That's quite a tall order these days.'

Holly tilted her chin, aware that her cheeks were burning, but meeting his gaze head-on.

'It always was a tall order,' she retorted hotly. 'But then so is climbing mountains. If you don't like spectator sports and you're bent on reaching a summit not many people aspire to, why is your love life so second-rate? If your affair with Chiara was anything to go by, your relationships with women are the emotional equivalent of those beds in public gardens where they change the display every season. Personally, I would rather have a single *Worsleya procera* than an acre of showy bedding plants.'

The scorn in her voice made him grin. Angry as she was, it didn't diminish her awareness of the buzz she felt when his lean cheeks formed two deep creases and his lips curled back from those sexy white teeth.

'What's so special about *Worsleya procera*?'

'It's a beautiful blue amaryllis…a type of lily. One bulb costs a hundred pounds and often it takes years to flower. It's a connoisseur's plant…but I don't think where women are concerned you are a connoisseur.' As soon as she'd said it, she realised this wasn't the way to talk to a man who was offering her a commission every garden designer on both sides of the Atlantic would regard as a giant plum.

CHAPTER SIX

'Do you consider yourself the female equivalent of a blue amaryllis?' Pierce asked, his tone sardonic.

Holly's colour deepened. 'Far from it. Chiara might have been that, given different nurturing, but I'm nothing out of the ordinary. What I meant is that—'

Hearing footsteps crunching on gravel, she broke off. The driver had come back early, but he didn't enter the house. She saw him pass the front door, going in the direction of the car.

'I know what you meant,' said Pierce. 'I may not be a connoisseur but I'm quick on the uptake. You're wrong about Chiara, you know. In botanical terms, she's a rose, a climber, the kind with a short flowering season. As for you, except that you're self-supporting, I'm not sure yet what you are.'

Surprisingly, his eyes, which she'd thought would be cold with displeasure at her far too outspoken criticism, were undeservedly friendly.

'My label should tell you what I am,' she said, on a note of contrition. 'I'm afraid I'm sometimes as prickly as my namesake. I don't usually flare up at clients, but sometimes you make it hard to remember that you are a client…or may be a client. If we haven't much time left, I think we should go round again, on a more businesslike basis.'

'There's no rush. As I said on the phone, we can spend the night locally.'

Holly said, 'I left Parson plenty of water, but I don't have any near neighbours to come round and give him his supper and he's probably already eaten all the extra food I left him.'

'In that case, if we can't get back, he'll have to go out and catch himself a mouse or two,' said Pierce. 'Maybe you should have brought him with you. I did warn you about the weather.'

'It doesn't look like closing in at the moment. It's as warm as September.'

'As we came in for lunch, I noticed some cloud building up over to the west. But don't worry. If I can get you back to Norfolk I will…even though a quiet dinner here at the pub would be a nice end to the day.'

For once Holly had no difficulty reading his mind. He was thinking of another agreeable way the day might end. Tuning into his thoughts started a flutter in the pit of her stomach: Why couldn't she be like other women she knew? Although not as brazenly promiscuous as her stepsister, they didn't hesitate to go to bed with men they fancied. They didn't need to be *in* love to make love. It wasn't a big deal to them in the way it was to her.

The fact that she *was* in love with Pierce didn't make it easier. If anything it made it harder. How could she enjoy being in bed with him, knowing that numerous girls had shared the experience before her, and many more would succeed her? If he loved her, it wouldn't matter about his past. That would be something that had happened before she'd known him. Only their shared future would be important.

But not only was it difficult to imagine Pierce falling in love; she found it impossible to see him confining himself to one woman for the rest of his life.

As they were leaving the house, he said, 'Where does a

garden designer start? Explain to me how you begin the making of a garden.'

'It depends what exists already. Sometimes there's not even topsoil, just a battlefield left by the builders. Nowadays the better builders don't lay waste to their sites. If mature trees and shrubs don't interfere with construction, they leave them where they are, knowing they'll help to sell the properties. Some of the big-name developers even have landscaping done before the houses are advertised.'

'Your shoelace has come undone. Stand still. I'll fix it for you.'

With the supple ease which characterised all his movements, Pierce dropped to a crouch and took hold of the ends of the lace.

Looking down at the top of his head, she felt an almost overwhelming desire to reach out and stroke his thick hair. Controlling the impulse took such an effort of will that when he stood up and said, 'Sorry, I interrupted you,' her mind went blank and she couldn't remember what she had been saying.

Perhaps it showed in her face that something had wiped out her train of thought.

He said, 'With one of those battlefield gardens, how would you start?'

'First by talking to the owners…finding out what they wanted—a low-maintenance garden to laze in, or a hobby garden, or a place for their children to play. Ideally, a garden should be an outdoor room, an extension and reflection of the house. So we usually begin with a grid based on the external architecture. It's a very complex process to explain in a few minutes.'

He nodded. 'I realise that. What interests me is that when you start to talk about it your manner changes. Suddenly you're confident and authoritative. But when you're not being professional you're rather reserved and constrained. Or is that only with me?'

'Probably. You are rather an…overwhelming personality.'

Pierce looked amused. 'I wish I could overwhelm you. There's nothing I should like better. But each time I try you close up…like a tender seedling trying to resist being eaten by a large and voracious slug,' he said drily.

Holly couldn't help laughing at the analogy. Without pausing to consider whether it was wise to pursue this line of talk, she said, 'Oh, not a slug…one of those snails with an attractive shell…but just as voracious as a slug.'

'Not voracious at all, actually.' As he said this, his tone was light. But then, his manner changing, he went on in a more serious way. 'You have me filed in the wrong slot. What I was when I knew Chiara is not what I am today. People change, Holly. At that time my working life was unsatisfying and my private life was a reflection of it. For some years I've been ready to try a long-term, stable relationship, but the problem is finding a partner whose life will combine well with mine.'

'Perhaps the solution is for you to become more flexible. It sounds as if you expect all the concessions and adjustments to be made by your partner.'

'As I'm likely to be the primary breadwinner, is that unreasonable? When a woman holds that position, it's logical for her career and her preferred way of life to take precedence. But my work is of real importance in a global context and I shall be doing it for a long time to come, probably past the normal age for retirement. If the woman I marry doesn't take it as seriously as I do, and accept the demands it makes on me, I don't think we have much chance of making a go of it.'

'I'm sure she would respect what you're doing,' Holly

answered. 'But, even if her work weren't as important as yours, it could mean a lot to her.'

'Certainly. I accept that, and I'd want her to keep up her career, making the appropriate adjustments when our children were young and needed a lot of attention. If I were called overseas, she would have to be there for them. You may say it wouldn't be fair for that to be her responsibility, however inconvenient. But the fact is that life isn't fair. Never has been and never will be.'

'I don't disagree with that. Women themselves are coming round to the view that having it all isn't always possible.'

'As the woman who thought up that credo wasn't practising what she preached, it's always surprised me that so many women swallowed the concept for so long,' said Pierce.

Holly had heard the same view expressed by her father and could have rattled off reasons why 'having it all' had seemed an attainable goal to women now in their thirties and forties.

But she felt it would be more productive to return to the point they had started from.

'Oh, look…Miss Willmott's ghost!' she exclaimed, pointing to a clump of *Eryngium giganteum*.

'Why is it called that?' asked Pierce.

'Because Miss Willmott used to scatter the seeds as she walked round other people's gardens. She's been dead a long time…since 1934, I think…but she'll never be forgotten by gardeners who like eryngiums. I'm very fond of them myself. There's a lovely bright blue one which may be around here somewhere. The thing about a garden like this is that you really need to watch and wait for a whole year before you can tell what you've got in it. That's what

I'd recommend you to do, especially if the house is going to take time to renovate.'

'All right, that's what we'll do. We can come down together every two or three weeks and you can make notes and take photographs in the garden while I consult with the specialists about the interior restorations.'

'But you will also consult other garden designers? I'd feel happier if you did.'

'If you insist. Who would you recommend?'

'I'll jot down some names on the way back. You were right about the cloud building up. Ought we to be getting back to the airfield?'

Pierce laid a hand on her shoulder, the one furthest from him. 'If the idea of spending the night here really bothers you, then we'll go back at once.' He looked down at her, cocking an interrogative eyebrow.

'It bothers me, leaving Parson on his own,' she said. 'I know it wouldn't hurt him to miss a meal, but when bedtime comes he'll wonder why I'm not there.'

'What about the nights you spent in London? Who looked after him then?'

'I took him with me in his basket. He likes travelling.'

'I certainly wouldn't want Parson to be frantic with worry,' said Pierce, in a serious tone. And then he threw back his head and gave a shout of laughter.

He knew as well as she did that the reason she wanted to leave had nothing to do with her cat's peace of mind.

That night, tucked up in her own bed, with Parson kneading the quilt and emitting the satisfied purrs of a cat who has yet again proved his prowess as a hunter and is now in domestic mode with a tin of sardines inside him and his housekeeper back from her day out and gently rubbing his chin, Holly felt considerably less satisfied with life than her happy tabby.

From the moment they'd left Talavera, Pierce's manner had been noticeably brisk, as if, having failed to persuade her to stay over with him, he had lost interest.

When they had landed on the Norfolk airfield to which she had driven that morning, she had wondered if he might invite himself back for supper and, later, have another crack at coaxing her to let him supplant Parson as her sleeping partner.

But he hadn't. He had seen her to her car, offered his hand and, without so much as a social peck on the cheek, said goodnight.

Now, mulling over the day, she had a sinking feeling that by insisting he consult other designers she had lost a commission she wanted more passionately than any of her previous heart's desires.

The only thing she longed for more than to restore the garden at Talavera was for Pierce to fall in love with her. That, she knew, was crying for the moon. But the garden could have been hers, and now, more than likely, she had lost it.

The days that followed seemed interminably long as she waited for him to call her. Yet why should he call her? He had talked about visiting Talavera every few weeks, but with Christmas now in the offing he might be otherwise occupied.

For someone like Pierce the festive season would bring many invitations. Probably he would be spending Christmas in some exciting way. Skiing, perhaps. Or flying to a place in the sun to join a house party of important men and alluring women.

For her, Christmas was a lonely time. She had no one

but Parson to spend it with. Once, when Chiara had been involved with a married man who had gone home to his family for Christmas, she and her stepsister had spent the holiday together. But Eric was divorced from his second wife and would very likely be taking Chiara to the Costa del Sol.

A week after the trip to Devon, Holly had another visit from Ben. He took her out to lunch at a country hotel he had noticed while driving his grandmother.

Holly was surprised and puzzled by this second visit. Although she liked him very much and thought he felt the same way, she was almost certain he wasn't attracted to her. So why had he come? Could Pierce have asked him to come? But for what possible purpose?

The motive behind Ben's visit emerged during lunch.

He said suddenly, 'Holly, I have a problem I'd like to discuss with you. I need an outside opinion, but it's not so easy to find someone whose advice is worth having. Although we haven't known each other long, I feel I can trust you to keep my affairs to yourself and to make sensible comments.'

'You can certainly trust my discretion, but I can't claim to be at all wise, except perhaps a little about gardening.'

'This has nothing to do with gardens,' he said, smiling at her. 'It's a love problem.'

'In that case why not ask your grandmother…or Pierce? They both know a lot more about that sort of problem than I do.' She couldn't resist asking, 'Have you seen him recently?'

'Not for a while. He's a very busy guy. He'll call when he has a space in his life. There are one or two details to finalise before we go to Argentina. After that, I must settle down and get my future organised. The trouble is, I don't

know what I want to do with my life but I do know who
I want to share it with.'

He paused, looking out of the window beside their table.
Watching him, Holly was struck by the refinement of his
face with its subtle combination of East and West. In a *Star
Wars* film, he would have been ideal casting for the part
of a superior being from a planet where all Earth's problems had been overcome.

As she was thinking this, Ben turned troubled dark eyes
on her.

'A year ago I fell in love with an English girl. She feels
the same way about me. But because I'm half-Japanese I'm
unacceptable to her family.'

'But that's ridiculous,' said Holly. 'Have they met you?
Has she taken you home?'

'I've met them several times. On the surface, they were
very nice to me. But as soon as they realised we were
serious they insisted we stop seeing each other.'

'Why? For what possible reason?' To Holly's way of
thinking, any parents who, having met Ben, didn't welcome
him as a son-in-law had to be out of their minds.

'It's a complex situation,' he said. 'Charlotte's parents
are well-to-do people…or were until a few years back.
Then her father was involved in the great Lloyd's disaster.
Do you remember that?'

Holly nodded. 'A lot of people were ruined by it. It was
front-page news for a long time.'

'Charlotte's parents would have been ruined,' said Ben.
'They lived, and still do, in a large house with lots of land.
All their children went to expensive schools. They were
only saved from disaster by Charlotte's grandmother. She
married a guy with a title and acres of real estate in the
centre of London. She's very grand and very rich. She
bailed out Charlotte's father and she holds the family purse-

strings. The trouble is, she hates the Japanese. If she knew Charlotte wanted to marry one, she'd blow a gasket.'

'Why does she hate the Japanese?'

'In World War Two, her father was a prisoner in Japanese hands. He was treated badly and came back to Europe a wreck. All this time later, his daughter is still breathing vengeance. That the West took a horrible revenge when they dropped atomic bombs on Hiroshima and Nagasaki means nothing to this mean old lady. She's still consumed by a hatred going back fifty years. Until she dies—and she isn't seventy yet—there's no way I can marry Charlotte.'

'Have you discussed this with your grandmother?'

'She thinks painful and unpleasant situations should be avoided. As she can't see any solution, she thinks we should resign ourselves to the impossibility of finding a way through our difficulties.'

'And what does Pierce think? Have you talked to him about it?'

'No, I haven't discussed it with him. I already know what he'd think. He would regard Lady Bletchley as a domestic tyrant. If he were me, he would marry Charlotte without her family's approval. She's twenty. She doesn't need their consent. Knowing Pierce, he would say the financial aspect is her parents' problem. He probably wouldn't be convinced the old lady would cut off the help she's giving them. But what do you think, Holly?'

'I can't go along with your grandmother's point of view. If you're right about what Pierce would think, I disagree with that too. Families are important. If Charlotte loves her parents, naturally she doesn't want to do anything which may cause them hardship. They've been through enough as it is, and the present situation, of being dependent on Lady Bletchley's handouts, must be very difficult for them.'

After a pause for thought, she said, 'Is there any way you could meet her? I'm sure if she spent a little time with you she couldn't fail to like you. She might not revise her ideas about the past, but it could make her realise that people of our generation can't be held responsible for what happened long ago.'

'That's what Charlotte says,' Ben replied. 'You and she are very alike. I'd like you to meet...but I don't see any way I can meet Lady Bletchley. It's obvious to anyone that one of my parents was Japanese. That would be enough to put her off me.'

'She may be grand and rich, but she can't be very intelligent,' said Holly. 'If she'd read any history, she'd know that every nation on earth has committed the most ghastly deeds at some time in its past, and those things are still happening today. She ought to be up in arms about present horrors, not seething about her father's sufferings. How fond is she of Charlotte?'

'She adores her. She's her favourite grandchild.'

'Then how about Charlotte telling her that she's fallen in love with a wonderful American but her parents don't approve of him? She doesn't have to say why and, if Lady Bletchley asks them, they don't have to give the real reason. They could say they don't want Charlotte to go to America where they'll hardly ever see her. Then Lady B will insist on seeing you for herself and maybe...just maybe...you can charm her out of her prejudice.'

Ben gave her a wry grin. 'I think you overrate my charm. She would most probably take one look and have me thrown out. But I guess we could give it a go. In an impasse like this, anything's worth a try.'

When they got back to her cottage, Holly was amazed to see Pierce sitting on the bench outside the front door with an open hamper on one side of him and Parson lying with folded front legs on the other.

'Why didn't you let me know you were coming?' she asked as she opened the wicket-gate.

He rose to his feet. 'I thought I'd surprise you,' he said. 'But I'm the one who's surprised.' He was looking past her at Ben.

Perhaps it was her imagination, but the steely glint in his eyes didn't seem the right expression for a man about to greet a close friend with whom, in a few weeks' time, he was going to share a small tent on a mountain notorious for its capricious weather.

'Hello, Pierce.' Ben came up the path, shook hands and clapped his friend on the shoulder, obviously not receiving the hostile vibrations that Holly thought she had sensed. 'How long have you been here?'

'About an hour and a half.'

'If you'd shown up a little sooner you could have joined us for lunch.' He noticed the hamper. 'Oh, you brought some with you. Too bad I got here first.'

'Don't worry about it. I didn't have to eat alone. I had this guy for company.' Pierce reached down to run his hand along the cat's glossy back. 'But I do have some things I'd like to discuss with Holly in private. As you've had her to yourself since before one, perhaps you wouldn't mind my having her to myself for the rest of the afternoon. A lot of what we have to talk about wouldn't be of interest to you.'

It was pleasantly said but there was no mistaking the firmness underlying the suggestion. Expressed in a courteous way, it was basically an order for Ben to take himself off and the sooner the better.

'Oh...right.' At first taken aback, Ben quickly adjusted his expression. 'I'll be off, then. See you around.'

But as he was turning away Holly grabbed his sleeve. 'Wait...I haven't thanked you for lunch yet.'

'It was my pleasure, Holly.'

After a slight hesitation, he bent to kiss the cheek she offered him.

When he had gone, Holly said, 'That wasn't very friendly.'

'I'm not feeling friendly,' said Pierce. 'How many times has he been here?'

'Only twice. Why?'

'I shouldn't like to see him hurt.'

'I'm not going to hurt him.'

'The only way to be sure of that is to be unavailable next time he wants to date you.'

'Today wasn't a date. It was just a friendly lunch.'

'There's no such thing as a friendly lunch between men and women who find each other attractive.'

'I don't find Ben attractive. I mean, I do in a general way, but not personally...and I'm sure it's the same for him.' She was tempted to add, I *know* it's the same for him, but felt that might lead to questions she couldn't answer without breaking Ben's confidence.

'You may be sure, but I'm not,' was his clipped reply. 'You underestimate yourself. You're very beguiling and Ben is very susceptible.'

'Is he? What makes you think so?'

'Fujiko says he's unhappy. A love affair has gone wrong. He could fall for you on the rebound. He could fall for you, period.'

'I can assure you he won't. We like each other very much, but only as friends. There's no special spark between us.'

'I'm glad to hear it. How about making me some tea?'

'With pleasure.' She unlocked the door. 'I'm sorry your plan fell flat. It's a good day for a picnic.'

The cottage had no hall. The front door opened into the living room which was adequately but simply furnished. Holly had been free to put her own stamp on it with books and other personal possessions from a trunk she had acquired before leaving the house which had once belonged to her father but had later become her stepmother's property.

The kitchen led off the main room. While she was filling the kettle and laying a tray, Pierce wandered about, looking at her books and the paintings hanging in place of the cheap and cheerful prints put up by the owners of the cottage.

'This looks like a Seago. Is it?' he said, looking at a small oil painting of an Arab market.

'Yes, it's the medina in Marrakech. My father bought it…an extravagance he never regretted. I think by now it must be worth many times what he paid for it, but I could never part with it. The painting next to it, of Venice, was my mother's. It's by Glynn Boyd Harte. My parents went to Venice for their honeymoon and she kept a diary in a notebook my father bought her on their first morning there. One day, when I can afford it, I'm going to have a holiday in Venice and go to all the places they went to.'

Pierce had moved on to look at the titles of the paperbacks filling some hanging shelves.

Her memory jogged, Holly clapped a hand to her mouth. 'Oh, hell's bells…I've never thanked you for sending me Daddy's books. I meant to write you a letter and it went clean out of my head. How bad-mannered you must have thought me.'

'We all forget things,' he said easily.

'I bet you never do.'

'I have a PA to remind me.'

'I feel horribly ashamed of myself. It was such a nice gesture on your part.'

He swung to face her. 'Then how about a reciprocal gesture from you…? A kiss would be pleasant.'

He had her cornered, with no gracious way of evading him.

'All right,' she said, outwardly calm, walking towards him. 'But I am very sorry I haven't thanked you before.'

As Pierce didn't bend his head, in order to put her lips to his cheeks she had to rise on her toes and steady herself with her palms on his chest.

'Thank you now,' she said, before kissing him.

He put his hands on her waist, preventing her from backing off. 'A peck on the cheek wasn't what I had in mind. You can do better than that.'

Now he did bend his head, finding her mouth and sending a surge of pleasure through every nerve in her body. She didn't resist him. She couldn't. This was where she wanted to be, held securely in his arms, her mouth parting under his.

It was Pierce who, some time later, put her away from him.

'I think the kettle will have boiled by now.'

Relieved to be let off so lightly, for she knew that already she had lost the power to resist him, she hurried back to the kitchen, hoping her movements didn't betray how dizzy with longing he had made her.

He followed her. 'I'll take the tray. Where do you want me to put it?'

'On the table by the windows, please. I'll open them. We'll still get the sun and the chairs are more comfortable than the bench outside.'

While he was carrying the tray, she found a packet of chocolate digestive biscuits and a plate to put them on. She had never felt less like snacking, but arranging the biscuits in an orderly circle gave her a reason not to join him until she felt more composed. She wasn't used to handling these feelings he had aroused in her.

'I'll pour the tea, shall I? You might spill it,' said Pierce once they had both sat down.

When she flashed a quick glance, he was smiling. He knew the effect his kisses had had on her, damn him.

'I have an apartment in Venice,' he went on. 'We could spend our honeymoon there.'

For some seconds she couldn't believe he had said what she thought he had said.

Reading her mind, Pierce added, 'Yes, that was a proposal of marriage. Not a very romantic one, perhaps, but I can promise you a romantic honeymoon. Venice is the most romantic city in the world…as I expect your mother's diary records.'

'I can't believe you're serious!' Holly exclaimed. 'Why would you want to marry me, of all people?'

Pierce placed a cup of tea in front of her. 'You're the only one, of all people, I have ever wanted to marry.'

'But you're not in love with me…are you?'

'I don't think being in love is the best basis for marriage. Liking makes better sense. I like you very much, Holly. I knew you were the woman I'd been waiting for when you fell in love with Talavera. Falling in love with a house is different from falling in love with a person. A love affair with a house almost always lasts a lifetime. Where's the pot from Talavera you told me about?'

'It's on the large bookcase.' She went to fetch it and give it to him.

Pierce turned it over to look at the words painted on the base. 'Perhaps one day we'll go to Talavera together and choose some more pottery there. You are going to say yes, aren't you?'

'I need time to think about it. You've taken me completely by surprise. I—I thought you only wanted to get me into bed.'

'I do want to do that…very much. I think you want to be there with me. But perhaps it might add to our enjoyment if we postponed that pleasure until our wedding night. Which won't involve waiting very long. When is your birthday?'

'The day before Christmas Eve.'

'Then why don't we get married on your birthday and spend Christmas in Venice?'

'That's less than a month away.'

'So?'

'It's terribly rushed. We've only known each other a short time.'

'But our minds aren't clouded by the usual illusions that cause so much trouble later when they start to fade and reveal all the faults and flaws which were overlooked before. I know you can be prickly. You know I like my own way.'

Holly started sipping the hot tea, hoping it would have a steadying effect. 'I know I couldn't bear being married to a man who was unfaithful to me…even if it wasn't a love match,' she said, in a low voice.

'I shan't be unfaithful. I shall have no reason to stray. On the whole, men don't, if they have all they want at home.'

'I'm not sure that's true,' she said. 'Some men are compulsive gamblers or drinkers and some are womanisers.'

'Any unattached virile man is going to make the most of his opportunities until he finds a wife,' said Pierce. 'We're driven by a powerful urge to perpetuate the species.

The fact that we can control the outcome of our couplings doesn't alter the strength of that driving force. Once we have a woman of our own, the force has a focus. If I give you my word I won't stray, you can trust me to keep it. You trusted me with your life when you flew to Devon in the chopper. Can't you trust my promise that from now on you'll be the only woman in my life?'

'I don't know,' she answered honestly. 'At the moment my head's in such a whirl that I don't know what to think.'

'How long d'you think you will need to recover your equilibrium? A few days? A week?'

'How can I say? It's been such a bolt from the blue.'

'Call me when you've made up your mind. Now I'd better call up the taxi service I used to get here. If I stay, I'll be tempted to use undue persuasion,' he said, his eyes caressing her.

He had made his phone call and was replacing the aerial when Parson joined them, jumping onto the third chair and starting to groom a paw.

'I wonder what he and Louisa will make of each other…assuming you decide to join forces with me?' said Pierce.

'Joining forces makes it sound more like a business merger than a marriage.'

'Marriage is a merger.' Suddenly he reached across the table and captured one of her hands. 'It would be very easy to sweep you off your feet, Holly. But I don't want to do that…not yet. I'd rather reserve that for Venice. In the meantime, I'll only say that, if you do decide to spend the rest of your life with me, I'll do my utmost to make the future a happy one.'

The seriousness of his tone brought a lump to her throat.

How could she refuse what he offered? It might not be the fulfilment of her secret dreams, but it was far more than her rational self had expected.

CHAPTER SEVEN

FOR two days Holly grappled with conflicting thoughts and emotions. Her head was at war with her heart and she had no one to turn to for wise advice.

Usually, when she had a problem, she would imagine talking it over with her father. Invariably, from among all the things he had said to her while she'd been growing up, there would be something to guide her to the right decision.

But her present dilemma was so far removed from anything she or he could have visualised happening to her that none of her father's codes of behaviour nor anyone else's seemed to cover it.

A marriage of convenience—which was what, basically, Pierce's proposal boiled down to—had been nothing out of the ordinary in past times when women had been dependent on men from the cradle to the grave.

But now, in the closing years of the twentieth century when, even if not in all countries, women had climbed every summit of achievement and no doors remained closed to them, such marriages were an anachronism.

Today, with the exception of gold-diggers like Chiara who would marry for money, women married for love. Which, judging by the divorce statistics, was no greater guarantee of happiness than marrying a man selected for you by your parents, Holly thought, with a sigh as, for the second night in succession, sleep eluded her.

Next morning she overslept, waking with a headache and the insoluble problem still looming over her.

While she was fixing her breakfast, she turned on the radio to hear the weather forecast, forgetting that, as she was up late, she wouldn't catch the programmes she usually heard.

A man with a quiet voice not unlike her father's was giving a talk. For some minutes, with Parson stroking her legs with his furry body and her mind on what she was doing, she listened to the pleasant timbre and good diction rather than to the subject matter.

Then the speaker began to recite some lines she had first heard at Stratford-upon-Avon, at a performance of Shakespeare's *Julius Caesar*.

'"There is a tide in the affairs of men,
Which, taken at the flood, leads on to fortune;
Omitted, all the voyage of their life
Is bound in shallows and in miseries."'

The melodious voice continued but Holly was no longer listening. Suddenly, her mind was made up.

Why hadn't she seen before what now, all at once, seemed obvious? Loving Pierce, she had no choice but to marry him. And perhaps, if she made him happy and helped to realise his dream of how Talavera could be, one day he would find that he loved her.

Wondering if, by this time, he would have left for his office, she tried his private number. After three rings, he answered.

'Sutherland speaking.'

'It's Holly. Am I calling at a bad moment?'

'There are no bad moments as far as you're concerned. How are you?'

'I'm fine. How are you?'

'I'll answer that when you've told me what you've decided. I take it you have decided?'

'Yes. Is your offer still open?'

'Of course.'

'Then I'd like to marry you…I'd like it very much.'

There was silence at the other end of the line.

Wondering if, despite his assurance, when it came to the crunch he might be having second thoughts, she said anxiously, 'Pierce…are you there?'

'I'm here. I'm wishing you were. There are better ways to seal this kind of agreement than by talking. As bad luck would have it, I can't come to you today and I have a raft of appointments tomorrow as well. But I'm free this evening. Could you come and have dinner with me?'

'With pleasure. What time would suit you?'

'Be here by six if you can. We have a lot to talk about.'

'Until six,' she said. 'Goodbye, Pearce.'

'And Holly?' he said, with some urgency, in case she rang off.

'Yes?'

'Thank you.' He had lowered his voice to a more intimate tone. 'If you still have lurking misgivings about your decision, it's the right one, I promise you. We're going to be very happy together.'

'I hope so…for both our sakes.'

'You can be sure of it. Bye now.' It was he who cut the connection.

In case she should need to stay in London more than one night, Holly took Parson with her. As the train was half-empty, she let him out of his basket to sit on the seat beside her, hoping that if a ticket inspector came by he wouldn't insist on the cat being put back inside his travelling container.

From Liverpool Street Station, she took the underground to Marble Arch and from there walked the short distance to an inexpensive bed and breakfast establishment frequented by members of the Women's Institute and similar organisations when they came up from the country to attend their annual conference or have a day's shopping followed by a visit to the theatre.

The reason she hadn't rung Chiara and asked to put up with her was that Holly didn't want to break the news to her stepsister until she had talked to Pierce again and become more used to the idea that by the end of the year she would no longer be Holly Nicholson but Holly Sutherland.

When she arrived at the B and B place, the woman who ran it looked at the furry face peering through the window in the basket and said, 'We can't take pets here, I'm afraid.'

'He won't be here for very long,' said Holly. 'I'm taking him out to dinner with me. He's very quiet and well-behaved. He won't scratch your furniture, I promise you.'

'What about doing his business? Where's he going to do that? Not in one of my bedrooms,' the landlady said severely.

'Of course not. He has a lead. I'll take him for a walk last thing and again first thing in the morning. The thing is, I'd nowhere to leave him and tonight I'm celebrating my engagement,' Holly explained.

The landlady's face softened slightly. 'There's a shed at the back he could sleep in without doing much harm. But not if he's going to start caterwauling and disturbing my other guests.'

'Neutered tom-cats don't caterwaul. Parson might miaow a few times while he settles down, but you see how quiet he's being now. He never made a sound on the tube.'

'Well, all right, I'll make an exception,' the landlady conceded graciously. 'But kindly keep it to yourself. I don't want myself inundated with people's cats, do I?'

Holly arrived at Pierce's front door at five minutes past six. She was tense with excitement, her insides quivering as they had before playing small parts in school theatrical productions and before her college interview.

When Pierce opened the door and saw what she was carrying, he said, 'Is your acceptance conditional on your cat liking my cat?'

'It will be awkward if they don't get on.'

'They'll get on,' he said confidently, taking the basket from her with one hand and cupping her chin with the other.

'Hello again.' He touched her lips lightly with his in a kiss of such unexpected tenderness that it took her breath away.

'It's cold out. Come in and get warm.' He ushered her into the house. 'I debated booking a table at a ritzy restaurant, then decided it would be nicer to eat at home, by the fire. I hope that's all right with you.'

'Anything that suits you is fine with me.'

Pierce laughed. 'I'll remind you of that rash statement in twelve months' time when you may be feeling less compliant. But I'm glad you feel that way now. Let me take your coat.'

He had put Parson's basket down on a hard-seated chair and as he was waiting for Holly to undo her buttons the sound made by a hostile cat drew their eyes to the doorway.

Louisa, who had come to see who was arriving, had noticed the basket and its occupant and was showing every sign of extreme displeasure.

'She may think he's a randy tom who will make unwel-

come advances,' said Pierce, ignoring his cat's arched back
and indignant face. 'She'll calm down when she finds that
he isn't.'

'Perhaps I shouldn't have brought him, but there seemed
no alternative,' said Holly, as he took her coat. 'I'm not
staying with Chiara this time. I wanted to see you before
telling her what's happened.'

'Where are you staying?'

'At a small guest house. If you're serious about getting
married on my birthday, I shall need to buy some clothes.'

Pierce hung her coat in a cupboard and then, picking up
the basket, put a hand on her waist to steer her towards the
studio. There, an elderly man in a black coat and pinstriped
trousers was placing a bucket of ice with a bottle in it on
the table in front of the sofa facing the blazing fire.

'This is Hooper, who looks after me,' said Pierce.

Holly smiled. 'Good evening.'

The manservant bowed. 'Good evening, miss.'

'Hooper, you are the first to know that Miss Nicholson
has agreed to marry me.'

'Allow me to offer my congratulations, sir. I wish you
both every happiness.'

'Thank you very much,' said Holly.

'Perhaps your cat would like some water,' he suggested.

'Yes, take him away and give him a chance to compose
himself. He was quite rightly shocked by Louisa's display
of bad manners in the hall just now,' said Pierce. To Holly
he added, 'Don't worry. By the end of the evening they
may be sharing her beanbag.' The glint in his eyes added
a subtext she pretended to be unaware of.

In spite of what he had said the day he'd proposed this
strange engagement, about waiting till they were in Venice
to make love to her, he might have changed his mind since
then. If he wanted to make love tonight, she had no real

grounds for refusing other than an instinctive feeling that it would be wiser to wait.

Although she had some experience, it hadn't amounted to much. If he found her disappointing, he might begin to regret his precipitate proposal. The thought of losing him, before she had had time to learn how to please him, sent a shiver of panic through her.

'Go and sit by the fire if you're still cold,' said Pierce, with a nod at the cushioned club fender. 'Did you walk? Why didn't you take a taxi? Are you short of funds?'

'No, no, I just felt like walking.'

'Well, don't do it again…not in London, not after dark. I don't like the idea of you wandering about on your own, especially encumbered with a cat basket. Women don't have to be wearing a fur and expensive earrings to be targeted by street thieves these days.'

She perched on the fender. She was wearing a straight black skirt with opaque black tights and black leather loafers. Her top was a cream silk shirt, one of Chiara's cast-offs.

Holly's pearl studs and single-strand necklace had belonged to her mother. They were cultured pearls, too discreet to make any kind of statement except that of conventional good taste. But none of the ethnic jewellery, bought from market stalls, which she usually wore to go out had seemed right for this occasion. Pierce was accustomed to women who dressed to a high standard of elegance. She didn't want any detail of her appearance to seem cheap to him.

He brought her a glass of champagne. 'To us…to a lifetime of sharing everything life has to offer.'

'To us,' she echoed as they touched glasses.

After tasting the wine, Pierce sat down at the other end of the fender, leaving a space between them.

'As you have no family to speak of and mine is across the Atlantic, I suggest we get married very quietly in my local register office. Or would you prefer a church service?'

'My father was an atheist. We never went to church. I'm happy with a register office.'

'Right, that's the first item settled. What about witnesses? Would you like Chiara to be one?'

'I think she'll be away…in the south of Spain. What about Mrs Shintaro and Ben, as we both know them?'

'No, I think not,' he said. 'I'll ask my two closest friends. There'll be time for you to meet them beforehand. I have a lot of people I want you to meet later on.'

Holly wondered if, despite his friendship with him, Pierce could be jealous of her affection for Ben.

'After we've done the deed,' he went on, 'we'll go to Claridge's for lunch and then fly to Venice. You can buy most of your trousseau there. There are some excellent shops and I'll enjoy helping you choose. Which reminds me…your ring. I had a jeweller whose work I like send round a selection for you to look at. If none of them appeals, they can go back and we'll look for something you do like. I'll fetch them.'

He crossed the room to one of the banks of books, where he touched something, causing a section of shelf to swing forward, revealing a safe. A combination lock opened the thick fireproof door. From the interior Pierce took a shallow box covered with leather. He brought it to the table in front of the sofa and beckoned her to join him. When he opened the lid, Holly saw that the box was lined with black velvet and divided into many small sections, about a dozen of them holding the selection of rings.

'You have beautiful hands. I noticed them the first time we met…I mean the very first time,' he added.

'Really?' said Holly, astonished. She had always taken

care of her hands, wearing barrier creams and gloves to prevent their becoming ingrained with soil like those of many keen gardeners. But she was amazed that he should have noticed them approvingly the night she had thought he disapproved of her.

'Try this one,' said Pierce, taking her left hand and slipping a ring over the third finger. 'No, that's not right. How about this?' He selected another.

'They all look gorgeous to me,' she said, and meant it.

Any one of the rings would have pleased her. They had a distinctive style quite different from conventional engagement rings.

He tried all the rings in the box, fitting them on her finger and studying the effect, unaware that for her it was not the beauty of the jewels which entranced her but the way he was holding her wrist in one hand and trying on the rings with the other. Merely to sit beside him, with one of his long, hard thighs inches away from her lap and his lean fingers circling her wrist was an exquisite pleasure which made her mind boggle at the thought of what she would feel when he made love to her.

'I think this is the right one, but you may not agree,' said Pierce.

'It's lovely. But isn't it frighteningly valuable? What if I lose it or damage it?'

'It will be insured,' he said casually. 'What matters is that you like it. Perhaps you've set your heart on something quite different. If so, you have only to say.'

'I haven't set my heart on anything…except trying to be a good wife,' she said, in a low voice.

His fingers tightened on her wrist. 'Anyone hearing you say that would think you were marrying me for love.'

Holly could not meet his eyes for fear he might see the truth. 'I'm not marrying you for any ulterior motive…unless you count Talavera. But even to have that garden I wouldn't marry just anyone.'

'I'm relieved to hear it,' he said drily. 'Now, to get back to this ring, are you certain you're happy with it?'

'It's beautiful. Thank you, Pierce.'

'Good. That's something else settled. Tomorrow or the day after you can go and confer with the designer about what kind of wedding ring you'd like to go with it. We won't be exchanging rings because I prefer not to wear one. For a climber they can be dangerous.'

He closed the box and took it back to the safe. While he was putting it away, Louisa strolled to the fireside and sat down on the large Persian rug, where she extended one back leg at an angle of forty-five degrees and began some energetic grooming.

Suddenly, pausing, she looked up, fixing large kohl-rimmed eyes on the place, near the back of a chair, where Parson was lurking, looking unwontedly nervous.

Coming back to the sofa, Pierce said, 'Finish what's left in your glass and I'll give you a refill. There's no kick in tepid champagne.'

Obediently Holly drained her glass, her attention on the two cats. 'I think Parson is scared of her.'

'More fool he,' was Pierce's succinct comment. 'It's fatal to let a female of any species feel she can dictate terms. That isn't what they want. It makes them capricious and cruel. If Parson knows what's good for him, he'll come and show her who's boss.'

Holly felt her hackles rising slightly. 'Are you including women in that statement?'

'It's particularly applicable to women. They can't stand a man who dithers. They want him to be in control. If he isn't, they'll give him hell. Your sex is still programmed by nature to need a protective male to stand between them and any threat to their safety. If they find out a man is a wimp, they'll delight in tormenting him. I have an example of that situation among my staff at the moment. An accountant working for us is living with a woman who makes his life miserable. As he's not legally bound to her, it's a wonder he doesn't walk out. But that's part of the problem, of course.'

He stopped speaking, his eyes on Parson who, having retreated behind the chair, now appeared on the other side of it and was investigating the uprights of the fender, pretending to be oblivious to the baleful glare focused on him from the centre of the antique rug.

'That's better,' Pierce said approvingly. 'Pretend you couldn't care less. Louisa's not used to being ignored. Five minutes of the cold shoulder and she'll start making up to you.'

'Let's hope you're right,' said Holly, watching her cat stroll past the fire to sniff the fringe of the rug and then the valance of a slip-covered chair on the other side of the hearth. After satisfying himself that there was nothing hiding beneath it, he jumped onto the chair and gave his shoulder a light lick in the manner of a man who has noticed a speck of something on his immaculate suit.

'D'you mind him sitting there?' asked Holly.

'Hooper doesn't approve of Louisa sitting on chairs, but I don't mind and I don't think this is the moment to undermine Parson's dignity,' said Pierce.

'What did you mean about it being part of the problem…the accountant's problem?' she asked.

He leaned back and crossed his long legs. 'Women have gone along with living together and having children together without any formal commitment. But I'm not sure that, deep down, they're really comfortable with it. I suspect they feel they've lost out. If I had said to you—putting it rather more gracefully—Let's shack up together, what would you have said?'

'Putting it rather more gracefully, Get lost!' she told him, with a flicker of amusement. Then, more seriously she went on, 'My father thought living together was a cop-out…an evasion of responsibility. The irony is that, if he and my stepmother had merely joined forces instead of marrying, when their relationship broke down he could have ended it without, as they say, being taken to the cleaners.'

'If he'd been thirty, or twenty, or ten years younger, he probably wouldn't have married her,' said Pierce. 'The possibility of being taken to the cleaners looms very large in the male mind these days. It's the fundamental reason why, if they can, a lot of men would rather dodge marriage and settle for cohabitation. That doesn't protect them entirely but they usually get off more lightly than a legal spouse.'

'Doesn't the thought of being taken to the cleaners bother you?' she asked.

'It did…until I met you. Then I knew I had found the kind of person who, if, in a place where no one was watching, she found a wallet stuffed with twenty-pound notes but no identification, would go straight to the nearest police station.'

'So would any honest person.'

Pierce crooked a cynical eyebrow. 'People as honest as that are not too thick on the ground, my love. You and I are not going to split, but if we did I don't think you'd run to a lawyer with instructions to take me for every last penny. I think you're the kind of woman who wouldn't even keep that.' He indicated the engagement ring.

Holly was silent, winded by the shock of being called 'my love' in that easy way, as if they were a normal couple to whom endearments came naturally.

Could she bring herself to use loving words to him? Somehow she didn't think so. Not yet anyway.

'It would be nice to think that one day our daughter will inherit it. The pearls I'm wearing tonight belonged to my mother. They're not very special by your standards but they have great sentimental value for me.'

'Understandably,' said Pierce. He reached out to put the tip of his forefinger behind the lobe of her ear and then ran it gently down the side of her neck.

The light caress had an effect as stirring as if he had touched her breast. She sat very still wondering what he might do next, but just at that moment Louisa rose from the rug and walked to the front of the chair where Parson was sitting. As they watched, he folded his forelegs, bringing his face almost to a level with hers. After a moment both cats extended their necks and, with noses almost touching, gave each other a cautious sniff. Then Louisa turned round and, with a flourish of her tail, like a *belle époque* courtesan flirting a large feather fan, strolled away to another part of the room.

'I'm no expert on feline body language, but that looked like the beginning of a mutually tolerant relationship, don't you think?' Pierce asked.

'Yes, I do,' Holly agreed.

Hooper reappeared. 'Shall I serve dinner, sir?'

'By all means.' Pierce drained his glass and stood up. While the butler was lighting the candles on the same table where they had lunched but which tonight was more formally laid with a damask cloth and napkins folded to look like water lilies, Pierce said to him, 'Tomorrow I want Miss Nicholson to choose a wedding ring. I can't go with her myself. You'll be taking the ring box back. Would you pick her up from where she's staying?'

'Certainly, sir. Where is Miss Nicholson staying?'

Pierce looked enquiringly at Holly who gave the butler the address of her B and B place.

While Hooper went away to fetch the first course, Pierce drew out a chair and seated her. 'Let's finish the champagne, shall we? Do you like it, or is it too dry for you?'

'I like it. I've never had this champagne before.' She had noticed the label. 'I can see why it's famous.'

'You'll be drinking a lot of it in future. Now…what else do we need to settle? The rings…the form of the wedding…the lunch party afterwards… Oh, yes, the announcement. How shall we word it? "The marriage has been arranged and will take place shortly of…" I'd better write it down.' He felt in an inside pocket of his coat and produced a pen and a diary. 'What was your father's first name, or did he prefer his initials for anything formal?'

'Professor Peter Nicholson.'

As he jotted it down, Pierce said, '*The Times* and *The Telegraph* naturally. What about local papers? The one where you went to school, for instance?'

'That isn't necessary.'

She was beginning to realise what should have been obvious already—that in marrying Pierce she was entering a different world, a milieu involving formalities which had not been a part of her past. Her father, although a don at a major university, had lived in a more modest style than many of his colleagues.

The adjustments she would have to make didn't unnerve her. She was confident she could cope with the public side of their life together. It was merely a matter of studying how things were done.

But the private aspects of their relationship did worry her. Would she be good enough in bed? Would she be able to keep him amused and interested when they were not in bed but were on their own together?

The meal Hooper served was delicious: chestnut soup with the tang of fromage frais in it, a roast pheasant with slices of truffle under the skin of its breast and, to finish, caramelised pears on a bed of juice-soaked sponge cake.

They had coffee in front of the fire while, with almost soundless efficiency, Hooper cleared the table. About half an hour later, while they were listening to music, the butler came back to tell Pierce that he was going home and to ask Holly what time it would be convenient for him to call for her.

After he had gone, she was very conscious that they were alone in the house. By this time Parson had come to sit on her lap, as he usually did in the evening. Louisa, it seemed, was not a lap cat, perhaps because she had been discouraged from settling on her owner's legs.

'If you like you can leave Parson here overnight,' Pierce suggested. 'I should think he'd feel more at home in the conservatory with Louisa, where he can use her litter tray, than in the place where you're staying.'

'They weren't very keen on having him,' Holly admitted. 'Are you sure you don't mind his staying here? I don't think he'll be a nuisance. He's a very adaptable cat and he has met you before, so he'll know I haven't abandoned him.'

'As long as he doesn't expect to sleep on *my* bed,' Pierce said drily. 'It would be a good idea to debar him from yours from now on…get him used to the idea that after we come back from Venice your bedroom will be forbidden territory.'

'What will the weather be like in Venice?'

'It varies. Often it's wet or misty. Sometimes it's very

cold when the wind is blowing straight off the mountains to the north. Or it can be mild and sunny. Whatever it's like, it's one of the world's magic places, especially in winter when the Venetians have it more or less to themselves. I love it whatever it's like. I'm looking forward to showing you all my favourite corners of it.'

'I'm looking forward to going.' The wine and the food and the warmth made her stifle a yawn.

'Time you were in bed,' said Pierce. 'I'll run you back.'

He leaned towards her, scooping Parson from her lap and holding the startled tabby suspended in his strong hands for a moment before putting him gently on the floor.

Parson gave an offended shudder, adjusting the set of his fur before looking over his shoulder and fixing Pierce with an old-fashioned look, so plain in its meaning that Pierce laughed and said, 'Sorry, old boy, but you might as well accept you're not the top cat any more. I am.'

Parson's expression had made Holly want to laugh, but she had suppressed her reaction, not wishing to add to his sense of indignity.

When he turned round to face her, it looked for a moment as if he might dispute Pierce's authority over him by jumping back on her lap. But he thought better of it and stalked off, his tail—held upright when he was pleased with life—now indicating displeasure by waving from side to side.

'Don't worry; he's too intelligent not to accept the situation. I like him very much. I'll make it easy for him.'

Pierce put his arm round her shoulders and drew her against him. With his mouth near her ear, he whispered, 'More than Louisa, as a matter of fact, but I shan't let her know that.' Then, using his free hand to turn her face towards his, he kissed her.

It felt as deliciously sensuous as a mouthful of chocolate. As her lips opened to his, he used the tip of his tongue to caress the inner edges of her mouth. But there was no thrusting invasion of the kind that had happened before, when she hadn't been ready for it. Nor did she feel his hand fumbling to open her shirt in the peremptory way other hands had. His fingers were touching her throat, exploring the delicate area behind her ear and down the side of her neck.

Suddenly, just when other parts of her body were beginning to tingle responsively, he brought the kiss to an end. Disengaging himself, he stood up. 'I'll go and get your coat.'

He left her surprised and disappointed. She hadn't wanted him to stop and didn't know why he had. There could be two reasons. He had found her response disappointing. Or he was deliberately keeping things under control until he was free to go as far as he liked with her.

But he was free to do that now, if he wanted, she thought, trying to recover her self-possession, not wanting him to come back and find her visibly disorientated.

When Pierce took longer than she expected to bring her coat, she thought it might be because he knew she needed a space to recover, or because he was himself aroused. Men, as she had cause to know, did get aroused very quickly by physical contact with females. Both the previous men in her life had reached boiling point in seconds, making her wonder if she was unnaturally slow.

When Pierce did return, he said, 'I don't want to offend you, Holly, but most brides have parental backing and I know your finances can't be too fluid. In the circumstances, would it affront you if I ordered you the use of my accounts at Simpson and Liberty? They should have something you'd like for your wedding dress. If not, I also have an account at Harvey Nichols.'

'I'm not in the least offended. It's nice of you to suggest it. But I wasn't planning to buy anything wildly expensive. You don't mind if I dress for your wedding at my normal price level, do you?'

'If you buy your dress at a thrift shop, it won't worry me,' he said smiling. 'You seem to be someone who always looks right for the occasion…whether it's a party or a day in the country.'

'Thank you.' She didn't tell him that the only party outfit he had seen her in had been borrowed and must have cost as much as the clothes worn by the women he normally mixed with.

While she was fastening her coat, she said, 'I'll just say goodnight to Parson.'

At first there was no response to the pursed-lip squeaks which usually brought the cat hurrying to see why he had been summoned. Then, at a less eager pace, he appeared round the corner of the sofa.

Holly crouched down to pat him. 'I'm leaving you here tonight. You'll be quite all right and I'll see you tomorrow. Be a good pussy.' She picked him up to give him a hug and a kiss on the top of his head.

He followed them to the garage where, not ungently, Pierce made him stay in the passage while he closed the door. Plaintive miaows could be heard as he opened the passenger door for her. Before entering the car himself, he switched off the garage light. As he got in beside her, he said, 'I expect you feel the same way as mothers whose children go to boarding-schools. I've heard a lot of them say it's an agonising business consigning your darling to the care of other people. Do you think, when I get back to him, a sardine or two might make him feel better about being separated from you?'

'If you have some, it probably would.' To her vexation, her voice came out slightly husky.

Pierce used the gadget which opened the garage door. As it swung slowly upwards and outwards, he switched on the motor.

'Are you going to lie awake, worrying about him?'

'No, of course not. I know he'll be fine. It's just that he was dumped by someone when he was a kitten. I wonder if he remembers that? I wonder if he thinks I'm leaving him?' To her greater chagrin, her eyes filled with tears and she had to look out of the side window in case Pierce should see them.

They were cruising along the street now and a warm hand closed on her thigh and gave it a squeeze. 'Don't cry, darling. Cats aren't like elephants. They don't have long memories. Have you got a hanky on you?'

Darling. To hear him say it, as if she really were his darling, made her want to burst into tears.

'Yes, thank you.' She felt for the tissue she knew was in her coat pocket. 'I'm sorry to be such an idiot. But you see…since my father died…Parson has been like a person to me. I know it's silly to love him as much as I do…but I can't help it.'

The car glided to the kerb. Pierce pulled on the hand-brake and put the gear in neutral.

'Of course you can't help it.' He leaned over to put both arms round her. 'Everyone needs someone to love.'

At that she did burst into tears. 'Oh, dear…it's the wine,' she gasped. 'I don't…make a habit…of this.'

'Don't worry about it. I grew up with sisters. I'm used to tears,' he said calmly, holding her against his shoulder.

His kindness dissolved her completely. The stress she had been through before deciding to marry him, the strain of concealing her love for him, her uncertainty about the future all came welling up to the surface in a burst of uncontrolled weeping.

After perhaps half a minute of letting it all out, with an enormous effort she overcame her emotion and managed to swallow her sobs and bring the outburst to an end.

Drawing away from him, she said shakily, 'Now you'll be wondering what on earth you've let yourself in for.'

'On the contrary, I think the fact that you've managed to let your hair down is a good omen.' In the light from a nearby streetlamp, she could see the flicker of a smile curling the corners of his mouth. 'My father, who's a very wise man—I'm sure you're going to like him—once gave me a kind of summary of what he'd learnt about women from spending the past forty-five years with my mother. One of the things he told me was that if a woman starts crying, whether they're five or eighty-five or any age in between, but especially if it's your wife, the right thing to do is to put your arms round her, not pretend not to notice, or walk away, or get angry. My dad thinks that men should cry more. He says it's a great safety-valve. Are you feeling better now?'

'Much better...and thank you for being so understanding.'

'That's what a husband is for,' he said gently. And then, in a lighter tone, he added, 'I'll be there for Parson too, if he's feeling down when I get back. Come on; you've a heavy day tomorrow. Buying a wedding dress is a big event. Do you prefer shopping alone or would you like someone with you? I suppose all your friends are working.

How about Fujiko? I'm sure she'd be delighted to go with you if you wanted her.'

'I don't mind going on my own. I'd rather be by myself.'

He hadn't suggested the most obvious person to accompany her, she noted. She wondered how Chiara would receive the news of their engagement. She had an ominous feeling that her stepsister wouldn't approve.

CHAPTER EIGHT

'YOU'RE kidding me!' said Chiara, when they met for lunch on the fourth floor at Harvey Nichols.

'I'm serious. I know it's amazing. I can't believe it myself,' Holly admitted.

'I'm gobsmacked,' her stepsister declared.

Inwardly, Holly winced. Perhaps that ugly expression was one that Eric used and Chiara had picked up from him. It might be a good thing if she did take up with the donor of the aquamarine. He might be less coarse and uncouth than her present lover. Chiara had always been influenced by the people she associated with. At school she had fallen in with a group of girls to whom lessons had been a boring interruption to their after-school activities. It was they, to some extent, who had steered her in the direction she had gone.

Deliberately, Holly had kept her woollen gloves on while they'd settled themselves at their table, one of the last few vacant in a restaurant beloved by the store's chic clientele as a rest-stop between bouts of shopping.

Now she took her gloves off, knowing it wouldn't be long before her stepsister spotted the striking ring on her left hand.

As she'd expected, only seconds passed before Chiara gave a smothered shriek. 'Did Pierce give you that? It's gorgeous. My God! That must have set him back a few thousand. Did you choose it, or did he? He always despised things I bought when he wasn't with me. Oops! I guess it's not very tactful to remind you I had him first.'

It struck Holly that there was a perceptible tinge of bitchiness in Chiara's pretended apology.

She said quietly but firmly, 'Pierce is thirty-five and very attractive. It stands to reason that you were one of many. But that's in the past. If you want a place in my future, Chiara, you'll have to stop making gaffes like that outsize brick you just dropped.'

Her stepsister pouted. 'You've become very dictatorial all of a sudden,' she said sulkily. 'If you're going to start being big-headed, I don't know that I want a place in your future, as you put it.'

Holly reached across the table and put her hand over her stepsister's. 'I'm not being big-headed. I'm just telling you straight that although I might excuse your tactlessness I know Pierce won't. I think it would be a great shame if the fact that he had an affair with you years ago meant we couldn't go on being part of each other's lives. You're the only family I've got now.'

After a pause, during which she scowled at the table-cloth, Chiara looked up and said, 'I'm sorry. The fact is, I'm jealous that you've got a wonderful guy who's going to marry you and I'm stuck with a rich layabout who only wants to—'

Holly was fairly well inured to her stepsister's casual use of four-letter words. Fortunately the noise level in the restaurant made it unlikely that two older women lunching at the next table had overheard a word they might have found offensive.

'You're not stuck with him, Chiara. The world is full of men much nicer than Eric. But, if you want one of them to love you, you can't spend the next five years being somebody's popsy. You have to stand on your own feet...make a life for yourself.'

'Doing what?' Chiara said glumly. 'People much brainier than I am are losing their jobs every day. Can you see me working in a shop, living in a bedsit in some dreary suburb, stewing on the tube twice a day? I couldn't take that grind. I'm used to better things. Having lunch here, for example. Let's have a drink.'

When the drinks and their lunch had been ordered, she said, 'I'm pinning my hopes on this guy at Sotogrande. We're going down for Christmas. I'm hoping he'll still be there. I'm not like you, Holly. I don't have a talent for anything. I wasn't tall enough to go in for modelling. I didn't have the right contacts to get into films or television. I'm doing the only thing I can do to have a share of the good life. I know you think I'm a tart, but there aren't too many options for people like me. If guys like Eric are prepared to pick up my bills for half an hour in bed when they feel like it, I think that's better than slogging away as a typist or behind a counter. When are you going to be married?'

'On my birthday.'

Chiara blinked at that. 'Why the mad rush?'

'Pierce sees no point in waiting.'

Holly was tempted to tell her about Talavera, but decided not to. Chiara wouldn't understand the appeal of such a place.

'I hope you know what you're up against,' said her stepsister. 'I'm not trying to put you off. He's a catch...a big one. But living with him won't be easy. He's what they call a control freak...wants everything his way...no argument. I suppose you're madly in love with him. Knowing you, you wouldn't be marrying him if you weren't. I just hope he doesn't hurt you.'

'So far he's been wonderfully kind.'

'Aren't they all, in the early stages?' said Chiara. 'It doesn't last. Hey, I'm going to miss your wedding. I'll be in Spain on your birthday. Where are you going to be married? What are you going to wear?'

Late the same afternoon, Holly found her wedding dress in the Oxford Street branch of a chain which had built its reputation on inexpensive versions of high fashion.

She had trawled all the stores Pierce had mentioned, not with the intention of charging her purchases to his account, but to see what styles women who could afford to shop there were buying at the moment.

The dress she took back to her B and B place in a large carrier was going to need some minor alterations. Better buttons. A hand-sewn hem. The ends of the sleeves turned up an inch. After that, it would take an expert eye to distinguish it from a similar style she had seen on a display model in Harvey Nichols priced at ten times what she had paid for her dress.

A message from Pierce was waiting for her. He would pick her up at half past six and would like her to have her case packed and be ready to leave.

These unexplained orders did seem to support what Chiara had said at lunch about his being a control freak. But after the way he had handled her breakdown last night Holly was prepared to accept that whatever he had in mind had to be in her best interests.

However, it was Hooper, not Pierce, who called for her in a taxi.

'Mr Sutherland would prefer you to stay somewhere more comfortable, with a telephone in your room, Miss Nicholson,' the butler explained. 'He asked me to apologise to you for not being here with you now. He's been held up at his office. By the time you have unpacked and resettled yourself, he will be at your hotel. He's arranged for you to dine there before going to the theatre. He thought you would like to see the new play at Wyndham's.'

'That sounds lovely,' said Holly. 'How has Parson behaved himself, Mr Hooper?'

As he looked to be in his late sixties, she felt it was inappropriate to use only his surname as Pierce did.

'As I told you this morning, when you rang up, he gave every sign of having slept well and his behaviour today has been exemplary. From time to time he has miaowed in a way which I took to indicate that he was thinking about you and wondering when he would see you, but he seems to be a sensible cat, a good influence on Louisa who's inclined to be temperamental.'

'Do you have any pets, Mr Hooper?'

'No, Miss Nicholson. My companions are antiquarian books. My father was a second-hand book dealer so old books are in my blood, so to speak.'

Holly told him about the discovery of some of her father's books in Pierce's library and they chatted companionably until the taxi arrived at their destination, a hotel occupying a row of elegantly-porticoed town houses in a square in the part of London where Pierce lived.

There Hooper handed her over to the care of the hotel staff and very soon she was unpacking in a luxurious bedroom with its own bathroom and a view of the gardens in the square and the early Victorian houses beyond them.

A brochure and tariff inside a leather folder on the dressing table told her the price of the room. It was far beyond her own pocket, but obviously Pierce was going to pay the bill for her. It made her feel slightly uncomfortable to be staying here at his expense before they were married and she wondered what Hooper thought about the arrangement.

She had never known either of her grandfathers and, had they lived, they would have been older than the butler. But she felt he was a cultivated man whose view of the world and its ways would be similar to that of her grandfathers, one a schoolmaster and the other the editor of a weekly newspaper. In Hooper she might find someone to replace those two gaps in her now non-existent family circle.

She spent the day Christmas shopping for Pierce. It was difficult if not impossible to buy a major present for a man who already had everything so she had come up with an alternative she hoped would at least amuse him on Christmas morning.

Wearing the same clothes she had worn the night before, she was ready and waiting in the lobby when he strode through the hotel's entrance.

As she rose from the chair where she had been sitting, he saw her and changed direction.

'Hello, darling. Had a good day?'

Before she could answer, he bent to kiss her on both cheeks in a perfect imitation of a normal fiancé greeting his bride-to-be.

'A lovely day, thank you. How was your day?'

'Tedious. I need a pick-me-up. Let's go to the bar.' He took her elbow and swept her in that direction. 'I'll have a stiff gin and tonic. What would you like?'

As soon as he had ordered their drinks, he turned and gave her a slow, caressing appraisal. 'You have the glow of a woman who's enjoyed an orgy of shopping...second only to that other well-known glow effect. Hopefully, while we're in Venice, you'll radiate even more beautifully.'

The implication made Holly blush, but she found herself thinking that what she would like, instead of dinner, would be to be taken upstairs to her luxurious room and made to glow like that tonight.

'I've arranged for us to have our first course and main course before the theatre and come back for the rest after the play,' he said. 'Now tell me what you've been doing. Where did you go and what did you buy?'

She told him about the film star who had been auto-graphing copies of a probably ghosted autobiography in Hatchards, and seeing a royal duchess buying presents in Harrods toy department.

'What were you doing there?'

'Just having a look. Then I met Chiara for lunch and told her my news.'

'How did she react?'

'With amazement. They're going to Spain for Christmas so she wasn't offended at not being asked to our wedding.'

'I have to tell you that the slob she's with at the moment will never be welcome under any of my roofs,' Pierce said bluntly. 'Of course you're welcome to see her as often as you wish, but as I am never likely to enjoy her company it would be sensible, if you ever want her to stay with you, to have her when I'm abroad.'

'Will you be abroad a lot?'

'Fairly often. Sometimes you can come with me. But in many Third World countries there are health risks I would rather you weren't exposed to, particularly when we decide to have children. I think we should start by having a year or two to ourselves. How do you feel about that?'

'In the circumstances we probably do need more time to get used to each other than an ordinary couple. Anyway Talavera won't be ready for two years. I assume that will be our main home, once it's ready.'

He nodded. 'The pollution level in London makes it no place for babies, if there's a better alternative. I had a coun-try childhood. I'd like the same for my children. Which reminds me—I called my parents today to tell them about us. Later my mother faxed a letter to you.' He felt in an inside pocket and produced an envelope. 'Don't read it now. Keep it for later. If you want to write a reply, the hotel will fax it for you. The number is on the letter.'

'How nice of your mother,' said Holly. 'Wasn't she rather upset at your marrying someone they haven't met?'

'She trusts my judgement. Her main reaction was pleasure that I've finally found a wife. I'm the last of her brood to marry. She was getting worried I was never going to meet Miss Right,' he said, smiling.

His mother wouldn't be pleased if she knew the truth, thought Holly. But clearly he hadn't explained that. Somehow she didn't think he would lie to his parents and wondered what he had said to convince them that she was Miss Right while avoiding saying he was in love with her.

During dinner, at a corner table sufficiently far from its neighbours to make private conversation possible when the staff weren't near, he returned to the subject of children, this time raising the question of which of them should be responsible for the postponement of her first pregnancy.

It wasn't a matter which, at this stage of their relationship, she found easy to discuss.

Seeing her embarrassment, he said, 'You have had a close relationship with a man before, haven't you?'

At her nod, he went on. 'Then I'd guess it was you who made sure no unplanned babies resulted. From what I know of you, I can't see you taking any chances.'

It struck her as a strange remark in view of the fact that, in marrying a man who didn't love her, she was taking a gigantic chance.

She was glad when the discussion ended for, although she knew it was important to talk over everything affecting their future together, in some respects she felt as shy of him as if she had had no experience. His assurance, his air of authority, the deference with which he was treated all combined to remind her that although eleven years was not a huge age gap it gave her a lot to catch up with in terms of sophistication and *savoir-faire*.

'Have you found your dress yet?' he asked, on the way to the theatre.

'Yes, but don't ask me where. I want it to be a surprise.'

'You will have to tell me the colour so that I can order suitable flowers. Or perhaps you'd rather I put you in touch with the florist so that you can discuss it directly.'

The play they saw was a revival of a comedy of upper-class manners first produced in the fifties. The characters' witty repartee and the actresses' glamorous clothes put the audience in a happy mood. But although she enjoyed the performance there were moments when Holly's attention wandered from the stage to the tall man sitting beside her. Although, the night before, she had wept in his arms and been warmed and reassured by his sympathy, he was still very much an enigma to her. She felt it might be years, if ever, before she penetrated the deepest recesses of his nature.

When, back at her hotel, they had concluded their meal, he didn't linger.

'I expect you're missing Parson and I'm sure he's missing you. Come round tomorrow morning and reassure him that you haven't vanished from his life. Come and have breakfast with me.'

They said goodnight in the lobby where, this time, he took her hands and kissed them both in turn.

When she returned to her room, Holly remembered the envelope in her bag. The thick envelope bore the name and address of Pierce's organisation, but the single sheet of thin thermal paper inside carried a New England address.

The letter was typed but began with a handwritten 'Holly—what a pretty name'.

It went on:

I can't tell you how happy we are to hear that our youngest son has finally found the person he needs to make his life complete. Of course we are longing to meet you and hope that will happen very soon after your honeymoon.

Pierce tells me you have lost both parents and have been on your own for a long time. Soon you will be a most welcome member of our large family and, from what my son tells me, a wonderful addition to it. Has he mentioned my garden and how much pleasure it gives me? How wonderful to have a daughter-in-law who not only shares that interest but is a trained garden designer. I can't believe my luck.

Robert, my husband, joins me in wishing you both as much joy as we have had since we married forty-five years ago. We think marriage is still the best recipe for happiness.

It was signed 'Marianne'.

Holly was touched and encouraged by the warmth the letter conveyed. That Pierce came from a large close-knit family seemed a good augury.

She felt she should reply at once and sat down at the writing table to compose an appropriate answer. After several false starts, she wrote:

Dear Mrs Sutherland,

It was so kind of you to write and welcome me to your family. Your son is such an exceptional man that I can't help wondering if I am up to his weight. But I shall do my very best to be a good wife to him. I, too, hope that it won't be long before we meet. Thank you again for your kindness in writing to me. Yours very sincerely, Holly.

The writing paper provided by the hotel included headed sheets and blank sheets. She used one of the latter to copy out the letter in her neatest writing, putting 'Working at' and her Norfolk address at the top.

By now it was after midnight, but she took the lift down to the lobby and asked the night porter if the letter could be faxed immediately, knowing that now, in New England, it was early evening and her future parents-in-law might be having a drink before their meal.

'Certainly, madam,' said the porter. 'And your room number, please?'

Holly went back upstairs, where she used the electric kettle on the side table to make a cup of hot chocolate and also ran a warm bath. But they didn't combine to make her drowsy. She was wound up to a high pitch of excitement, not only by the unaccustomed taste of London night life and the realisation of how different her future as Pierce's wife was going to be, but also by a disturbingly strong longing not to be lying on her own but to have him with her, or to be with him in his bed.

An unsatisfied longing for love was something she had felt before, but never very strongly. Engrossed by her work, often tired out by hard physical labour, she had never been obsessed by sex as some of her friends from her college days seemed to be whenever she was in touch with them.

Perhaps it was partly because she wasn't wound up by sexy films and the books they laughingly called 'bonkbusters'. She never went to the cinema, hardly ever watched TV, and mainly read gardening books.

But tonight was different. Several hours in Pierce's company had left her with the feeling that the evening hadn't ended as it should. She had wanted to feel his arms round her, his lips on her mouth, his fingers stroking her neck as they had the night before.

Lying in the darkness of the unfamiliar room with its double-glazed windows and heavy interlined curtains shutting out any traffic noises and her own quickened breathing the only sound she could hear, she wanted more than the controlled caresses he had given her so far.

She found herself longing, urgently, for the night of her birthday when he wouldn't need to restrain himself. What he might do to her then, what feelings he might arouse sent a long, delicious shudder through her. As her body quivered and burned in anticipation, she began to wonder if Pierce might hold the key to the emotional equivalent of a locked room, a part of herself no one else had ever discovered and even she hadn't realised was there.

Next morning Parson greeted her with loud purrs and loving head-butts against her legs as she crouched down to talk to him.

She had picked him up and was cuddling him in her arms when Pierce said, 'If I had rung you last night, an hour after I left you, would I have woken you?'

'No, I was still awake…thinking about the play,' she added untruthfully.

'I was thinking about you…wishing I had stayed with you, or brought you back here.'

She flashed him a startled glance then looked quickly away, unable to meet the fierce light in his eyes.

He came close to where she was standing with the cat in her arms.

'Will you hold me like that?' he asked softly.

Holly's throat seemed to close up. Even if she had known

what to say, the constriction would have prevented her from speaking.

He came closer until Parson was like the filling in a sandwich. Taking her face between his hands, Pierce said commandingly, 'Look at me.'

She obeyed and was instantly mesmerised by the look he bent on her. Once, at the very beginning, she had thought his eyes cold. Now they seemed like windows into a fiery furnace.

'I want you,' he said, in a low voice. 'I've wanted you from the moment I called you a prig and you damn nearly lashed out and hit me. But I'll wait till we get to Venice, till you're my wife. I don't like to run with the herd. I like to do things my own way.' Softly, he traced the line of her cheekbones with his thumbs. 'We're probably going to be the first and last couple in years who haven't been to bed before the wedding. But it'll be worth the waiting. You're going to remember your wedding night for the rest of your life…I promise you that.'

It was Parson, beginning to wriggle, who brought an end to the moments of motionless silence which followed that husky-voiced pledge. Pierce removed his hands from her face and stepped back to allow the cat to drop lightly to the floor.

At the same time Hooper appeared with a tray of breakfast things.

After Pierce had indicated that she should follow the butler, Holly said, 'I think I'll go back to Norfolk this afternoon. I've got a few more things to buy…tights to go with my dress and so on…but I am still a working woman and can't take too much time off if I'm taking a long break at Christmas.'

The butler was on his way to a large, light conservatory. While he was transferring the things on the tray to a breakfast table already spread with a crisp cotton cloth, Pierce asked her, 'With a project like the one you're working on now, how are you paid? In instalments?'

'Yes. The clients wanted me to oversee the job from start to finish but obviously, during the winter, there are periods when the weather holds up progress. I worked out what it would cost me to live locally and added what I felt was a reasonable fee for the time I was likely to be actively involved. They accepted the total and we arranged to split it into three instalments. They're out of the country themselves at the moment. As soon as they're back, I'll explain what's happened. I'm sure they'll be very understanding and it shouldn't make a lot of difference.'

After being dropped by Pierce in Bond Street, Holly spent the morning buying underwear for Venice. She didn't waste money on an expensive nightdress which she knew she wouldn't be wearing, but she did buy herself a new dressing gown: not a frilly feminine number, which she didn't think Pierce would like, but a plainly styled robe of silky-looking striped rayon, the predominant colours violet and deep dark red.

After a sandwich lunch, she went back to the hotel, from which she had checked out earlier, to collect her case from the baggage room. Then she took a taxi to Pierce's house to put Parson in his basket and say goodbye, for the time being, to Hooper and Louisa.

On the afternoon before her wedding, she returned to the same hotel in time to bath and change for a dinner party given by Mrs Shintaro. Ben was going to be there and Holly was curious to know what was happening to his love life. He hadn't called her since the day they had lunched together and Pierce had been markedly cool towards him.

In the interval since her last visit to London, Pierce had called her every day, but his manner had been matter-of-fact. He had never repeated the things he had said to her on the last morning at his house, or made any similar remarks.

When he arrived to take her to Fujiko's apartment, she was wearing an outfit she had happened to see in the window of a country dress shop after mailing her Christmas cards from the nearby post office.

It was a colour she never normally wore—the bright red of holly berries. But at this time of year it seemed appropriately festive. Surprisingly cleverly cut for the price, it clung to her figure in a way that contradicted the long sleeves, the conservative length of the skirt and the modest depth of the V-neck.

When, having stayed in her room until notified of Pierce's arrival, she stepped out of the lift and walked to where he was waiting, he didn't come to meet her. She could see that he was surprised, but whether favourably or unfavourably she couldn't be sure.

Her wrap, a black lambswool shawl with a braided edge, was folded over her arm. In her other hand she had a small black purse with, inside it, the slip of plastic which unlocked the door of her room.

'Hello,' she said, smiling, lifting her cheek for his kiss.

'Hello.'

As he bent towards her, she caught an elusive whiff of some fresh-smelling aftershave. He always looked and smelt cleaner than other people. She had never seen him with hair that didn't look recently washed. His nails always looked as immaculately scrubbed as a surgeon's.

'I've never seen you in red before. That's a terrific dress.' He was looking at the way it was moulded to her breasts and hips.

'Thank you.' She shook out her wrap. 'It was mild when I arrived but perhaps it's colder out now.'

He had come in a taxi, no doubt in order to drink more freely than he would if driving. Outside the hotel, the same taxi was waiting to take them on to the party. As she stepped in and settled herself in the far corner, Holly wondered if, on the way there, he would kiss her again.

The interval since their last meeting had seemed far longer than it had actually been. He had stirred something in her which now wouldn't leave her in peace. She had thought of little else but their honeymoon and his promise to make their wedding night unforgettable. Now their arrival in Venice was less than twenty-four hours away.

'Did you drop Parson at the house? I haven't been back since this morning. I knew I'd be running late so I took a change of clothes to the office and had a shower there,' he said as the taxi moved off.

'Mr Hooper told me you had a lot on today. Are you bushed? Is a party the last thing you want?'

'The sight of you in that red dress revitalised me. I just wish this trouble in Africa hadn't blown up right now. There's been enough strife there already without a fresh outbreak.'

Holly had seen a newscast on the TV in her room. But, preoccupied by this important juncture in her own life, she hadn't paid much attention or realised that trouble in one of the African countries might affect his organisation.

'We could postpone our trip if you feel you ought to stay here,' she said.

'Are you kidding? Postpone my honeymoon? Not damn likely.'

He moved to the centre of the seat to take possession of one of her hands and hold it in his on his thigh.

His fingers were warm and, close to him, she could sense

the strength of his vitality almost as tangibly as the heat from a radiator. It took more than a long, busy day to diminish his driving force.

'This time tomorrow we shall be in my place in Venice,' he said, lowering his voice, although the glass partition behind the driver was closed and he couldn't hear them. 'You'll be the first person to stay there. It's a part of my life I've never wanted to share before.'

Somehow this made her feel such a strong rush of love for him that she couldn't control the impulse to snuggle against him, bending her cheek to rest on his shoulder for a moment as she said, 'I'm longing to be there.'

'Do you mean that, Holly?'

The sudden tightening of his fingers made her suppress a gasp.

'Of course I mean it. I—' She bit back the words on her tongue. Straightening, she said, 'I've learnt a few words of Italian. Just "please" and "thank you" and so on. I suppose you speak Italian fluently?'

'Yes.' His tone was abrupt.

Sensing his displeasure, Holly wondered if her instinctive gesture was not what he wanted from her. Perhaps it had been too childlike, or too much like Parson's displays of affection. Perhaps what Pierce wanted from a woman wasn't that kind of gesture but only signals of desire. Perhaps he was holding her hand on his thigh in the hope that she would caress him in a more exciting, inviting way.

But he must know she wouldn't do that…couldn't do that…not yet. They were not on those terms. She could imagine if he loved her, casting inhibitions to the winds and becoming as wanton as he wished. But a one-sided love was not the right climate for total abandonment, except, perhaps, when the lights were turned out in their bedroom.

It wasn't far from her hotel to Fujiko Shintaro's apartment. On arrival, a liveried doorman came forward to open the door and Pierce sprang out and turned to help her alight. While he paid the fare, Holly rearranged her wrap.

'Not so cold tonight, miss,' said the doorman. He was young and his smile was admiring.

Holly smiled back, as she did at everyone who was pleasant. 'It doesn't look as if there's going to be a white Christmas after all.'

'There's snow in the north.' The doorman's eyes were saying that he fancied her.

At that moment Pierce turned round, intercepted the look and gave the young man an arctic stare which made him redden and look down.

To Holly's astonishment, when they entered the lobby where an older member of the apartment block's staff was on duty, he said, 'Your doorman needs some more training in keeping his thoughts to himself. He'll explain what I'm talking about. Have a word with him, will you?'

'Yes, sir. Certainly, sir.' If the man was baffled, he didn't show it but ushered them into the lift.

On the way up to the penthouse, Holly said, 'Wasn't that rather severe, Pierce? You could get the doorman into trouble.'

'He's asking for trouble, looking at women like that. He's lucky I didn't swat him.' Pierce sounded and looked tense with anger.

As the doors of the lift slid apart, Holly felt a frisson of apprehension. Long ago, in one of his talks about life and how to live it, her father had warned her about jealousy.

She could still remember his words. 'Jealousy is a sickness…a mental illness. People who suffer from it see the world through a distorting lens. They suffer terribly themselves and they make other people's lives hell. No matter how much you like someone, if you see signs of jealousy, steer clear of them, Holly. They're dangerous people to mix with.'

As she removed her wrap, she looked up at the face of the man she was going to marry at half past eleven tomorrow and saw little knots of sinew at the angles of his jaw and a stormy look still in his eyes.

Was this the first intimation that Pierce was one of the people her father had warned her about?

CHAPTER NINE

IT WAS a party for twelve and almost everyone present had, like Pierce and herself, been born in a different country, even the married couples being a combination of nationalities. Only the hostess and her grandson had visible links with the same culture. When they went into dinner, Holly found herself next to a Frenchman many years older than herself.

'You are the beautiful garden designer who has swept Pierce Sutherland off his feet, so Fujiko tells me,' was his opening gambit.

'I wouldn't say that, but we are engaged to be married,' Holly said, smiling.

'You are too modest, *mademoiselle*. Were I thirty years younger, I should also be at your feet.'

He flirted with her all the way through the first course. But when Holly glanced down the table to where Pierce was sitting, wondering if he was aware of the Frenchman's light-hearted attentions and was taking them seriously, he caught her eye and gave her a friendly wink.

Perhaps he had the sense to see that although her neighbour was playing the part of the gallant Frenchman for all he was worth, it was only in fun, and he had a very attractive Irish wife with whom, from time to time, he exchanged affectionate glances.

With the arrival of the second course, they both turned to their other neighbours, Holly's being a Swede in his forties. From him she learnt that in the far north of Norway, because of the long hours of daylight and the effect of the Gulf Stream, rice could be grown. She filed this away to tell Pierce, hoping it would interest him, if it wasn't something he already knew.

It wasn't until after dinner that she had a chance to talk to Ben, although only in the company of other people, so that she couldn't ask what she wanted to know.

Presently, he said to the others in the group. 'Would you excuse us? There's a Japanese painting Holly wants to see. It's in another room.'

On the way there, he said, 'As you probably guessed, I want to talk to you privately. We'll go to my grandfather's study. We shan't be disturbed there.'

'I wasn't sure you would be here tonight,' said Holly. 'I thought you might have gone back to America.'

'I've been in the north of Scotland, trying out the tent Pierce and I will be using on Aconcagua.' He opened a door, feeling for the light switch before standing aside for her to precede him into a room lined with books and furnished with a large desk and two comfortable chairs on either side of a library table.

'When he died, my grandfather was writing the second volume of his definitive work on the artists who specialised in carving netsuke,' said Ben. 'Do you know what they are? Come over here and I'll show you some.'

He gestured towards a glass-fronted alcove between the rows of massed books. When he touched another switch, the alcove illuminated, the better to show a display of small carvings in ivory and wood.

'Netsuke—it's spelt N-E-T-S-U-K-E but pronounced *netski*—the toggles are used to anchor medicine boxes and purses to traditional Japanese costume,' he explained. They're an important art form. If you want to see a very fine collection of them, go to the Victoria and Albert museum.'

After giving her a minute or two to admire the carvings, many in the form of rats, mice and other small animals, he said, 'I want to thank you for the advice you gave me when I came to see you in the country. We did as you suggested and it worked. It turns out that Charlotte's grandmother is no longer as violently anti the Japanese as she used to be. Do you remember the VJ celebrations in the summer of 1995?'

'Of course,' said Holly, who had seen on television the parades and other functions commemorating the end of World War II in the Far East.

'It seems the old lady saw a programme on TV which made her realise how much the Japanese had suffered. Charlotte's parents hadn't grasped that her attitude has changed. It's a subject they've always avoided discussing with her so they didn't know her outlook has mellowed.'

'That's wonderful, Ben. I'm so glad for you. Does that mean that you and Charlotte will be emulating us pretty soon?'

'I hope so. I may even return to my father's law firm. I never wanted to before, but now it seems more attractive. Anyway, I'm grateful to you, and I hope, soon after you come back from your honeymoon, I can get you together with Charlotte. She's very keen to meet you. This is from both of us.'

He put his arms round her and hugged her.

It was a spontaneous gesture to which Holly responded with real affection, hoping that the young American and the girl he loved would become lasting friends.

As they drew apart, smiling warmly at each other, a voice from the doorway said, 'Is this a private party, or can anyone join in?'

Holly was startled into an audible gasp. Ben had steadier

nerves. Without any visible surprise, he said, 'Come on in. I've been showing Holly some of the netsukes. Is the party starting to break up?'

Pierce said coldly, 'Not that I've noticed, but it's time she and I left. Holly has a big day tomorrow.'

'At least you aren't having a huge wedding with all the strains that involves,' Ben said, smiling at her, apparently unaware that his friend's tone had not been friendly. 'I hope when I tie the knot I can persuade my bride to do it quietly and privately. Aside from the massive cost of a fashionable wedding, who really enjoys that kind of three-ring circus?'

Neither Pierce nor Holly made any comment on this. They all left the room, Ben switching out the lights and closing the door behind them.

When Holly said goodnight to their hostess, inwardly she felt a good deal of embarrassment because Mrs Shintaro had not been invited to the wedding or the lunch at Claridges afterwards.

Whatever Fujiko felt inwardly about being excluded, there was nothing but warm affection in her manner during their parting exchange.

Going down in the lift, Holly said nothing, waiting for Pierce to break the silence. But he didn't speak.

A different doorman from the one who had annoyed him earlier was on duty now and within moments of their leaving the building a taxi had seen this doorman's signal.

Stepping into it, Holly knew that even if Pierce chose to ignore the incident upstairs she couldn't let it pass.

For several minutes after the taxi had set off, she waited for him to initiate the kind of discussion about the party people normally had after going out together. But the minutes passed and he said nothing, staring out of the windows on his side of the vehicle with his face turned away at an angle which emphasised the slant of his cheekbone and the clean, taut line of his jaw.

At last she could bear no longer the unspoken tension between them.

She said, in a quiet, even voice, 'Are you going to make a habit of following me every time I disappear with another man...even one who's a close friend of yours?'

For some seconds she thought he was going to ignore the question. That irked her even more. Sulking drove her to distraction. She had thought it a hateful weapon since seeing her stepmother use it against her father.

But then Pierce spoke. 'I wasn't aware that you had disappeared until I looked round and you weren't there. I assumed you had gone to the bathroom, but you were away so long that I began to wonder if you weren't feeling well. When I spoke to Fujiko, she said you had left the room with Ben. Not very civil behaviour by anyone's standards.'

'That's ridiculous,' Holly said crisply. 'Ben had something to tell me that wasn't for public consumption. If I'd seen you leave the room with Fujiko, I would have thought nothing of it.'

'Fujiko is older than my mother. Ben isn't an elderly man. He's not much older than you are.'

She could no longer repress her mounting indignation. 'He's your *friend*. He's been testing the tent you're going to share on Aconcagua. Can't you trust him to spend ten minutes alone with your fiancée? Can't you trust me?'

'You misunderstand my concern,' he said coldly. 'I warned you before that you underestimate yourself. The way you look tonight, every man there was admiring you. You should be aware of your power and use it more circumspectly.'

Holly decided that, even though Ben hadn't told Pierce

his news yet, if he knew the trouble it was causing he wouldn't object to her being the one to tell it.

She said, 'I could be the most alluring woman in the world. It wouldn't have the smallest effect on Ben. He's still in love with someone else and it's going right for them now. That's what he wanted to tell me. That's why he was giving me a hug. Because he's relieved and happy and he thinks I helped him get over his problem.'

'How did you help?' Pierce asked.

'It's a long and complicated story. I'll tell you some other time. At the moment I'm too upset by the way you've behaved. You went over the top about the doorman and you were obviously furious when you saw Ben and me exchanging a perfectly innocent hug. If that's how you're going to be for the rest of our lives, I have to ask myself if I can live with a man who starts being suspicious and angry with so little reason.'

He shot out a hand, grasping her by the wrist, his fingers painfully tight. 'I don't like it when other men leer at you in my presence. He was out of line and deserved a sharp reprimand.'

'Ben didn't deserve to be glared at. It's the second time you've been foul to him for no reason…and you're hurting my wrist.'

'I'm sorry.' His fingers slackened, but he didn't let go.

In the half-light of the taxi, its interior intermittently brightened by the beams from streetlamps and shop windows, they stared each other down.

Although in her heart she felt a sick despair that all her bright dreams of making him love her seemed about to blow up in her face, Holly refused to be routed by the fierce gleam in his eyes.

If she didn't stand her ground now, she was giving him

tacit permission to ride rough-shod over the rest of her life…if, after this, they could make a life together.

'I don't think Ben noticed,' he said. 'He's not as sensitive as you are.'

'Then you admit you were jealous?'

'Yes, for a moment, I was. Is that a crime? Would you rather I had been indifferent?'

At this point the taxi pulled up outside the hotel, where a couple in evening dress were waiting for transport. Even if they hadn't been there, waiting for Pierce and her to vacate the taxi, Holly wouldn't have been able to reply immediately. She needed time to think how best to answer.

The doorman opened the door and she stepped out first, moving out of the way while Pierce paid the fare and the other couple got in. He must have given the driver a twenty-pound note and the man was short of change and took a little time to find the necessary money.

Holly looked at Pierce's broad shoulders and remembered the night she had leaned against him and wept. She wished she understood him. Was it madness to marry a man she couldn't rely on to behave in a way she found acceptable? Was the brutal pressure of his fingers on her wrist the first intimation that, given what he considered sufficient provocation, he might even be physically cruel to her? Or was that horrible possibility a figment of her imagination, prompted by an article on domestic violence in the paper she had read on the train this morning, plus a bad case of pre-wedding jitters?

She heard him say goodnight to the driver and then he turned towards her, his expression inscrutable.

'We have to talk this out. I'll come in with you.' Inside the lobby, he said, 'Would you like some coffee?'

'Why not?' said Holly. 'It's not going to keep me awake. I'm unlikely to sleep much anyway.'

Pierce ignored the rider, turning towards a quiet corner of the large entrance lounge, having first made a sign to the night porter that he would require service.

Within moments of their sitting down in two armchairs arranged at right angles to each other, a waiter appeared. 'Yes, sir?'

'A pot of coffee and two glasses of Remy Martin brandy, please.'

'Certainly, sir.'

'Now,' said Pierce, when the man had gone, 'let me repeat my question. Would you prefer me to ignore other men's attentions to you?'

'You didn't go overboard when the Frenchman I was sitting next to at dinner was flirting with me.'

'I know him. He behaves like that with every attractive female. It doesn't mean anything.'

'You should have known that Ben hugging me was equally harmless.'

'Did I suggest that it wasn't?'

'You didn't say so…but you looked angry. Your whole manner was hostile.'

He was sitting with his elbows on the arms of the chair and his hands loosely clasped. Now he unclasped them, placing his closed fingers on either side of his nose and closing his eyes for a moment.

The gesture reminded her that he had already had a difficult day because of the crisis which had blown up in Africa. In spite of her own hostile feelings, suddenly she found herself wanting to put her arms round him and hold him the way he had held her when she had been overwrought.

Instead, she said, 'Perhaps, as I suggested earlier, we should put off the wedding for a bit. You have other things on your mind now. It's not as if a postponement would upset a mass of elaborate arrangements and disappoint scores of guests.'

He opened his eyes and dropped his hands. 'Is that what you want to do?'

'I want what's best for both of us. Maybe we've rushed into this. Maybe we need more time.'

'You may,' he said. 'I don't. I never go back on decisions. I only make them when I'm sure that what I'm planning is right.'

The waiter came back. They watched in silence while he arranged a coffee-pot, sugar, cream, cups and saucers, two balloon glasses of brandy and a dish of chocolates.

'Are you staying here, sir?'

'No, but Miss Nicholson is. It can go on her account,' said Pierce, handing him a tip.

'Thank you very much, sir.' The waiter offered her a pen to sign the bill.

After she had poured out the coffee, she said, 'I wish I had your confidence. It's such a momentous step...marriage. People hope they've made the right choice but only time proves them right.'

Pierce drank some coffee and chased it down with almost the whole glass of brandy.

'You'd better sleep on it, Holly. I can't make up your mind for you. Perhaps your subconscious will. I'll say goodnight.'

He crossed the lounge and, without turning round when he reached the door, left the hotel.

On the day of her wedding—if it were going to take place—Holly was woken at nine by her alarm clock. In the early hours of the morning she had re-set it so when eventually she did fall asleep she wouldn't be woken up early.

First she had a shower and then, knowing it was served

until ten, she ordered a continental breakfast. That done, she dialled Pierce's number.

The call was answered by Hooper. 'Mr Sutherland's residence.'

She was too strung up to stand on ceremony. She said, 'This is Holly. May I speak to Pierce, please?'

'He isn't here, Miss Nicholson. He's in the park, on his roller-blades.'

'His roller-blades?' she echoed, astonished.

'Mr Sutherland has been roller-blading since the sport started in this country. He's extremely expert. He says it concentrates the mind. Did you just want to speak to him, or has some kind of hitch arisen? If so, perhaps I can help?'

'There's no hitch. But I do need to talk to him. Does he have a cellphone on him? Can you make contact?'

'Unfortunately not. He prefers to be undisturbed. But I'll ask him to call you the moment he returns.'

'Thank you. Before he went out…did he seem his usual self, Mr Hooper?'

'I would say so, yes.' After a slight pause, he added, 'Are you feeling nervous this morning?'

'Yes,' she admitted. 'I'm wishing my father were here to calm me down.'

'Perhaps, if you wouldn't think it impertinent, I can offer some reassurance.'

'Please do, if you can.'

'A long time ago I was married myself,' he said. 'Unfortunately we had no children and my wife died young…in her forties. But until then we were very happy…and I'm sure you and Mr Sutherland are equally well suited. It's very natural to feel nervous in the last hours before your wedding. In a few days' time, when you're together in Venice, you'll look back and smile at this morning's feeling of stage fright. Naturally, Mr Sutherland doesn't discuss personal matters with me, but I know him well enough to be sure that he's been a much happier man since he met you, Miss Nicholson. If that also holds true for you, as I'm sure it does, can there be any doubt that much happiness lies ahead of you?'

'Thank you, Mr Hooper...thank you.' She was too moved to say more.

It was half an hour later, and she had finished her breakfast, when the telephone rang.

'Hello?'

'It's Pierce. You wanted to speak to me.'

'Only to say good morning...and that it seems a long time till half past eleven.'

'You're going to be there, then?'

'Yes, I'm going to be there.'

'Good. I was hoping you would be. How did you sleep?'

'Not very well. And you?'

'Hardly at all. But tonight, with you in my arms, I'll sleep a lot better. Until half past eleven...'

Holly left for the register office escorted by Pierce's friend, whom she had met before. He made all the right remarks about her outfit—a simple cream dress and a cap of Christmas roses with clusters of golden stamens among white silk petals. From then on the day, after starting slowly, suddenly switched to fast forward.

The short wedding ceremony, the lunch with the witnesses, the drive to the airport, the unaccustomed luxury of the first-class lounge, the short flight to Italy, the final lap of the journey in a fast launch from the airport across the lagoon all seemed to follow in rapid, dream-like succession. None of it felt like real life, except that, when she looked at her left hand, there beside her lovely engagement ring was the plain gold ring symbolising her new identity as a married woman. All that remained was for Pierce to make her his wife in the fullest sense—an act which most bridegrooms performed a long time before the wedding but he, for reasons of his own, had chosen to delay.

Italian time being an hour ahead of London time, it was dark before they reached Venice, which was first seen as a shimmer of lights which seemed to rise from the sea like those of some magical city in a fairy tale.

The runways at Gatwick had been wet from a steady drizzle, but here it was a dry, clear evening and not too cold to stand outside the cabin and breathe in the salty air and watch the city take shape.

Pierce put his arm round her shoulders, drawing her close to him. It seemed to her that she could feel the warmth and vigour of his body even through their thick winter coats.

'By this time tomorrow,' he said, 'I hope you'll feel the same way I do about this extraordinary place. From the first time I saw it, I loved it. But perhaps if I lived here the magic would dissipate. It's better to come and go and never to stay too long.'

The launch slackened speed to enter a canal just wide enough to allow two-way water traffic. Tall houses loomed on either side, the lights from their windows reflected in the water.

'A lot of Venetian apartments, especially the ones on the upper floors of the old *palazzi*, have very low ceilings,' said Pierce. 'For somebody tall that's not comfortable, so I bought a place with more headroom. I hope you're going to like it.'

'I'm sure I shall love it. Oh, Pierce!' Her exclamation was caused by the launch gliding under a bridge and leaving the canal behind as it swung to the right and presented her with a view she had seen many times in paintings of

Venice but which held her spellbound as she took in the busy waterfront and what she knew had to be the mouth of the Grand Canal itself.

They went in a different direction, passing a point of land and cruising along another waterfront on one side of a wider channel.

'You can get your bearings tomorrow,' said Pierce. 'This evening the names don't matter. You must be tired. It's been an exhausting day for you.'

'I can think of a lot of people who wouldn't mind being exhausted in such nice ways,' she said, smiling. 'Who looks after your place for you?'

'A maid comes in every morning when I'm here and twice a week when I'm not, to keep an eye on things. Apart from breakfast, I eat out. Tonight we'll stay home and picnic, if that's OK with you. My secretary called Lucia and gave her a list of stuff to leave in the kitchen for us.'

His place was part of a building which had its own watergate. The launch drew alongside the mossy step and the boatman made fast while Pierce helped her to step out, leaving the boatman's assistant to deal with their luggage.

'Alone at last,' Pierce said, smiling, when the cases had been brought up, the bringer of them tipped and the outer door closed behind him. 'Come on, I'll show you round and then you can either unpack or lie in a hot bath while I make a cup of tea or fix you a drink. Whatever you want, you shall have, *bella signora*.'

The main room, where they were standing, was so full of interesting things that she couldn't take them all in, but only formed an impression of treasure trove from his travels or perhaps found here in the city, like the eye-catching bust of a Moor with a black marble face and rose marble turban and tunic.

'The bedroom is through here.' He led her along a cor-

ridor, lined with books and lit, in the daytime, by a window
of small leaded panes the size of saucers, to the most romantic bedroom Holly had ever seen or imagined.

Its side walls were lined with panels of antique mercury
glass. Behind the bed was an enormous landscape, painted
on unstretched linen, of islands in a blue sea. The bed itself
had four posts, each about four feet tall and topped with a
gilded swan spreading its wings.

'What a wonderful bed! Is it Venetian?' she asked.

'Yes, but not an antique. I had it made for the flat. The
wood is cherry and the swans were inspired by the finials
on Gabriele d'Annunzio's bed in the Casetta delle Rose.
My swans are slightly more streamlined.' He put his hand
on the one nearest to him. 'No one else has ever slept here
apart from myself. I had the bed made as a marriage bed.
Perhaps I had a premonition that it wouldn't be long before
I met you.'

It was a romantic thing to say, and he looked romantic
as he said it, his hair ruffled by the breeze blowing across
the lagoon, his tall frame now coatless, an open-necked
shirt under a coral sweater making him look younger than
the formal suit he had worn earlier in the day.

She had an almost overpowering longing to fling herself
into his arms and tell him she loved him. But she mastered
it, saying only, 'It's a beautiful bed. I'm honoured to be
the first woman to sleep in it.'

He beckoned her to him. 'Do you realise we haven't even
kissed each other properly yet? That peck in the register
office hardly counts.'

'I know.' His hand was still on the swan when she
stepped close to him and put her arms round him.

She couldn't say what she felt, but she could show it,
and would, in every way possible. Now that she was his
wife, she needn't hold back from physical displays of love

even if the words she wanted to speak would be an embarrassment to him until he started to feel the same way about her.

From now on she was determined not to think of *if* but *when*…

Looking up at him, she said, 'You know that saying—Life isn't a dress rehearsal? Well, this morning, when I was dressing, I felt that until today my life *has* been a dress rehearsal…and tonight is the opening night of a show which is going to run for the rest of my life.'

Pierce put his arms round her. 'If you go on saying things like that to me and looking so lovely…' His arms tightened, crushing her to him.

CHAPTER TEN

'WHAT are you writing now?' Pierce asked.

They were sitting in the sun in a *caffè* in one of the city's many squares, the only foreigners there, because although people came to Venice for Christmas and New Year they did not come in their thousands as they did for the famous carnival and during the hot summer months.

At this time of year, Venice belonged to the Venetians and to the connoisseurs who knew the city intimately, not the hordes of tourists who stayed for a day or a few hours, often spending more time peering through their viewfinders than imprinting La Serenissima's beauty on their minds' eyes.

Holly had been writing a couple of postcards, but now was scribbling in a notebook, using a pencil and doing a lot of erasing with the rubber on the end of it.

'I'm trying to write a poem,' she said. 'But please don't ask to see it. I haven't got it right. I may never get it right.'

'Do you often write poetry?'

'I don't often have time...or the inspiration.'

'What's inspiring you now?'

'I've called it "Venetian Days...Venetian Nights".' She gave him a saucy grin. 'It's a rather erotic poem.'

In matters relating to sex, she could talk to him freely now. Her last shred of shyness had evaporated. You couldn't be shy with a man whose finely sculpted body you knew as well as your own. The only taboo, the only unmentionable word—at least in any personal context—was love.

'In that case I'd better keep quiet and let you commune with your muse.' Pierce returned his attention to the book, bought an hour earlier at the Libreria Internazionale, which he had been dipping into while they drank coffee.

But a smile lingered round his mouth for a moment or two before he became reabsorbed in the text. She knew she had pleased him with her tacit acknowledgement that Venetian nights in the swan bed had given her life a new dimension.

Occupying one of their table's four chairs was yet another of the many large, stylish carriers they had taken back to the flat since their arrival.

On their first full day in Venice, they hadn't got up until lunchtime. In the afternoon he had taken her to the Missoni shop, buying her a long knitted coat combining a dozen colours in a pattern so vivid yet so subtle that it glowed like a priceless rug and felt as warm as her tweed coat but as light and cosy as a sweater.

Every day since then he had insisted on buying her other lovely things. Perhaps because he couldn't yet give her his heart, he seemed to feel a strong need to lavish her with all the material delights Venice had to offer.

But although everything he had bought her was of the finest quality and would last many years—she expected still to be wearing the Missoni coat when she was middle-aged—it was the hours in his arms which had been his best, most memorable gift to her.

He had taken her gently, impatiently, fiercely, swiftly, leisurely—in all the ways a man could make love to a woman.

More than that, he had shown her how to make love to him, which she had known in theory but never put into practice. When she did, it astonished her to find how much pleasure it gave her. Perhaps that was partly because his body, when he was naked, was even more splendid than she had guessed it would be—lithe, lean and still lightly tanned from a September holiday walking in the Picos de Europa.

His clean, smooth skin was as delicious to taste as it was to touch with her fingers. Sometimes, when she was revelling in the freedom to caress him in ways which would have seemed unbelievable only a few weeks ago, he would suddenly give a low groan and his shoulders would come off the bed as he pushed her onto her back and did the same things to her, driving them both wild.

Remembering those moments made her long to repeat them. 'Pierce…can we go home now?' she asked.

'Of course. Is anything the matter?'

'Nothing that half an hour in bed won't put right.'

He lifted a quizzical eyebrow, then signalled for the bill.

When, arm in arm, with him carrying the shopping, they were walking back to the apartment, he said, 'I've been propositioned before, but I've always suspected the motive.'

'How do you mean?'

'I've felt the suggestion was made to please me, rather than because the propositioner really wanted to go to bed with me. I'm beginning to believe that you do.'

'Of course I do,' she said fervently. 'I think I've missed my vocation…that I was born to make love. But only with you, Signor Sutherland.'

'But not only in Venice, I hope.'

Holly looked up at him. 'It will always be special in Venice because this is where it began and the mirrors and the swans make it seem like a wonderful dream from which I'm afraid to wake up.'

'You aren't going to wake up. It will be the same wherever we are. If you want to have mirrors and swans at Talavera, it can be arranged.'

They had come to the entrance to a long covered alley, one of many such passageways in the city. This one was too narrow for them to walk comfortably abreast. Before going ahead of him, Holly stopped and said, 'Perhaps we could have a different kind of swan bed for Talavera, made in the Regency style…you know, *faux* bamboo and painted swans. But the bed isn't really important. It's the person in it who matters. I'd be happy in any old bed as long as you were there with me.'

She knew that her heart was in her eyes as she said it and turned quickly away to hide a message which, if he read it, she hoped he would intercept as corporal rather than emotional.

It seemed that he did. A little way along the passage, she felt his hand on her shoulder, forcing her to a standstill. Turning her round, he pushed her against the wall and held her there with his body. Then he kissed her hard and hungrily on the mouth.

To two Venetian housewives, the sound of whose heels tapping on the flagstones brought the embrace to an end, they might have looked, seen in silhouette from the far end of the passage, like a pair of illicit lovers snatching a few moments' privacy to give vent to frustrated passion.

As Pierce let her go, Holly realised that, but for the interruption, in a few more moments she would have reached the high pitch of ecstasy that belonged somewhere secluded, not in this public place.

Profoundly shaken, she forced her trembling legs to carry her forward, averting her face and keeping close to the wall as she passed the two women coming the other way, one behind the other.

When they emerged into sunlight, by the side of a narrow canal with a stepped bridge crossing it further along, she said, 'You are a devil, Pierce. Do you know what you almost did to me?'

'No more than I did to myself. You could drive a man insane.' He seized her hand and began to walk very fast, his long stride forcing her to run to keep up with him.

'Stop...stop...you'll give me a stitch,' she protested, with a breathless laugh.

He did stop. A moment later, she was in his arms, being carried.

'Pierce...you can't. What will people think?'

'Who cares what they think? If I want to carry you, I will.' He lowered his voice to add softly, 'I will do whatever I want with you, but it will take more than half an hour. It could take all afternoon.'

On their last evening in Venice, they dined at a restaurant which stayed open later than most in a city whose citizens kept early hours, especially in winter.

Afterwards they strolled home through almost deserted streets and over bridges reflected in motionless water. It was almost full moon, although not much moonlight penetrated the narrower streets and canals, where the buildings cast such black shadows that, even though Venice was a safe city at night, in places it had a sinister atmosphere for anyone imaginative.

Then they came out into the great open space of the Piazza San Marco and for once there was no one about. Even the pigeons had gone to their roosts on the ledges and friezes of the surrounding buildings.

'Let's have a last cup of chocolate at Florian's,' Pierce suggested.

'They'll have closed...hours ago,' said Holly regretfully.

Of all the pleasures of Venice, she had particularly liked the city's oldest *caffè* with its many little rooms inside and, outside, musicians playing on an awning-covered dais, their music sometimes mingling with that of the rival *caffè* the Quadri, on the opposite side of the square.

But at this hour, both would shut and, by the time they reopened, she and her husband would be on their way to the airport. The honeymoon would be over.

'Do you know any old-fashioned dances?' Pierce asked as they were crossing the Piazza. 'The waltz and the tango, for instance?'

'Strangely enough, I do. My father showed me how to waltz and I learnt a bit of the tango—not the very complicated steps—for a show we put on at college. Do you know any ballroom dances?'

'I've been to a few formal balls. I can put on a reasonable show. Would you like to try me?' He turned and assumed the posture of a dancing partner.

As they had the square to themselves, Holly didn't hang back. She thought they would take a few turns and then he would kiss her and hustle her home for their last night in the swan bed.

'They say that one of the cafés is haunted,' he said as she put her hand on his shoulder. 'People living around the square or walking home in the small hours have sometimes heard music playing. But when they look out from their windows or come round the corner it suddenly stops.'

'It sounds like something cooked up by the tourist office,' said Holly, knowing he wouldn't believe in such a story.

He drew her closer, beginning to whistle one of the slow sweet numbers from the *caffè* musicians' repertoire. As he put his cheek against her temple, Holly closed her eyes, the better to concentrate on what her feet should be doing.

Then, as they slowly revolved and he shifted his hold on her hand to interlace their fingers, she heard a violin starting to pick up the melody, and then a cello and a piano.

Her eyes flew open. She looked round. The arcade in front of Florian's was now alight and on the dais, also lit up, three musicians in overcoats and fur hats were smiling and nodding to her.

'Did you plan this? Is it just for us?'

Pierce was grinning from ear to ear like a delighted schoolboy who had pulled off a great practical joke.

'Just for you, my lovely. Something special to remember when we're back in the everyday world.'

'Oh, Pierce, it's *all* been special…every single minute. You told me I'd fall for Venice and I have…head over heels.'

And for you, too, my darling love.

She almost blurted it out but just managed not to.

They danced to a half-hour medley of waltzes and tangos, Holly's confidence growing as she found that their physical harmony also extended to dancing. Anything he did, she could follow. In the end they were whirling and twirling like a couple of professionals.

When the music finally stopped and she rested, breathless, in his arms, the musicians applauded. One of them had brought a large flask of hot chocolate and some of the pastries sold in the *caffè* by day, and a bottle of *grappa*, a spirit that seared Holly's throat but made her attempt more polite remarks in Italian than she might otherwise have done. Pierce, of course, spoke it fluently and was able to thank them more graciously than she could, before they all said goodnight.

'I'll remember it all my life,' she told him, on the way home. 'I'll tell our grandchildren about it. ''When we were on our honeymoon, your grandfather hired an orchestra to dance with me in the Piazza.'' I wonder if anyone else has ever done that? I shouldn't imagine so. Most men would never think of it.'

Whereupon, to her dismay, she burst into tears and had to pretend she was crying from happiness.

But the real reason was that she found it unbearably painful to have everything in the world any woman could possibly want, except the freedom to say those three little words, 'I love you'.

In the time between their return to London and his departure with Ben for Argentina, Pierce was away a great deal. His absences allowed Holly to get on with her work in Norfolk, taking Parson with her for company. But, fond as she was of her cat, he was an unsatisfactory proxy for her husband.

In late January, Pierce managed to make time to take her to spend a long weekend with his parents. She hoped they liked her. She liked them even more than she had expected to.

Soon after this came the day when they had to say goodbye for five weeks. To Holly it seemed an eternity of loneliness and anxiety. Although the mountain the men were tackling wasn't comparable with the great peaks of the Himalaya, it was sufficiently hazardous for more than a hundred people to have died attempting to reach the summit.

While he was gone she went down to Talavera and began a comprehensive survey of the grounds. It wasn't a job which could be completed quickly, but she hoped to have it ready to show Pierce when he came home…if he came home.

From Mendoza, the city in western Argentina where those attempting the climb had their last taste of civilisation, he called her. She managed to sound bright and cheerful. It wasn't the way she was feeling.

As soon as he had rung off, she wished she had told him she loved him. What did it matter that he didn't feel the same way? At least, if something should happen to him, she would have told him the truth, held nothing back. Not knowing where they were staying, she couldn't ring him. The opportunity was lost and might never recur.

The feeling that she had been wrong to conceal her feelings oppressed her more as the time passed. It passed interminably slowly. Every night she watched the newscast with mounting dread that one of the last, minor items in the catalogue of death and disaster would be a fatal accident on Aconcagua. Every morning she switched on the radio feeling the same apprehension.

Hooper, who sensed her anxiety, although she tried to hide it, would boost her morale by citing examples of his employer's ability to get himself out of trouble, including several sticky situations in central African conflicts.

Every week she had a call from her mother-in-law whom she knew was equally anxious although, like Holly, she didn't admit to it.

One day, while they were talking, Marianne Sutherland said, 'It was such a relief to me when Pierce fell in love with you. I was beginning to wonder if he would ever find someone to suit him…if he had passed the stage when he was capable of falling in love. And then he called us to say he had met this amazing girl who was everything he'd ever dreamed of…but that she didn't like him.'

This was followed by hoots of maternal laughter at the idea of anyone being able to resist one of her beloved sons.

Holly managed to laugh too. 'Did he really say that about me…even before I changed my mind about him?'

'Oh, yes, he was plainly besotted. In fact we were a bit

worried. For someone like Pierce to fall headlong in love at first sight seemed out of character. We wondered if it could last. But once we had met you we understood.'

'I wish I did,' Holly answered. 'I know why I love your son, but why he should love me is baffling.'

And even more baffling is why he should tell *you* he loves me, but never tell *me* he loves me, she was thinking.

'I don't think people ever recognise why they themselves are lovable,' said her mother-in-law. 'The lucky ones, like you and me, who are loved by very special men just have to accept that it is so and be eternally grateful.'

After that conversation, Holly debated flying out to Mendoza to be there when Pierce got back. It was Hooper who dissuaded her, pointing out that if there had been any change of plan she might find it hard to locate him, especially as she didn't speak Spanish.

On the day before they were due back, Chiara rang up. Immersed in her own concerns, Holly had hardly given a thought to what might be happening to her stepsister. Now she learned that Eric had been dropped and Chiara was living on the yacht of the man who had given her the aquamarine. She sounded on top of the world.

'He's gorgeous…and he's crazy about me…wants me to meet his family. They're in Australia. His father's a motor-cruiser tycoon and his mother comes from Indonesia, which explains why, when I saw him, I thought Bradley might be a sheikh.'

'Are you going to Australia on his yacht?' Holly asked, a good deal relieved that Chiara's new man was Australian and not from a culture where attitudes to women were completely different from those in the West.

'No, that would take too long,' said Chiara. 'Bradley and I will fly there. The yacht can be shipped back the same way it came to Europe. So it doesn't look as if you and I'll be seeing much of each other in future, Hol. Bradley's had Europe, he says. He wanted to have a look round but he likes his own country better. He says the future is with the Pacific Rim countries. He says…'

She talked about Bradley non-stop for the next ten minutes. If he was only half as opinionated as she made him sound, he must be a world-class bore, thought Holly. All the same she was glad Chiara had met the man she had always wanted: rich, generous, handsome, pleasure-loving and besotted with her.

Perhaps down under she could make a fresh start, as so many others had. If the relationship lasted, Australia could be the making of her.

'So it's goodbye for now, but I'll give you a buzz every now and then,' Chiara promised.

'Yes, do that. Don't let's lose touch. Take care of yourself.'

As she replaced the receiver, Holly had the feeling it could be goodbye for a long time, if not for ever.

It was five o'clock in the morning when Pierce rang from Mendoza to say they had made the summit and would soon be flying to Buenos Aires and then back to London.

'Have you been OK, Holly? I've been worried about you.'

'I've been fine, but missing you badly. I can't wait for you to come home. Saying "I love you" on the telephone isn't the same as saying it in person.'

When he didn't answer, she had a sinking feeling that they had been cut off in mid-call.

Then his voice came through, strong and clear. 'Say it again anyway.'

'I love you. I've always loved you. Perhaps from the first time we met, when you belonged to someone else.'

'I never belonged to anyone till that day at New Covent Garden when you made it clear me you hated my guts. From that day on I was hooked.'

'Do you realise you've never said so?'

'Neither have you, until now.'

'I know…it's been driving me crazy…that something awful might happen and I would never have told you in so many words.'

'It's been the same for me, I pictured you getting run over…being in a train smash. Why the hell am I up here, stuck in this damned tent with Ben, when I could be in bed with Holly? I kept asking myself.'

'Pierce, have you called your parents? They've been as anxious as I was.'

'I know and I'll do that next. But you had priority. You're more important than anyone. I'll be with you as soon as I can. Until then, take care of yourself.'

Why it had been a problem to be open about their feelings was something that they discussed some hours after their reunion. By then they had made rapturous love and Pierce had caught up on some sleep.

The exertion of the ascent combined with limited food had made him lose weight. He was all bone and sinew—too spare, in her opinion, but even more exciting with his lean face deeply tanned by the Argentine sun and his hair overdue for a cut.

'Until I was stuck on that mountain, unable to make contact with you, I'd never been in a situation where, if something went wrong, I would leave a dependant…someone I wanted to be with for the rest of my life,' Pierce said thoughtfully. 'Before that I was hell-bent on inducing you to love me, which I didn't think you did.'

'Why did you think I married you?'

'Partly for Talavera. Partly because of the sexual attraction between us. Partly because you were lonely. Put together, those factors seemed enough for you to persuade yourself that marrying me was a sensible thing to do.'

'It *was* a sensible thing to do,' Holly said, smiling. 'Men like you aren't thick on the ground. Any woman who meets one is a fool if she hesitates…even if there is a downside.'

'What's the downside?' Pierce asked, amused.

They were having a late breakfast in the conservatory, with Parson and Louisa sunning themselves on the long, cushioned window-seat and a vase of early daffodils flown in from the Scilly Islands on the table.

'The downside is having to bite one's nails when you're risking your neck on the other side of the world. But if all our reunions are going to be like this one I guess it's a small price to pay.'

'It wasn't much of a risk and I may give up doing these things now that my home life has become more exciting,' he said, reaching for her hand and pressing it to his cheek. 'I love you in ways there are no words to explain.'

He hadn't shaved yet and she felt a tingle of response to the masculine roughness of his bristles against her palm. She knew that being married wouldn't change him and she didn't want him to change. His energy and his daring were two of the many reasons why she loved him.

Why such a man should love her must remain forever a mystery.

Cathy Williams is Trinidadian and was brought up on the twin islands of Trinidad and Tobago. She was awarded a scholarship to study in Britain, and came to Exeter University in 1975 to continue her studies into the great loves of her life: languages and literature. It was there that Cathy met her husband, Richard. Since they married Cathy has lived in England, originally in the Thames Valley but now in the Midlands. Cathy and Richard have three small daughters.

TO TAME A
PROUD HEART
by
CATHY WILLIAMS

CHAPTER ONE

FRANCESCA WADE was not a person given to nerves. She had the resilient self-confidence which came naturally to those who were good-looking or wealthy. In her case, both.

Right now, though, with her eyes dutifully glued to Kemp International's promotional magazine on her lap, she was feeling decidedly tense. She might have impulsively made the decision to come here, but she was discovering fast that this was the last place she wanted to be, and the temptation to take flight was enormous.

She kept reading, glancing covertly at her watch every so often, wondering where the hell The Man was. She had been shown into his outside office forty minutes previously, had smilingly been informed that Mr Kemp would be with her shortly, and here had she sat since. Waiting.

When the door opened she glanced up hopefully, and tried to wipe the growing resentment off her face.

'Mr Kemp will see you now.' It was the same smiling face that had ushered her into the office—neat grey little bun caught at the nape of her neck, navy blue suit, plumpish figure. She stood aside and Francesca made an effort to smile pleasantly back as she was led along the corridor to an intimidating mahogany door.

Suddenly the nerves gave way to something else—something more like alarm—and Francesca's mouth was dry as the door was pushed open.

The stylish designer suit which she had plucked from the wardrobe and donned because she thought that it conveyed the right image of businesslike efficiency now felt starched and uncomfortable. She was not accustomed to being so carefully dressed. She preferred casual clothes. She nervously smoothed down the skirt and looked around her, her eyes settling on the figure in the chair, his back towards her.

Behind her the door closed deferentially, and the figure in the chair swung around.

What had she expected? She realised that she had no idea—vague impressions, yes. She had spent weeks listening to her father's well-placed insinuations that it was time she found herself a job, that she couldn't sit back and indulge in useless creature comforts for ever, to him telling her that he knew someone—the son of a friend of his, a charming fellow.

It had been a quiet game of gradual persuasion, aimed at eroding her objections—the age-old water-dripping-on-a-stone technique—so that now, standing here, she found that she could hardly recall any recent conversation with her father which hadn't been vaguely permeated with descriptions of the wretched Oliver Kemp.

'He's a self-made man,' her father had told her in his early, enthusiastic phase, before her constant, stubborn refusals to have her life sorted out for her had obliged him to take a more subtle stance. 'Grabbed the proverbial bootlaces and hauled himself up, inch by inch, until now he's worth millions.'

That had conjured up images of a sour-faced young man grappling up the face of a cliff, growing ever fatter on the way as he made money and did all those wonderful things which had clearly awed her father.

The man facing her was not fat. Nor was he sour-faced. He had a disturbing brand of good looks—the sort of good looks which she had never before encountered among her young rich set. Every feature was strong and aggressive and his light blue eyes were mesmerising, hypnotic.

He stared at her openly, not blinking, until she lowered her eyes. 'Sit,' he commanded—a coldly uttered monosyllable that made her flinch.

He gave no apologies for having kept her waiting, but then he didn't strike her as the sort of man who went in much for apologising. Probably, she thought, he didn't even know how to spell the word.

She sat down opposite him, across the gleaming boardroom table, at one end of which was a word processor and several sheets of paper.

'How did you hear of this job?' he asked bluntly. 'It wasn't nationally advertised.'

'From my father,' Francesca confessed reluctantly, already on the defensive for reasons which she couldn't even identify.

'Ah, yes.' He stared at her, and she thought irritably, What does *that* mean?

'He mentioned that you were a friend of his and that you were looking for a secretary.' She was even more irritated to find herself rushing into a little explanatory speech. 'He thought that I might be interested.'

'I had lunch with your father weeks ago,' Oliver informed her coolly. 'How is it, if you're that interested in finding work, that you've only now decided to come here for an interview?'

Interview? she wanted to ask. What interview? This was more like a cross-examination. What exactly was she *guilty* of? she wondered.

'Unless, of course, you've been busy going to other interviews?'

He let the question hang in the air challengingly, while he continued to look at her with coolly polite indifference.

'Not as such,' Francesca admitted, disliking him more with each passing minute.

'*Not as such*? What does ''not as such'' mean? Either you've been going to interviews or you haven't.'

'This is the first,' she muttered, trying to comfort herself with the thought that she didn't really want this job anyway, that she had been goaded into it by her father.

'And how long is it since you left college?' He appeared smilingly vague. Did he, she wondered, think that she had been born yesterday? He would know exactly how long it was since she had left college because her father would have told him.

'Several months.'

'So, if you haven't been working or even, as you tell me, looking for a job, what were you doing for ''several months''? Resting?'

'Look, Mr Kemp,' she said, through gritted teeth, 'I came here for an interview. All these questions you're asking me aren't relevant to whether or not I'm capable of doing the job, are they?'

'Miss Wade—' he leaned forward and there was a soft, cold threat in his voice '—you don't decide what's relevant or what's not. I do. If you don't like it, then the door is right behind you.' He stared at her, and for a split second she was seriously tempted to leave, but strangely she didn't want to be browbeaten by this man.

'So,' he said with the same unsettling softness in his voice, 'are we going to continue?'

She nodded. There really was something very threatening about this man, she thought. It sat on his shoulders like an invisible cloak.

'Shall I tell you why you haven't bothered to stir yourself into getting a job sooner, Miss Wade?' he asked with pointed casualness. 'Your father is a rich man, and rich girls have no need for jobs. No doubt jobs get in the way of late nights, partying, men—'

Francesca's head shot up at that one. 'That's an insult, Mr Kemp!' she snapped. 'You have no right to make assumptions about my character!'

He shrugged negligently and stood up. She watched him as he strolled across to the window, one hand casually thrust into his trouser pocket, his face half turned away as he idly surveyed the scene outside.

There was a panther-like grace about him. His body was lean, muscular, as much of a threat as his dark good looks. All in all, she didn't like him—about as much as he didn't like her. He had no intention of employing her, of course. No doubt the only reason he had agreed to see her in the first place was because he vaguely knew her father. She should never have let herself be emotionally railroaded into this.

'You need to settle down,' her father had told her the evening before. 'You're a bright girl—too bright for a life of constant parties and holidays and shopping.'

For the first time she had sensed a certain amount of irritated despair in him. There had been no gentle teasing in his voice, none of the sly nagging in which he took great amusement.

He was right, she had thought reluctantly. She had left her expensive private school at eighteen, with three A levels under her belt, had sailed through a very expensive secretarial course, which she had taken simply because she couldn't face the thought of going to university, and ever since then had done very little about finding a job.

She frowned at the image her mind threw up of herself—too rich, too pretty, content to drift along with her crowd of friends who appeared to fritter their lives away happily doing nothing in particular, or else indulging in sporadic bursts of fruitful energy when they would do a course on photography or cordon bleu cookery, or anything else that enjoyably absorbed a bit time but didn't inconveniently leave an aftertaste for something more.

She wasn't like that. She knew that. But if she wasn't why had she allowed herself to flow with the tide instead of taking her life in her own two hands?

Oliver Kemp had turned to face her. His back was to the window now, and the harsh, winter sun threw his face into angular shadows.

'The fact is, Miss Wade, that I don't know precisely what your motives are in coming here, but if the only reason is to get your father off your back then you've come to the wrong place.'

He hadn't smiled once, she realised, since she had walked into this office.

'Of course that's not the reason why I'm here—' she began, reddening because there was too much truth in his observation for comfort, and he cut in abruptly.

'Really?' The ice-blue eyes raked over her thoroughly, and clearly disapproved of what they saw.

'I apologise for taking up your time, Mr Kemp,' Francesca said stiffly, standing up. 'But I'm afraid I made a mistake in coming here; I'm afraid that I can't accept any job you have to offer.'

'Sit back down, Miss Wade, and kindly do not think about leaving until I am through with you.'

'I have no intention of sitting back down, Mr Kemp,' she replied equally coldly, 'and kindly do not patronise me by treating me like a child.'

'I wouldn't,' he said smoothly, 'if you would start acting like an adult. Your father mentioned that you needed to settle down, that he was at his wits' end with you. God only knows what sorts of high jinks you've been getting up to, but I can well imagine. The fact is that I don't really give a damn what you do or don't do in your personal time, but my company isn't a rehabilitation clinic and I'm not in the business of setting wayward children back on the straight and narrow.'

Francesca actually only managed to absorb part of this. Her mind seemed to shut off when he got to 'high jinks', and anger flooded through her like a crashing tidal wave.

'I am not,' she managed to splutter, 'some kind of charity case, Mr Kemp. I was not obliged to come here and you are certainly not obliged to give me this job!'

'No,' he agreed, but his expression was shuttered.

'And for your information I am not a wayward child!'

'Really?' Mild disbelief bordered on downright indifference, but he wasn't about to let her put her point across. He pointed to the word processor on the table.

'Let's dispense with the histrionics,' he said coolly, making her sound, she thought furiously, like a candidate for the local mental asylum. 'I might as well find out if you're qualified for the job anyway. I want you to type the document at the side of the computer, and then I'll dictate some letters to you.

'Your father said that your secretarial skills were excellent but—' he looked at her with enough disbelief to make her teeth snap together in anger '—whether that was paternal pride talking is left to be seen.'

Francesca smiled sweetly at him and rose to go over to the terminal. 'Indeed,' she said. This at any rate was one area in which she was supremely confident. 'And, forgetting paternal pride,' she said, sitting down and quickly switching on the machine, 'anything I learnt at secretarial school might well have been forgotten after six months of partying, late nights and—what was it? Oh, yes—men. *And* high jinks and debauchery. Wouldn't you agree?'

She threw him another sweet smile. He didn't smile back at her, but there was a sudden shift in his expression, and she glimpsed behind the powerful, aggressive face a suggestion of charm that was an unnerving as his insolence had been.

She looked away quickly and began typing, her fingers flying smoothly over the keyboard. She could feel Oliver Kemp watching her, perched on the edge of the boardroom table, one hand resting lightly on his thigh—watching and waiting for her to sink obligingly to the level of his pre-conceived notions of her.

She glared at the word processor. True, she had come here of her own accord; true, her father, although he hadn't actually arranged the interview himself had hinted long and hard enough. He had also caught her at her weakest moment.

She frowned, and wondered whether she would be sitting here now if she had not spent that one misguided night with Rupert a few days before. Dear Rupert—tall, blond, carefree, with more money than sense most of the time. Her father thoroughly disapproved of him, and when he had discovered her whereabouts he had hit the proverbial roof. It had made not the slightest difference that Rupert Thompson held about as much sexual allure for her as a baked potato.

Her eyes slid across to where Oliver was sitting. If her father absolutely had to interfere, she thought, the least he could have done would have been to recommend her to someone halfway human—someone easygoing and amiable. Oliver Kemp, she decided, was as easygoing and amiable as a cyclone.

She printed the five pages of typed document and handed them to him with a blankly polite expression.

The cold blue eyes skimmed over them, then he read

them more slowly. Checking for errors, she thought. No doubt hoping for them. If any existed he could go back to her father with a rueful shake of his head and say, in all truth, that she just had not got the necessary skills to work for him, but that he would keep his ear to the ground as a favour to him.

Maybe, she thought suddenly, I should have inserted enough mistakes to have guaranteed that rueful shake of the head. But her only thought at the time had been to show the damned man that she wasn't the completely frivolous nitwit that he obviously thought she was. Shame. The best ideas, like the best retorts, always came to mind after the event.

'Not bad.' He deposited the sheets of typed paper next to him and walked across to the door, expecting her to follow, which she did, brushing past him then following him towards the office where she had sat for forty minutes earlier.

His own office was through the connecting door. It was huge, with two desks, one of which was his, the other housing a computer terminal and printer. Extending along one side of the room was a floor-to-ceiling bookcase, handmade in the same rich dark wood as the rest of the furniture, with rows of books on electronics.

Kemp International had cornered the market in sophisticated electronic equipment, and had always managed to stay one step ahead of its rivals.

Francesca eyed the books and wondered whether this was Oliver Kemp's personal taste in literature as well. Was he one of those men who ate, slept and dreamt work?

'I would expect you to be au fait,' he said, following the direction of her eyes, 'with the contents of most of the books on those shelves. Working for me isn't simply a question of being an adequate typist.'

'So you've decided that I'm good enough for the job, Mr Kemp?' she asked, with an expression of surprise. She didn't know whether to be astounded or dismayed by this. 'Does this mean that you don't think my father's verbal curriculum vitae was based entirely on paternal pride?'

He sat back in his swivel chair and linked his fingers together. 'Sarcasm is not a trait I admire in a secretary,' he drawled.

Oh, dear, oh, dear, oh, dear, Francesca felt like saying; then we might as well call this a day, mightn't we? But she swallowed down the rejoinder. Her father would be elated that she had taken him up on his suggestion, that she had landed this job through her own skills in the end, and she dearly loved him.

'I do apologise,' she murmured, and he frowned at her.

'You've proved,' he said, giving her reply the benefit of the doubt, 'that you can type.'

'And that I can read,' she pointed out. 'I shall consume the contents of those books avidly.'

His eyebrows flew up at that, and she hurriedly began stammering out a suitable apology.

He waited patiently until her voice had fizzled out into a series of fairly inaudible noises.

'Good. Because when clients call with queries you will have to respond to them in a coherent, knowledgeable fashion.'

He paused, and she said into the silence, 'What happened to your last secretary?'

'My last secretary,' he said lazily, 'emigrated to Australia to live with her daughter three years ago. Since then I've been subjected to a string of women ranging from the downright dim to the misplaced intellectual.'

So you wouldn't describe yourself as fussy? Francesca

wanted to ask. 'I see,' she said, only, in fact, seeing a series of hopeless confrontations ahead of her.

'You, at least, have started off in vaguely the right direction. You can spell at any rate.' He looked at her through his lashes, his face expressionless. 'Which brings me to the obvious question. Why are you here?'

'I thought you knew why I was here,' she answered, bewildered by the question. 'I'm a spoiled brat who—'

'Why are you *really* here?' he interrupted impatiently. 'What are you doing here when you could have got yourself a job at any number of companies if you'd wanted. Your father informed me that you had excellent A level results. Why didn't you go to university?'

Francesca looked at him resentfully, not liking the way he was manoeuvring her into a position of self-defence.

'Your father wanted you to go to university.'

'He did,' she agreed.

'He wanted you to study economics, I believe.'

'Did you talk about anything at this lunch of yours apart from me?' she asked with irritation. 'I suppose you also know what dress size I am, and what my favourite colour is as well?'

She hadn't expected a response to that, but he looked at her very carefully, his eyes roaming over her body and sending a reeling sensation of alarm through her. Men had looked at her before—in fact she was quite used to interested stares—but she had never felt this nervous prickle down her spine.

'Size eight, and, with your hair, probably green—dark green.'

'I didn't go to university,' she said hurriedly, flushing, 'because I wanted a break from studying.'

'A break to do what?'

'To enjoy myself,' she muttered feebly, feeling like a cornered rat.

'Ah, now we're getting to the heart of the matter, aren't we?'

'Are we?' she asked, already feeling her hackles beginning to rise.

'You may have all the qualifications for this job, and God only knows I've seen more than enough internal applications by way of comparison, but don't for a minute imagine that I shall tolerate your personal life spilling over into your professional one. Working for me isn't going to be a game to be endured simply to humour your father. I don't want to see you enter this office either late or the worse for all-night partying. Do I make myself clear?'

'As a bell,' she said coldly.

'Nor do I expect you to spend your time rushing through your work so that you can get on the telephone to your numerous admirers.'

'I don't have numerous admirers, Mr Kemp,' she snapped. 'And I can't believe that Dad would have told you that I did.'

He shrugged. 'He mentioned some playboy who was always in tow, and playboys tend to travel in packs, don't they? They don't feel complete unless they're enjoying their wild times in the company of like-minded individuals.' There was contempt on his face.

'You don't approve of me, do you, Mr Kemp?' she asked stiffly.

'No, I don't.' His words were blunt. He was not the sort of man to beat about the bush, nor was he the sort to parcel up unflattering thoughts underneath pretty wrapping.

'I grew up poor, Miss Wade, and I made it on my own. I don't approve of playboys who can't see further than having a good time. Nor do I approve of women like you, who were raised in the lap of luxury and swan through life thinking that hard work is something best left alone. You obviously have the brains to do something for yourself, but that doesn't appeal, does it? Hard work is rarely glamorous to those who don't have to do it.'

That stung. She felt angry hurt prick the back of her eyes but she didn't say anything. She could hardly deny that she had been indulged all her life, could she? By the time she had been born, late in her parents' lives, her father had already made his first million and had been well on his way to making several more.

Would things have been different if her mother had lived? Probably. But in the absence of a mother her father had spoilt her, doted on her, bought her everything that her heart had desired. There was so much, she later realised, that he had wanted to make up for—for the lack of a mother, for the long hours he worked and, most of all, it had been his way of showing her how much he loved her.

But maybe Oliver Kemp was right. Maybe showering her with material things had taken away from her that hungry edge that drove people on to succeed. She thought of her friends—all pampered, all the indulged products of wealthy parents, charming enough people to whom hardship was unknown and suffering was measured in terms of missed skiing holidays.

'But those are my personal feelings,' he said coolly, breaking into her introspection. 'Personal feelings have no place in a working environment, though. Just so long as you do your job competently then we'll get along just fine. Abuse your position, my girl, and you'll soon discover the limits to my tolerance.'

They stared at each other, and she felt panic rise up in

her throat. This was never going to work out. He disliked her and he disliked everything that she stood for.

'Thank you for making me feel so warmly welcomed into your organisation, Mr Kemp,' she said stiffly, and his lips curved into an unwilling smile which totally altered the forbidding angularity of his face.

He stood up to show her into her office. 'I see,' he murmured over his shoulder, their eyes meeting, 'that that biting tongue of yours might be something I shall *have* to tolerate. However,' he continued, turning away and walking into the outer office, 'there's no need to dress in designer clothes.'

He sat on the edge of her desk, waiting for her to sit down, then he leant towards her. 'I say this for your own benefit. The people with whom you'll be mixing don't come from such a rarefied background as you do.' He reached out to finger the lapel of her expensive shirt. 'Too much of this and you might find yourself distanced by a group of very nice people indeed.'

She didn't pull away from his touch, but she wanted to. Instead, as he strolled back into his office, she found that her body had become rigid, and she only began to relax as she sorted out the stack of typing which lay at the side of the computer.

At twelve o'clock he emerged from his office and informed her that he would be out for the rest of the day. She watched as he slipped on his jacket, adjusted his tie, and breathed a sigh of relief when the door closed behind him.

He made her tense and it wasn't simply due to the insults which he had flung at her. There was something watchful about him—something that stirred a certain uneasy wariness in her. He was like a shark, circling the water around her, content to watch, but she would do well to remember that sharks bit.

He had left her enough work to fill her time until five o'clock, but in fact she stayed on until nearly six-thirty, familiarising herself with his filing system, and familiarising herself also with some of the books on the shelf which he had informed her would have to be read, digested and memorised.

She had no idea how much of that had been said because he contemptuously believed that she would never manage such a task, but if she was to stay working with the loathsome man then she would make damned sure that by the end of her stint he would have to swallow everything he had said.

Her father was not at home when she got back—tired, but oddly elated at having spent the day doing something productive—but Rupert was. Bridie had let him in and Francesca found him in the sitting room, on his second glass of gin and tonic.

He looked at her as she walked in and said without preamble, 'Nasty rumour has it that you've got a job.'

Francesca looked at him and grinned. She was very fond of Rupert Thompson. She had known him casually for two years, but it was really only in the last seven months that they had become close, much to her father's disgust. He had no patience with men like Rupert. He thought that he should buckle down and find himself a job or, failing that, join the Army—as if joining the Army would suddenly change sunny-tempered Rupert into an aggressive work-machine.

The only thing that held him in check was his daughter's repeated reassurance that nothing was going on between them. Rupert was fun. He didn't want her as a passionate lover and the feeling was mutual.

She took off her coat, tossed it onto a chair and went across to the bar to pour herself a glass of mineral water.

'Nasty rumour,' she said, sitting down on the sofa, kicking off her shoes and tucking her feet underneath her, 'is right.' She looked at him. 'You could always follow my example,' she added, and he grinned at her infectiously.

'And lose my reputation? Never.'

As it happened, he did have a job of sorts, but in typical Rupert-style he had long ago decided that delegation was a talent that was much underrated. And, in fairness, it worked for him. His parents had died ten years ago, leaving him a fortune, along with a vast estate which he had happily left in the efficient hands of the managers who had looked after it from the year dot.

He signed things that needed his signature, spent enough time at his country home to ensure that things were being run profitably, and there his input ceased. He made sure that all his employees were treated well, received unstinting loyalty in return, and cheerfully had his good times on some of the immense profits that came his way.

'So tell all,'' he commanded, settling back comfortably with his drink, and Francesca obliged, carefully editing out the unpleasantness of her interview. She wasn't given to confiding private feelings to other people—a legacy, she had always assumed, of having been the only child of a single-parent family.

'Kemp,' Rupert murmured thoughtfully. 'Kemp, Kemp, Kemp. I know that name.'

'Their electronic stuff is all over the country, Rupert,' Francesca said drily. 'And they're branching out all the time,' she heard herself saying. 'They've moved into Europe and are hoping to capture the Far East fairly soon.' One *day*, she thought suddenly, and I sound like an advertising brochure. Had Oliver Kemp been that successful in influencing her thoughts? She found the idea of that slightly disconcerting.

'No, no, no.' He waved aside the explanation. 'What I mean is this—I've heard of that man personally.'

'Really?' She felt a sudden rush of curiosity which, she told herself, she had no intention of satisfying. Oliver Kemp was an arrogant bastard, and whatever he did in his private life had nothing to do with her. She would work for him because a combination of pride and guilt would make her, at least for the time being, but beyond that her interest stopped.

Rupert, immune to subtle shifts in atmosphere, blithely ignored this one and continued in the same thoughtful voice, 'Oliver Kemp. I've seen him around.'

'You've seen most people around,' she pointed out. 'You're hardly one of life's shrinking violets, are you?'

He laughed, pleased at that. 'Good-looking chap,' he said, draining his drink and eyeing the empty glass meaningfully. She ignored the hint. As far as she was concerned he drank too much anyway, and she had no intention of assisting the situation.

'You can have some mineral water, Rupert,' she said eventually, and he sighed in resignation.

'Too much of this stuff is bad for you,' he said when she handed him the glass of water. 'Haven't you heard that?'

'No, and nor have you.'

'A glass of wine, according to the experts, does wonders for some organ or other. Heart, I believe.'

'I would sympathise if your input was restricted to one glass per day.'

'Oliver Kemp,' he said, not commenting on that one, 'was in the gossip columns not too long ago. That's why the name rings a bell. Don't you ever read the gossip columns?'

'Too trivial,' she replied airily, and he laughed with great humour.

'Ever since they announced that we were about to become engaged?'

'Stupid people.' Her mouth tightened as she remembered all the fuss. One casual shot of them leaving a nightclub in London had been enough to propel them into an item, and it had been that silly drama which had led to all her father's unfounded suspicions that his daughter was about to do something utterly ridiculous.

'Well, they had their facts right about Oliver Kemp. He's engaged to a woman—Imogen something or other. There was a picture of them taken at their engagement party not too long ago.'

'Oliver Kemp is engaged?' Her voice was high and incredulous, and Rupert looked at her with some surprise.

'Sattler,' he said, nodding, delighted at this triumph of memory. 'Imogen Sattler. She's one of the city's top businesswomen. They squeezed in a few lines of background on her. Born up north somewhere.' He frowned. Instant recall was not one of his strong points and he didn't pursue it. 'Girl makes good, type of thing. You know what I mean—parents not well off, daughter very clever, gets into Oxford University, ends up sitting on the board of one of the top companies in the country.'

That made sense. Oliver thought that she was frivolous, an intellectual lightweight who spent her time enjoying her father's wealth—'Daddy's money' would probably be the term he would use, she thought with sudden bitterness. She was a decorative little bauble who had suddenly found herself catapulted into his sphere.

Rupert was standing up, ready to leave. He had only

really dropped by, he told her, to ask her out to dinner. 'Now that you're earning,' he said, 'I shall expect you to pay your way.'

'Rupert, I always pay my way, and let's not go into those times when your wallet has mysteriously been absent without leave.'

They laughed, and arranged a place to meet tomorrow— at seven, so that she would have time to leave work at six, dash back to the house, and quickly change.

She knew that she didn't need to justify herself in the eyes of Oliver Kemp, but some part of her wanted to prove to him that she wasn't the brainless dimwit he thought she was.

He had expected her to falter over that typing test, she realised, and he probably confidently expected that she wouldn't last the course in the job. He would think that she would get bored or that she wouldn't be able to cope, or both.

She went upstairs to have a bath, and by the time she emerged she had gone from simmering irritation over his contempt for her to downright anger. She had also found herself giving far too much thought to this fiancée of his.

She had no idea what Imogen Sattler looked like, but her imagination provided her with all the details—tall, hard, eyes as condescending and intolerant as his—the sort of woman who was only happy when discussing the stock market or the economy, the sort of woman who never *spoke* but *held forth* to an audience. The sort of woman, in fact, who would be ideally suited to a man like Oliver Kemp. And, of course, they would share the same hard edge of people born without comforts and destined to make their own.

Her father came home just as Francesca was finishing her meal and settling down to a cup of coffee. It took a great deal of effort to maintain a calm expression, to convince herself that working for Oliver Kemp was worth it when she saw how his face lit up at the thought that his dear little daughter had taken the bull by the horns and got herself a job—and one that he had recommended at that.

And he must have known Oliver Kemp's character more than he had originally suggested, because he was visibly relieved when she told him that the job was fine, that the boss was fine, that everything would work out, she was sure. She kept her fingers crossed behind her back all the while.

'He's a very highly respected man,' her father said, prepared to be just the tiniest bit smug.

Francesca made agreeing noises and thought, Respected by whom? Vampires and other creatures of the night?

But then, she later thought in bed, he wasn't coldhearted, was he? Not with a fiancée tucked away in the background.

She tried to imagine him as a hot-blooded man of passion, and that was so easy that by the time she finally fell asleep she no longer felt just angry and resentful towards him, she also felt vaguely disturbed.

CHAPTER TWO

'SO YOU made it here on time.'

Those were the first words that greeted Francesca as she walked through the office door at five minutes to nine. She had planned on arriving earlier, but her body had become accustomed to late mornings, and trying to put it through its paces at seven-thirty had been torturous.

She looked at him, keeping her temper in check, but he wasn't looking at her at all.

'I see you managed to finish all the typing that was on your desk. What time did you leave last night?'

Francesca sat down at her desk. She had dressed in slightly more conservative clothes today—navy blue dress, straight and fairly shapeless and far less obviously designer.

'Around six,' she murmured vaguely, and his eyes slid across to her with irony.

'There's no need to become a workhorse,' he said mildly, reaching down two volumes from the shelf of books and putting them on the desk next to her. 'I want hard work out of you; I don't want a nervous breakdown.'

'What is that supposed to mean?' she asked, eyeing the books.

'What it's supposed to mean is that I don't want you working over-long hours and then complaining of exhaustion by the end of the week.'

'I'm not a complaining sort, Mr Kemp,' she answered, truthfully enough, and he shrugged, not really interested

25

in what she was or wasn't, she supposed, just so long as it didn't intrude on work.

It was a novel situation. She had always been accustomed to provoking a reaction in men. She had the extraordinary looks of a blonde with contrasting dark eyes and eyebrows. She looked at him from under her thick lashes and saw that as far as her looks were concerned she might well be as alluring to him as the umbrella stand in the corner of the office.

'I want you to get a start on these two books,' he said, pushing his hands into his pockets. 'They'll give you some background information on what the company does. Before that you'd better come into my office and we'll go through my work diary for the next six months.'

She followed him into the office and obediently compared her thick diary with his, slotting in meetings and conferences which had obviously been arranged since the departure of his last unsuccessful temp.

When he had finished he sat back in his chair and looked at her steadily.

What was it, she wondered, about this man's eyes? They were quite cool, quite calculating, but somewhere in the wintry depths there was also something else—something offputtingly sexual.

'I never got around to asking you whether you have any questions about the company,' he said, 'or, for that matter, about your role in it. Have you?'

'What did your last secretary do?' Francesca asked 'I mean, the one who left three years ago. What duties did she have?'

He looked at her with a trace of irony on his mouth. 'Do you intend to fill her shoes?' he asked. 'No one else has managed that.'

'I'm willing to give it a try,' she said evenly. 'I know you don't think very much of me—'

'Oh, but I think your secretarial skills are surprisingly as good as your father described.' His voice was cool and his choice of words blunt enough to leave her in no doubt as to where the remainder of his thoughts lay.

Francesca kept her temper. She was normally an even-tempered person, but then, admittedly, no one had ever been quite so abrupt to her before. She had only been in the job one day but already she was beginning to realise exactly how cushioned her life had been. When she walked into the building she was surrounded by people purposefully going somewhere, hurrying to jobs because, no doubt, they needed the pay-packet that came with employment.

'Irene,' he said into the silence, 'was my right-hand man. She not only typed, she also knew the workings of this company almost as well as I do. When I asked for information on a client she could provide it almost without needing to go to a file for reference.'

'Sounds a paragon,' Francesca said wryly.

'I think it's called devotion. The assortment of secretaries I've had since then have been in the job simply for the money.'

'Which,' she pointed out, 'is one thing, at least, you can't accuse me of.'

'No,' he returned without emphasis, 'but your lack of need to earn a living does mean that it's fairly immaterial what you bring to this job, wouldn't you agree?'

'You're not prepared to give me a fighting chance, are you?' she asked, and he shrugged, neither confirming or denying that. He simply continued to look at her steadily, shrewdly, with cool judgement in his pale eyes.

'How did you start all this?' she asked, changing the

subject because she didn't want to let him get under her skin. Again.

'With a loan from the bank,' he replied drily, as if it had been a particularly stupid question because the answer was so self-evident.

'And after the loan from the bank came what?'

'A small outlet in the Midlands. Our products were good, though, and we moved in at a fortuitous point in the market. Any more questions?'

He waited politely and she clamped her teeth together. It wasn't difficult to tell that he found her a bore. She stood up, shaking her head, and when she looked back towards him as she left his office his attention was already elsewhere, his face frowning as he skimmed through something on the computer on his desk.

She quietly closed the door behind her, feeling for almost the first time in her life that she had been politely rebuffed.

When you thought about it, she decided, it was funny— funny to have the shoe on the other foot, not to be the focus of admiring attention. Except that she didn't much feel like laughing, even though she knew that her reactions were childish and that she would have to stop acting like a damned spoiled brat who sulked when she was not in the limelight. She had never before considered herself a spoiled brat and it was silly acting like one, she told herself, just because Oliver Kemp, a man whom she didn't like anyway, found her uninteresting.

At ten-thirty the outer door opened and one of the managers strolled in. He was in his mid-thirties, fair-haired, and the minute he saw her his eyebrows flew up.

'Well,' he drawled, darting a quick eye at the connecting door and then obviously deciding that the coast was clear, 'where have you been hiding yourself, my lovely?'

Francesca stopped what she was doing and said calmly, 'You must be Mr Robinson. Mr Kemp is expecting you. I'll just buzz and tell him that you've arrived.'

'Brad. And no need just yet. I'm five minutes early anyway.' He eyed the door again and adjusted his flamboyantly coloured tie.

Francesca watched him in silence as he perched familiarly on the edge of her desk and leant towards her. She knew this type, this make and model.

'When did the wind blow you in?' he asked.

Probably married, she thought, but still felt as though he was entitled by divine right to do just whatsoever he pleased. Probably, she decided, he felt as though it was his duty to spread himself around the female population, or at least around those remotely presentable.

'I've been here since yesterday,' Francesca answered coolly, 'and I wasn't blown in by the wind.'

'No, but you look as though you should have been. Ethereal, almost, with that hair of yours.' He reached out to touch her hair, and she saw Oliver Kemp watching them with widening eyes. How long had he been standing there? She hadn't heard the click of his door opening.

'Mr Kemp,' she said, standing up, 'I was just about to show Mr Robinson in.'

Mr Robinson had gone an embarrassed shade of red and had hopped off the desk as though suddenly discovering that it was made of burning embers.

Oliver didn't say a word, and his dark-fringed, pale eyes were expressionless. He simply turned his back. The now very subdued manager bustled in behind him and the door was firmly shut.

Francesca released a long breath. She felt inappropriately as though she had been caught red-handed doing something unthinkable.

When an hour and a half later Brad Robinson hurried out of the office, making sure not to look in her direction, she found that she was concentrating a little too hard on what she was doing, and when Oliver Kemp moved across to her desk the colour flooded into her face.

'I do apologise,' she began, stammering, and he looked at her with raised eyebrows.

'By all means. What for, though?'

She had been so sure that he had been going to say something to her, in that coldly sarcastic way of his, about not flirting with management that his question took her by surprise.

'I didn't invite Mr Robinson to sit on my desk...' she began, faltering and going a deeper red. 'He—'

'He's an inveterate flirt, Miss Wade,' Oliver cut in un-smilingly. 'I've caught him sitting on more desktops than I care to remember, but he's a damned good salesman.'

'Of course,' she murmured with relief.

'That's not to say that I condone a lot of time-wasting during office hours,' he added.

'No.' She paused. 'Though I know how to handle men like Brad Robinson, anyway.'

'I'm sure. I expect you're quite accustomed to men who flirt the minute they clap eyes on you.'

He didn't say that as a compliment and he was already looking at his watch.

'I've got a few files here,' he said, moving round the desk and perching next to her. Her eyes travelled along his muscular forearms to where his sleeves were rolled up to the elbows, and she felt a sudden twinge of uneasy awareness.

'Yes, sir,' she mumbled, disconcerted by her reaction.

His dark-fringed eyes slid across to hers and he said drily, 'You can call me Oliver. I don't believe in a hierarchical system, where my employees salute every time I walk past. Bad for the morale.'

'You've studied psychology?' Francesca asked, and he raised his eyebrows. 'I'm sorry,' she said, flustered, 'I...'

'Don't mean to be sarcastic all the time?' He sat on the edge of the desk. 'I suspect that that's because you've never had to curb your tongue, have you?'

'What do you mean?'

'What I mean, Miss Wade, is that your privileged background has opened a great many doors for you. People are often subservient to wealth, and I suspect that you've come to expect subservience as part and parcel of everyday life.'

'That's not true,' she said in a weak voice, but there was more than an ounce of truth in what he was saying. She had not gone through life demanding special treatment, but on the other hand it had frequently been given to her.

'This is your first job,' he continued relentlessly, 'and probably for the first time in your life you're going to have to realise that no one here is going to treat you as anything other than another employee in this organisation.' She felt his cold blue eyes skewering into her dispassionately.

'I don't want to be treated any differently from anyone else,' Francesca said defensively. She looked away from the hard, sexy contours of his face, which anyway was only addling her mind still further, and stared at the stack of files on which his hand was resting.

'I'm glad to hear it.' He slipped off the desk and turned his attention back to the files. 'There are letters in these which need typing and I've highlighted a few things which I want you to sort out. You'll have to phone the regional managers and arrange appointments for them to come and see me. As far as the Smith Holdings one is concerned, make sure that you get Jeffrey Lake to see me no later than lunchtime tomorrow.' He looked down at her. 'Any questions?'

'I don't think so,' Francesca murmured, and a ghost of a smile crossed his face.

'You're very confident, aren't you?'

'Don't tell me that there's something wrong with that!'

'Nothing at all.'

She looked up at him and their eyes met. 'I guess you'd be able to analyse that trait in me as well? Wealth breeds self-confidence, doesn't it? Maybe you start off from the vantage point of thinking that everyone is inferior, so it's an easy step towards thinking that you're capable of anything.'

'Very good,' he drawled, and his expression was veiled. 'Too much self-confidence is as bad as too little, though. I'm sure you wouldn't like to fall flat on your face just because you're too proud to ask questions.'

'I don't intend to fall flat on my face,' she returned calmly, 'and I'm not so completely stupid that I don't realise the value of asking questions when I need to.'

'Good.' He walked towards the door and she watched his loose-limbed stride with angry fascination. 'I won't be back for the rest of the day,' he said over his shoulder. 'If you need me I'll be contactable on my mobile phone until seven, then anything after that will have to wait until to-morrow.'

Once he had gone she turned to the computer and methodically began working her way through the files, calling the regional managers, arranging appointments.

Every so often, though, her mind would flit back to him. It irked her that he treated her like a child—an over-indulged child who appeared capable of handling the job but of not much else beyond that. There was always a cool dismissiveness in his voice when he addressed her, and even when he had perched on the desk and offered her his little pearls of insight into her personality the basic unin-terest had still been there. To him she was a case study in everything that he disapproved of. Someone who would either do her job well or not.

Her father, had he known, would have had a good laugh at that, she thought.

She worked steadily through lunch, and it was only when the door was pushed open that she realised with some surprise that it was after four.

'Hi.'

One word—a monosyllable—and Francesca knew instantly that she wasn't going to warm to the girl standing by her desk, looking at her with assessing eyes.

'What can I do for you?'

'Could you give these to your boss for signing? I take it he's not in.'

'No. Who shall I say left them?'

'Helen. I work in the accounts department.'

She looked, Francesca thought, as though she had been wildly miscast. She looked, in fact, as though she should have been working at the cosmetic counter of a large de-partment store. Her hair, dyed jet-black, was carefully styled and hung in a straight bob to her shoulders, and her face was impeccably made up in an assortment of shades which gave her the look of a highly painted doll—she was attractive in a very obvious sort of way, and was clearly in no mood to hurry on, from the way she was standing looking around her.

'Actually,' Helen said, dragging a chair to sit opposite Francesca, much to Francesca's dismay, 'we've been cu-rious about you. One minute Oliver had given his temp the boot and Cathy was filling in, and the next minute here you are. How did you manage to land the job?'

'Oh, usual way,' Francesca lied vaguely, but the other girl let that one go past. She was clearly not madly interested in the ins and outs of how Francesca had found herself working for Oliver Kemp. But she wanted something, because she still made no move to depart.

'We're all dying of envy, anyway,' Helen said, narrowing her blue eyes. 'I'd do anything to work for Oliver, but my typing skills are lousy.' She picked up a paperweight from the desk and idly turned it over while Francesca wondered what this bizarre conversation was leading to.

'Well, I'm sure your job must be very interesting,' Francesca said politely, and Helen laughed—a hard, brittle sound that jarred.

'Oh, riveting, dear.' She plonked the paperweight back down and stood up. 'Well, I'm off; just thought I'd come and see what the competition was like.'

'The competition?'

'Oh, yes.' She opened her eyes wide and failed to look guileless. 'Thought you might be the brainy type that Oliver goes for, but you're not. Still, just between the two of us, he can't be that immune to a pretty face, can he?'

'And, if he isn't, you want to make sure that you're the one in the firing-line?'

'Got it in one.' She smiled but without humour. 'I'd give my right arm to get into the sack with him.'

'Really?'

'Wouldn't you?'

'No,' Francesca said coldly. 'Now, if you don't mind, I've got a lot of work to do.'

'Sure.' Helen walked towards the door. 'He in tomorrow?' she asked, and Francesca nodded. 'Tell him

I'll come by to collect that stuff in the morning.' And she was gone, leaving an unpleasant taste in Francesca's mouth.

That, she thought acidly, was office politics—something else of which she had no experience.

She was ready to leave by five-thirty, and it was something of a relief to see Rupert at seven—sweet, uncomplicated Rupert, who wouldn't know the meaning of 'connive' if it jumped in front of him waving a sign in neon lettering.

'You look tired,' he said as they walked towards his car—a sleek red Jaguar which he had obligingly parked in the very centre of the courtyard. 'Tired yet extraordinarily gorgeous, considering all we're doing is going out for a meal. Sure you won't change your mind about coming out to a nightclub with me? We could dance till dawn and drink until at least midnight.'

Francesca laughed. He was incorrigible. He was also easy company. They drove to the restaurant—a French bistro in the theatre district—and he entertained her with a barrage of fairly trivial chat, which was quite amusing nevertheless. Rupert had always felt uncomfortable with pregnant pauses in conversation, and consequently he was adept at making small talk, which, she thought as they went into the restaurant, was just what she needed.

The restaurant was dimly lit, in accordance with someone's clever notion that subdued lighting was conducive to a romantic atmosphere.

The proprietor knew them well and showed them to a little table in the corner, much loved by aficionados because it offered an excellent view of the other diners. Rupert liked it. From there he could watch the comings and goings of the largely pre and post theatre crowd who were wealthy enough to afford the exorbitant prices the place charged.

Privileges, Francesca thought suddenly—all those privileges that money could buy.

She had never known what it was like to have her choice of restaurant narrowed down to a hamburger bar because of financial considerations. Of course, she had eaten hamburgers, and she had enjoyed them, but then she had chosen to. She frowned and wondered why she was devoting so much time to these questions when they had never really bothered her before.

She was subdued over the meal, listening to Rupert ramble on in his harmless, amusing fashion. He was typical of all her friends—out for a good time, ever game for harmless, mostly expensive fun. But they all lacked something, didn't they? she thought. It was as though reality hadn't quite impinged upon them.

Then she thought of Oliver Kemp, and that irritated her. He was hardly what she would call a role model of a caring man—at least not as far as he had shown her—but still, he was somehow more substantial than anyone else she had ever met, wasn't he?

Rupert was saying something and she nodded amiably enough, letting her eyes drift through the crowded restaurant, and she saw him just as he saw her. Their eyes tangled in the dimly lit room, and then, with a feeling of sinking horror, she watched as he and his companion walked towards their table.

At first she hardly noticed the woman with him. The only thing her eyes could focus on was the masculine figure in his dark suit with a cream silk tie around his neck.

'Oh, God, Rupert,' she whispered nervously. 'Here comes my boss.'

They watched until Oliver had approached the table,

then Rupert, ever ready with a tactless opening statement, said, smiling broadly, 'So you're the slave-driver I've been hearing so much about!' He stood up, unruffled by Oliver's cool, speculative expression, and said expansively, 'Why don't you pull up a couple of pews and join us?'

'I'm sure Mr Kemp has a table booked,' Francesca said, mortified, while the woman with him watched the cabaret with a pleasant smile.

'We'd love to join you,' she said, still smiling, and for the first time Francesca looked at her fully.

Was this Imogen Sattler—the tall, hard woman she had envisaged from Rupert's vague description? The self-made woman who had climbed to the top of her career?

She was small, with short, curly fair hair and an intelligently serious face.

'I take it you've just come from a play?' Rupert asked them both as they sat down, and Oliver nodded, looking at Francesca with amusement, as though the playboy man in her life was just precisely as he had imagined.

'I'm Rupert Thompson, by the way,' Rupert said with limitless *bonhomie*. 'General wastrel but with a heart of gold.'

The woman laughed and said brightly, 'What a novel introduction. I'm Imogen Sattler.' She looked at Francesca. 'And I'm so glad to meet you. I hope you work out as Oliver's secretary. He seems to run through them at a rate of knots.' She glanced at him fondly, and Francesca felt a spurt of confused emotion which she could neither explain nor rationalise.

'So I understand,' she said politely, looking at Oliver from under her lashes.

'Miss Wade is still in the enthusiastic phase,' Oliver said coolly. 'She's trying to prove herself.'

That amused Rupert. He beamed, took a generous sip of port, and said, grinning, 'That must be new to her. You've never had to prove yourself to anyone before, have you, Frankie?'

If he had set out to confirm everything that Oliver suspected of her, he couldn't have done it better. Oliver gave her a dry, knowing look, and she said defensively, 'Of course I'm not trying to prove myself. I just feel that if I'm employed to do a job of work then I should do it thoroughly.'

'Well done!' Imogen said, laughing. 'Just don't let him take advantage of you! He's notorious for taking advantage of his secretaries. Why do you think they all leave with such alarming regularity?'

'Now, now,' Oliver murmured, and his light eyes slid across to his fiancée, 'you make me sound like an ogre.'

The waiter approached to take their order and Rupert said, speaking for all of them, 'Just the bill. Our friends here have decided to come to a nightclub with us. Haven't you?' He looked at Imogen and murmured breezily, 'It would be a shame to waste such a glamorous outfit on a badly lit restaurant, don't you agree?'

She looked delighted at this turn in events, but Oliver's mouth had thinned and he said abruptly, 'I don't think so.'

'I'd really like to just get home, Rupert,' Francesca said, alarmed, but he waved aside both protests as if the thought of their turning down his kind invitation was hardly conceivable.

'Nonsense, Frankie. Just because you've got a job it doesn't mean that you have to give up all of life's little pleasures.'

'It would be fun,' Imogen said, turning to Oliver, and he looked at her with grudging indulgence.

They might not be all over each other, Francesca

thought, but there was a thread of real emotion there between them, evident in the way they looked at one another. Was this love? She abruptly drained her glass of port and felt a little dizzy.

Rupert stood up and held his arm out for Imogen. 'You don't mind my escorting your lovely fiancée to the door, do you, old man?'

Oliver was beginning to look mildly irritated, and when he fell into step with Francesca he said in a low, harsh voice, 'Can't you keep a rein on your lover?'

'Rupert is not my lover!' she said angrily, and he shrugged.

'Whatever, then. Playmate.'

'You make us sound like a couple of children.'

They were walking towards the door, and ahead of them Imogen was laughing, highly entertained by whatever Rupert was saying. He could be a superb conversationalist when he chose—witty, warm, direct, and with a boyish charm that could halt a charging rhino at a hundred paces. Francesca had seen it in action often enough before.

'And it's hardly my fault that Rupert's commandeered your fiancée, is it?' she added tartly.

'Oh, Imogen is a big girl,' Oliver drawled lazily. 'And intelligent enough not to be taken in by your little playmate's oily charm.'

They stepped outside into the freezing air, and Rupert immediately hailed a taxi while Imogen smiled coaxingly at Oliver over her shoulder. 'We never go to nightclubs,' she said persuasively, her eyes bright. 'It might be fun!'

Francesca thought that going to sleep sounded rather more fun, and her mouth was tight by the time the taxi pulled up to the nightclub and deposited them outside.

Rupert was well-known there, not that it would have mattered. Oliver's presence commanded such immediate awe that they were ushered in like royalty, and Francesca looked around at the familiar haunt with a sinking heart.

Had she really enjoyed frequenting these places—loud music, beautiful people frenetically talking and looking around them, eyes ever open to spot anyone they knew?

'I'm awfully sorry about this,' she murmured to Imogen once they were inside, and the other woman turned to her with wry humour in her eyes.

'Why? It makes a change for me. My head is normally so full of business that I find it hard to relax.'

Oliver, with an ease which he seemed to accept without question as people made way for him, had gone to the bar for drinks, and Imogen took her arm confidentially.

'You come here often, I gather?'

'Oh, all the time,' Francesca said, airily. 'My head is so devoid of business that I find it terribly easy to relax.'

'I wasn't meaning to be offensive,' Imogen said with gentle sincerity, and Francesca blushed.

'No, of course not; it's just…'

'That Oliver's been giving you a hard time because of your background? He told me that your father is terribly well off.'

'And what else has he told you?' She pictured them together, talking about her, and winced.

'He's a hard man,' Imogen said, 'but I expect you'll get used to that in time. If you stick it out, that is! Must be something of a culture shock, though,' she added thoughtfully, 'if you're used to a man like Rupert.'

'Rupert,' Francesca began defensively, 'is—'

'A type of person I've never met in my life before!' Imogen laughed, and Francesca felt the beginnings of real warmth towards her. She watched as Rupert took her to the dance floor and reluctantly sat down in a secluded corner with Oliver.

Out of the corner of her eye she could see the attention he was receiving from other women in the room—sidelong glances of interest which he either chose to ignore or else genuinely didn't notice.

'I can understand why your father was worried about your lifestyle,' he said, leaning towards her.

Amidst the noise and push of people there was something disturbingly intimate about his husky voice, and she looked at him and felt a twinge of something uninvited begin to stir inside her. She pushed it aside and said crisply, 'I never intended to make this kind of thing a permanent feature of my life.'

'You just spent the past few months allowing yourself to be persuaded into it?'

'That's hardly fair! You don't know me.'

'I know enough.' He looked around him and there was a condescending glitter in his pale eyes which made the blood rush to her head angrily.

'Your fiancée seems to be enjoying it,' she snapped.

'The element of novelty has its temptations for a limited period of time.'

'You sound as though you've never had a moment's fun in your life before.'

'Is that what you think?' He refocused his attention on her, and she felt her head begin to swim a little.

'Well, have you?'

'I didn't spend my whole life in front of books before joining the army of people out to earn a living,' he replied, his deep, low voice cutting through the tinny sound of the music.

'You just decided somewhere along the line that fun was something you could do without?' She cradled her glass in her hands, unwilling to drink another drop because she already felt a bit giddy.

'No, I just decided that this sort of thing was an exercise in stupidity.'

'Which I suppose is another criticism of me?'

He shrugged. 'You can suppose anything you like.'

'You don't really care one way or the other.' For some reason that stung.

'That's right.' He leaned back in his chair and looked at his watch.

'I'll make sure that I'm at work on time tomorrow,' Francesca said, abandoning her principles and taking another long gulp of her drink.

'Of course you will,' he murmured easily, 'if only to prove that you can burn the candle at both ends and still function.'

'I don't have to prove anything to you,' Francesca lied, not meeting his eyes.

'Well, then,' he said, not bothering to look at her, 'maybe to yourself.'

CHAPTER THREE

'I'M LEAVING home.' Francesca's father looked at her with anxious consternation, and she knew that it wasn't because of what she had just announced but the way she had announced it. She knew that her mouth was tight, her words abrupt, her expression hard, but she was just so angry that anything else was quite beyond her.

How could he?

'I've found a flat,' she carried on, not quite meeting her father's eyes but not looking away either. 'It's small but it'll do, and I shall move at the weekend. You're away for a couple of weeks so I won't get under your feet.'

'What's the matter?'

'What's the matter?' She stood up and walked across the room to the window, then she turned to face him, her hands on her hips. 'Dad, how *could* you?'

Two months, she thought furiously; two months of working for Oliver Kemp and now this. She didn't quite know how the sudden flare-up had happened. She had got into work the morning before and had known the minute she had clapped eyes on him that he was in a foul temper.

Whether it had been his mood or a reaction to two months of his stunning indifference to her, which, she had managed to persuade herself, suited her just fine, she didn't quite know, but she had snapped.

All she could coherently remember was Oliver leaning across her desk with a filthy expression on his face and telling her that the document which she had typed, which she had spent *hours* typing, would have to be redone because some of the facts were inaccurate, and that she should have known better. As if, she had thought at the time, she were on some uncanny hotline to Divine Company Information.

David Bass had dictated the facts. How could she have known that some of them weren't on target? She had said as much to Oliver.

'Oh, I've had a few words with David Bass,' Oliver had said grimly, and then she had snapped.

'How could I *what*?' her father asked now, and she glared at him. The memory of what Oliver had told her was still humiliatingly clear in her head.

'How could you have blackmailed Oliver Kemp into hiring me?' she wailed, angry with her father, herself, Oliver and the world at large.

She had spent the last two months working hard, proving herself, foolishly believing that she had got the job on her own merit, and she knew that she would have continued harbouring the illusion if she hadn't goaded Oliver into revealing the truth.

Her father was looking uncomfortable, clearing his throat and attempting to placate her, but Francesca was in no mood to forgive.

'I only did it for your own good, my dear,' he offered.

'You knew his father very well, didn't you, Dad?' she said bitterly. 'This was no passing acquaintance you bumped into accidentally. You grew up with his father! You both went to the same school, except that when you left to go on to a private school to finish your education he left to support a family of nine!'

'He was a very clever man,' her father murmured ruefully, which to her seemed quite beside the point.

'I don't care if he was Einstein!' Francesca shouted, on the point of tears. 'Oliver said that when his father died you sent them money—money so that Oliver could have the education he deserved. You sent me to him like a mouse to a trap, knowing that he would have no option but to employ me.'

'You went of your own free will,' her father pointed out, and Francesca ignored him.

'You put him in a position of obligation. I was a debt.' Her voice sank to a whisper. 'A debt to be paid off.'

'I knew you could do the job,' her father said.

'In that case you should have let me prove myself,' she retorted immediately, and her father reddened.

'My dear—' he began, and she cut him short with a wave of her hand.

'No,' she said, gathering herself together. 'It's done, but I shall never forgive you for this.'

'You're making a mountain out of a molehill. If Oliver had thought you incompetent he would have sacked you, debt or no debt.'

'The fact is you shouldn't have blackmailed him.' She walked towards the door. 'Please tell Bridie that I'll be in over the weekend to get my things together.' She didn't want to meet her father's eye. Her anger was so great that it pushed aside everything else. It consumed her.

'I can't possibly continue working for you,' she had told Oliver the day before, shaken and humiliated by his revelation.

And he had said curtly, 'Don't be a complete fool. I won't accept a resignation from you.'

'Why?' she had taunted bitterly. 'Because you're honour-bound to keep me here?'

'And stop,' he had said, unwittingly focusing on the one thing guaranteed to make her feel even worse, 'acting like a child.'

She felt like a child now, but she couldn't help herself.

Her self-respect had been whipped away and she felt naked and vulnerable, and she certainly wasn't about to be persuaded by her father to be reasonable.

She didn't want to be reasonable. She wanted to fling things about, and before she could do that she left, slamming the door behind her and bringing Bridie rushing down the stairs to see what was wrong.

Francesca was still fuming the following morning when she got to work, and as soon as Oliver walked in and saw her face he said tightly, impatiently, 'For God's sake, Francesca, drop it.'

'Drop what?' She watched as he took off his jacket, then slowly turned around to face her.

'Let's get one thing straight,' he said, moving across to her desk and propping himself on it with his hands. 'If I hadn't thought that you could do the job I wouldn't have hired you.'

'Sure,' Francesca muttered under her breath, and he gripped her chin with his fingers, forcing her to look at him.

'I can't stand people who feel sorry for themselves,' he grated, and she met his eyes with an angry glare.

'Since you can't stand me anyway,' she said, 'I don't think any further criticisms of my character will have any effect.'

He shook his head and looked as if he could willingly have slapped her, but instead he stood up and strode into his office, slamming the door behind him.

By the time Friday rolled around Francesca's nerves were jangling from the silently aggressive atmosphere between them.

Her work was as efficient as ever, but her body tensed

the minute he came near her, and there was a tension in him too that didn't help matters. She still hadn't told him that she was moving house, and she delayed that until she was ready to leave on the Friday evening, when she said coolly, not looking at him, 'I don't know whether I mentioned this to you or not, but I've decided to leave home.'

'Why?'

She shrugged and headed towards the door, but he was there before her, and he positioned himself right in front of it so that she had to stay where she was.

'I've decided that accepting charity from you is bad enough, but accepting it from my father as well is just compounding the situation.'

'And what exactly is the situation, Francesca?' he asked unsmilingly. 'That you've been knocked off course by something I shouldn't have said, and you're not big enough to believe me when I tell you that it doesn't really matter?'

'Yes, that's it,' she said flippantly. 'I'm not big enough.'

His lips thinned. 'Your father once did me a favour, and in return I did him one. Leave it at that.'

Francesca remained silent, her face quietly stubborn, and he shook his head with impatience.

'You're about to tell me that I'm acting like a child,' she said to him. 'Aren't you?'

'You read minds as well, do you?'

'Only yours,' she retorted, saying the first thing that sprang to her lips, and there was a thick silence in which an intimacy which had not been there before seemed to take shape and hover between them.

'Don't blame your father,' he said, looking away from her with a dull flush on his cheeks. 'He only did it for you.' He paused. 'I'll need your address for Personnel. They'll have to have their files updated. I'm on my way to see Sally now, so I'll tell her.' His voice sounded odd, but when he met her eyes again it was with his usual expression of inscrutability.

She rattled off the address, which she knew he had no need to write down because he stored things in his memory with prodigious ease.

'Take a couple of days off,' he said, stepping aside from the door so that she could leave.

She replied immediately, 'No, thank you.'

'No,' he murmured, 'I thought not.' Then he walked back into his office and shut the door behind him, and she cranked her mind away from him and onto the matter at hand—the move.

It didn't take long. By seven-thirty the following evening she had transferred everything she was taking with her from her father's house to the flat.

Now, for the first time, she sat down on the tiny two-seater sofa squashed beneath the bay window and looked around her. It would take some getting used to, that was for sure. If her father's house had been a sprawling mansion, this in comparison was a doll's house.

It had one minuscule kitchen with a fridge that could hold a carton of eggs and not much else, one small bedroom with a bathroom adjacent to it, and a living room with a rather tired-looking sofa, two chairs, and a Persian rug which she had brought from her own bedroom and which looked arrogantly glamorous on the floor in front of the fireplace.

The ceilings were high, though, because it was a Victorian house, and although the place had been chopped about to accommodate six little flats, nothing could detract from the graceful lines of the building. She sat back and smiled a slow smile of pleasure.

This, she thought, was the first taste of real freedom she

had ever had, and although an unfortunate combination of events had brought her here it still felt good.

Money, her father had once told her years back, was a trap. She had never given the observation much thought, but now she could see how true the statement had been.

If you let it, money would give you everything, but it would also form the bars of your gilded cage, and there you could remain for ever, unable to break free.

There was a sharp knock on the door and she jumped up in some surprise to answer it. It couldn't be Rupert. He had ruefully told her that he was going out on Saturday night, and she hadn't as yet told any of her other friends that she had moved. Most of them would think her completely deranged, and she had lost touch with quite a few, anyway, since she had started work and no longer had time to fritter away the days.

Oliver Kemp, however, was the last person she had expected to see. She pulled open the door, and as soon as she saw his tall dark shape in the hall she felt her heart begin to thud.

He watched the fleeting expressions on her face and lounged indolently against the doorframe. 'Are you going to invite me in?' he asked. 'Or would you rather we just stand here and look at one another?'

Francesca dutifully stepped aside and he brushed past her, his powerful frame dwarfing the small dimensions of the room.

'What are you doing here?' she asked, shutting the door behind her. She felt scruffy in her jeans and faded blue and white checked shirt and at a disadvantage.

'I thought I'd bring you a house-warming present,' he said, prowling around the small sitting room and, en route, placing two bottles of cold champagne on the table in front of the sofa.

'That was very thoughtful of you.' She didn't move and he finally turned around to face her.

'Your voice rings with sincerity,' he drawled. 'Mind if I sit down?'

He did anyway, tossing his coat and jacket onto one of the chairs and rolling up the sleeves of his shirt.

'When you told me that you were moving into your own place, I have to admit that this wasn't quite what I had expected.'

'Oh, really?' She picked up the bottles of champagne, and eyed him warily through her lashes. 'Did you think that I would have found myself somewhere larger and more luxurious?'

'The thought had crossed my mind,' he admitted.

'I may have been born into luxury,' she said, still not willing to forgive him even though she had simmered down a little. 'It doesn't mean I'm addicted to it.'

'*Touché*' He stood up and went across to the kitchen, and after a while he emerged holding two glasses of champagne.

'You really don't have to stay here…' she began, unconsciously making sure that their fingers didn't touch as she took the glass from him.

'Do you want me to leave?'

'N-no, of c-course not…' Francesca stammered, feeling thoroughly out of her depth.

'Have you got someone else calling round?'

'No.'

'I wanted to make sure that you were all right,' he said, his fingers lightly caressing the stem of the glass.

'Why shouldn't I be?' She sipped some of the champagne.

'Because you're like a nervous thoroughbred, overreacting to things, rearing up at imaginary obstacles.'

'Thanks so much for the vote of confidence,' she snapped, ready to argue if that was what he wanted, but he unexpectedly laughed.

Francesca took another mouthful of champagne. She had never been a great lover of champagne. As far as she was concerned it was a hugely overrated drink, but she had to admit that its bubbles went to her head faster than lightning.

He looked at her over the rim of his glass.

'Why are you here, anyway?' she asked in hurried confusion. 'Where's Imogen?'

'Imogen,' he said evenly, 'is out. With your boyfriend, as a matter of fact.'

Francesca's mouth half opened in surprise. 'Rupert?' she asked stupidly.

'Do you have more than one boyfriend?'

'What is she doing with Rupert?'

'They've gone to a nightclub.'

'They've gone to a nightclub?'

'You sound shocked. What sort of relationship do you have with this man if you don't know what he does when you're not around?'

She was still too amazed to find a suitable retort to that. 'So that's why you're here,' she said, nodding her head slowly, and feeling deflated. 'You don't care about my mental welfare. You've come to have it out with me just because your fiancée has been seeing Rupert behind your back.' Actually, after a couple of glasses of champagne on an empty stomach, *she* was beginning to lose interest in her mental welfare as well.

His dark eyebrows flew up and he laughed. 'Have it out with you? Don't be puerile. Imogen tried to drag me along to the damned place but I decided I could do without the dubious pleasure of loud music and the inevitable head-ache.'

'But don't you mind?' Francesca asked, proffering her glass for some more champagne, and wondering how she had ever got so worked up over Oliver's revelation to her a few days before.

'Don't I mind what?'

'That your fiancée is out on the town with another man?'

'I'm not a jealous man, and besides—I think I told you this before—I trust Imogen. She's also a free being. I don't believe in putting someone under lock and key and claim-ing possession of them.'

'How very liberal-minded.'

She had hardly had anything alcoholic to drink for weeks, and her three glasses of champagne had gone to her head with alarming speed.

She tucked her feet back under her and heard herself saying, with the sudden insight of someone who has had one glass too many, 'Did you think that I might need bol-stering at the thought of Rupert on the town with another woman?' She laughed, throwing her head back so that her hair spilled over the back of the chair in white-blonde disarray. 'Hardly! Rupert and I aren't lovers!'

His eyes narrowed on her, but he didn't comment. He said conversationally, 'How did your father react to your moving out?'

'He didn't try to stop me,' Francesca answered, circling the rim of her glass with one finger, then taking another sip from it.

'Would he have succeeded if he'd tried?'

'No.'

'Then he's a wise man.'

'When I told you that I wanted to leave I meant it,'

Francesca murmured, with a logic that only made sense to herself.

'Of course you didn't mean it.' She didn't look up but she could feel those amazing eyes on her. 'You like working for me, whether you want to admit it or not.'

'And do you like *me* working for *you*?' Francesca asked, topping up her glass with the remainder of the champagne from the bottle. 'You don't approve of me; you could have got rid of me for any number of reasons once you felt your debt had been paid in full.'

'I may not approve of you,' he said lazily, 'but I would have to dislike you personally to want that.'

Why didn't that make her feel any better? she wondered. Because, a hazy little voice murmured, you don't want to occupy that limbo between like and dislike, you want to be actively liked; in fact you want to be actively desired.

She felt her skin burn at the illogicality of that.

'Shall I open the other bottle of champagne?' she asked, not pursuing the unwelcome thought. She didn't wait for an answer. She went into the kitchen, opened the bottle, closing her eyes as she yanked the cork out and heard the distinctive pop, and then poured them both another glass.

Her legs felt wobbly, and she knew that he was frowning slightly, but she didn't care. The past week had been traumatic and she deserved to relax.

She was also feeling a little piqued. For the past two months she had told herself that what mattered most to her was that he should accept her professionally, but right now, right here, a part of her craved something else.

Instead of going back to the chair, she sat down on the sofa next to him. Was it her imagination, or did he take a swift, barely audible breath?

She looked sideways at him but his expression was bland.

'I don't think,' he murmured, 'that it's a very good idea for you to consume any more alcohol. What have you had to eat today?'

'Let's see…' She frowned. Her knee, she realised, with a little quiver of forbidden excitement, was nearly touching his thigh. 'I had some fruit for lunch and a bowl of soup earlier on.'

'And that's it?'

'And that's it,' she agreed, smiling at him. The lighting in the room was dim, and she looked at his face with surreptitious pleasure—the strong, smooth lines, the angle of his jaw, the sweep of his black hair.

She only realised that he was staring back at her when he said softly, 'All done?'

She didn't answer. There was a stillness in the room that made the hairs on the back of her neck stand on end. She reached out for her glass and immediately his hand snapped out and circled her wrist.

'I don't think so.' His voice was still soft but there was the hard edge of command in it.

She said irritably, 'Why did you bring me champagne if you didn't want me to drink it? You should have brought two bottles of orange squash.'

'I would have if I'd thought a bit harder about it,' he said, his hand still on her wrist.

Francesca shrugged and lowered her eyes, and he removed his hand.

'I think it's about time I left, don't you?'

'Why?'

He looked at her intently. 'I think you know the answer to that. Come on.' He stood up and she raised her eyes to his, confused.

'Where?'

'To the bedroom, my girl. I think you need to sleep this one off.'

Before she could utter a word of protest he bent down and picked her up, carrying her to the bedroom as if she weighed nothing. Of course, he was right. She was behaving in a crazy way, she knew that. With a little sigh she rested her head against his chest, hearing the steady beating of his heart, and half closed her eyes.

She couldn't remember having ever felt so frighteningly aware of anyone in her life before. But then, she thought, it wasn't as though her life had been cluttered with sexual exploits, was it? In fact, what she felt now stemmed from the dizzy Olympian heights of total inexperience.

She might have appeared on the surface to have enjoyed an uproarious few months, but she had never involved herself in all those things that seemed to go hand in hand with an uproarious life.

He placed her on the bed and switched on the side-light, and immediately the room was bathed in a warm glow. She lay back on the pillow and her eyes drifted across the dark wooden furniture, which looked so much nicer in this half-light than it did under the harsh light of day, when its cracks and grooves were so discernible.

Then her eyes drifted to his face.

'May I have a glass of water?' she asked, sitting up. 'The kitchen is…' She waved vaguely and he shot her a crooked smile.

'I don't think I need a map and compass to find my way to the kitchen.'

He left the room and returned before she had had much time to get her thoughts into order.

'Sit down,' she said, drinking the water, and after a little pause he sat next to her on the bed.

'How did you find this place?' he asked conversationally. He was such a formidably controlled person, she thought. What would it be like to see him out of control?

'Luck, aided and abetted by anger. I was so angry with Dad for involving me in his schemes, and with you.' Not that she felt angry now. She paused. 'Where do you live?'

'Hampstead. Not all that far from here, as a matter of fact.'

He began to stand up and she said quickly, not wanting him to go, 'Don't leave, not just yet.' In the silence her voice was almost a whisper and he sat back down, but with the expression of someone doing something against his better judgement.

Most men, she thought, would have jumped at the opportunity to be in a room with her. She had had enough blunt invitations before in her life to know that.

'Scared?' he asked. 'Is it the first time you've ever been on your own?'

'Yes,' she answered defiantly.

'Well, it's got to be done. Now, I think it's time you closed your eyes and went to sleep. Will the door self-lock behind me when I leave or do I need a key? I wouldn't like to leave you in here with the place wide open.'

'Why not?' She opened her eyes wide. 'Do you think someone might creep in in the dead of night and have his wicked way with me?'

'Or steal your television and video recorder, at any rate,' he said drily, raising his eyebrows. 'Better to be safe than sorry.'

'You needn't give me lectures. I've lived in London all my life! I know how to take care of myself.'

'You may have lived in London,' he said patiently, 'but you've been wrapped up in cotton wool. What would you do if a man broke into this place because you were stupid enough to forget to lock your door, or because you decided to keep the window open because it was a hot night?'

'What would anyone do?'

'I might have guessed you would answer a question with a question.' He laughed, and that irritated her.

'Do you think I'd be at any more of a disadvantage than if a burglar broke into your girlfriend's flat?' she asked, her mouth downturned at the corners.

'Imogen may look small and gullible, but she's far more streetwise than you are.'

'Because she comes from a different background?'

'This conversation,' he said, his voice cool, 'isn't getting us anywhere.'

'The least you could do is answer my question.' Her head was feeling considerably clearer now. In fact, her brain appeared to be working remarkably well.

'All right, then,' he said, with an edge of impatience. 'Yes. Growing up without a silver spoon in your mouth does mean that you have to develop a certain hardness, and that's a damn good protection. When there's no one around to make sure that the back door's shut you damn well realise soon enough that you've got to shut it yourself.'

'You're never going to forgive me for being the daughter of a rich man, are you?'

'I didn't realise that I had to forgive you for anything. You work hard and that's the bottom line.'

'I'm surprised you care whether you lock the outside door or not,' she muttered, irritated with herself for being perverse.

'I would care about leaving any woman alone in an open flat, especially in the state you're in.' He spoke evenly, making sure that she got the message.

'They're more likely to steer clear of me if they come in and find me collapsed on the bed,' she said, biting back the silly temptation to goad him into some response other than complete, polite indifference.

'You think so?'

'What do you mean?' Her head was beginning to swim a little again.

'Fishing, Francesca?' he asked, amused. 'Don't tell me that I'm the first man to point out that you're a very attractive girl.' He patted her hand and glanced at his watch.

'Not attractive to you, though,' she said, and there was silence.

'Do a few glasses of champagne usually have such an effect on that tongue of yours?'

She shrugged. She felt as though she was on the edge of something, as though some long-awaited event was about to happen—although she couldn't work out what this long-awaited thing was. She just knew that her pulses were racing and her skin felt hot and tingly.

She raised her hand, and even though she felt muddled, like someone floating softly above the clouds, a part of her still knew that what she was about to do was insane.

She began unbuttoning her shirt, her eyes locked with his. She had never realised that there were so many buttons on this shirt. It seemed to take for ever but eventually she reached the end, and she pulled aside the shirt, exposing her breasts, full and round, her nipples erect. Her breathing felt laborious.

'What the hell are you doing?' he asked on a sharp breath, and she reached out and grasped his hand, guiding it towards her aching breast. A sort of primeval instinct seemed to have taken over, and as his hand made contact with her skin she groaned and wriggled slightly.

He leaned forward, his eyes glittering in the semidarkened room, and his breathing, like hers, was quick and uneven. It gave her a heady sense of power to see that some of that self-control had slipped.

When his mouth met hers she felt her body arch up against his, and her lips parted to allow the forceful entry of his tongue. His fingers had curled into her hair and he pulled her head back while, with his other hand, he cupped her breast.

He rubbed his thumb across her nipple and thousands of little electric currents seemed to fly through her. Through half-closed eyes she followed the progress of his dark head as his lips trailed downwards to her breasts, but she closed her eyes when his mouth encircled the swollen pink nipple and he began to suck it hard, pulling it into his mouth while his tongue licked the hardened tip.

Her eyes were still closed when he lifted his head to look at her, and it took a moment or two before she realised that he had straightened and was sitting up on the bed.

'What's wrong?' she asked, suddenly feeling freezing in the room now that the savage heat of his body had been taken away.

'You are,' he said curtly. 'Button up your shirt, for God's sake!'

She propelled herself into a sitting position and hurriedly pulled the gaping sides of her shirt together, hugging her arms around her.

He had stood up, and now that reality was revealing her humiliation in slow motion before her she wished that he would leave, but he didn't. He remained standing at the foot of the bed, staring down at her coldly.

'Was that the drink just then, Francesca, or do you make a habit of throwing yourself at whatever man happens to be around at the right time?'

His words cut into her like a whip and she raised her eyes to his. 'I do not sleep around!'

'Sure? That wasn't the impression I got just then.'

'I've never slept with a man in my life!'

That was the first time she had admitted it to anyone. Her friends, she knew, had all been involved in physical relationships, and it felt slightly odd that she was still a virgin. But she had never been seriously tempted.

Not, that was, until now, because she knew that if he had continued his love-making she would not have tried to stop him. She had wanted him with an intensity that was frightening, and, worse, she realised, with horrified mortification, she had wanted him for a long time now, and while the drink might have loosened her inhibitions it certainly hadn't provided the motivation.

He shook his head and raked his long fingers through his hair. 'You're looking at the wrong man if you want to broaden your experiences,' he said, leaning forward and resting the palms of his hands on the foot-board at the bottom of the bed.

She didn't say anything. She couldn't meet his eyes and she looked away in miserable confusion. Was that what she had wanted? No! Not in the way he had said. She hadn't wanted a man to broaden her experiences; she had wanted him.

'You're a good-looking girl,' he said tonelessly, 'and I admit that I was tempted to take what was on offer, but you're barking up the wrong tree. I might as well have this out with you once and for all. You aren't my type. No more, I suspect, than I am yours.'

'And what type do you see me with?' she asked lightly, even though her mouth felt cold and stiff.

'You're a child, Francesca. I have no time for children.'

They stared at each other in silence, then he spun round

on his heels and walked out of the room. She heard the
click of the outer door, and then she fell back on the bed
and covered her face with a pillow.

Her mind was alive with torturous thoughts of how she
had thrown herself at him. What had she hoped to achieve?
she wondered. She remembered the feel of his hands on
her breasts with a shudder of hot embarrassment.

When she had found out the real reason she had got the
job with Oliver Kemp her pride had been crushed, but
deep down, she realised, she had known that however she
had managed to get the job she had succeeded in proving
herself.

Now his rejection of her had shattered that bit of her
pride which was irreparable. She had never been rejected
in her life before, and what she felt now was a mixture of
bewilderment, anger and hurt.

'I hate you,' she said aloud, and her words reverberated
in the silence and then in her head, over and over and
over, until sleep caught up with her and pulled a dark blind
over her emotions.

CHAPTER FOUR

FRANCESCA felt tired and nervous on Monday morning when she walked into the office building. She had fallen asleep on Saturday with a gut-wrenching feeling of misery, and precisely the same feeling had stayed with her since.

She had made a decision, though. She might have thrown herself at Oliver Kemp, and he could make of that what he wanted, but there was no way that she would make that mistake again. Every time her mind replayed the scene she wanted to close her eyes and find herself a dark little corner where she could hide until her embarrassment faded.

And she didn't care what interpretation he chose to put on what had taken place. Let him go ahead and think that she had succumbed to the influence of drink, or even that she had wanted to lose her virginity to him for no better reason than that she had selfishly wanted the one man she knew she couldn't have, because she was little more than a spoiled, wilful child.

Just so long as he never suspected, even for a minute, that she was devastatingly attracted to him and had been long before she had even begun to put words to how she felt in his presence. That, she knew, he would find uproariously amusing. He might even—and she winced at this—be tempted to confide all in Imogen.

She met him, as luck would have it, in the lift, and as it slowly emptied he turned to her and said, his face unreadable, 'Feeling better?'

'Yes, thank you,' she answered, with a stiff smile. 'Yesterday my head felt as though someone was having a fine time jumping around inside it, but I took two aspirins and it soon felt better.'

He nodded, and as the lift stopped on their floor she said awkwardly, 'I want to apologise for Saturday night.'

He pushed open the office door to allow her past him, and even that brief brush by his body made her feel hot.

'No point talking about it—' he began in a cool voice.

She cut in swiftly, 'I think there is. I mean, I agree that there's no point in dwelling on it, but I'd just like to clear the air.'

'Go ahead, in that case.'

He looked at her and she wondered whether he was seeing her with her blouse open, her breasts exposed, straining towards him for the feel of his wet mouth. It took a great deal of effort not to wilt at the thought of that.

'I know you probably think the worst of me, but that sort of episode will never happen again. I can only think that the champagne must have gone to my head quicker than I thought, and I guess I was feeling a little maudlin, worrying about the way Dad and I parted company, wondering if I hadn't acted too recklessly.' It sounded the most rational excuse, and she made sure that her voice was very composed when she spoke.

'We all make mistakes,' he said, shrugging and turning away from her to riffle through the post on her desk.

'I'd fully understand,' she continued quietly, 'if you wanted me to leave.'

'Why should I?' He raised his light eyes to hers. 'I think the best thing is if we both relegate that unfortunate incident to the past, don't you?' He walked towards his office. 'Did you manage,' he asked, and she realised that he was already moving on, 'to finish working on that Peterborough file?'

She nodded and he said, taking it from her outstretched hand, 'The damned man's been on the phone again, wanting to know when we can complete our stock for him. I don't think he understands that phoning on an hourly basis isn't going to get things moving any quicker than they are already.'

She laughed dutifully at that, but she knew that already there had been a shift in their relationship.

Before the weekend they had been relaxed with one another. He had begun to take her competence for granted, which she had rather enjoyed, and although their private lives had remained huge, unspoken areas between them at least they had settled into a good working routine.

Now everything had changed. She was blindingly aware of him, and she knew that even though he had resumed his polite, distant manner things had been said, things had been done which had altered the surface calm.

It was as though something dangerous had been thrown into a pond, and although calm stillness had resettled on the water you knew that there was something there— something in the depths which would change the way you looked at that pond for ever.

He emerged at eleven o'clock to tell her that he would be out for the remainder of the day, and at twelve, when she was sitting in front of the computer, staring at the words on the screen, the telephone rang.

It was Imogen.

'I wonder if we can meet for lunch?' she said, and Francesca paled. Had he said something to his fiancée? She had hardly thought of the other woman on Saturday. It had been as if something had possessed her, leaving no room at all for thoughts of anyone else, and certainly not for the fact that he was involved with someone. Her face reddened now in guilty shame.

'Sure,' she said, clearing her throat, and listening while Imogen made arrangements as to where they could meet.

At five to one Francesca was waiting in anxious expectation at the wine bar which was only a stone's throw from the office. If Oliver had told his fiancée about what had happened, then she knew that she would have no alternative but to stop working for him.

She had been a thoughtless fool, she knew, and when Imogen finally arrived, ten minutes late, she was already feeling on the brink of confessing all and waiting for the axe to fall, knowing that it would be a well-deserved punishment.

But Imogen, smartly dressed in a navy blue suit and carrying a tiny black bag just large enough to hold her wallet and chequebook, did not look like a woman with an axe behind her back.

Francesca looked at the neat, intelligent figure and felt a sharp pang of bitter, unbridled jealousy, made all the worse by her knowledge that the qualities which Oliver saw in his fiancée were ones that she herself could never hope to achieve in a million years.

Her life, she realised, had been so uncomplicated before she'd met Oliver Kemp. She had skimmed merrily along the surface, like a water-skier flying across the waves, happily unaware that there were dangers under the sea waiting to engulf her.

After ten minutes her mouth ached from the strain of having to smile and chat, and she only surfaced into the conversation with any real interest when Imogen told her that she needed some advice.

'What about?' Francesca asked, surprised, and Imogen looked at her thoughtfully.

'Clothes. I want to change my wardrobe a bit and I

thought, Who better to ask than you? You're such a gorgeous dresser.'

'Why do you want to change your wardrobe?' Francesca asked, bewildered. 'In your position—'

'Oh, I know that. Power-suits for work. The problem is I can't seem to break out of the power-dressing ethos.' She laughed, as if astonished at her desire to do so. 'I need some bright colours, some variety.'

'Why? Doesn't Oliver love you the way you are?' That took a great deal of effort, and she felt quite sick after she had said it.

'Oh, a change is as good as a rest, don't you think?' Imogen answered ambiguously, smiling and sipping some of her orange juice.

'He may not think so,' Francesca said, with a tight little smile.

'Then again,' Imogen murmured, 'he might be pleasantly surprised.' But she had lowered her eyes and, with a little shrug, Francesca chatted briefly about where she shopped, giving her names of people who would happily kit her out in whatever she wanted.

Her mind conjured up images of the other woman dressed seductively, images of Oliver finding that a pleasant surprise, images of them making love, and it was with relief when she parted company from Imogen outside the wine bar.

Over the next two days Francesca kept her head down, barely glanced in the direction of Oliver, and tried desperately to reason with herself.

What she felt for him, she told herself—this terrible pull—was foolish and pointless, and, having recognised that, she should be able to shrug it off to experience, but every time he came near her her body went into overdrive.

When he leaned by her to show her something she had to keep her hands tightly clenched by her sides so that he couldn't see how much they were trembling. When he spoke to her she had to make sure that her eyes didn't meet his because she didn't want him to read the message waiting there for him.

'What's the matter with you?' he asked on the Wednesday evening as she was about to leave. He had called her into his office to go through some files with her, and he sat back in his chair and looked at her carefully through narrowed eyes.

'I feel a bit ill,' she replied quickly. 'I think I must be coming down with something. There's a lot of flu going around.'

'You're working too hard,' he said without emphasis. 'Do you ever have a lunch break?'

'Occasionally. I met your fiancée for lunch the other day. We went to the wine bar down the road.'

'Yes. She told me.' He didn't appear to want to pursue that.

'She wanted some advice on clothes, so she came to me. Who better? Anyone can see that my forte is knowing how to put an outfit together.' She couldn't help it. Her voice was laced with bitterness, and she could have kicked herself for the little slip in her well-maintained façade.

He frowned. 'If that's what you think of yourself then it won't be too difficult for the rest of the world to fall in with your opinion, will it?'

'I suppose not.' She laughed shortly and stood up. 'If it's all right, I think I'll call it a day now. Unless you want these letters typed urgently?'

'They can wait.' His eyes were still on her and she nervously looked away and moved towards the door, half expecting him to call her back, half wanting it, in fact, but he didn't, and when she looked back at him, his head was downbent reading reports.

She felt so angrily miserable as she let herself out of his office that she was almost happy when she looked up and saw Brad Robinson by her desk.

She had seen him often enough over the months, and she had become quite accustomed to his brand of outrageous flirtation. She still smilingly disregarded all of it, but she no longer found it as oppressive and disagreeable as she had done the very first time she had met him.

It had helped, she supposed, that, contrary to her initial judgements, he wasn't married. He still thought himself a creation handmade for the benefit of the opposite sex, but at least there wasn't some poor woman in the background, building a life around him.

'You look terrible,' he said, his eyes sweeping over her appraisingly as they always did.

'I feel terrible,' she answered, clearing her desk and automatically pushing him off his perch by the computer terminal. 'My head aches, my back aches, my eyes ache.'

'Would an all-over body massage be the thing?' He flexed his fingers and shot her a wolfish, enquiring look which brought a reluctant grin to her lips.

'Well,' she said, not looking at him but still grinning, 'that certainly beats all the usual clichés I've heard from you in the past, Brad.'

'Doesn't it?' he asked, giving that some thought. 'Perhaps I could incorporate it in my repertoire.'

Before she could comment on that one he had moved behind her, and she felt his hands on her shoulders, his thumbs pressing against her muscles.

'Feel good?' he asked in her ear, and she had to admit that it did.

'Just so long as those hands of yours don't develop any

wanderlust,' she said, tilting her head back and half closing her eyes.

'I'll try to keep them in check,' he said, and she didn't have to see him to know that he was grinning. 'But they can sometimes be bad little boys when it comes to the opposite sex.'

'Oh, good grief,' she murmured, flexing her shoulders. Neither of them heard the connecting door open. When Oliver spoke his voice was like the crack of a whip, and they sprang apart.

'Are you here for something in particular?' he asked Brad, his mouth drawn into a tight line. He stood where he was and folded his arms, and every muscle in his body was taut with suppressed aggression. 'Because if you are then say so, and if you're not you can get back to your office and do what you're so lavishly paid to do.'

'We were just on our way out,' Francesca said, her colour high, and he rounded on her.

'No. You've got it wrong. Mr Robinson here is on his way out, and you, my girl—in my office. Now!'

He spun round on his heels, and she could feel her anger mounting as she followed him into the office and closed the door behind her. 'That was unnecessary!' she burst out, watching him angrily from a distance, alarmed by the black fury on his face.

'Don't you tell me what's necessary and what's unnecessary in my own damn company! Do you understand me?'

'He only came for a chat before we left,' she mumbled, and he strode towards her and took her by the shoulders. She felt the grip of his fingers and winced in pain.

'This is not a playground,' he muttered, his black brows drawn together in a harsh frown, 'and I don't pay my employees to cavort during office hours! Is that clear?'

'Brad always flirts,' she said, looking away guiltily because she knew that she should have discouraged him, and would have if she hadn't been feeling so low. 'You told me that yourself when I first joined.'

'That's no excuse to abuse my trust, is it?' he snarled. 'I don't damned well expect to find you fornicating on the office floor just because you imagine that you can get away with it.'

Her head shot up. 'I'd hardly call it that!' she snapped, her colour high. 'And you're hurting me!'

He released her abruptly but he didn't move. He remained where he was, his hands thrust into his pockets.

'And you expect to be taken seriously?' he asked, with a sneer in his voice. 'If you insist on behaving like an adolescent, then please tell me, and I'll gladly hand you back over to your father, and he can find himself another school of correction for you—debt or no debt.'

Their eyes met and, oddly, he was the first to look away. He stalked across to the window, then turned back to look at her.

'It won't happen again,' she muttered, realising that she was shaking all over.

'Good. Because if it does then you're out, and so is he.'

'You wouldn't!' She looked at him, appalled by the savagery of the threat. 'He's a good salesman. You said so yourself!'

'You heard me.' He turned away and stared out of the window, waiting for her to leave, and she did, after a moment's silence.

She had never seen him so furious. What had got into him? Had he exploded over that little incident because he was looking around for an excuse to get rid of her? she wondered. He might have told her that they could put her stupid, childish indiscretion behind them and continue working together, but had he really meant it?

She was still frowning, turning over the problem in her mind as she let herself into her block of flats, and in the gloomy entrance hall she didn't see the umbrella lying on the floor. One minute she was hurtling towards the staircase and the next minute she was on the floor. She stood up and then sat back down and began massaging her ankle.

It hurt like mad, and she eyed the offending umbrella with loathing. Eventually she tentatively tried to stand up again and found that she could just hobble up to her flat, with much clinging to the banister, and only very slowly.

The only bright spot was that her throbbing ankle did succeed in diverting her thoughts from Oliver slightly. She prepared herself a light supper, which turned out to be a one-hour job and left her feeling exhausted. At eight she telephoned her doctor, a family friend, who asked her a series of detailed questions on the phone, told her that she had just sprained the ankle, that the pain would subside but that she could take aspirin if she found it helped.

'Thanks very much, Dr Wilkins,' she said tartly. 'I already feel a lot better.' He laughed at that, told her that he would telephone her in the morning, and to have a good night's sleep.

It didn't feel a whole lot better in the morning, and with a sigh of resignation she phoned through to the office and connected immediately with Oliver on his direct line.

'I'm afraid I can't come in,' she said, twisting the telephone cord and wondering how his presence could fill the flat when he wasn't even in the room.

'Why not?' No words of concern, no sympathetic cluckings. Had she expected otherwise?

'I've twisted my ankle,' she admitted. 'I can hardly walk.'

'Careless,' he said briefly. 'Especially as I need to go over those pending files with you.'

'I really do apologise, Mr Kemp,' Francesca said in a syrupy voice, scowling down the line. 'Next time I'll try to plan my accidents for more opportune moments.'

'That would be useful,' he agreed, and she gritted her teeth together in frustration. 'However, all's not lost. I'll drop by this evening after work, say about six-thirty.'

'Drop by…?' she asked, horrified at the prospect of that, but he had already hung up, and she heard the dead dialling sound of the phone in her ear with annoyance.

She spent the remainder of the day in a state of tense anticipation. Rupert's appearance at lunchtime was almost irritating. She hadn't seen him for a while, and now she was beginning to find him trivial. He was amusing, but sometimes she didn't want to be amused, and he would never understand that. For him life was one long, enjoyable, never-ending game, but that got tiring after a while.

She found herself looking at her watch more than once, and when he stood up to leave he said, sharply for him, 'Sorry I disturbed you by dropping by, Frankie. When I phoned your office and I was told about your ankle I thought you might appreciate the company.'

'I'm sorry, Rupert,' she said, meaning it. 'But I've got a lot on my mind,' she added, meaning that too. Rather fervently.

'So have I,' he surprised her by saying, and he hesitated. He was thinking about whether to confide in her, she realised. It was the first time she had ever seen so much as a frown cross his amiable face, and she immediately felt ashamed that she hadn't been paying more attention to what he had been saying.

'Anything you want to talk about?' she asked, giving

him her undivided attention, and he shrugged, with the same hesitation in his manner.

'Not really,' he finally said. 'Usual woman troubles.'

'Usual? Rupert, you never have woman troubles.'

He laughed, and she realised what she hadn't noticed before, that he had been worried when he had first arrived.

'I know,' he agreed, nodding. 'Bit of a shame I'm having to find out about them now, at my ripe old age.'

But that was as far as she got, because he left without really saying much more to her, and very soon she forgot all about the conversation.

Of course, as she might have expected, Oliver didn't arrive until after seven, by which time tension had given way to anger. Having decided, she thought mutinously, that he could invade her flat just because he needed some work doing, he now thought that he could walk in at whatever time he pleased.

When she heard the sharp knock on the door she hobbled across and pulled it open, her mouth tightly set.

He eyed her very slowly, from foot to head and back to swollen foot, then picked her up bodily, ignoring her protests.

'There,' he said, depositing her on the chair, then removing his coat. It was raining outside—a steady drumming beat against the window panes. 'I've brought us food,' he said, and she noticed the brown bag. 'Chinese. I hope you like it.'

Something in his manner alarmed her, although she couldn't quite put her finger on it. It was like trying to reach for a shadow—something elusive but disturbing all the same. She wondered whether she wasn't imagining it because she had been living in a state of such heightened awareness recently.

'That was very thoughtful of you,' she said awkwardly, remembering how disastrous his last appearance at her flat had been.

'I didn't think that you'd get around to cooking in your state,' he pointed out, vanishing into the kitchen and emerging a couple of minutes later with two plates and some cutlery.

She watched, nervously silent, as he fished the little foil containers from the bag and undid lids.

'Doesn't look very appetising, does it?' he asked, handing her the plate, and she smiled.

'Smells good, though.' She looked at him from under her lashes, feeding on his devastating male sexuality like a foodaholic greedily looking at a plate of food. It was a terrible, forbidden pleasure but she couldn't resist it.

Now that she had acknowledged her attraction to him everything about him was an impact on her senses—the strong lines of his face, the power of his body, the way his black hair curled against the nape of his neck. She took it all in, adding it to her little store of images which had swelled and multiplied over the months without her even realising it.

She looked at him when she thought that her hunger would go unnoticed, but she felt like a thief in the night, stealing something that didn't belong to her.

'How are you settling in?' he asked neutrally. 'Any regrets?'

In between mouthfuls of food she chatted to him, answered his questions, told herself that the only threat to her peace of mind was herself. And he was, not all that surprisingly, easy to talk to. He had the rare gift of being able to listen attentively, and after a while she found herself talking to him more freely than she would have expected.

Why, though, was he being so nice, so charming? The little question kept floating into her head intermittently, but she chose to disregard it.

'You know all about me, though,' she said eventually, putting her plate on the table in front of her. 'You know my background,' she said, 'and heaven only knows what else, thanks to my father.'

'So I do,' he agreed smoothly.

'So why don't we get down to work? If you leave the dishes in the sink I can do them later.'

He nodded, and for the next hour they went through files. She deciphered her shorthand jottings, made notes of things that she needed to do as soon as she got into the office, and when they were finished he sat back and said, 'In case you're wondering why I came over here, the reason is that I shall be abroad for the next three weeks. Urgent business.'

'Ah.' That made sense. He had needed to discuss work because he wouldn't be around, and she didn't know whether the news of his absence from the office filled her with relief or disappointment.

'I'll be in touch, of course, every day, but you'll have to carry on without me. Can you manage?'

'What do you think?'

He looked at her thoughtfully. 'I have no doubts that you can,' he murmured, giving her a crooked smile that sent little shivers through her. 'Does it feel good to you, knowing that I was wrong about you? I'm not usually wrong in my judgements of people, but I have to admit your work has been superb.'

'Is that the sound of a man eating humble pie?' she asked, and he laughed.

'I think I'll pass on that question. Humble pie tends to give me indigestion.'

He stood up and she thought that he was going to leave, but he wasn't. He went into the kitchen, fetched them both some coffee and handed a cup to her.

'Thank you,' she said, taking the cup, surprised. 'I wouldn't have thought that you had a domesticated streak in you. First the food, now this.'

'Making a cup of coffee isn't quite beyond me,' he replied drily, sitting back down and raking his fingers through his hair. 'I can even do a halfway decent meal when pressed.'

'I suppose you had to when you were at university,' Francesca commented, not looking at him.

'And before. My mother was quite ill before she died. I had to do all the household chores, in between studying like crazy. I became a dab hand at wielding a vacuum cleaner and revising statistics at the same time.'

She laughed and wondered fleetingly how a man could be so hard, so aggressive and yet so witty when he chose to be.

'It must have been hard,' she said, 'being on your own.'

'I learnt pretty quickly how to stand on my own two feet.' He shrugged. 'It's no bad lesson to learn.'

Here we go, she thought. Here come the veiled criticisms.

'I don't suppose there are too many people who would disagree with that,' she said lightly. 'Not when they see what a success can be made from it.'

'Success is a dubious beast,' he murmured, and this time when he looked at her his eyes held hers for a fraction longer than was necessary. 'Success, sadly, breeds suspicion. The more money you make, the narrower becomes the circle of people whom you can trust. You must have found that.'

'Not really,' she answered, thinking about it.

'Because you lived in an exalted world far removed from reality.' It was more a statement of fact rather than a question.

'It wasn't one I chose,' she pointed out, not willing to spoil the pleasant atmosphere between them. She stood up to carry the cups into the kitchen and to stretch her muscles, which felt as though they were slowly seizing up on her, and as she bent down to retrieve his cup from the ground he reached out and caught her wrist in his hand.

'You shouldn't be moving about,' he said softly.

Her heart began to thud. She felt that familiar excitement course through her and she tried to look at him calmly, without letting her body dictate her responses.

'M-my ankle feels m-much better already,' she stammered, and he pulled her gently down onto the sofa next to him.

'Let me have a look at it,' he said, and she looked at him in panic.

'There's nothing to look at,' she protested. 'It's just a bit bruised.'

'How did you do it? I never asked.'

He gently lifted her leg onto his lap and shoved up her long skirt so that her ankle was exposed. It was ridiculous but she felt as exposed and vulnerable as a Victorian lady being stripped. She also felt confused. Why was he doing this, behaving like this? She remembered his cold words of contempt when she had thrown herself at him, and she pulled her leg, but he held it firmly in place.

'Well?' he asked, looking up at her, and she had to think before she remembered what his question had been in the first place.

'Oh, I tripped over an umbrella.'

'Novel.' He bent his head to inspect the ankle, and very carefully he stroked it with his hand.

'What are you doing?' Was that her voice? It sounded like a terrified squeak.

He ignored that. 'What did the doctor say?'

'It should be better tomorrow, or else definitely by the day after.'

'I'm glad to hear it.' He gave her a slow, lazy smile and she finally realised what her subconscious had been telling her all along. Oliver Kemp was flirting with her.

It was so unexpected that it was almost shocking. She glanced down at her entwined fingers and felt rather than saw his eyes roaming over her.

She felt oddly at sea with this frank appraisal from a man who had hardly so much as glanced in her direction in the past, and, when he had, had done so with the indifference of a man who saw no sexuality in the woman at whom he was looking.

There was no rush of longing on her part, though. She had flung herself at him with the naïve optimism of inexperience, and now that same inexperience, when faced with this sophisticated game of seduction, was pulling her back. She felt bewildered and defensive.

She gave another tug of her foot and he asked in a low, casual voice, 'Do you want me to leave?'

There was silence—a silence so profound that every little sound in the room was amplified a million times over. The gentle spitting of the rain against the window-pane became a drum roll; the ticking of the clock on the mantelpiece sounded like a time bomb about to go off.

'What time is it?' she heard herself ask for want of anything better to say, and there was dry irony in his eyes when they rested on her.

'Time to leave or time to stay. Tell me which.'

'I don't understand what's going on,' she said evenly. 'When you were last here—'

'You had had too much to drink,' he said, but she had the uneasy, fleeting feeling that he wasn't telling the whole truth.

She lifted her leg from his lap and rested it gently on the ground, and then stared at it in apparent fascination.

She was so aware of the man sitting next to her that she could hardly breathe. Her blonde hair hung across her face like a curtain, hiding her expression, for which she was glad because the last thing she needed was to have him read the thoughts flitting across her face.

'Why,' he asked, sweeping her hair back with his hand, 'don't you look at me?'

He didn't move his hand. He curled his fingers against the nape of her neck and she reluctantly faced him.

'Is it a stupid question to ask whether you've been drinking?' She attempted a light laugh which emerged as something of a choked noise.

'Very stupid.'

Now that she had her eyes firmly fixed on his face she found that she couldn't drag her gaze away. 'I'm afraid I'm missing something here,' she whispered. 'None of this makes any sense.'

'Some things don't,' he murmured, and she had that feeling again, as though there was a thread of meaning behind his words which she couldn't quite comprehend.

'Are you scared?' he asked, and she didn't say anything. 'Do you,' he continued, 'want me to make love to you, Francesca Wade?'

CHAPTER FIVE

FRANCESCA wasn't so green that she hadn't understood the signals coming from Oliver, but now that the words were out of his mouth, now that he was staring at her with that glittering intensity in his eyes, she found that she couldn't think at all.

'W-what?' she stammered.

He didn't repeat what he had said. He just continued looking at her and the blood rushed to her head with such force that she thought she was going to faint.

'What about Imogen?' she asked faintly, and that drew a short, humourless smile to his lips.

'Imogen and I have decided that we need to think things over.'

'You mean you've decided to split with her? Why?'

'Why do people ever split up?' he asked, with a hint of impatience in his voice now, as though they were drifting from the matter at hand into waters that were only marginally relevant and certainly did not warrant much explanation.

'You and she were so well suited,' Francesca said, frowning and trying to read all the meanings behind this revelation—meanings hidden underneath his silence.

'I didn't realise you knew me so well,' he drawled with amused sarcasm.

Know you well? she thought suddenly, looking across at him. I don't know you at all.

'You still haven't answered my question,' he said softly, but before she could say anything he raised his hand. 'No, don't answer. Not yet.' Then he leaned across to her and she closed her eyes before his mouth touched hers. She felt the warmth of his lips as they took hers in a kiss that lingered persuasively, then, as her mouth parted, hungrily moved in a kiss that made her feel as if she was drowning.

She groaned and tried to pull back.

'What's the matter?' he asked, releasing her, but only slightly so that, although she could speak, the sheer power of his sexuality still kept her in its grip.

'You don't find me attractive,' she said unsteadily. Her mouth obligingly said one thing, but her body said another, because she still grasped his shirt, and she knew that however many questions were unanswered, however many doubts she had that what she was doing was right the pull she felt for him was just too strong.

'Maybe I find you too attractive,' he murmured, his eyes veiled. He trailed his finger along her spine and she felt her body begin to melt.

This time when he bent to kiss her her answer to his question was there in her response. He held the sides of her head with his hands, pushing her back.

'I want to hear you tell me that this is what you want,' he whispered roughly into her ear, and she felt the tingling of his warm breath with a shudder of deep excitement.

'It's what I want,' she said, in barely a whisper. It's what I have wanted for so long now, she could have added. It's what I've wanted all my life.

He swept her up and carried her towards the bedroom, kicking open the door with his foot, and this time when he lay her down on the bed there was naked desire in his eyes.

He hadn't bothered to switch on the bedroom light, but he had left the door to the small sitting room open so that

the light filtered into the room from there, giving the bedroom a shadowy, mosaic feel.

'You're so damned young,' he muttered, and she anxiously wondered whether this marked the beginning of a
retreat.

'I'm not,' she denied. 'I'm not young and I know what
I'm doing.'

'Oh, I'm not talking about your age,' he said. He was
sitting next to her, and he placed his hands on either side
of her supine body, so that she was in a cage. She reached
out and put her hands on his arms.

'What, then?' she asked, trying to be calm, already trying to step over the pain of his leaving, if that was what
he was going to do.

'You're very ingenuous,' he said. 'Not at all what I
imagined when your father first described you. Oh, you
have the social *savoir-faire* that comes to a woman born
into wealth, but underneath you're like a child.'

'And you're so experienced,' she said huskily. 'You
sound like an old man, but you're not, are you?'

'Sometimes I feel as though I am.'

'Old and with a string of lovers behind you?' She made
herself laugh, but she wasn't laughing inside. Inside, her
heart was twisting with jealousy at all those imaginary
lovers that had passed through his life.

'Not a string,' he murmured, stroking her face with his
finger, tracing the contours of her cheek-bones, her eyebrows, the outline of her lips. His touch was light and
feathery, and she knew that her breathing had quickened
and that the strings deep inside her were becoming more
urgent.

'I've never made a habit of moving from one warm
body to another.'

'No?' she asked, lowering her eyes.

'No.' He laughed under his breath.

'But I'm sure you must have had countless offers,' she said.

'Oh, countless. Any more questions?' He laughed softly again, then bent to kiss her neck and she wrapped her arms around him, pulling him towards her.

If there were any more questions, she couldn't think of them. Come to that, she couldn't think of anything at all. Thinking was proving to be beyond her.

He pushed up her shirt, pulling it over her head, then he stood up and she watched, feverish, as he slowly took off his clothes, never taking his eyes off her face, enjoying her frank appreciation of his body.

Whatever he had said about not having had a string of lovers, there was no doubt that she was watching a man well-versed in the art of making love.

His nudity made her gasp with sudden, wild yearning. Physically he was perfect, as lean and muscular as an athlete, even though she knew that he didn't do any exercise—he didn't have the time.

He slipped onto the bed next to her, but before she could begin removing her long skirt, he asked, 'Are you protected?'

'Protected? Protected against what?' She couldn't imagine what he was talking about. What should she be protected against? The only protection she could think of was when she had started travelling abroad at the age of six and had had vaccinations.

'What do you think?' he murmured. 'Pregnancy, of course.'

'Of course.' Her brain engaged and she said swiftly, 'Yes, I am.'

'Good.' Even as he said that he unzipped her skirt and she wriggled free of it, but when she went to slip off her lacy underwear he put his hand over hers and said roughly, 'Not yet.'

Not yet? It was agonising having any clothes on, even underwear. She wanted him so badly.

He lowered his head against her breasts, sucking them, playing with them, rolling her nipple between his fingers, then he moved his hand lower, against the flat planes of her stomach, and she parted her legs with a little groan of pleasure.

When he cupped her underneath the briefs with his hand she felt her body shudder, and she moved spontaneously against him, moaning as his fingers found the moist depths of her femininity.

But he wouldn't let her reach that pinnacle of satisfaction. He slowed the rhythm of his strokes and slipped off her underwear, then guided her hand to his throbbing masculinity.

She turned on her side to face him, but he gently pushed her flat, bending over her so that his exploring mouth could follow the seductive path of his fingers. His tongue teased and she closed her eyes, feeling her body lift to regions which she had never dreamt possible.

When he finally entered her any momentary pain was swamped by her sheer need for him, and the mounting rhythm of his movements sent her spinning at last beyond imagination, beyond thought.

In fact, thought processes only began once again when they were lying next to one another. Did the earth move for you too? she wanted to ask him. Did lightning strike? All those clichés which she had heard about and read about now seemed to possess an accuracy which she would never have thought possible. Was physical attraction *this* strong? she asked herself, vaguely perturbed.

She didn't ask him, though. In fact, she said with utter banality, 'What time do you leave tomorrow?'

'Early,' he replied, stroking her hair. 'Why?'

'No reason.' She swept her hand along his side and wondered whether he would miss her. She thought not. He might not believe in casual sex, but that didn't mean that he considered her his destiny, did it? That didn't mean that he loved her.

She felt a momentary jolt of shock. What had love to do with anything? she wondered, trembling. Nothing? Or everything?

'What happens when you get back, Oliver?' she asked hurriedly, feeling a bit like someone whose boat had capsized and who was trying desperately to clamber back on, and he frowned.

'What happens about what?'

'About us?'

His eyes narrowed but he continued stroking her. 'I run my business; you work for me; we make love.'

'You make it sound so simple.'

'Isn't it?'

'Nothing in life is simple,' she said, and he gave her a slow, amused smile.

'You sound like an adult now,' he murmured.

She said in a sharper voice than she had intended, 'I am an adult.'

'Then as an adult you should know how it stands between us without my having to spell it out. I'm not looking for commitment.' There was a hard edge in his voice when he said that.

'Just fun.'

'It's a philosophy you should be well acquainted with.'

She couldn't begin to put into words how ill acquainted she was with any philosophy of the sort. She might have spent months avoiding responsibility and having fun, but none of it had involved sex.

'I guess so,' she said lightly, and was it her imagination or did his body relax? 'Was it just fun with Imogen?'

'Imogen was—is—a very special person,' he said thoughtfully. 'On paper we were the ideal couple, which just goes to prove that nothing in life is a certainty. We were on the same wavelength, our experiences had been pretty much the same, we were made from similar moulds, you might say—but in the end it wasn't enough.'

'Are you bitter about it?' she asked, but tentatively, because she felt rather than knew that at any point when he decided that her questions were none of her business he would switch off.

'Why should I be bitter?' And again there was that hard edge in his voice. 'It happened. And, like all experiences, I've learnt a lesson from this one.'

'Which is?' She had no idea why she bothered to ask the question, because she knew what he was going to say even before he said it.

'That marriage is something for other people.' He laughed, but there was no humour behind the laughter. 'Now, aren't there more interesting things we could be doing, apart from talking?'

He cradled her breast in his hand and her body made the decision before her mind even had time to think about it. She sighed, nodding languidly, and this time when he laughed there was warm amusement there.

'You're a passionate little creature, aren't you?' He aroused her nipple into hardness, and she needed no asking to take his manhood in her hands, to tease him as he was teasing her. When hunger began to replace the lazy amusement in his eyes she felt a surge of power that she could do this to him.

Their love-making this time round was slow and easy, and less one-sided. They built each other up with caresses that seemed to have no beginning and no end.

Where did this wanton passion spring from? she wondered, but she knew the answer to that one. The answer had been lurking just out of reach, but always there—the uninvited guest waiting to come in. Now the guest had entered, and Francesca knew with shuddering certainty why she had made love to him.

Underneath the physical pull was something stronger, more powerful, less manageable—a burning love, a dark fire that would not go back whence it came. She could have fought against simple desire, but what weapons did she have against what she was feeling now? And did she, she wondered tremulously, want any?

She lay on him, letting her full breasts hang temptingly to his mouth, smiling when he caught one provocative nipple and began suckling on it while his hands gripped her waist, almost encircling it completely. When she eased her body onto him she found a rhythm of her own and arched back as the rhythm took her again and again to sexual fulfilment.

It was only later, when he said that it was time for him to go, that she looked at the clock by the bed and saw that it was after midnight.

'I've got to pack,' he said, standing up. He looked at her. 'I'm going to have a quick shower. I'd invite you along, but if I did I'm not sure I'd make it out in time to do any packing at all before I leave.'

She smiled drowsily and lay back, hearing the distant sound of the shower going and letting her thoughts take their course, stray wherever they wanted to.

He didn't want commitment. That should have sent her

spinning into despair and regret, but it didn't. How could she regret what had happened between them? All he wanted was uninvolved fun, and, much as she craved something way beyond that, part of her had already decided—when, she couldn't say—that she would take what he was offering, because the alternative was to walk away from him and she didn't know if she could do that.

In the end she would be hurt. That was as inevitable as day following night, but at least her pain would come in the wake of something which she had spent her life waiting for.

Maybe, she thought, if she hadn't slept with him she could have walked away, but now she had given too much.

She looked at him as he emerged out of the shower, drying his hair roughly with a towel, and just wished that he wasn't about to disappear from the face of the earth— or as good as anyway—for three weeks. Three weeks was such a long time, but it couldn't be helped.

He was opening a subsidiary and it would need time to get sorted out, he had told her. The preliminaries would have to be done by him, because when he worked he worked to a level of perfection which he couldn't trust anyone else to achieve.

That, she knew, was why he had done so well in life. He never took short cuts and he never accepted anything less than the best. Was that what had finally made things fail between him and Imogen? She watched as he slipped on his clothes and wondered whether he had expected that relationship to attain a level which was out of reach.

When he came to stand by the bed he bent down and kissed her lightly on her forehead—a goodbye-and-sweet-dreams kind of kiss that made her smile.

'I'll be in touch every day,' he said, and she nodded.

'What shall I do if I run into a problem I can't handle?'

'Send me a fax. If it's really urgent I guess I can return, but I'd rather get this thing over and done with, without breaking off in between.'

She desperately wanted to ask him if he would miss her, but already she knew what questions were permissible and which ones weren't, and that one was definitely in the no-go zone.

He left quietly, and she lay in bed for a long time, awake and empty, thinking that she would never be able to sleep, but eventually she did.

When she awoke the following morning it was nearly ten o'clock and, after some internal debate, she decided to take another day off so that her ankle could heal up completely before she went in.

It seemed strange when she did make it into work the following week to be in that office on her own. She had become accustomed to listening out for him, to knowing that he was close by.

After three days she realised that the only thing that kept her going was his daily phone calls. Then his voice seemed to bring him into the same room with her.

'Missing me?' he had asked lightly down the line the day before.

She had laughed as lightly as he had spoken and said, 'Of course! There have been a lot of queries I would much rather you had dealt with.'

She wasn't going to show him how deep her feelings for him ran, even in the occasional passing remark, and a small part of her optimistically hoped that in time fun would develop into something else. She didn't like dwelling on the thought that it might not, that he might tire of her the way a child tired of a toy that had outlived its welcome.

You didn't have to be a genius to know that any relationship that existed solely on sex would eventually run out of steam, and as far as he was concerned sex was the only thing that drew him to her. She certainly was not his ideal woman the way Imogen had been, and if that had failed what chance did they stand?

But she avoided thinking along those lines. Instead she told herself that nothing in life was beyond reach, not if you tried hard enough.

She was clearing her desk to go home, two weeks after he had left—each day mentally ticked off on her calendar—when Helen walked into the office.

Francesca had not seen the other girl for quite some time—at least five weeks or so—even though she occasionally met her in the cloakroom, which served two floors. At times like that she made obligatory polite conversation, because bad atmospheres were not a good idea in an office environment, but that was all—a 'Hello, how are you? Oliver will have that stuff you phoned about for you later today,' and then a quick escape.

Now she looked at the other girl warily, keeping her hands busy with her tidying, letting it be clear that she was about to leave so that Helen would not invite herself into conversation.

It didn't work. Helen looked at her with her hard eyes and said brightly, 'How are you coping without your big, bad boss?'

'Fine.' A bit more meaningful tidying.

'Rumours have been floating around the building about him…' Helen picked up a pen and scrutinised it.

'Really?' Francesca answered, her body tensing even though she kept her voice casually uninterested.

'Really.' The pen was deposited and Helen gave her a long stare.

Her face, as usual, was heavily made up, which made her eyes look even more alarming, and she was dressed inappropriately in a very short black skirt and a long-sleeved top which left precious little to the imagination. The etiquette of office dressing had obviously passed her by, because Francesca had never seen her in anything that did not look as though it should be worn in a nightclub instead of at a desk. No doubt the men appreciated that, and no doubt Helen didn't object in the slightest.

'Rumour has it that he and his girlfriend are no more.'

'Is that a fact?' The casualness in her voice was slipping a little. She didn't want to discuss any of this, not at all.

'Sure is. Rumour also has it that the reason they hit the rocks was because she found someone else.'

'Oh? People shouldn't believe everything that's said.'

'Seen, actually. At a nightclub. With some fair-haired guy.'

'Fair-haired guy?' Francesca asked sickly. She was beginning to sound parrot-like, she knew, repeating everything as though she were hard of hearing. 'Who told you that?'

'Friend of a friend. I kind of wished that I had been there. I can't imagine Miss Imogen High and Mighty living it up, can you?'

Yes, Francesca thought, I can.

'This friend of a friend knew someone who knew the guy she was with. Vaguely. Rupert something or other. Old flame of yours, I believe.'

The heavily made-up eyes were slits, and Francesca nodded without saying anything. It hadn't even crossed her mind that Rupert had not been in touch with her for weeks. It hadn't crossed her mind because there had been so much else there filling it up.

Now she remembered the last time she had seen him, when he had mentioned in passing that he was having woman problems. No wonder he had felt reluctant about going into details. How could he have when the problem was a bit too near home for his liking?

'I wonder how Oliver took it?' Helen asked herself.

Without thinking Francesca said, 'He didn't seem too crushed.' The minute the words were out she felt herself go bright red.

'He's been confiding in you?'

'I have to go now, Helen. Was there anything else you wanted?'

'He's not the sort to confide, not from what I've seen of him. So how come you know about his personal life?' She followed Francesca to the coat rack like a bloodhound on the scent, and Francesca kept her head averted, putting on her coat. Eventually, though, she had to turn round, and when she did Helen asked sharply, 'Have you slept with him?'

Instead of protesting, which was what she should have done, she hesitated, and that brief hesitation was enough. Helen looked at her viciously and nodded.

'Decided to get in there while the going was good, did you? You little bitch!'

'Don't be silly,' Francesca said weakly, knowing that it was too late, that her moment's silence had cost her dear.

'Took advantage because he was on his own? Or did he decide that you would do, you would tide him through a bad night?'

'I'm going.' Francesca began walking towards the door, hoping that the other girl would not pursue her down to the ground floor, because in a lift there would be no escape.

'I should have known that that butter-wouldn't-melt-in-my-mouth face of yours was a put-on,' she spat out, and Francesca saw with distaste that the venom there was a case of the cat thinking that its cream had been heartily lapped up in its absence.

'I'll make sure that everyone within a twenty-mile radius knows what's going on,' she said, with a cold smile, and Francesca stopped in her tracks.

She hadn't wanted this argument, but now that she was embroiled in it, she felt angry blood rush to her head. 'If you do,' she said quietly, 'I'll make sure that Oliver knows exactly who started the gossip, and you'll soon find yourself out of a job.'

She had never threatened anyone in her life before, and she was shaking like a leaf. They stared at each other wordlessly for a few seconds, and she could tell that Helen was digesting that, wondering whether spreading her story was worth her job—her no doubt highly paid job.

'I'll make sure that you pay,' she contented herself with saying. 'Somehow.'

The lift came and Francesca hopped in, pressing the ground-floor button and breathing a sigh of relief when she realised that the other girl was not going to step in with her.

She still felt hot at the thought of that conversation. She should have denied it all; she should have left the office before they'd even got to that stage; she should have laughed off the suggestion. She should have, should have, should have. But she hadn't.

Helen Scott was basically an unpleasant person; Francesca had always known that from the very first moment that she had set eyes on her. She shuddered at the thought that that sly, curling mouth might start rumours snowballing through the building.

When she got into her flat the telephone was ringing, and Francesca picked up the receiver, balancing it under her chin while she tried to wriggle out of her coat. It was Oliver.

'I'll be delayed by a bit more than a week,' he said, with his usual lack of preliminaries. His voice sounded distant and hollow, and there was a slight crackle down the line. 'Things are moving slightly slower here than I had imagined.' There was a sigh, and she could imagine him rubbing his eyes with his thumbs.

'No problem,' she said brightly, feeling utterly dejected at this piece of news. 'I'm doing fine at work. I've been in touch with Ben Johnson about that contract and I shall fax him the information he wants tomorrow first thing.' She thought of Helen and wondered what he would say if she told him that on another front things weren't humming along nicely at all.

'Good,' he said in a clipped voice. 'And how are you?'

'Nice of you to ask,' she replied, suddenly happy. 'I'm fine.'

'So you're fine and work is fine.' There was a touch of harshness in his voice and she speculated on what that meant. Was he missing her? Had he hoped that she wouldn't be fine, that she would be missing him? She couldn't hear him very well, though, and long-distance lines distorted voices, but if her imagination was playing tricks on her then her imagination was also doing a good job of improving her mood.

Not that she was about to tell him how she was really feeling. She knew that he wanted to be casual about their relationship, and she intended to be as casual about it as he was. If he got the slightest idea that she was playing a game of deadly seriousness, then he would turn his back on her faster than the speed of light.

'Shall I postpone all those meetings that were lined up for you on your return?' she asked, still in her cheerful voice.

'Of course,' he said briefly. 'I can hardly be in two places at once, can I?'

They chatted about work for a while longer, and when he rang off she was feeling distinctly happier than she had been an hour previously.

On the spur of the moment she decided to give Rupert a call, and after a few sheepish apologies from him about not being in touch recently she talked him into coming over.

'You can share dinner with me,' she said temptingly. 'Corned beef sandwiches.'

'Irresistible.' He laughed. 'I'm on my way.'

Actually—and she told herself that that had not been the point of the phone call—she wanted to ask him about Imogen.

And he had expected that. She could tell from the expression on his face the minute he walked through the door. It was a mixture of guilt and wariness, and as soon as he had been settled with a glass of wine—the only alcohol in the place—he said, obviously taking the bull by the horns, 'I meant to tell you, I'm going out with someone you know. Imogen Sattler.' There was hearty bluster in his voice, but his face was red.

'Really?' Francesca said, raising her eyebrows expressively, and he battled on, not drinking, his hands cradling the glass.

'I would have told you sooner, but you know how it is…' His voice fizzled out and she smiled.

'Naughty, naughty Rupert. Imogen Sattler was spoken for.'

'The engagement is off.'

Francesca looked at him, frowning, thinking. Earlier, speaking to Oliver on the phone, she had pushed aside any uncomfortable thoughts about what had happened between him and Imogen. Now she found herself wondering. She found herself thinking of Helen. 'Did he decide that you would do; you would tide him through a bad night?'

'Neither of us meant anything to happen, Frankie.' The bluster had given way to earnestness, and he leaned forward. 'I thought she was fun, not like the other girls I've met in the past.' He frowned, and tried to be more descriptive than that. 'When I first saw her I didn't think she was that attractive. I mean, I thought she was a very nice-looking girl, but...'

'But not along the lines of Linda Baker,' Francesca filled in wryly, and he gave her a dry look in return. Linda Baker had been one of his past girlfriends—an impeccably beautiful girl with an impeccable background and not much happening between her two ears. If the rooms in Imogen's head were all filled and busy, there had been quite a few in Linda's which hadn't been opened up for a while—if ever.

'But not along the lines of Linda Baker,' he agreed. 'I also thought that she was humouring me when she told me how much she enjoyed the nightclub—you know, the time I dragged her and that boss of yours along.'

Francesca nodded. 'And things just went on from there, Rupert?'

'She phoned me up. We chatted. I telephoned her. I happened to be passing right outside her office one day and we went out for a drink. It was all above board, honestly.'

'You don't have to convince me of anything, Rupert,' she said mildly. 'I'm not here to sit in judgement on you.'

'I feel badly about Oliver Kemp, though,' he muttered, and she knew that he would. It was not in his nature to steal other men's girlfriends, but theft, in that instance, would have been a two-way affair, wouldn't it?

'We just had so much to talk about,' he clarified helplessly. 'She was different. She had more intelligence in one little finger than all the other girls I'd ever been out with combined. I couldn't understand what she saw in a lump like me. I don't suppose I ever will.'

There was such genuine wonder in his voice that Francesca had to smile. It would not occur to him that what he had was unique—his good nature, his thoughtfulness, his happy, carefree disposition. It was a different kind of appeal from the overt aggressive masculinity that Oliver had, but she thought, it carried its own weight.

'I began to think about her all the time,' he carried on. 'I stopped going out. I felt that I needed to be by the phone in case she called. We weren't sleeping together,' he felt compelled to add, 'but we both knew that it would happen, and we both knew that she had to break off the engagement.

'She told me that she and Oliver had been friends for years, but that the engagement had been a mistake. Friendship had never matured into love. At least not for her. She had thought at the time that it would be enough, but then she met me…' He couldn't prevent a small, satisfied smile from forming.

'So there you have it. As it turned out, Oliver called the whole thing off anyway. Told her that she deserved to pursue what she wanted.' He sipped some of the wine and sat back with his fingers entwined on his lap. 'Any questions?'

He sounded like a professor addressing his students, and Francesca shook her head. No questions. None that concerned him, anyway.

She listened while Rupert spent the next couple of hours chatting, mostly about Imogen, but things were going around in her head, and as soon as he left she began thoughtfully tidying the room.

Oliver had broken the engagement, true enough, but from where she was standing, with the jigsaw pieces neatly slotted together, it seemed very much like an act of generosity propelled by circumstance. His lover had wanted to be free and he had given her her freedom before she could demand it.

'Did he decide that you would do?'

A man on the rebound could be very undiscriminating, couldn't he? Was that why Oliver had come to see her? The woman he loved had told him that she was not in love with him, was going out with someone else, in fact, and he knew where he could find a willing woman with whom he could drown his sorrows? He hadn't looked like a man with a broken heart when he had come round, but then, thinking about it, Oliver Kemp was not the sort of man to walk around with a long face, was he?

No wonder he had told her that he wasn't interested in commitment. He was committed somewhere else—that was the reason.

On the rebound, she thought to herself. I had flung myself at him once, and he had walked away because his heart was somewhere else. He knew where to come; he knew that I would not turn him away. He didn't know why, but that didn't matter.

What mattered was that she would now have to face the truth. Oliver Kemp wanted a body—temporarily—and she was no longer happy to be a yielding one just because she had optimistically believed that time would make love grow. The soil there was barren. Nothing would grow.

Oliver Kemp loved Imogen, with her intellect, her gritty rise from rags to riches. He probably loved her more now that she was out of reach and for ever would be.

He could never love me, Francesca thought, with my cosseted upbringing and an intellect that has never had to strive to attain anything.

Now she was glad that he wasn't going to be back on schedule—glad that she had been given time to compose herself and do what she knew she had to do.

CHAPTER SIX

'YOU look sick,' Helen said with a sort of nasty satisfaction. They were in the cloakroom and Francesca was staring at her reflection in the mirror and wondering whether a dab of lipstick might improve her green complexion.

'I feel fine,' she muttered, lying. She felt awful. In fact, she had been feeling awful for the past fortnight, thinking about Oliver and that resignation letter which he would find on his desk when he returned the following morning.

'Could have fooled me.' Helen stood behind her so that their eyes met in the mirror. 'Claire Burns said that you looked like death warmed up when she came to see you the other morning.'

Claire Burns, thought Francesca, wouldn't have been snide with it.

'You should be feeling on top of the world, what with your lover coming back tomorrow.'

Francesca couldn't help a furtive look around to make sure that the cloakroom was empty, even though she knew that it was, and Helen laughed slyly.

'The coast is clear,' she said, sneering. 'Just the two of us and our little secret.' Which only made Francesca feel sick all over again, and she rushed into the toilet, only just managing to slam the door behind her.

When she emerged Helen had gone, and she slowly made her way back to her office. Her resignation letter was sitting in the top drawer of her desk like an unexploded bomb, and it had been there ever since Rupert had visited her at the flat, ever since her mind had been made up for her, and she had been drained of all reason for living. Or so it seemed.

It was just as well that she had never let him suspect her feelings for him, and just as well that she had kept their telephone conversation for the past weeks on a cheerful, impersonal note, never once betraying how much she yearned for those few minutes every day when she would hear his distant voice down the line.

In fact, since she had made up her mind to resign she had made sure that her voice was downright cool. That way she could prepare herself for the inevitable.

Nevertheless, Francesca was highly nervous the following morning when she arrived at work. She had left her unexploded bomb on his desk, so that he could read it and digest it without her standing in front of him like a tense schoolgirl.

She still had to face her father about her decision, and the quicker she left, the quicker her life could carry on.

I'll get over him in no time at all, she told herself, hanging her coat on the peg and walking across to her desk. She hadn't quite made it there when the connecting door opened, and she half turned, feeling a sick feeling in the pit of her stomach when she saw Oliver standing there, looming in the doorway, his eyes cold.

The impact of seeing him again after more than four weeks only made her realise how devastatingly handsome he was. She had forgotten how tall and overpowering his physical presence was, though she hadn't forgotten the sort of effect he had on her. He was having that effect now. She looked at him and felt that rush of awareness, that excited sensitivity to every last little detail of his appearance.

She also had a sudden, very sharp and very unwelcome

memory of the last time they'd seen each other, naked and in bed after the most wonderful night she had ever had in her entire life—a night when foolish optimism had been born and cold reality had been conveniently shoved into the background.

Foolish optimism, she thought, was hardly a worthwhile emotion, but she would certainly have preferred it to the lurch of dread that washed over her now, making her feel dizzy.

'Come into my office.' His face was unsmiling when he said that, and before she could say anything he had turned his back and vanished.

Francesca took three deep breaths to steady herself and followed him, quietly closing the door behind her. Then she sat down on the chair facing him and folded her arms on her lap.

'Did everything go all right on your trip?' she asked when the silence had stretched so taut that she could feel nervous perspiration breaking out all over her.

He was sitting staring at her, his eyes hard, his elbows resting on his desk. 'What does this mean?' He ignored her pleasantry, which she had known he would, and picked up the letter between two fingers as though it were contagious.

'Oh,' Francesca replied, her mind going blank, 'so you've read it.'

'No,' he answered, his deep voice thick with sarcasm. 'I've called you in here so that I could play a guessing game with you. Of course I've damn well read it.' He stood up so abruptly that she jumped, and then he stalked across to the window; he perched on the ledge and looked at her, his arms folded.

She had rehearsed this little scene quite a number of times in her head, but now, reluctantly staring up at his menacing figure, she realised that no amount of dress rehearsals had prepared her for this.

'Might I ask why you've decided to resign?' he asked coldly, and she licked her lips.

'Ah.' She frowned and struggled to remember her little speech. 'I've decided that this isn't the sort of job that I'm looking for,' she said, which bore no resemblance at all to her rehearsed speech.

'Too uninteresting?' His mouth curled.

'No. It's very stimulating,' she responded quickly, truthfully.

'Not well paid enough?'

'No, of course not! I have no idea where I could get a job with a bigger salary.'

'So why are you leaving a stimulating job with an incomparable pay cheque?'

Good question, she thought miserably, trying to come up with an equally good answer. 'It's just not what I'm looking for...' was all she could find to say, and his brows snapped together in an angry frown.

'Oh, let's stop playing games, Francesca, shall we? Why don't you admit that the reason you're leaving is because we slept together.'

There was a heavy silence, and the colour crept into her face.

'That has nothing to do with it,' she muttered, and he banged his fist on the table.

'Stop it!'

'All right, then!' she snapped, her head flying up. 'I admit it. I'm leaving because we slept together.'

'Well, at least we're getting somewhere now.' He sat back down at his desk. 'What difference does it make to your job whether we went to bed together or not?'

'I can't work with you and...'

'Oh, grow up, Francesca,' he said impatiently. 'Do you think that I'm going to make passes at you the minute you set foot inside the office?'

'No!' This was another one of those verbal traps, she thought. He was very good at that. He should have been a lawyer.

'Then…?' He gave her a cool, stripping look, and she had to force herself not to launch into a mumbling, incoherent explanation.

'It's just that I've decided that I'm not attracted to you. When I first came here you told me in no uncertain terms that I wasn't your type, and I guess you're not my type either.' She was sure that he would see through that; she was sure that anyone would see through a lie that was as big as a house, but his expression didn't change, and when he replied the temperature in his voice had dropped by a couple of degrees.

'I see,' he said with glacial politeness. 'I still can't see what that has to do with your resigning. Have you now decided that I'm so repulsive that you can't bear to be anywhere near me?'

There was deep distaste in his voice when he said that and she wondered whether he was thinking that she was nothing more than a rich young thing, utterly immature, who had thrown herself at his feet only to retreat hurriedly once the plunge had been taken. In the real world, she knew, they would shrug and carry on, with life settling back into its normal routine, and their one night together relegated to history.

She couldn't begin to know how to answer his question, and he stared at her, waiting, for such a long time that she eventually dropped her eyes and gave a small shrug.

'Look,' he said, and his voice was that of someone older and wiser addressing a recalcitrant child. 'You're a good secretary, and it's taken me a hell of a long time finding one. Believe it or not, I'm not going to take advantage of you. We slept together once, but don't think that I see that as some kind of perk to which I'm now automatically entitled.'

He leaned forward. 'Francesca, why don't you open your eyes and wake up to the real world? Men and women sleep together for all sorts of reasons, and they make mistakes. Life carries on, though.'

'I know that.' So she was a mistake. He couldn't have cut her deeper if he had pulled out a ten-inch carving-knife and run it through her heart. The pain was so intense that she had to take a deep, shaky breath to keep from collapsing.

'You'll have to find me a replacement,' he continued, and she knew that she should be overjoyed that the situation had been resolved, but she had to bite back the tears. So this was how that subtle game of sexual courtship was played. In a game without love, indifference made retreat so easy.

'Of course.' She nodded, struggling to think of a suitable platitude that might restore her self-control, and discovering that platitudes were never around when you needed them. 'Have you got any specifications?'

'Someone,' he said in a hard voice, 'who is prepared to view the job as a long-term proposition.'

'I'm sorry…' she began, faltering, and he cut in harshly.

'Forget it. If I'd known that you'd react to what happened between us in such a hysterical way, I wouldn't have come near you.'

'But you couldn't resist, could you?' Bitterness restored some of her spirit, and she looked at him without flinching.

His eyes narrowed. 'What the heck are you talking about now?'

'Imogen ended your relationship and you just couldn't resist sleeping with me as an afterthought, because you knew that I would be willing.'

'So that's what this is all about.' He leaned back in his chair, looking as sympathetic as a cobra about to strike. 'You're quitting because of a case of severe pique.'

If he had intended to make her feel ten years old, he couldn't have succeeded more. She flushed and looked away, and he laughed under his breath. It wasn't a pleasant sound.

'No one likes to be used,' she muttered.

'You seem to enjoy every minute of it,' he drawled. 'Or did I misread the situation?'

'I was a fool.' If I was your mistake, she thought, then you can be mine—or at least that's what I shall let you believe.

'What were you hoping for after one night together, Francesca? Love and marriage?'

That was so near the mark that she had to fight not to betray her emotions. 'No. But I didn't think at the time that I was a fill-in for someone else—someone who was no longer available.'

'I'm not some kind of sex-crazed animal,' he said coolly. 'I wanted you and the feeling was mutual. We slept together. End of equation.'

'And now you think that we can continue working happily together as though nothing had happened?'

'Nothing *has* happened,' he said. 'But this is a pointless argument. I'm not going to persuade you to stay; you've already made your mind up and I have no intention of beating my head against a brick wall. There's some correspondence still to be finished. Once you've done that, and, of course, found someone to replace you, you can leave.'

'Thank you,' she said, wondering what she was thanking him for exactly. For ruining her life? For treating her as a disposable object of desire? She knew that she could hardly blame him for that, not when she had so readily made herself available, no questions asked, no answers expected, but she did anyway.

She stood up and let herself out, and immediately went to the cloakroom, where she had to fight down the desire to be sick. Again.

When she got back to her desk he had gone, and there was a note with some instructions, and three letters to be typed.

She ignored all of them. She telephoned the employment agency instead and lined up four interviews for the afternoon. Keep busy, she thought. Time enough to make misery your companion.

It was with some uncertain relief that she found two of them proved very promising. One was a woman in her mid-thirties, who was returning to work after some years of rearing children, and the other was a middle-aged woman who had moved down from the north with her husband, who had had a company transfer. They both looked capable and easy to work with.

As soon as Oliver returned at five-thirty that afternoon she told him.

'Hire whichever seemed better,' he told her, making his way past her desk into his office, and she spun around, astonished.

'But don't you want to see them for yourself?'

He stopped at the door and looked back at her. 'Trust your instinct,' he said, with a cold smile. 'It may have let you down in one department, but I'm sure it's working well enough in others.' And he closed the door behind him.

So she telephoned the agency, told them which of the two she had decided to take on, arranged a starting day, contacted the personnel department, and then remained working for another hour, busily doing as much as she could because she now had the impression that Oliver wanted her out sooner rather than later. He had tried to keep her on, and, having failed in that, had washed his hands of her and her infantile scruples.

Well, that suits me fine, she thought to herself, banging away on the keyboard and wishing that it was Oliver Kemp's head.

He left shortly before she did, nodding briefly in her direction, and when she next glanced at her watch it was after six-thirty and she was feeling light-headed and ill with hunger.

She stopped off at the supermarket—or rather at what optimistically called itself a supermarket when in fact it was little more than a corner shop with a stock supply of the most basic tinned food, and a selection of vegetables that always looked as though they had seen happier days.

It was only later that night, after she had consumed a large, hastily prepared meal and was lying in bed, that her wayward thoughts began to take a different direction. By the time she fell asleep she knew that she would have to leave the company the following day if possible.

Francesca arrived at work late the next morning—the first time since she had started—and immediately went into Oliver's office, after knocking and pushing open the door.

He was on the telephone and he pointed to the chair facing him, carrying on his conversation, his voice clipped and authoritative. She watched him surreptitiously, imprinting on her mind for ever the taut lines of his body, the curve of his mouth, the wintry grey-blue of his eyes. And she wondered.

'Yes,' he said to her as soon as he had replaced the receiver.

'I've found a replacement,' she told him without preamble. 'A youngish woman with two small children. She's been out of the workforce for a few years, but I gave her an impromptu typing test and she sailed through it. She's worked in this sort of field before, though it was a long time ago, but she's bright and enthusiastic and I think she'll catch on without too much difficulty.'

'What's her name?'

'Jessica Hines. She'll start tomorrow.' Francesca paused and looked at him in the eye. 'I've brought everything up to date, and I thought that if I spent the rest of the week showing her the ropes I might make Friday my last day.'

He shrugged and said, 'Sure.'

She stood up, ready to leave, but before she could turn the handle of the door he was standing next to her. He leaned against the door, looking down at her. When she breathed, she breathed him in—that masculine aroma that was as powerful to her senses as incense.

'I'm not around for much of the week,' he said in a low voice, 'so I want to say something to you before you go now, in case the opportunity doesn't arise again.'

'What is it?'

'Look at me,' he commanded, and she steeled herself to do it, to raise her eyes to his.

'I don't want you to leave here thinking that the only reason I made love to you that night was because I was suffering from a broken heart and I needed a bit of female companionship.'

'There's no need to explain anything to me,' Francesca retorted, with a spark of bitter anger in her voice.

'Yes, there is. Emotionally you haven't grown up, and this is the sort of thing that you could dwell on until it assumed proportions way beyond control.'

'Thank you for being so thoughtful,' she said sarcastically, wincing at the unintended insult. The fact that he had not meant to offend her by describing her as a child at the beck and call of her emotions only made the offence worse.

'What we did that night was totally spontaneous. When I touched you I wasn't touching Imogen in some maudlin, nostalgic way.'

'You loved her, though.'

'Is that a question or a statement of fact?'

'An observation.'

He didn't answer that. Instead he said, angling his head away from her, 'I would rather you didn't leave.' There was a dark flush on his neck and a certain harshness in his voice that made her realise that he was uncomfortable. Was this the first time that he had ever asked anyone to do something; the first time that he had not told, knowing that he would be obeyed?

He had risen through life the hard way, had never had doors opened for him. He had had to open them all himself, and in the process he had become accustomed to forging forward, to taking steps that needed to be taken in order to gain what could be gained.

She felt a powerful, searing pang of sheer wanting—wanting to listen to him, to stay in a job she enjoyed, to feed her addiction to him. But, of course, all that was impossible. Youthful optimism had been shed for ever, and now she couldn't even really remember how she could have nurtured any wild hopes that he would one day love her if she persevered hard enough.

'I can't stay,' she said flatly, and he pulled back, shoving his hands in his pockets.

'Fine. In that case I won't keep you further.' He walked back to his desk and sat down. 'You have a list of my meetings for the rest of the week,' he said briefly, not looking at her but flicking through a file on the desk and extracting bits of paper from it. 'I shall be out for most of the day, but if you need to talk to me I'll be accessible on my mobile phone or at the client. You can arrange for me to have lunch with Mrs Hines tomorrow. I should be able to manage that.'

'Of course.'

'Good. You can go now.'

He hadn't looked at her once, even though she stupidly knew that she was hovering a bit by the door.

'That's all, Francesca,' he said, looking up, and she nodded and left his office.

Well, she thought, sitting down in front of her computer terminal, that's that. Life goes on. Time heals. There were countless clichés she could think of and none of them gave her a scrap of comfort. What she saw ahead of her wasn't life carrying on, or time healing. It was a dark tunnel—because everything had changed, and it was as if she had now found herself in a strange new world where she no longer knew the rules. What was going to happen now?

She didn't want to think about it. Not now. Not yet. There would be time enough for that.

Not for the first time she desperately wished that her mother was still alive. She could share most things with her father, but what she was going through now needed a woman's wisdom. She could understand for the first time why her father had felt compelled to try and make up for her mother's absence from her life, why he had felt guilty that although he could give her a lot it would never be enough.

The following day Jessica came, bright and keen and like a breath of fresh air.

Oliver had her in his office briefly, but he was virtually on his way out. It was enough time, though, to leave quite an impression on Jessica, who emerged, sat next to Francesca at the desk, and said in a slightly shell-shocked voice, 'He's awfully overpowering, isn't he?'

'You'll get used to it,' Francesca replied, reaching for the top file on the desk and spreading it open between them. She didn't want to talk about Oliver Kemp.

'Did you?'

'Yes,' she said tonelessly. She wondered whether she really would have if she had needed the job and the money as desperately as Jessica needed it. Her husband was a painter and decorator—a job which depended largely on all sorts of things beyond his control—and he was finding work thin on the ground at the moment. The money that Jessica earned would be vital to their standard of living.

'He may work you hard,' Francesca said, brightening up her voice—after all, there was no point in spreading doubts and tarnishing the other girl's enthusiasm—'but he's very fair and he's very patient at explaining things.' Bit of an exaggeration, that last one, but she said it anyway, and it seemed to have the desired effect of relieving some of Jessica's anxiety.

They worked non-stop for the remainder of the day, apart from the break when Oliver took Jessica to lunch, and by the time Friday rolled around enough had been explained so that Francesca could make her departure without thinking that she had left someone floundering in the deep blue sea.

At five-thirty she found herself taking her time with her coat, taking her time looking around the office for the last time, hoping that Oliver would stride in so that she could have one last look at him before he vanished out of her life for ever. But there was no sign of him.

She had hardly seen him at all that week. Meetings had kept him out of the office most of the time, and when he had been around he had liaised with Jessica, with Francesca only a background presence, there to clarify bits and pieces.

She was leaving the building, hurrying in the direction of the Underground, when Helen appeared from no-where—materialised, Francesca thought with an inward groan of despair, like a vampire.

'How are you?' Helen asked, falling into step with her.

'Fine,' Francesca said tightly. It wasn't anywhere near the truth, because she had never felt worse in her life, but the question was not one that required a truthful answer. As with most things that Helen said to her it was a prelude to something altogether nastier.

'Sure? I don't believe you!'

'That's fine by me.'

They had arrived at the station and they both joined the queue for tickets. On a Friday night, at rush hour, the place was packed, and the crowds, the harsh fluorescent lighting, Helen's presence there at her elbow all combined to make Francesca feel giddy and sick. She could feel Helen's sharp little eyes on her, watching the sudden pallor of her skin.

'I hear that you're leaving,' she said conversationally, and Francesca didn't say anything. 'What brought about that sudden decision?'

Francesca wished that the queue would move a bit fas-

ter. There were at least fifteen people ahead of her, and
naturally the man at the counter, as luck would have it,
was taking an inordinately long time because he couldn't
find his wallet.

'Still—wise, I suppose,' Helen said conversationally.
'I'd have done the same. He only slept with you because
you were there at the right time in the right place.'

There was a thread of bitter envy in her voice. Helen
must know, Francesca thought, that Oliver Kemp was simply not interested in her, was probably totally unaware of
her existence, in fact, but that didn't stop her from taking
a malicious delight in spoiling what she saw as a relationship she could have had.

'A girl's got to have her pride. What are you going to
do now?'

'Get another job,' Francesca said shortly. The man had
at last found his wallet, after what seemed like an all-out
search through every nook and cranny of his overcoat, suit
jacket and briefcase, and the line was moving swiftly forward. Thank God.

'But will you be able to?' Helen asked softly from behind her, and Francesca felt her body stiffen in alarm.
What did that mean?

'There are lots of vacancies for secretaries,' she said,
still feeling that dreadful flutter of alarm move around inside her.

She paid for her ticket, turned around, and said, in a
final parting shot, 'I should forget Oliver Kemp if I were
you. He's not interested in you and he never will be.
You're wasting your time.'

'So we're more alike than you care to think, then?'
Helen said, but her eyes were hard stones. 'Still, best of
luck with what you move on to do.' She smiled that feline

smile. 'And I know you'll be pleased to hear that your leaving has made way for me.'

'What are you talking about now?'

'Oh, nothing really. Nothing that affects you now, anyway. Just that I saw Oliver today and I managed to persuade him to let me take over your job. After all, my typing may need a bit of home improvement, but I *do* know an awful lot about the company, and I *do* know an awful lot about the clients. Jessica is going to slot into my old department. He's going to tell her on Monday.' Sly eyes gleamed from under heavily mascaraed eyelashes. 'Wasn't it sweet of him to give me a go?'

Francesca didn't say a word. She turned her back and almost ran to her platform. She felt hot, sick and desperate to get back to her flat.

Employing Helen Scott behind her back seemed the ultimate betrayal. Would *she* end up in his bed as well? Francesca wondered feverishly.

She spent the next week hibernating, too lethargic to do anything and with too many thoughts on her mind. They weighed her down, made her sluggish and tearful.

She didn't want to think about Oliver, but she did. She didn't want to think about Helen Scott, but she did. And then there were all those other equally consuming worries—like how she was going to cope and how she could tell her father. An uneasy silence now lay between them—her doing, she knew, but uneasy silences were the hardest to break, and this news was the worst possible way of breaking this one.

She was sitting with a cup of tea on Friday night, with the television switched on, half following a complicated plot which seemed to involve a lot of running around and a lot of baffled faces of detectives trying to solve a string of murders but mostly thinking, when there was a sharp knock on the door.

She took a deep breath, frowning at the intrusion, opened the door and stood still in shock.

'What are you doing here?' she whispered, with panic in her voice.

Oliver's pale eyes were cold, but his mouth smiled, and he said lightly, 'Is that any way to greet your ex-boss?'

Francesca made no move to pull open the door. 'Why have you come?'

'To find out how you are, of course,' he said in the same light voice, while his eyes remained cool and hard. He reached out and pushed back the door, and then walked into the room, leaving her two options—either to close the door behind her and muster up some kind of self-composure, or else to stand by the open door and yell at the top of her voice that she wanted him to leave.

She closed the door behind her and he prowled around the small room, pausing to look out of the window, which offered a particularly uninspiring view of the street below—not a tree within sight, no patch of green, but then this was London.

'Would you like a cup of coffee?' she asked awkwardly, and he nodded.

'If it's no bother.'

'No bother at all.' They sounded like two distant acquaintances who had unexpectedly found themselves thrown together in an artificial situation and were trying to make polite conversation.

She made a cup of coffee, handed it to him, then sat down on the chair, hitching her legs up, and contemplated him with as much detachment as she could muster. Wasn't facing a problem, she told herself, the first step to curing it?

'So how are you?' he asked, sipping some of his coffee and giving her the full blast of that off-putting stare of his.

She said a little defensively, 'I'm fine.'

'Told your father that you've left?' he asked, still casually, and she shook her head.

'I haven't spoken to him since… Well, I'll do that next week,' she murmured vaguely.

'Difficult breaking bad news, isn't it?' He gave her a cold smile and stared at her, which made her feel uncomfortable and suddenly very resentful of his presence in her flat. She had not asked him to come. She had certainly not wanted to see him. All she wanted was to forget about him.

'Have you started looking for something else?' he asked, and she shook her head.

'I'll start next week,' she muttered.

He said with heavy sarcasm. 'Busy week ahead of you, wouldn't you say?'

'Yes,' she agreed. She felt oddly threatened by his tone, like someone who had suddenly spotted a shark in the swimming pool.

'There's a vacancy at the company,' he said, looking at her closely. 'Maria Barnes has left to work for her brother-in-law, and Gerald Fox, one of the financial directors, is looking for a replacement. The job is yours if you want it.'

'No!' She spoke quickly and loudly. Return to that company? It was utterly impossible. She couldn't have taken that job if she had been down to her last penny and had nothing else in the offing.

'No?' He shook his head, and she could tell from the expression on his face that her answer had not surprised him in the slightest. He had expected it.

She wished that he would go. She felt so nervous that

her fingers were gripping the sides of the chair and the heavy beating of her heart was making her feel faint.

'Why did Maria decide to leave?' she asked, licking her lips and knowing that if she could keep the conversation on an impersonal level she might be able to get through it. 'I thought that she liked working there.'

'Oh, she did,' Oliver agreed, running his finger round the rim of the cup. 'But her brother-in-law's firm isn't doing too well, and he can't afford a full-time secretary even though he needs one. She's going to take a big cut in her salary, in return for which they're going to give her the top floor of their house so that she doesn't have to pay any rent.' He raised his eyes to hers, and there was hard irony there. 'Desperate situations sometimes need desperate solutions, don't they, Francesca?'

He stood up and placed the cup very gently down on the table in front of him. 'You look a little tired,' he said, moving across to her. 'Shall I leave you in peace now?'

She nodded, relieved, and he said, still very calmly, 'I won't come round again, if you'd rather I didn't.'

She nodded again, putting her feet to the ground to see him out, but he said immediately, 'Don't get up. Please.' He smiled, and there was definitely something very alarming about that smile now. He leaned forward, over her, resting his hands on either side of her chair.

'We wouldn't want you to tire yourself even more, would we, Francesca?'

'What do you mean?' she asked faintly.

'What do I mean? I'll tell you what I mean. Did you think that I wouldn't find out? You're pregnant, aren't you?'

CHAPTER SEVEN

IT TOOK a little while for that to register. For a few seconds
Francesca's mind went completely blank, but then it
started working again and her face whitened.

'Who told you?' There didn't seem any point playing
games. For one thing the dark rage on his face, which she
realised now had been lurking there all along, was frightening her, and for another he would be able to find out
easily enough that she *was* pregnant. All he had to do was
watch her, and as sure as day broke and night fell he would
see her putting on weight.

When she had found out that she was pregnant her immediate thought had been that she had to resign, but her
thought processes seemed to have ended there. Now they
sensibly moved one step further, and she realised that there
was a good chance that he would have found out anyway.
He knew her father, and no doubt they would have arranged to meet again, and then it would all have come out.

She had not planned on telling her father the identity of
the baby's father, but that would have been immaterial.
Oliver would have worked it out for himself. It would only
have taken some elementary mathematics.

She put her hand to her forehead, and he pulled it away
and pinned it to the chair with his fingers.

'How did you find out?' she asked faintly, and he bared
his teeth in a cold smile.

'Does it matter? Helen Scott, one of the girls who works
in the company, mentioned that you had been looking sick

119

for the past couple of weeks and said that she thought you might be pregnant.'

That was a bitter pill. She closed her eyes and wondered when these little confidences had taken place and where. At his desk, with her sitting provocatively on the edge? Over a drink in a bar somewhere? In bed?

She should have known that Helen would have suspected, and now that little cryptic comment at the station about finding another job—whether she would be able to—made a lot more sense than it had then.

At the time she had thought that the other girl had been making some guarded, spiteful remark based on an ill-founded suspicion that the reason she was leaving was because she couldn't handle the job, but she had been much closer to the mark than that, hadn't she? In fact, she had scored a bull's eye on the first shot.

'Why didn't you say what you wanted to say the minute you walked through the door?' Francesca asked resentfully. 'Why the charade?'

'I thought I'd give you time,' he said savagely. 'I thought I'd beat around the bush enough so that you would come right out and tell me, if that was what you intended doing, but you didn't.'

'Why should I?' Francesca asked tightly, looking up at him. 'It's not your concern.'

That, she realised, had been a poor choice of words. His face darkened, and she began to stammer incoherently. 'What I mean is…what I meant to say…'

'I know exactly what you meant to say, Francesca. But you'd better get it through that head of yours right now that it is my concern!'

'It's your baby,' she agreed heatedly, 'but that's about it. I don't want anything from you. In fact, I wish you'd just vanish out of my life. I wish you'd never come here in the first place!'

She really did too. He would never understand how he had ruined her life, because what she had given him was much more than a night of love-making, and she couldn't see how she would ever be able to recover from the wreckage and start piecing her life together again if he saw the baby as his concern, and decided that he was to be a permanent fixture on the scene.

If at the beginning she had not seen beyond handing in her resignation and optimistically thinking that he would never find out, her thought processes had now jumped ahead by several leagues, and she imagined a life ahead of her with him appearing in it regularly, so that he could keep in contact with his child—keep in contact even when another Imogen Sattler came along. How was she going to face that?

If Helen had wanted to deliver a final piece of misdirected spite, she could not have chosen a more effective way—to usurp her job and to disclose her pregnancy. He had allowed the first and now he would destroy her for the second.

'Well, I'm here now, lady, and if you think that you're going to get rid of me then you're mistaken.'

'But why…?' she asked in a raw voice. She rubbed her wrist where he had been holding it, and risked another quick glance at his face to see whether some of his anger had subsided. It hadn't.

'Why? You must think I'm a number-one bastard if you believe I can casually get a woman pregnant and then walk away from my responsibility as though it didn't exist.'

So this is what it feels like to be someone's responsibility, she thought. Not a very pleasant feeling. Almost as gut-wrenching as being someone's mistake.

He raked his fingers through his hair and went back to the sofa, sitting down heavily, leaning forward with his elbows on his knees and his hands lightly clasped together.

The funny thing about dreams, she thought, was that they rarely ever bore any resemblance to reality. She had always dreamed when she was young that life would pan out in a very normal manner for her—she would fall in love, she would get married, she would start a family, and every step of the way would be wondrously happy.

Yet here she was—in love all right, but with the wrong man, and starting a family all right, but in a loveless relationship. What a laugh. Except she wasn't remotely amused by any of it. She felt utterly miserable.

'You said that you were using contraception,' he said, breaking into her thoughts, and she looked across at him with an expression that was half defensiveness and half guilt.

'I lied,' she admitted, twisting her fingers together. 'I didn't think that anything would happen.' She saw his expression of impatient disbelief and rushed on, more in defence now than guilt, 'Well, it's not as though I sleep around! Why should I be using any contraception? On the off chance? Anyway, I didn't think that I would have the bad luck for this to happen on the one and only time I made love.'

'Well, it's happened, and now we've got to decide what we're going to do about it.'

'"Do about it"? "*Do* about it"? What does *that* mean? If you think that I'm going to get rid of it somehow, then you're wrong!'

'Don't be bloody stupid!' he bit out harshly. 'That's not what I'm saying at all.'

'Then what are you saying? It's too soon to start talking about visitation rights. Why don't we wait until it's born?'

He ignored that as if he wouldn't dignify the remark with a response. 'Like it or not, I'm the father of the child,' he said calmly, 'and there's only one thing for it—we're going to have to get married.'

'No!'

'Why not?'

'We don't love each other—' she began.

'Stop living in a dream world, Francesca,' he cut in harshly. 'This is reality, and the best thing we can do is get married. We can break it to your father in the morning.'

'We are not going to do any such thing!' Did he really think that she would agree to marry him, knowing that the only reason he was doing so was because of the baby? 'Shotgun marriages are always doomed to failure,' she informed him, and he laughed, but without much humour.

'And where do you get your statistics?'

'Everyone knows that,' she muttered stubbornly. 'I can manage perfectly well on my own. I don't need any financial help from you. I'll go back home and—'

'You will *not* go back home,' he said before she could finish. 'You will *not* use your father's money to bring up a child of mine.'

'Don't tell me what I can and can't do!'

They stared at each other silently, and after a while he said, getting up, 'I'm going to make myself a cup of coffee. Would you like one?'

'I've gone off it.'

'A glass of juice, then?'

She shrugged and nodded, and hoped that he would take his time, because she needed to get her thoughts into order.

He came back into the room eventually, handed her a

glass of orange juice, and after a few minutes said conversationally, 'Feeling better now?'

She could see that even if she wasn't he most certainly was. There was no longer that violent anger on his face. He had regained that formidable self-composure and was looking at her over the rim of his cup, his eyes veiled.

'Shall we continue this conversation without any hysteria?' he asked, which made her bristle with resentment, but she didn't say anything and he carried on with calm confidence, 'I agree you don't need any financial help from me, but that doesn't begin to solve your problems. For instance, what do you think your father is going to say about your condition?'

'He won't be overjoyed, I know that,' Francesca muttered, looking down into her glass as if searching for inspiration. 'He'll be shocked and disappointed.'

Which, she thought, was putting it mildly. He had always tried so hard to do what was right for her, to compensate for the lack of maternal guidance.

Through all his long, hard, working hours he had always made time to come to her little school functions, to be there whenever it mattered. That was why he had been so worried when she had finished her secretarial course and had started going out with what he'd seen as entirely the wrong crowd. That was why her rift with him would now be causing him anxiety.

'He'll be even more shocked and disappointed when you tell him that you won't marry me even though I want you to,' Oliver murmured smoothly, and she glared at him.

'He'll understand.'

'Will he, though?'

'He'd rather I married for love than for all the wrong reasons.'

Oliver's lips thinned and he said silkily, 'Then I shall

just have to convince him how much I love you, shan't
I?' And now her eyes were helpless. 'There are worse
things in life than marrying for the sake of a baby,' he
said in a hard voice, but there was an angry need to persuade her there as well that made her frown. 'Two people
can start out with stars in their eyes and the marriage can
break down in a matter of weeks because there wasn't
enough there to start with. At least we know each other.'

'In a manner of speaking.' Francesca put in with a certain amount of bitter sarcasm. 'Besides,' she continued,
thinking about it, 'Dad would see through my phoney ba-
loney about love in a minute flat.'

'No, he wouldn't. People are very good at believing
what they want to believe, and, face it, I'm not exactly the
human equivalent of the bubonic plague, am I?'

'Oh, very modest,' she snapped, and he laughed, and
this time there was a great deal more humour there.

Although she would never admit it, he was right; they
did know one another, perhaps better than she cared to
say. Or at least *she* knew *him*. Wasn't that why she had
fallen in love with him? She had seen the warm charm,
the wit, the sense of fair play which were all there underneath the aggressive, terse exterior.

He'd implied that *he* knew *her*, though. But did he? He
had thought her a child—a spoiled child who had sailed
through life on the wings of money.

And she knew that he had not been initially attracted to
her at all. She had not been his type. Maybe physically he
had revised his opinions, for reasons which she did not
know for certain but could make an educated guess at, but
she still wasn't his type. If it hadn't been for the baby, he
would never have dreamt of asking her to marry him. He
might have continued sleeping with her, but it would have
only been a temporary arrangement.

'Your father would prefer to know that you were being taken care of, rather than think of you as a single parent, emotionally struggling on her own to bring up a baby. You're still a child yourself, for God's sake.'

'There you go again! Thank you very much,' Francesca muttered.

'Think about it.' He put his cup on the table and stood up. 'I'll pay you a visit tomorrow morning.'

After he had gone she sank back onto her chair and stared sightlessly in front of her, thinking about what he had said.

She didn't think of herself as a child, but she could understand what Oliver meant. She had behaved impulsively with him, and with foolish naïvety had found herself in a situation that was going to catapult her into maturity whether she liked it or not.

It would worry her father knowing that she would be bringing a baby into the world without the security of a family unit. She had been born into a great deal of love, and if she had been the daughter of a single-parent family herself then it hadn't been his choice.

She also worried about how her father would cope with having a newborn baby in the house. He wasn't an old man, but sleepless nights could tire the most vigorous individual and he would feel obliged, she knew, to do his fair share—not out of duty but out of love.

When Oliver knocked on the door the following morning at eight o'clock Francesca looked as tired as she felt.

'Have you had any sleep?' he asked immediately, and she stepped back to let him in.

'Not much,' she admitted. 'Did you expect me to, after our conversation last night? I've been thinking about it, wondering what to do.'

'Have you had any breakfast?' he asked, changing the subject, and she shook her head.

'So in other words you're behaving in exactly the sensible manner any doctor would heartily recommend. No sleep, no food.'

It was Saturday so he wasn't dressed for work. He was wearing a pair of jeans and a cream shirt, and she hurriedly looked away so that he wouldn't see the pull of attraction on her face.

'Come on,' he said, chivvying her along, she thought sullenly, like a recalcitrant child. Had he treated Imogen like that? she wondered. No chance.

'Let me get you something to eat.' He settled her into the chair and she obediently remained there because she was feeling rather faint and sick—as she had been for what seemed to be an eternity. Presently she heard the sound of pans and cutlery, and he emerged after a while with a plate of scrambled egg and toast. Then he sat down and watched while she ate the lot. Making sure, she thought, that she didn't tip it all into the plant next to the chair, no doubt.

'Thank you,' she said when she had finished. 'That was very nice.' She walked into the kitchen and looked round her in disbelief.

'How many pans did you use to concoct this?' she asked incredulously.

'I mentioned I could cook,' he murmured, closer to her than she'd expected. 'I never said anything about being a tidy cook.' He took the plate from her and began washing up in a fairly slapdash manner, stacking the crockery onto the draining-board in an inelegant heap, so that she had to grab a teacloth and hurriedly dry it to prevent breakage.

'Now,' he said when they had finished, 'get dressed and let's go and pay your father a little visit.'

'He'll be out.'

'No, he won't. I telephoned him to tell him that we were coming over. He's been worried, waiting for you to get in touch. He was delighted.'

'What?' She stared at him, aghast. 'How could you?'

'You have to tell him sooner or later about the pregnancy,' he replied evenly in that voice of his which she had come to recognise from working with him—the voice that implied that arguments were useless.

'Of course, and I intend to! I just don't need pushing.'

'You do,' he said mildly. 'You needed pushing to get a job and you need pushing to do this, or else you'll put it off until it overshadows every waking moment. You stormed out on your father over a piece of nonsense and you can't face the thought of returning with this revelation. That's how family feuds develop.'

Francesca ground her teeth together. The fact that he had a point only made her angrier.

Why had her life suddenly become so complicated? She might not have spent her time in the past single-mindedly heading towards a goal; she might have been somewhat ingenuous in her outlook that dilemmas were things that happened to other people, and that she could merrily trundle through life without too many worries to disturb the flat surface, but why had things now gone so completely awry?

She would dearly have liked to blame him, but that was impossible, and she was not enough of a believer in fate to blame that either.

Perhaps her father's enormous wealth had insulated her even more than she could ever have imagined. She had never had to face any hard knocks in her life and now she found herself in a situation with which she could scarcely cope.

Still, that didn't mean that Oliver Kemp was entitled to push her around, did it?

'I might as well tell you that I haven't made any decisions about...about what we talked about. Or rather what *you* talked about,' she said once they were inside his car and heading towards her father's house. 'So I have no idea why you want to come along with me to see Dad.'

He averted his attention from the road briefly to glance at her, and there was an unyielding expression on his face.

'I don't trust you to tell him,' he said bluntly.

'Stop interfering in my life!'

'You opened the door, Francesca,' he told her.

'Are you trying to tell me that this is all my fault?' she asked, on the verge of tears. 'Oh, isn't that typical of a man?'

'Stop being a fool,' he said, shoving his handkerchief across to her, and she blew her nose noisily into it.

'I'd feel happier explaining things if you weren't hovering there in the background. This is a very personal thing.'

'And one that concerns us both,' he reminded her grimly.

He swung his car through the gates that led up to the courtyard outside the house and then waited for her, his hands in his pockets, the stiff, cold wind blowing his black hair across his face, giving him a dark, rakish look.

Her father was waiting for them in the sitting room. Bridie bustled them through, casting suspicious glances in Oliver's direction whenever she thought herself unnoticed, wondering what this stranger was doing in the house.

'Hello, darling,' her father said hesitantly. 'I'm so very glad you're here.' He came across, and Francesca smiled automatically, but she felt dreadfully nervous inside. She had had enough time to steel herself for the inevitability of this, but now that the time had actually arrived she felt as desperately anxious as someone standing on a platform about to address hundreds of people only to find that she'd lost her notes.

'Oliver,' her father said, shaking his hand, 'what's this all about? Sit down the both of you.' He gestured vaguely to the sofa and Oliver sat down, patting the spot next to him, which made her father's eyebrows shoot up in surprise. 'Would you like some tea? Coffee?'

He didn't wait for an answer. He went across to the door, shouted for Bridie, who obviously was close at hand because she appeared within seconds, and asked her to fetch some coffee, 'and a few croissants.'

'Dad...' Francesca said in a faltering voice. 'I'm sorry about...about what happened. I accused you of things and...and I apologise.'

'It's already forgotten,' he said briskly, but there was a sheen in his eyes. 'Now,' he continued, once they were sorted out with something to eat and drink, 'whatever is this all about? I hope you haven't come to tell me that Francesca isn't up to the job, Oliver.' It was as if, she thought, that uncomfortable silence between them had never existed. If only everything could be resolved as painlessly as that.

'I think,' Oliver said calmly, 'that Francesca would like to break the news to you herself.'

He sat there, she thought, sipping his coffee, not looking in the slightest bit nervous. Was he made of steel? she wondered resentfully.

'News? What news?' her father asked a little more sharply, turning to her, and Francesca tried a soothing smile.

'Nothing to get excited about, Dad,' she said. 'It's just...quite simply...that...' Oh, God, she thought, taking refuge in her coffee which tasted quite revolting to her. She could feel their eyes on her and her stomach gave a lurch. 'What I'm trying to say here, Dad, is that...'

She looked helplessly at Oliver, who said calmly, 'Francesca has resigned.'

'What?'

'Dad!' She could feel herself in deep water now, without a lifebelt in sight. 'I... Yes, I've resigned.'

'Why?'

'Ah. Why?' she said, pointlessly playing for time. 'I don't quite know how I'm going to tell you this,' she continued, in the manner of someone looking for divine inspiration and not finding it, 'and I know that you're going to be shocked and disappointed...' at this point, she didn't dare meet her father's eyes, because the last thing she wanted to see was his shock and disappointment '...but I've been rather silly...'

'Not from my point of view,' Oliver murmured from next to her, and she felt the brush of his arm as he extended it along the back of the sofa behind her.

Her father wasn't looking too shocked or disappointed at this juncture. He just looked bewildered.

'Dad,' she blurted out, 'I'm pregnant.'

There was a deathly silence, and when she sneaked a glance at her father she saw that his mouth was half-open. It would have been comical in any other situation.

'And before you collapse on the spot,' Oliver said smoothly, taking it all in his stride, as though breaking news like this was a daily occurrence, 'we're going to get married.' He bent across to kiss the side of her face, and she went scarlet.

'I haven't—' she began.

He cut in swiftly. 'No, we haven't set a date yet, but it'll be sooner rather than later. Won't it, darling?' he said, and she could feel from the warmth of his breath on her face that he had turned to her.

Her father had still not come up for air, but eventually he said, 'Frankie? Pregnant? Getting married? What has been going on here?'

She began to splutter out that yes, she was pregnant, but that no, marriage was not on the cards, but she hardly had time to formulate a coherent sentence when Oliver said, still in that controlled, unfazed tone of voice, 'We're both a little surprised at how things have turned out, but we're also delighted, aren't we, darling?'

She wasn't so stunned that she couldn't detect the note of warning in his voice. All of a sudden she felt as though she had completely lost the reins on her life. Things were lurching about wildly—a surreal situation that made everything spin around her.

'Well,' her father said, releasing his breath. 'Well, well, well. I don't quite know what to say.' He still looked dazed. 'Of course, I'm stunned; it's all so sudden, isn't it?'

'These things can be unpredictable, can't they, Francesca?' Oliver said lazily, and she threw him her own dazed look.

'Of course,' her father was saying, with some semblance of having re-entered planet Earth, 'your mother and I knew within minutes of meeting that we were meant for one another. I guess it was the same for you.'

'Exactly,' Oliver said smoothly, with a smile in his voice, and Francesca felt faint.

'Well,' her father said again. 'Frankie, darling. Too late, I suppose, to tell you about the birds and the bees? Bit like shutting the door after the proverbial horse has bolted.' She could see that he was coming round to the idea, and she realised with panic that Oliver had been right—the prospect of marriage between them had taken the sting out of the situation. Oliver was a brilliant catch— the biggest fish in the sea—and just the sort of man her father would have wanted for a son-in-law.

He had also put her in an awkward position. How could she tell her father that she didn't want to marry Oliver?

For the next thirty minutes or so she listened with a swirling head while they chatted, but as soon as her father had gone she turned to Oliver and said coldly, 'Thank you very much.'

She stood up and walked across to the huge patio doors and stared, unseeing, out towards the impeccable stretch of manicured lawns. A gardener came twice a week to look after the garden. Her father had once told her that when he'd first been married he had been used to doing a lot of gardening—her mother had loved it—but that when she'd died he'd lost the heart for it.

Francesca had never mowed a lawn in her life.

'I never told you that I wanted to marry you!' she said in a high voice, and the tears were pricking the back of her eyes. 'It's wrong,' she continued, turning around to face him.

He lounged against the mantelpiece, his mouth taut. 'Why? Why is it wrong?'

'You don't love me,' she said bitterly. 'We don't love each other!' Saying that made her wince inside, but she continued to look directly at him. 'People don't get married nowadays for the sake of a baby.'

He walked towards her, taking his time, and there was scathing disgust in his eyes. 'Listen to yourself,' he said tightly. 'Do you really believe that a child should pay for our mistake?'

'No,' Francesca answered, feeling cornered and resenting his implication that she was somehow without morals.

'But you'd end up hating me for having put you in a situation where you felt compelled to marry me,' she said, holding her ground and looking up at him.

'Don't try and analyse me,' he said harshly, and he reached out to hold her shoulders. He looked as though he wanted to shake the living daylights out of her, but she refused to be intimidated.

What would it be like? she thought with despair. Living with him, married to him, bringing up their child, and having to hold her love deep inside her day after day?

'I'm not,' she whispered. 'But it would be a mistake. We have nothing in common.'

'It's too late in the day to start drawing up lists of what we have in common and what we don't,' he said, but the harshness had left his voice and his fingers weren't gripping her quite so fiercely. 'You and that Rupert character had a lot in common. Would you rather the mistake had happened with him?'

'Rupert?' That almost made her laugh. 'I wouldn't have been so stupid.'

Oliver's brows met. 'There's no point debating the issue,' he said shortly. 'Unless, of course, you want to tell your father that you've decided to go it alone.'

'You shouldn't have forced my hand,' Francesca whispered stubbornly.

'Is that what you find most upsetting?' he asked coldly. 'The fact that I forced your hand?'

'No one likes to be pushed into a corner.'

'Life isn't always about doing what you like,' he said in a hard voice, and she felt a rush of tears. She made a helpless, shrugging motion with her shoulders, and he drew her towards the sofa with a sigh.

'Look,' he said, sitting her down and then settling himself next to her and dabbing her streaming eyes with a handkerchief, 'you're going to have to stop finding hidden meanings behind everything I say.'

'I can't,' she said in a trembling voice, taking the handkerchief away from him and doing a better job of wiping her wet face. 'I know how you feel about me. You're critical of me, of everything I represent. I know that life isn't about just picking out the things you like and pretending that unpleasantness doesn't exist, and I know I haven't had much practice at facing lots of things that other people have to face, but I can't bear the thought of being married to you.'

'I see,' he said expressionlessly. 'Why did you make love to me, Francesca?' he asked.

'Because…' she struggled to think of how she could explain it without giving herself and her feelings away in the process. 'Because you're an attractive man.'

'If you really can't face the thought of marrying me, then I won't force you.'

'No.' She tried to feel relieved at that and couldn't.

'But then sit back and try to think clearly of the alternative. Bringing up a baby isn't going to be a piece of cake, however much money your father has.'

'I know that,' she said in a small voice.

'You can look at any marriage we go into as a business arrangement,' he said flatly. 'You may well bitterly regret what's happened, but you should have thought about that before. That fact is that what's happened has happened, and we both have to accept it and do whatever is going to be best for the baby.'

'How can you be so calm about it all?' she demanded in an anguished voice.

'Because I don't see the value in hysterics,' he told her bluntly. 'You're pregnant, I'm the father—and I'm not about to relinquish my responsibilities.'

Francesca listened to him but her thoughts were on herself, on the enormity of raising a baby without help. He'd said that she could consider any marriage they went into as a business arrangement, which said a lot about how he felt about her, but he was right—she wasn't the one at stake here.

'All right,' she said tiredly, defeated. 'I'll marry you.'

'I'll arrange it,' he said, sounding neither relieved nor overjoyed.

'I don't want a big wedding. Dad will try and get us to have a grand affair, but I won't have it. That would be too much of a farce. I just want a register office, and I won't wear white.'

'No one's asking you to,' Oliver murmured, his eyes veiled. 'You can wear screaming scarlet for all I care.'

'Good!' she said, as though she had scored a point.

He stood up and looked down at her. 'Shall I drop you back at your flat?' he asked, and she shook her head slowly.

'I'll stay here for a while,' she said. 'I'll make my own way back.'

He hesitated for a while, but finally he shrugged his shoulders and told her that he'd be in touch on Monday. 'We'll get it all sorted out by the end of next week,' he said, and she gasped and raised her eyes to him. 'Then you'll move in with me. How much notice do you have to give your landlord?'

'Two weeks,' Francesca said, feeling as though she had stepped onto the roller coaster once again. 'But we don't need to move so fast,' she protested faintly.

'Yes, we do. If we don't you'll change your mind every other day and in the long run nothing will be sorted out at all.'

'I wish you wouldn't treat me like an idiot child!' she told him with a burst of energy, and he laughed shortly.

'But that's what you are, isn't it, Francesa? A child who wanted to grow up at the hands of a man she was temporarily attracted to. A child who's finding it difficult to realise that there's such a thing as cause and effect.' He shot her an odd look and then he was gone, and she lay back on the sofa with a sigh of relief.

She wanted to cry again, but what would be the point? So she let her mind go blank and tried to distance herself from the painful thought that Oliver Kemp could give her everything—a ring on her finger, a united family for the baby; he could give her everything but the one thing she wanted. He couldn't give her love.

CHAPTER EIGHT

FRANCESCA hadn't had a great deal of time to think about whether she was doing the right thing or not in getting married. Oliver had come round on Monday evening to her flat and told her that they were going out to dinner.

'What for?' was the first thing she'd asked. He had still been in his business suit—an expensively tailored dark grey double-breasted suit which made him look over-poweringly masculine.

'To have a meal, of course,' he'd said drily. 'Isn't that what most people do when they go out to a restaurant? We need to discuss a few things and we need to eat. It seems a simple enough equation.'

So here they were now, in a cosy French restaurant in Hampstead.

'Have you spoken to your father again about it?' he asked, sipping from a glass of white wine while she toyed with her extremely dull glass of orange juice.

Francesca nodded. 'A lot,' she admitted, contemplating the glass. 'I spent last night there and we talked for hours. I told him that we would be married in a register office, which he wasn't too thrilled about, but he's been fine mostly.'

'He loves you,' Oliver said gently. 'You worked your-self up into a lather wondering what his reaction would be without realising that love can forgive and forget almost anything.'

She didn't want to talk about love. She didn't want to remind herself that that was an emotion which she would have to learn to live without, so she said hurriedly, looking away from those light, penetrating eyes, 'I'm still not sure, though, that we're doing the right thing.'

Their meal came—a fishy affair with lots of creamy sauce—and she fiddled with the attractive array of vegetables, concentrating on her plate rather than on the man sitting opposite her.

'Eat up,' he said, eyeing her lack of enthusiasm for the food, and she glared at him, which made him laugh under his breath.

'I hope you don't intend to order me around when we're married,' she muttered, and he laughed again.

'It would take a brave man to do that, Francesca,' he murmured.

'And what does that mean?'

'It means that you have the sting of a viper.'

'I'm not sure I like that,' she said, frowning, but not feeling as nettled by his remark as she knew she should have—perhaps because there had been a smile in his eyes when he'd said it, and that smile had made her feel warm and foolishly happy.

She began eating, and discovered after a few mouthfuls that she was hungrier than she had thought.

'I've made all the arrangements for the wedding,' he said casually when she had closed her knife and fork on a plate that had been scraped clean. 'Day after tomorrow.'

'Day after tomorrow?' She looked at him, astounded at the speed with which he had moved, and his eyes narrowed.

'No arguments,' he said. 'You can invite a few friends, but the smaller the better, as far as I'm concerned. Then there's the question of our honeymoon.'

'Honeymoon?' Francesca's eyes widened in horror at the thought of that. Honeymoons, she thought, were for lovers, not for two people propelled into marriage by circumstance. 'We don't need a honeymoon,' she said quickly. 'Can't we just get the wedding over and done with and then carry on as normal?'

'You mean as if nothing major had happened?' There was a thread of anger in his voice which puzzled her. 'I realise that you wish you could forget what's happened. It's not a pretty thought to live with, is it—that you jumped into bed with a man purely for physical reasons, and that that one simple, natural action has led to a series of events which you'd like to pretend haven't changed both our lives dramatically?

'But that's what's happened. We're getting married, and we're going to go on a honeymoon. For starters, what do you imagine your father would think if we didn't? He's a conventional man and you've already probably shaken him to his foundations.'

'Oh, so *you've* decided that we need a honeymoon so that we can continue the charade that everything between us is all roses and light.'

'Stop being so damned argumentative,' he rasped. 'You could do with a break abroad somewhere, anyway.'

'I'd prefer—'

'You've already told me what you'd prefer,' he cut in harshly, ignoring the waiter who was hovering at a respectful distance with the dessert menus in his hand. The waiter sidled off and Oliver leaned towards her, his face dark and disturbing.

'We'll spend a week abroad somewhere sunny. The Caribbean, perhaps, or the Far East. Which would you prefer?'

'Oh, the Caribbean, I suppose,' she said with bad grace, and he shot her a dry look.

'Most women would hardly need persuading to take a

holiday in the sun and get away from this filthy British weather that's trying to pass itself off as summer.'

'Well, I'm not most women!'

'No, that you most certainly are not,' he said, looking at her from under his lashes, and she wondered whether this was another little dig, but she decided not to make a point of it. She might as well learn to be civil to him, and to stop cross-examining every little word, every little gesture.

She knew why she did it. She did it because although she didn't regret having given in to that strong, physical impulse to sleep with him, she couldn't forgive herself for her stupidity in having fallen in love with him. For him it was all so much simpler. The woman he was in love with—had been planning to marry—had walked into the sunset with another man, and she, Francesca, had been available—in the right place at the right time.

You could change lots of things in your life, she thought, but the one thing you could never change was your past.

Francesca spent the following day coming to terms with what had happened and what now presented itself on the horizon—a wedding, a honeymoon, a baby in a little over seven months' time. This was reality, and reality had drained her of her youthful optimism and showed her what an utter fool she had been when she had thought that she could hold life in the palm of her hand.

The wedding, in the end, was something of an anticlimax. One minute she was Francesca Wade and the next minute she was Francesca Kemp, and there was ring on her finger, announcing the fact to the world at large.

They had jointly asked a few friends, although her father had made up for the lack by inviting a good few of

his own—people who would, he assured her, be devastated
if they knew that his only little gem had got married and
omitted to include them in the happy event—and after the
brief ceremony they went back to her father's house,
where, frustrated by the lack of a grand affair, he had laid
on an elaborate buffet.

Amongst the guests were Imogen and Rupert, and
Francesca did her best to avoid looking at Imogen, because
every time she did she wondered what was going on in
Oliver's head when he looked at the woman he had lost
to someone else.

She didn't want to surprise any unguarded looks of
longing for what might have been if things had turned out
differently. But the effort of averting her eyes and pretending that she was happy made her feel stiff and miserable.

'Cheer up,' Oliver ordered *sotto voce*, with his arm
around her, and she replied without looking at him.

'I'm smiling as hard as I can.'

'I know. I can tell.'

'No one else has noticed anything,' she pointed out.
There was a lot of laughing going on, and easy conversation, and her father was having a great time strutting
around proudly.

'No,' he said under his breath, 'but I'm learning to pick
up signals from you.' He kept his arm around her, and it
was only when the party was beginning to disperse that
she found herself face to face with Imogen.

'I've hardly had a chance to talk to you,' the other
woman said, drawing her to one side and sitting her down.
There was a warm smile on her lips and Francesca tried
to respond in kind. She felt tired and sleepy. Pregnancy
seemed to have made her feel permanently tired. What she
would really have liked was to be able to sleep for the

next few months and awaken only when the baby was due to be born, conveniently skipping the intervening period which threatened to be to a slow version of the Chinese water torture.

'I've been rushed off my feet,' Francesca said vaguely. Apart from her father no one as yet knew that she was pregnant. She still had her slim, coltish figure, and maternity dresses seemed a long way away as yet.

'It all happened so quickly, didn't it?' Imogen agreed, smiling. 'Bit like Rupert and myself. We're planning on getting married later on this year, and I shall be giving up my job to start a family and to help Rupert run the estate.

'I've already warned him that he's got to get used to staying in, because when a screaming baby comes along yours truly isn't going to be cooped up in his rambling manor looking after it all by herself!' She laughed and Francesca joined in, feeling a pang of envy at the thought of the blissful family life that awaited the other girl.

'I'm happy for Oliver as well,' Imogen said confidentially, her face sobering. 'We were so close, and I hated to think that what happened between us might have jaded his faith in the opposite sex.'

'Don't you feel a little bit…?' Francesca sought around for the right words to convey her curiosity.

Imogen helpfully said, 'Aggrieved? Not desperately. For a while I had felt that it would be something of a mistake to marry Oliver, but I couldn't put my finger on it so I drifted along with the idea. I only realised what was missing when I fell in love with Rupert.

'It's a bit like my career, I suppose. I always did very well academically, and I had a great deal of luck along the way. I got a good job from the start and found myself being promoted until I'd reached the pinnacle of success.' She shrugged. 'I shan't be too sorry to give it all up.'

Francesca looked at her thoughtfully, and then said, 'Would you and Oliver have had children, do you think, if you had married?'

'Oh, yes.' Rupert was beckoning to her from across the room, holding up his wrist and pointing to his watch theatrically.

She stood up and then said casually, laughing, 'Oliver's always wanted a family. I think he would have done anything to have had a child straight away. He didn't want to wait until he was too old. I think it affected him more than he liked to admit—the fact that both his parents died when he was relatively young. He wanted to make sure that he was around to see his children into middle age.' She laughed again. 'Not that there's ever any certainty about that!'

The guests were beginning to depart, and Francesca did her duty and waved them off with a smile on her face, but she understood better now why Oliver had propelled her into marriage. He moved across to her and put his arm around her. The happy couple, she thought; at least to the outside world. No one would ever guess in a million years that all of this was an elaborate charade, performed because of what lay inside her.

They left soon after for the airport, and in the car Francesca lay back with her eyes closed, not saying anything, thinking.

When Oliver had made love to her that night it had been because he had wanted her. And he had needed the warmth of another body next to his. Whatever he said, the more she heard, the more she realised that if Rupert had never come along Imogen would still have been the woman with his ring on her finger.

Doubtless, for all her silly hopes at the time, his desire

would have waned rapidly, because essentially what he had wanted had not been *her* but simply an attractive woman to tide him through a difficult period. They weren't on the same wavelength. That had always been what he'd thought, and he still thought that.

But the pregnancy had changed everything. It had transformed an ill-fated night of passion into a lifelong obligation.

She glanced across at his profile and knew that she would never have guessed how strong his desire for a child was if his ex-girlfriend hadn't obligingly provided the information. Everyone, she supposed, had their own peculiar vulnerability.

She closed her eyes, and the next time she opened them they were at the airport and he was shaking her gently by the shoulder to make her wake up, which she did, with a wide yawn and as effective a stretch as she could manage within the confines of a car.

'Ready?' he asked, with a grin in his voice. 'Or shall I carry the suitcases and put you on the trolley so that you can continue your nap?'

'It's not my fault,' she answered irritably, yawning again. 'It's the hormones.' At which he laughed outright and raised his eyebrows in a dry question.

'And how long will these hormones be responsible for whatever you do?' he asked, and she stole a sideways look at him. He looked relaxed and sexy. Very sexy. He had changed out of his charcoal suit into a pair of dark green trousers and an oatmeal-coloured shirt which made him look alarmingly handsome.

'Months,' she said, clicking open the door and throwing over her shoulder, 'Maybe years.'

He was still grinning when he emerged from the driver's seat.

The airport was crowded but not unduly so. They were travelling out of the peak period.

Oliver handled everything with the self-assurance of someone who was accustomed to going abroad, and he was treated with the exaggerated respect paid to first-class travellers.

Francesca simply skulked in the background, watching the toing and froing of everyone else, and wondering whether she was the only one in the airport who wasn't overjoyed at the thought of leaving the country.

It was an eight-hour flight and she was dreading it, but in the end she slept through most of it, and when she was awake she found herself reluctantly beginning to enjoy the prospect of a week in the sun.

They stepped off the plane into blazing sunshine. It was some time since Francesca had been to the Caribbean. She had forgotten how vivid the colours were. Everything had an unreal brightness about it. The greens of the trees were somehow greener, the flowers brighter, the sky flawlessly blue. And the heat was of a kind rarely experienced in England. It made you feel lazy and peaceful.

She had worn light clothes, but by the time they made it to the hotel she was perspiring and dying for a shower.

It was only when they were shown to their room that she remembered, with a jolt of alarm, that this was a honeymoon and that they would be sharing a bed. She had half forgotten that she was married, just as she had half forgotten what marriage from now on would entail.

She eyed the double bed warily from the door and Oliver said drily, stripping off his shirt, 'Stop hovering. You look as though you're about to be eaten.' He disappeared into the bathroom without bothering to shut the door, and she hurriedly began unpacking her stuff and ignoring the bed.

When he emerged he was naked except for a towel loosely draped over his waist, and she snapped awkwardly, 'Couldn't you have dressed?'

He stopped where he was and gave her a long look, then he moved very slowly towards her.

'Has it slipped your mind that we're married now, Francesca?' he asked with icy politeness. The relaxed charm that had been on his face less than an hour ago had vanished.

'In name only,' she retorted, and his dark eyebrows met in an angry frown.

'Is that what you think?'

'What else should I think? We both know that the only reason we're here is because of the baby, and now that there's no one else around I don't see why we have to continue pretending.'

The colour had risen to her cheeks, partly because she was as heated as he was, but mostly because he was standing so close to her. If she stretched her hand out only a little she would touch that hard, powerful torso. Not knowing what stupid impulse she might give in to, she stuck her hands behind her back and looked up at him.

'What do you suggest we do?' he asked softly, but there was a dangerous silkiness in his voice that made her shiver.

'We could go our separate ways,' she suggested nervously, looking away.

'And occasionally meet in passing in the restaurant?'

She didn't answer, and he reached out and caught her arm in his fingers.

'Now you listen to me,' he said in a very controlled voice. 'We're married. You can analyse the reasons behind it until you go blue in the face but that doesn't change a thing, and, believe me, I have no intention of not coming near you whenever there's no one around looking.'

'Wh-what do you mean?' she stammered.

'I mean, this is going to be a marriage in every sense of the word.' He paused, giving her time for that to sink in, and she looked at him with dismay.

'You can't mean that,' she said.

'Every word. If you think marriage between us is going to mean sharing the same roof while I go my own way with other women, then you're wrong.'

'So you're going to be faithful, are you, Oliver?' she asked tightly. 'To a woman whom you don't love? You expect me to believe that?'

'I have no doubt that you'll believe exactly what you want to believe.'

'And you don't care! And what about when temptation positions itself in front of you?'

He looked at her with a perplexed frown. 'What on earth are you rambling on about now?'

'Helen?' She felt quite wretched but took great pains not to show it. 'Helen Scott? You gave her my job without even telling me! What else did you give her?'

His lips thinned. 'You little fool! Is that what that troublemaker told you? She isn't working for me! Why do you blindly believe whatever you're told? Sometimes I feel I could wring your neck, woman! Now, shut up and look at me.'

She raised her eyes to his face and her pulses gave a leap.

'Go ahead,' he said in a rough voice. 'Touch me.'

'No. I can't.'

'Yes, you can.' His mouth twisted into a dry smile. 'You think that if you disassociate yourself from me you can pretend that nothing's happened, but you're still attracted to me, Francesca, aren't you?' His voice had sunk to a mocking drawl that brought a flush of colour to her cheeks.

'No, I'm not,' she lied, staring into his wintry eyes with an odd sense of animal panic. 'I hate myself for what's happened. I gave in to one crazy impulse and it wrecked my life. I know that we're married now, but I don't want anything to do with you.'

'What do you think is going to happen if you give in to me again?' he asked softly, tilting her chin up with his fingers so that she was forced to look at him. 'Do you think that the heavens are going to fall down on you?'

'I don't want to talk about this,' she whispered. 'It's pointless, all this talk.'

'Like it or not, we're going to have to talk about it,' Oliver said in a hard voice. 'You've never had to face anything unpleasant in your whole life, have you, Francesca? That's why you're finding it so difficult to face this.'

'Would Imogen handle the situation any better?' she asked bitterly. 'You're so eager to point out what a hopeless failure I am. Is that because you're measuring me against impossible standards? I'll never be like your ex-girlfriend.'

'Have I ever told you that you're a hopeless failure?' he asked with curiosity. His senses had sharpened, and she knew that she would have to tread carefully, or else she could very easily end up revealing much more than she wanted to.

'You implied it,' she muttered. 'I know I've had a privileged background. I can't help that.'

'Are you jealous of Imogen?' he asked. 'Just like you

were jealous of Helen Scott? What do you think that means?'

She pulled away from him and walked across to the bedroom window.

She had known that he was going to ask her that. She should never have brought Imogen into the conversation at all, just as she shouldn't have mentioned Helen. But she hadn't been able to prevent herself. She was blindly jealous. Helen, she realised now, was no more than a mischief-maker, but Imogen would always be a lurking threat.

'Well?' he asked, coming up behind her. 'Answer me.'

'Are you jealous of Rupert?' she asked him back, avoiding the question.

'You weren't engaged to Rupert,' he reminded her smoothly. 'Nor had you ever slept with him.'

She was glad that she wasn't looking at him, glad that she was staring in an unfocused manner at the stretch of lawns outside, because that meant that he couldn't see the play of strong emotion on her face.

'And if I had?' she asked quietly.

'That's a hypothetical question.'

'Pretend that it isn't.'

'All right.' He paused, and she wondered what was going through his mind. 'I can't be jealous of a man so obviously unsuited to you. If you had been engaged to him, it would only have been a matter of time before you came to your senses.' She felt rather than heard him turn away. 'Go and have your shower, Francesca, and then get some sleep.'

'Yes, I think I will.' She walked across to the bed, collected some clothes and headed for the bathroom, making sure that she didn't look at him *en route*. She felt drained—utterly drained.

She took a long shower, and when she emerged half an

hour later Oliver was no longer in the room. He had cleared the clothes from the bed, and she opened one of the drawers to find them neatly stacked away in separate little disordered bundles, which brought a reluctant smile to her lips. She cleared the lot out, folded them all, put them away again, then thought that she'd never get to sleep, but did as soon as her head hit the pillow.

Francesca opened her eyes to see Oliver standing over her in a pair of tan shorts and a T-shirt, and there was a wry smile on his mouth.

'How long have you been there?' she asked, sitting up and rubbing her eyes. 'Hovering. It's bad manners to hover.'

She felt better for the sleep. With a shock she realised that she had more than slept the clock round. She hadn't thought that she was particularly tired, but she must have been because she had been dead to the world for such a long time.

'You redid all my unpacking,' he said, lightly teasing, sitting on the bed next to her and depressing it with his weight. 'What was wrong with my efforts?'

'You're supposed to fold things neatly before you put them away,' she said, still feeling drowsy, and rather liking the way he was sitting there on the bed next to her when she didn't stop to think about it.

'Ah.' He nodded. 'Thank you for sharing that with me. I can honestly say that that will change the course of my life.'

She laughed, and then asked suspiciously, 'Why are you being so nice?'

'Isn't it easier than being nasty?' he quipped, which made her grin again, though warily. 'Now, come along,' he said, in the voice of someone hustling along a young child. 'The world is waiting outside for you—swimming pools, strange-looking plants, warm blue sea, white sand, lunch.'

'Lunch,' she said, slipping past him off the bed and heading towards the bathroom to change. 'I'm starved.'

She slammed the bathroom door behind her and had a bit of a do trying to get into her shorts, which were already too tight for her. She managed to zip them up, but only just, and she realised ruefully that tight waistbands were now more or less out of the question.

'Lunch on the beach, I thought,' he said as they left the room and headed outside, which seemed a wonderful idea to her. She stole a sideways glance at him from under her lashes and felt that familiar quickening of her senses.

He was right. There was no sense in being antagonistic towards one another, circling each other like adversaries. It was a great deal less effort and a great deal less wearing on the nerves to be pleasant.

'Sounds marvellous,' she said politely.

They walked through the gardens, past the turquoise swimming pool with its faithful cluster of semi-clad bodies stretched out on sun-loungers, past bright green hedges interspersed with brilliant red flowers, then down a few steps towards the beach—eight uneven, steep stone steps, and he turned around and held her hand, the gesture without any sexual undertones.

'There,' he said, turning to face her. 'What do you think?'

'Gorgeous, isn't it,' she said, looking from one end of the long beach to the other. The water was calm, almost without ripple, and blue—the sort of perfect aquamarine blue that you saw in photographs and suspected of being touched up here and there. There were a few sun-loungers with people lazily dozing on them, a few towels laid out on the white sand, but really it was virtually empty.

They walked towards a small round table, shaded underneath an umbrella which seemed to grow out of its centre like one of the bright flowers they had passed along the way. Behind them and a little to the right was a bar, with a barman incongruously kitted out in a red and black outfit, and a chef, also incongruously kitted out in a white chef's uniform and a chef's hat.

Francesca pulled one of the sun-loungers towards her, stretched out on it with a towel behind her head, closed her eyes and told Oliver that he could order her whatever he wanted to for lunch.

'I could eat a horse,' she said, wishing that she had brought a straw hat with her.

'I'll find out what kind they do,' he said seriously from above her, and she smiled. 'And cover your face with something,' he continued. 'You'll end up the colour of a lobster otherwise.' He tossed a newspaper over her, which made her yelp in surprise, but she took his advice and put it over her face so that it blocked out the sun.

She felt lazy and relaxed. It was the sun, of course. The warmth had the same effect as a glass of good wine. It made you feel mellow and easygoing. She lay perfectly still in her bikini, wondering if this was what a piece of bread felt like when it went into a toaster.

'Don't tell me the hormones are sending you to sleep again,' she heard him say in a lazy drawl.

'Sun and hormones are a bad combination,' she informed him, not bothering to take the newspaper off her face.

'Come on,' he said.

'Come on where?' She lifted the newspaper and peered

at him. He was pulling a lounger towards a clump of coconut trees.

'Somewhere a bit quieter,' he said, returning and waving her off the chair so that he could do the same with
hers. She followed him, clutching her bag with her suntan
cream and dark glasses.

'Food will be ready in about fifteen minutes,' he said,
pulling his T-shirt over his head. 'Two horse burgers and
chips.'

'Very healthy,' Francesca said, laughing. For some peculiar reason she felt suddenly very shy with him. 'We
don't want to start getting the baby into bad eating habits,
do we?'

Their eyes met and there was the briefest of silences—
a silence charged with all sorts of meanings, but mostly
with that bond between them that lay there inside her—
then he said in an oddly rough voice, 'We most certainly
don't. We can't have a baby screaming for a plate of cho-
lesterol the minute she comes out of the womb.'

Francesca smiled again, but she felt slightly unsteady.
For perhaps the first time she had thought of the baby not
as the catalyst to a host of problems but as a miracle growing inside her.

'Now lie down,' he ordered. 'On your stomach. While
you still can.'

'What are you going to do?'

He didn't answer. He squeezed some lotion out of one
of the tubes and she lay down, half closing her eyes as he
began to spread the suntan cream over her, his hands moving slowly and rhythmically—first her shoulders, then
along her back, along her waist, then down to her thighs
and legs. There was nothing sensual in what he was doing,
but a delicious sensation of contentment began spreading
through her.

The sun was making her fuzzy-headed, she thought languorously. It was so hot that even thinking of bristling at him for what he was doing made her feel tired.

'Right,' he said. 'Turn over.'

She wriggled onto her back and lay with her arms hanging down on either side. When she opened her eyes she could see the slight swell of her stomach—noticeable, she knew, only to her because she was looking for it—and his dark head, as he began spreading the lotion along her feet.

When his hands began their rhythmic movements along her thighs she knew that her breathing had quickened and that a moist awareness of him was spreading through her. She shifted so that her legs were closer together, but his hands were already working their way upwards over her stomach.

'You're beginning to put on some weight,' he said in a surprised voice. 'I hadn't noticed before.'

'It only shows because I'm wearing this,' Francesca answered self-consciously.

There was an intimacy now in what he was doing which she hadn't noticed there before. Or perhaps, she thought, she was imagining it. She looked towards the snack bar to see whether the chef was bustling his way across to them, but no one was coming, and in this secluded little area they were virtually unnoticed. Lower down, towards the sea, odd couples occasionally strolled by, but they hardly glanced in their direction.

'It suits you,' he said, circling her stomach with his hands, not looking at her face. 'Makes you look more rounded.'

The sun, pouring through the fronds of the palm trees above them, threw a dappled pattern over him which moved every time he did. Francesca could not tear her eyes away from the dance of sun and shade on his body. She felt spellbound.

He squirted some more cream onto the palm of his hand and worked his way over her ribcage.

'Your breasts are fuller too,' he remarked in the same slightly surprised voice.

Their eyes met, and in the peaceful rustle of the breeze she could hear her own breathing—soft and quick, like a gentle panting.

'Where on earth has our lunch gone?' she asked, in a desperate attempt to break the fascination he held her in, but she couldn't tear her eyes away from his, and it was no surprise when his hands moved to massage the roundness of her breasts, which were pushing against the flimsy material of the bikini top. She could feel her nipples harden and swell under his manipulation, aching for the rub of his fingers over them.

'Oliver…' she said, on a small, protesting sigh.

'Oliver, what?' he asked, smiling crookedly at her. 'Oliver, keep doing what you're doing? Oliver, I want you to make love to me?'

He trailed his finger along her cleavage and then outlined the throbbing contours of her nipples, taking his time.

'Oliver, stop,' she said weakly. She glanced across and sat up. 'Here comes our food.'

He laughed and followed the direction of her eyes. 'Saved by the bell,' he said lightly, mockingly, and she ignored him, waiting until their food had been deposited in front of them—two oversized beefburgers which smelt wonderful, enough chips to keep several people happy, and two tall, very cold, very colourful drinks, with a piece of pineapple wedged over the rim of each glass.

Her body still felt as though it was on fire, as though it

had been denied something which it had desperately craved.

She looked at him—a quick, veiled look—and wondered how she was ever going to fight this man who had been her lover, and was now her husband.

CHAPTER NINE

FRANCESCA knew precisely what was going on in Oliver's head. Or at least she felt that she could make a pretty accurate stab at it.

They were now husband and wife, and even though he wasn't in love with her he saw no reason why he shouldn't sleep with her. He had been at his most charming during the day—so charming, in fact, that it was difficult to believe that there was so much going on underneath that veneer of civilised pretence.

Because that, she felt, was what it was. This, she thought, was all very well for him, but what about her? She could see herself sinking ever deeper into the quagmire of her emotions if she let him make love to her, and then one day, probably in the not too distant future, when he had tired of making love to her, he would look at her and realise that, baby or no baby, he could never love her, and where would she be then?

He had told her that as far as he was concerned he intended their marriage to be much more than just a marriage on paper, but she knew with a sense of foreboding that no marriage could survive without the bond of love. It was a realisation that would come to him over time.

Being married to him would legitimise their baby, but it left her floundering in a frightening sort of limbo, too scared to commit even more than she already had, but equally scared that her feelings for him ran too deep for her to resist the pull of his attraction.

She felt torn between the devil and the deep blue sea,

not knowing what stand she could take, and too inexperienced even to begin to know how to tackle the problem.

If she were ten years older, she might have accumulated enough knowledge of the opposite sex along the way to enable her to treat their relationship with the same adult cynicism as he obviously treated it. But she wasn't. She could look back now and see how hopelessly naïve she had been to make her attraction to him so patently clear.

She had never slept with a man before, and her boyfriends had been playmates rather than anything serious. Temptation had been something she had never had to tackle, so when it had presented itself to her she had reacted in what she realised now to have been the worst possible way—she'd yielded.

Was it any wonder that Oliver couldn't see why there should be any physical barriers between them now? How was he to know that the reason she had made love to him in the first place had been because he meant so much to her—so much more than a transient, pleasurable flirtation?

She stood in the middle of the room, with the balmy ink-black night pressing against the windows, lost in thought, frowning, and she jumped when he said in a rough, mildly impatient voice, 'What's the matter with you now?'

She looked up to find him staring at her, and there was amused irritation on his face.

'Nothing's the matter,' she said hastily, which she feebly hoped might put an end to the conversation. 'I was just thinking,' she continued nervously.

He sighed and walked towards her, and she had to steel herself not to start backing away, or, worse, to rush towards him and bury herself in his arms.

'You,' he said, 'are the most moody, most bloody illogical person I have ever met in my entire life. Ten minutes ago you were laughing downstairs with me and now you're acting as though Judgement Day is just around the corner.' He put his hands on her shoulders and she froze.

There wasn't a bed downstairs, she wanted to inform him.

'Am I?' She tried a laugh. 'It's just that I seem to have developed a headache.'

'Oh, really?' he said drily. 'Surely you can do better than that, Francesca?'

'I have got a headache,' she insisted irritably. 'You talk about me reading hidden meanings behind everything you say. Well, why can't you take what I tell you at face value?'

'Because nothing you say is meant at face value,' he told her, idly massaging her shoulders with his hands. 'Nothing on a personal level at any rate. You can chat happily enough about books and music and the scenery, but the minute we get onto anything remotely personal your thought processes seem to take a nosedive.'

'I am not an irrational child, Oliver. I'm a woman carrying a baby!'

'Only here.' He touched her stomach with the flat palm of his hand and she felt herself shudder convulsively. He felt the quiver of her body and laughed under his breath. 'And here,' he murmured, dropping his hand further to feel the outline of her womanhood through her thin, floaty skirt.

She pulled away from him and snapped, 'This isn't a game, you know.'

'I know that.' His mouth tightened and he watched as she walked towards the window and began drawing the curtains together. She felt as though she had to do something—anything—to break the crackle of electricity that had sprung up between them. She wrapped her arms around herself and turned to face him, with her back pressed against the window-ledge.

'I can't sleep with you. I just can't,' she said, in a voice that wanted to be strong and firm, but had enough of a plea in it to make his brows snap together in a frown.

'Why not?' he asked bluntly.

'I wouldn't be able to face myself if I did; I'd hate myself,' Francesca answered quietly. 'I know you probably can't understand this. I know what I'm saying doesn't make a scrap of sense to you because we've already slept together, and it's a bit late in the day to start having scruples, especially since I'm carrying your baby, but—'

'But you slept with me once,' he grated harshly, 'and thought that everything would be wonderful afterwards and it wasn't. Is that it?'

'Something like that,' she admitted nervously. 'We both did things for the wrong reasons, maybe,' she floundered on, 'but that doesn't mean that we have to keep on committing the same mistake.'

'So, in other words, I'm to expect that our marriage won't be consummated?'

Put like that, she could see why he was beginning to show the stirrings of anger, but she maintained a long silence and refused to be browbeaten by that sharp mind of his, which could outmatch anything she could hope to come up with.

'You don't want me anyway, Oliver, not really. The woman you want is Imogen. You just happen to have landed yourself with me.'

'Leave Imogen out of this!' he roared, and she glanced quickly and apprehensively towards the door.

'Look at me,' he commanded, walking towards her, his

body swift and graceful. 'Look at me, in the face, and tell me that you're not attracted to me.'

He touched her face, and although there was anger in his voice his fingers were strangely tender, caressing. Her breathing quickened, and she looked down, concentrating her attention on the gleaming floorboards.

'That's hardly the point,' she muttered under her breath. 'Sleeping with someone just because you happen to be attracted to them is an animal instinct.'

'You make desire sound like a sin, Francesca. And we're not talking about sleeping with just anyone, are we? We're married now.'

'Unfortunately.'

He swore under his breath and said evenly, keeping his temper in check, 'I'm going to have a shower. I won't force you into anything, rest assured. You may be a desirable woman, Francesca, but your desirability has its limits.'

'Yes, I know that.' She could have told him that desire always had its limits. It burnt like a fire and then died out, because without love there was never enough to sustain it indefinitely.

She didn't look at him as he walked away towards the bathroom and shut the door quietly between them.

But as soon as the room was empty she quickly undressed and slipped on her nightgown—a Victorian affair of white lace which made her feel like a prim little virgin, but which she had had for years and was comfortable.

She was half-asleep when she felt him slip into the bed next to her, and she tensed immediately, wide awake now, wondering whether he would try and force his point home, try and make her admit to him just how much she wanted him, but he didn't. He turned away from her, and she waited for what seemed like ages, her eyes getting heavier and heavier until she was too tired to be tense, too tired to care whether his even breathing meant that he was asleep…

It was a little after three in the morning when she woke up. She knew that because the first thing she saw was the illuminated digital face of the travel clock on the little cabinet next to her bed.

Then she realised drowsily that the reason she had awakened was because Oliver's arm was slung over her body—a warm weight which she tried to wriggle free of. But wriggling only brought her closer to him. He was pressed against her with her back curved against his chest. She moved again and his arm tightened around her, but it was a reflex reaction, she knew, because his breathing was still deep and regular, and very gradually she turned around to face him so that she could free herself of the inviting pressure of his body.

It was only when she looked up that she saw that his eyes were open and he was looking at her, his face almost invisible in the darkness in the bedroom.

She gasped in shock and said unsteadily, 'You're awake.' Brilliant observation, she thought crossly to herself.

'So I am,' he said, moving his arm and preparing to turn away from her.

'It's cold in here,' she said, and immediately wondered why she was prolonging a conversation at three in the morning.

'Would you like me to switch the air-conditioning off?' Oliver asked, inclining his body slightly so that he was facing her once again, his voice polite.

'No. It'll get too hot, and I don't want to have the windows open. The mosquitoes can be vicious over here.'

'OK.'

'Did you bring any insect repellent?'

'No. Why are we having this conversation at this ridiculous hour of the morning?'

She didn't know. She just knew that she had liked the feel of his body next to hers and that she wanted to have the weight of it against her again. It was comforting.

'It wasn't a conversation, it was a simple question.'

'Well, this is an extremely odd time to start a question-and-answer game,' he replied. 'So goodnight. If I get too close to you again just shove me off.' His voice was cool but held no anger.

'Oliver...'

'What is it now?'

I wish I knew, she thought. I want you, she thought. I don't care about tomorrow, she thought; I just know that I can't spend my nights with you without touching that magnificent body of yours, without feeding my addiction.

She reached out and ran her hand along his side, realising with heightened excitement that he wasn't wearing anything, and she felt him stiffen under the slight caress.

He caught her hand in his and said coldly, 'Now is not the time for games like this.'

'I'm not playing a game,' she said huskily.

'You don't know what you're doing. One minute you're fighting me tooth and nail, and the next minute you want me to make love to you. It won't do, Francesca. I'm not some damned boy who's going to patiently indulge your whims.'

'No, you're not a boy,' she whispered unsteadily. She wriggled a bit closer and placed her mouth over his, running her tongue along his lips, darting it inside his mouth, but he didn't respond. He tightened his grip on her and she drew back.

'What's happened to all this self-hatred you claimed

you would feel if you laid a hand on me?' he asked icily, and she didn't answer. He let her go. 'Have you decided in the warmth of a bed, with darkness all around, that you can live with yourself after all?' There was enough of a sneer in his voice to bring the tears glistening to her eyes.

'I didn't think about it at all,' she said.

'That's your problem, though, isn't it?'

She turned away from him in blind anger and slipped off the bed.

She really hadn't thought anything except that she wanted him quite desperately, that she needed to reach out and touch him, and his rejection was like a slap in the face. It hurt.

'Where are you going, dammit?' He sat up, expecting her to vanish into the bathroom, no doubt, she thought, but she suddenly needed time to get her thoughts in order.

She felt utterly confused, like someone who had been whirling around on a roller coaster and now felt the need to step off so that her mind could catch up with her body.

She knew what she had told him, but logic and reason had played no part in the shared intimacy of a darkened bedroom. She wanted to protect herself, but was there any point in the end? Was there any point in playing the martyr, in waiting for the inevitable axe to fall on their relationship? Was the dubious benefit of knowing that he had no idea of how she really felt really worth the misery of denying herself the one thing that could bring her happiness, even if it was only temporary happiness?

The questions soared through her mind, like a jigsaw puzzle that had been splintered into a thousand pieces. She felt that if only she could put the pieces together she could arrive at a solution.

'I need to think,' she said in a high voice, and he only

began to get out of bed when he realised that she was
leaving the room.

She ran, imagining him as he sprinted towards the light
switch and began chaotically throwing on some clothes,
and her imagination made her run faster, through the reception area, which was quiet and empty, out into the gardens and down towards the beach.

Outside it was warm, the air heavy, and around her she
picked up all the small sounds of the night life—crickets,
frogs, insects which she could not put a name to but which
called to each other in the night from bush to bush.

She looked around and saw nothing, and ran faster, her
legs flying over the grass and her white nightgown billow-
ing around her. The long nightdress which had seemed
protective in the dangerous confines of the bedroom now
seemed positively useless, and she gathered up the bottom,
bunching the cloth in her fist.

In the pitch-blackness of the night she saw the strip of
sea and headed towards it, knowing that the beach would
give her the silence she needed to think things through.

She took one last look behind her, and saw Oliver racing
towards her—a silent, swift-moving figure, covering the
distance between them like an arrow. She knew that he
would have seen her as well, but he didn't call out. It
seemed somehow inappropriate to shout into the stillness
of the night.

Francesca turned round, stepped forward, and felt herself falling down the stone steps in what appeared to be
an agony of slow motion.

In daylight the steps had been uneven and steep. At
night they were treacherous.

She lay at the bottom in a heap, unable to move, and
closed her eyes, waiting for Oliver to arrive. It didn't take
him long. When she opened her eyes she looked up to see

him towering at the top of the steps, then he sprinted down to her.

'Are you all right?' he asked, his voice urgent. He tried to help her up and she gave a little moan of pain.

'I can't move,' she whispered.

'You little fool. What did you think you were doing, running off like that? Where do you hurt? Is it your leg? Have you twisted your ankle?' He didn't wait for her to answer. He scooped her up very gently, like a child, and slowly carried her up the steps back towards the hotel.

She closed her eyes and clung to him, hearing voices in a blur. He was talking to someone, his voice quick and commanding.

'We're going to get you to a doctor,' he said to her. 'Don't worry, you're going to be all right.'

'I didn't see the steps,' Francesca whimpered. 'I knew they were there, but I lost my footing on the top one and there was nothing to hold onto.'

He carried her across to a sofa in the reception area and sat down, still cradling her.

'I'll be all right,' she told him in a weak voice. 'There's no need to get a doctor out. It can wait until the morning.' She felt dreadful, bruised all over, but, more than that, there was a wrenching ache in her stomach, and her mind veered away from what that might mean.

'Listen to me, Francesca,' he said, gently and firmly. 'You're bleeding very slightly, and it won't wait until the morning. I've sent the receptionist off to get the hotel doctor. He only lives about fifteen minutes away from here. He'll be here shortly.'

'What do you mean, I'm bleeding?' She felt tears welling up into her eyes and she tried to sit up, but he held her against him.

'Francesca,' he said after a while, with a rough edge to his voice, 'I...I'm sorry. Dammit, this is all my fault.'

She opened her eyes to look at him. 'I shouldn't have run off like that,' she mumbled, and he put his finger over her lips, but although his face was as controlled as ever his finger trembled slightly.

The doctor arrived, took one look at her and told Oliver to follow him. He had a small but comprehensive office on the ground floor and they walked there in silence.

Through Oliver's shirt she could hear the beating of his heart—a rapid thud against her ears—and she had an overpowering desire to stay where she was, held close against him, because there was something so strong and reassuring about him. She felt safe. Ironic, she thought. It was thanks to him that her life was in the mess that it was, but right now she knew that no one could give her the comfort that he did.

'So what happened here, young lady?' the doctor asked, indicating to Oliver where to put her down.

Francesca looked at the small, wiry man, with his dark, intelligent face and said, 'I'm very sorry to have got you out of bed at this hour in the morning.'

'I wouldn't have become a doctor if I wasn't prepared for these sorts of things,' he said, his eyes busily registering her bruises while his fingers gently pressed her body.

'I understand you're pregnant,' he said, and she nodded. 'I'll want to examine you to make sure that everything is OK.' He looked at Oliver. 'You'll stay?' he asked, in a voice that implied that his presence in the room was taken for granted, and Oliver nodded quietly, holding her hand, brushing her hair away from her face.

She clung to his hand. Things seemed to have happened so quickly. One minute they were in the bedroom, and she was feeling that urgent, restless need to silence the thoughts in her head which were clamouring and driving her mad, and the next minute she was falling down those steps, feeling every little bump along the way, powerless to do anything to protect herself.

It hadn't been at all like tripping down a staircase. She had fallen down stairs once before, when she was fifteen. She had been at school, looking back over her shoulder, laughing, saying something to the girl behind her, and she had missed her footing and fallen, but it hadn't been serious because she had been able to hang onto the banister as soon as her legs gave way.

As soon as she had felt herself falling down the steps to the beach she had known that she had no option but to continue falling until she reached the bottom.

The doctor was asking her questions and she answered them, but listlessly. She felt as though she had exhausted her reserves of energy. Eventually, he straightened up and his face was serious.

'You've had an awkward fall, young lady. No broken bones, which is good, but you're bleeding and there's some possibility that you might miscarry this baby.'

It was what she had been dreading. Hearing your suspicions put into words was always awful because it made them real—it took away the little seed of hope that perhaps you were wrong, that perhaps you were imagining it all. She groaned and squeezed her eyes tightly shut.

She heard Oliver ask sharply, 'What do you mean a *possibility*? Can't you be more certain than that?'

Francesca wished that she could close her ears to what they were saying. She didn't want to hear. She wanted to be an ostrich and stick her head in the sand, but she couldn't. All she could hear was their voices, obliterating everything else.

'Normally a fall in pregnancy is nothing to worry

about,' the doctor was saying in a detached but sympathetic voice. 'The baby is well cushioned inside the amniotic sac, but sometimes, if the fall is awkward, it can precipitate a miscarriage. Your wife is bleeding, but we won't know anything for sure until she's had a scan.'

'Now,' Oliver said harshly. 'We want a scan now, this instant.'

The doctor said gently, 'It's impossible. I will arrange for you to take her to the hospital first thing in the morning.' He began packing his little black bag. Doctors always carried little black bags, she thought inconsequentially. Why not red, or green? Or purple?

He wrote on a piece of paper and handed it to Oliver.

'You'll see a Dr Girot,' he said. 'I'll call him so that he knows to expect you. In the meantime—' he looked at Francesca and gave her arm a small, reassuring squeeze '—no more night-time saunters to the beach, young lady. You go up to your bedroom and stay put. I've left my number with your good husband here; he can call me any time if you're worried, it's in the good Lord's hands now.'

It was nearly five by the time they got back up to the bedroom. Dawn was beginning to glimmer over the horizon. In three hours' time the hotel would be bustling once again with tourists going in and out, preparing themselves for another hard day of doing absolutely nothing under the baking hot sun.

Oliver placed her on the bed and she watched him, not quite knowing what to say. He stripped off his shirt, which had been haphazardly buttoned, and tossed it onto the chair by the dressing-table, then he sat on the bed next to her with an unreadable expression on his face.

'You've got to try and get some sleep, Francesca,' he said.

'I can't. How can I sleep?'

The doctor had given her two mild painkillers for her bruises, which felt sore and throbbing.

'I was a fool,' she said dully. 'You're right. I don't think before I act. Nobody else—' Imogen, for instance, she thought, with a twinge of pain '—would have rushed out of the room and ended up tripping down eight steps to the beach.'

'Stop whipping yourself. It's done. We just have to wait and see what happens in the morning.'

'If I lose this baby, it'll never be done for me.' She fiddled with her fingers, anxiously clasping and unclasping them, and he reached out and placed his hand over hers, stilling the worried little movements.

'Don't think the worst,' he said gruffly, but she could tell from the tone of his voice that he had already thought of that outcome himself.

'I have to. We both do.' She raised her eyes and looked at him evenly. 'We got married for the sake of the baby, and if there's no baby...' She paused because she knew that if she carried on her voice would break. 'If there's no baby,' she continued, taking a deep breath, 'then what's the point of the marriage?'

He didn't say a word. He stood up and prowled through the room, his hands thrust into his pockets—a tall, commanding, half-naked figure who looked as though he belonged to myth and not reality.

'I don't deal in hypotheses,' he said finally, stopping at the foot of the bed and staring at her intently.

'We can't pretend that it's not a possibility. You always tell me that I don't like facing unpleasantness, and I suppose you're right. I haven't got your strength.'

'You underestimate yourself.'

'Do I?' She smiled sadly. 'I don't think so. I feel as though I'm growing up at long last. As though I've spent my life inside a cocoon, and now I'm slowly having to break out of it.'

'You make that sound like a tragic inevitability,' he said, returning to sit on the bed next to her once again. 'There's nothing wrong with living in a cocoon.'

'Don't humour me, Oliver.'

'When I was young,' he said, 'I sometimes used to wonder what it would be like not to have to struggle for everything. I used to wonder about you sometimes.'

'About me?'

'You. I knew about you from my mother. I knew when you were born. I wondered what sort of life you led on the other side of the tracks.'

'A very different one from yours,' she said quietly. She wished that she had known him then. She wished that she could have been a fly on the wall and watched him as he grew from boy to man. Had he always had that supreme self-confidence, or had necessity given birth to it as he'd got older? A bit of both, she suspected. He had been born to succeed, with or without a moneyed background.

'We came from different worlds, Oliver, and that's where we must return. If the baby is lost there's nothing at all to keep us together.' She had to turn away when she said that because if she hadn't she would have burst into tears.

'You can have your freedom whatever happens,' he said abruptly, standing up again and walking restlessly across the floor, as though the energy in him couldn't be confined.

'I can?' There was no hope there in her voice, no exultation at this, what she had wanted all along, just despair at the thought that her freedom meant nothing to her without him near. He misread her question, though, because when he spoke his voice was cool but with an underlying savagery.

'Will you have a better rest now?' he asked, raking his fingers through his hair. 'Go to sleep, Francesca,' he said. 'We have to be at the hospital for nine, and that's less than four hours away. I'm going out for a swim.'

'A swim?'

'That's right.' His mouth twisted. 'You'll fall asleep quicker if I'm not in the bed next to you.'

'But you must be tired as well,' she protested, and he gave her a crooked, mirthless smile.

'You'd be surprised how easy it is to get used to having next to no sleep. I've spent my life working so hard that sleep is a pastime that I can usually take or leave.' He stood at the door and said as an afterthought, 'What were you doing while I was working my way up and doing without sleep?'

'Sleeping, I should think.'

He laughed and looked at her, and she thought for a split second that he was going to add something more, but he just said, 'I'll be back shortly. Get some rest.'

Then he was gone, and all semblance of laughter died from her face. She lay back against the pillows with her hands on her stomach and stared upwards at the ceiling.

There was the hurdle of the scan to get over, but all in all she decided that she should be feeling relieved. All that agonising over whether she had done the right thing in accepting his proposal of marriage, all that worry at the prospect of living with a man who didn't and couldn't return her love—it was gone now. She was free. She could return to England without the thought of that dark presence filling her life until she could stand it no longer.

But she wasn't relieved. She lay there, trying to imagine a life without Oliver Kemp in it, and she couldn't. It was as though he had embedded himself deep inside her—too deep for her to prise him out.

She finally drifted into a sleep of sorts, and was awakened by Oliver shaking her by her shoulder and telling her that it was time to get up. She hadn't heard him enter the room, but he must have been there for a while because he had showered and changed into a pair of trousers and a striped short-sleeved shirt.

'I must have a shower,' she told him.

'Be quick, then. The taxi arrives in fifteen minutes.'

So she hurriedly showered, noticing that she was still bleeding and already preparing herself mentally for what that meant. She wished that the hotel doctor, who had seemed so kind and efficient, was going to be there.

'Come on,' Oliver called through the door, and she hastily plaited her hair back and put on a light denim dress.

'Feeling better?' he asked as she joined him in the bedroom and grabbed her bag from the chair, and she shook her head.

'I'm dreading this,' she replied honestly. 'I'm not strong enough for this.'

'I'm strong enough for the both of us,' he murmured almost inaudibly, taking her hand and ushering her out of the room and out towards the taxi which was waiting downstairs.

When they arrived they found that the hospital was small, but they were efficiently shown through to the waiting room, by which time Francesca's nervousness was almost palpable.

There was a stack of outdated magazines on the table next to her, and she idly picked one up and began flicking through it, hardly seeing the print at all, very much aware of Oliver sitting next to her, and wondering what he was thinking.

The room was only half-full. Two heavily pregnant women sat opposite her, talking in their low, lilting accents, and next to them was a young girl who couldn't have been more than fifteen and who looked as though she should have been in school instead of in the maternity wing of a hospital.

When the doctor called her name Francesca automatically took Oliver's hand, which seemed to be waiting for her, and they went into the darkened cubicle.

'Relax,' the doctor told her. 'Legs flat on the bed, please. No need to be scared; this isn't going to hurt.'

He swivelled the machine round so that she and Oliver could both see it, and there it was. Fuzzy, tiny, but moving vigorously, and every single word the doctor said from then on was lost, because her whole mind seemed to have been taken over by the image on the screen in front of her. Her baby. Their baby.

'Looks fine,' the doctor said, not feeling the miracle that was unfolding underneath his blunt-headed instrument; it was just another scan in a morning full of them.

'I won't lose it?' she asked timidly, and he smiled at her for the first time.

'Shouldn't think so. But I'd try and stop throwing myself down steps, if I were you.'

Outside, fifteen minutes later, the sun was beating down. The taxi-driver had been instructed to wait, however long it took, and he was fanning himself with a newspaper, his windows rolled down.

Francesca looked around her. The world, she thought, was suddenly a wonderful place.

'Francesca,' Oliver said, once they were inside the taxi, 'we have to talk.'

CHAPTER TEN

BUT they didn't talk. Not inside the taxi. They travelled the distance in silence. Francesca stared out the window and saw the bright green trees, the bright blue sky, the picture-postcard prettiness of the scenery, but her thoughts were travelling round slowly in her head.

She knew what Oliver wanted to talk about—arrangements. They would have to discuss how the marriage was going to be annulled. She had no idea how one went about dissolving a marriage which had not even survived the honeymoon, but she didn't think that it would be difficult. A few forms to sign, perhaps, and then it would all be over barely before it had started.

Except, she thought, it had started long ago. It had started at the very moment that she had walked into that office—the very moment that she had set eyes on Oliver Kemp and something deep inside her had been ignited. And it would carry on too—long, long after a piece of paper told her that it no longer existed.

The taxi travelled slowly back to the hotel, and in the back seat of the car the distance between them seemed like a yawning chasm. Oliver was as preoccupied with his thoughts as she was with hers.

When the taxi-driver finally stopped outside the hotel and they got out she hovered indecisively by the car, waiting for Oliver, not knowing what she should do now.

'There's a bar overlooking the pool,' he said, not looking directly at her but taking her elbow, as though he thought that she might fall down without the support, although in fact she felt fine physically. The reassurance of the scan had given her a stamina that had not been there earlier on.

They walked to the bar, sat down at a small round table, and when their drinks had been brought to them she said in a rush, because she wanted to get it off her chest, 'I know what you want to discuss—arrangements for ending this and for visiting the baby once it's been born. Can't we leave it until we get back to England, though?'

It seemed horribly incongruous to be discussing things like that with the sun beating down, with lazy couples lounging by the pool, with the sound of the sea a distant, lapping noise, with birds flitting from flower to flower. The worst thing about beauty was that it made ugly things seem so much uglier.

Oliver didn't answer. He stood up, as though his restless energy needed some kind of release, and leaned against the veranda railing, staring down at the pool below. Then he turned to her, with his back against the railing, and said harshly, 'I'm not waiting until we get back to England. I can't.' His voice was flat and aggressive.

He had ordered a glass of fruit juice and he took a long sip, then carefully placed it on the table in front of him. She had ordered some variety of fruit cocktail, which had arrived complete with pieces of fruit, a miniature umbrella—the sort that children adored—and a cocktail stirrer, so she now stirred, staring down into the glass. She wished that he would sit down. When he loomed over her like that he made her nervous.

'Look,' he said abruptly, 'I can't talk here.' He picked up the glass again and drained the contents, and when she raised her eyes to his it was with more curiosity than nervousness.

There was something about his manner—something

edgy and slightly defensive which she couldn't quite put her finger on.

'But—' she began.

'Let's go for a walk on the beach.'

'In these shoes?'

She stuck one sandal-clad foot out and he snarled roughly, 'Leave the damn shoes by one of the tables on the beach.'

'There's no need to shout,' she snapped, standing up.

He muttered darkly, under his breath, 'Sometimes I think it's the only way to get through to you.'

'Thanks a lot! Any more compliments before we go?'

'I blame you,' he said almost inaudibly, moving off while she hurried to keep pace with his long strides. 'You always manage to turn me into someone I can hardly recognise.'

'So it's all my fault now, is it?' she threw at him. 'Will you stop running?' A couple who had been passing them from the beach to the hotel looked round at her tone of voice, and out of the corner of her eyes she saw the man smile—a sympathetic, amused smile that seemed to say, Women—aren't they always the same? Take them on an expensive holiday and they still manage to find something to shout about.

She lowered her voice and said, catching up with him, 'I'm not racing behind you on the beach. I don't see why we couldn't just stay at the bar and thrash this out, since you insist that it can't possibly wait until we get back to England.'

He didn't answer. He walked across to one of the umbrella-shaded beach tables and kicked off his shoes, then he rolled up his jeans a few times, stripped off his shirt and looked at her.

That, she thought, was another thing she wished he

wouldn't do—look at her. She could never get her thoughts straight when he focused those amazing light eyes on her. She removed her shoes, then walked alongside him with her hands clasped behind her back.

It was a very long beach. Just around the area of the bar, and by the sun-loungers, there were clumps of people lying on loungers or on towels on the sand, and a few in the water, but further along the beach was empty—an endless strip of unexplored white sand.

She wondered vaguely why people seemed to group themselves together on a beach when there was enough of it to spread themselves out, to lose themselves almost. Did they feel more secure if there were other people close by?

Oliver clearly did not believe in the group mentality. He was walking towards the far end of the beach, and she fell into step with him, unwilling to break the silence—not because she had nothing to say but because there was an absorbed tension in his body, in the tautness of his muscles.

'I told you that everything would be all right with the baby, didn't I?' he said, in an accusing, argumentative voice, and she looked at him from under her lashes.

'Why do you want to fight with me?' she asked. 'Do we have to? Can't we sort this all out in a civilised manner?'

'No, we cannot!'

They were far away now from the sun lizards, whose prostrate brown bodies were dots in the distance. He went across to a log and sat down, then he began doodling on the white sand with a thin twig.

It brought back a rush of memories for her—memories of a holiday in the sun with her father, when she had spent hours doing exactly the same thing—drawing on the sand, fascinated at the thought that everything she drew would be obliterated by the wash of the water.

Oliver, she suddenly thought, would make a wonderful father. She closed her mind to that anguished realisation and sat next to him on the log, prodding her toes into the warm sand and making a little mound like a molehill, which she promptly flattened only to start again.

'My father will be able to recommend a good lawyer…' she began, faltering.

'There will be no lawyer,' he bit out harshly, with his face averted from her.

'You mean that we'll do it all ourselves?' She frowned and looked across to him, and he met her eyes unwaveringly.

'I don't mean anything of the sort, Francesca,' he said grimly, and when she continued to stare at him uncomprehendingly he went on, 'Are you completely stupid? Do I have to spell it out for you? There will be no lawyer because there will be no divorce. Do you understand me now or do you want me to put it in writing?'

'But you said—'

'I know what I said! I'm not senile! But I've changed my mind. No divorce, Francesca.'

'Why? Because the baby is all right?' Tears stung the back of her eyes and she glared at him.

'Because,' he said, and a deep colour rose to his face, 'you belong to me and I have no intention of letting you go. Ever. Do you get my meaning? If you want a divorce, I'll fight you and you'll lose.'

'Why?' she whispered. 'Is it because Rupert took Imogen away from you? Is that it?'

He laughed—a harsh, grating sound. 'My God, woman. What Rupert and Imogen do is irrelevant.'

'Is it?' Francesca asked quietly. 'How can it be when you still love her?'

He shot her an incredulous look. 'Love her? Imogen? What I felt for Imogen might have been a hundred things, but it was never love.'

She felt as though someone had lifted her up and was swirling her around. 'Why were you planning to marry her, then?' she asked, dragging herself back down, reminding herself that the situation between them had hardly altered. 'Because you detested her?'

'Because,' he muttered, 'I was a fool—a blind, stupid fool who thought that fondness and superficial similarities provided sufficient grounds on which to base a lifelong commitment.' The challenge was there in his voice, as if he wanted her to dispute what he was saying so that he could argue with her.

How could she when she was too busy struggling to stifle the little seed of elation which was growing steadily inside her?

'And you think a baby provides those grounds?' she asked, and his voice, when he replied, was sober.

'No.'

The seed was rapidly growing into a plant. What was he trying to say to her now? It was as though wild hope was dragging her along to the answer, but before she could get there she kept bumping into an invisible wall which wouldn't allow her entry.

'What do you want me to say, Francesca?' he said tersely. He flung the twig away from him and she watched it scud across the sand to rest next to a coconut which had fallen from a tree. She felt a bit like that twig—whirling through space for a while before the inevitable bump back to earth. Reality was always just round the corner, she reminded herself sternly, waiting to trip you up.

For a while, once, when she had made love to him, when she had let her emotions dictate her responses, she had known what it was like to fly high above the clouds, but that hadn't lasted, had it?

'I just want you to make sense,' she told him.

'How can I make sense to you when I can't even make sense to myself?' he muttered. He stood up, stared out towards the sea, then sat back down, closer to her this time. 'You're hardly the type of woman I've been attracted to in the past,' he said roughly, and she went red with hurt anger.

'I know; you've already aired your thoughts on the subject!'

'You grew up in the lap of luxury. You've never known want or need or driving ambition. You've had life cushioned for you.'

'That was not my fault! I never asked to be brought into this world with a silver spoon in my mouth!'

'Oh, sure, you're a beautiful woman,' he went on, ignoring her. 'I can imagine that hundreds of men—boys, dammit, if that Thompson character is anything to go by—must have been enslaved by you.'

'Oh, thousands!' she snapped, knowing that she shouldn't let herself be rattled by what he was saying, or what he had said before in the past.

'But I thought I would be supremely immune to your brand of charm.' He looked at her then, and there was a savage fire in his eyes that sent a spark of flame leaping through her. She didn't dare say anything. It was as if time stood still, as if the earth had stopped revolving on its axis.

'I was wrong,' he said, catching her chin in his hand as though he was afraid that she might look away. 'When you started working for me I found myself stealing looks at you, and I told myself that it was because I needed to keep an eye on you, needed to see for myself whether you really lived up to the potential you'd displayed at that interview, but after a while I had to face the truth. I wanted to look at you because I was attracted to you. More every day.'

'You were?' Her eyes widened. 'You never showed it,' she whispered.

'I didn't want to admit it to myself, never mind admit it to you. I was engaged to a woman I thought was on my wavelength, then you walked into my life and suddenly nothing made sense any more. I kept telling myself that you weren't my kind of woman, but I was bewitched by you, Francesca.

'When I came round to your flat that night with the champagne it had nothing to do with being thoughtful. I just needed to see you, and then... God, when you invited me into your bed, when you undressed for me you were the most beautiful creature I had ever laid eyes on.' His face darkened at the memory and she felt a stab of pleasure course through her.

'You walked away,' she reminded him.

'I had to. You'd had too much to drink, but also I just needed to think, to try and sort out what the hell was happening to me. It was blessed relief when Imogen got herself involved with the Thompson fellow.'

She raised her hand and brushed his face with her fingers, and he caught her hand in his, opening it so that he could kiss her palm.

'I came back to you, and when I did I knew that I had to have you. I wanted you like I had never wanted anyone in my life before. I wanted to feel you against me; I wanted to possess you, body and mind. And just for an instant I thought that I had, but then everything started going wrong. I went abroad, and while I was there you started sounding cooler and cooler down the telephone, and it was driving me crazy.'

'I had no choice,' Francesca said quietly, even though there was a burning happiness inside her that made her want to grin and shout and laugh. 'I found out that I was pregnant. I also started thinking that the only reason you'd made love to me was because the woman you really wanted was no longer available.'

'How could you think that?' he asked. 'How could that even occur to you when it's you I love?'

Of course, she had guessed what he was saying in that roundabout, tortured fashion of his, but now his admission that he loved her spread through her like a fever, and she smiled and briefly closed her eyes.

'My darling,' she whispered, looking at him, her eyes bright. 'My darling Oliver. And I thought that I was suffering alone. Why do you think I started pulling back from you? Because I loved you; because I couldn't bear the thought that you would never return the feeling.'

He leaned forward and kissed her, his mouth hard and hungry, and she wrapped her arms around his neck, laughing as they rolled onto the sand. She traced the outline of his spine with her fingers and he groaned.

'You sent me to hell,' he murmured. 'I got back to a woman I thought I could tempt into my trap, only to find that she'd recognised the bait and was now running off in the opposite direction. When I realised that you were pregnant I also realised that the baby was my passport back to you. I made sure that you were married to me before you had time to think too hard about it, and I know that I used every legitimate trick in the book to get what I wanted.'

'Apology accepted,' she said happily, and he raised his feverish eyes to hers.

'Who's apologising? Tell me, Francesca; tell me that

you love me. Say it over and over again. It's your punishment for putting me through what I've been through.'

'I love you, Oliver Kemp,' she murmured obligingly, and she moaned as he pushed his hand under the opening of her dress to fondle the swell of her breasts.

'You don't know how I've longed to hear you say that. When you threw that accusation at me—that I'd hired Helen to take over from you behind your back—I could sense jealousy, and, God, how I wanted you to admit it, to tell me that you were madly jealous, because I would have been able to read what I wanted to in that.'

'I *was* jealous,' Francesca confessed. It seemed such a long time ago. 'I hated her when she said that she'd got my job.'

'Helen Scott will have to watch her step very carefully in the future,' he said grimly, then his features relaxed into a smile. 'Although she'll get her own due reward when my wife meets me at work to join me for lunch.'

'She'll hate that,' Francesca answered, but she felt so happy that it was impossible to harbour any bad feeling towards anyone.

'You can't imagine what I felt when I thought that you might lose the baby,' he said softly into her ear, 'when you told me that without the baby there was no need for a marriage.'

'You agreed!'

'Pride made me agree, but before the words were even out I knew that I couldn't let you go.'

She laughed with delight and he nudged her head back, kissing her neck, tugging open the remaining buttons on her dress so that he could expose an aching breast. His tongue flicked out and he licked the hard outline of her nipple, and she whimpered, wanting more.

'You're so different,' he said, looking up at her, and she

smiled at him—a dreamy, contented little smile; a smile that no longer struggled to hide the love beneath it. 'The more I saw you, the more I got to know you, and the more I saw every one of those differences as a revelation. I had no idea how grey my life had been until you came along; then it was like having a blast of sun in a dark, shuttered place. To start with I tried to ignore it, then I was suspicious, but eventually I couldn't hide from the truth. Life without you is meaningless.'

'Good.' She sighed as his hand caressed her leg, her stomach, her breasts.

How could she ever have thought that she would never be happy? How could she have seen herself in a tunnel without end? They said that the darkest hour was always just before the dawn, but she would never have believed that.

She looked at the tender, masculine face so close to hers, and knew that from this perfect moment on the life that was growing inside her would be born into love and happiness. The way it should be.

Diana Hamilton is a true romantic and fell in love with her husband at first sight. They still live in the fairytale Tudor house where they raised their three children. Now the idyll is shared with eight rescued cats and a puppy. But despite an often chaotic lifestyle, ever since she learned to read and write Diana has had her nose in a book—either reading or writing one—and plans to go on doing just that for a very long time to come.

NEVER A BRIDE
by
Diana Hamilton

CHAPTER ONE

'I'M AT the London apartment, so it won't be long before I can see you. Yes, Jake's away… No, no I haven't told him. We'll discuss it when I see you. Must go now, darling, but see you soon, I promise.' Claire Winter replaced the receiver, a tender smile softening the classical loveliness of her features before she felt her scalp tingle with warning, felt the skin on her face go stiff. She slowly turned on the silk brocade-covered sofa, her aquamarine eyes shocked by the accuracy of her precognition as they homed in on Jake's narrowed grey gaze.

'You're in Rome,' she babbled, and immediately hated herself for her inaccurate inanity, despised herself even more when her stupid remark gave him the excuse to hitch up one dark sardonic brow and drawl mockingly,

'Kind of you to put me right. I actually thought I was in Mayfair.'

She watched him lever himself away from the door-frame where he'd been leaning, listening… How much of her telephone conversation had he heard…? And God, but he was beautiful. Every time she looked at him she was struck anew by his male magnificence. He was the dark stranger who haunted every woman's secret dreams, a fantasy of masculine perfection come to life.

And he knew it. He had more sex appeal than was good for him, so his arrogance over the opposite sex was understandable. Every woman he met drooled over him, fell at his feet. Even her own mother looked at him with a definite sparkle in her eyes and she, more than most, had good reason to be wary of anything in trousers. He had the looks, the wealth, the power and personality to turn the sanest woman's head.

She was firmly on her feet now, perfectly in control, presenting the image he expected—no, demanded. Cool, expensive, exquisitely groomed, her silky black hair cut stylishly short, the black and white heavy silk two-piece she was wearing emphasising the elegant lines of her tall, slender body.

'I didn't expect you for at least another couple of days.' She schooled her voice to coolness but couldn't disguise the trace of accusation; it came through despite her best efforts and Jake picked it up, obviously, because he said drily,

'So I gathered. Who were you phoning? Or is that a question a husband shouldn't ask his wife?'

'Liz,' she answered, perhaps too quickly. Something made his narrowed grey eyes glitter. He didn't believe she'd been talking to her mother.

Watching him walk further into the beautiful main room of their London apartment, shedding the jacket of his exquisitely tailored grey suit, she lifted her chin, her eyes stubborn, giving no hint of the alarm she felt at the way her heart was behaving so unusually. It was thundering around inside her chest, frightening her.

'And how is she? Well?' He hooked a finger in the knot of his tie and dragged it away from the collar of his crisp white shirt. 'I find myself with two unexpectedly free days. Perhaps we should visit her? I could persuade her to divulge whatever it is you haven't been able to bring yourself to tell me yet.'

So he had heard. And the unmasked derision in the look he sent her made her face turn to fire. And she felt too disoriented to invent something on the spur of the moment so she chose to attack, her slender fingers reaching unerringly for the folded newspaper on the rosewood coffee-table. She had opened it, spreading the newsprint on her lap far too many times throughout this long, quiet Sunday, knowing she shouldn't yet unable to prevent it, like probing an aching tooth with her tongue.

The paper fell open to the right page, out of habit, she supposed, her eyes darkening as the now all too familiar photograph of her husband leapt out of the grey print, his arms around a woman who was achingly, unfairly beautiful.

'Stripping assets of the romantic kind?' The letters of the caption danced beneath Claire's eyes. 'Multimillionaire Jake Winter caught playing away from home with the darling of Roman society, the irresistible Principessa Lorella Giancetti.'

'The paparazzi must have had a field day,' she clipped, flicking the photograph with a pearly oval fingernail, her eyes frowning as she watched a tiny smile curl at the corners of his hard, beautiful mouth while he scanned the page, anger battering at the wall of her chest.

'Jealous, Claire?' Mocking grey eyes held hers for a second before lowering, drifting down over her elegantly clad body, the mockery still to be glimpsed, though shadowed by thickly tangled black lashes, because he was comparing her slender, definitely understated curves with the voluptuous ripeness of the *principessa*'s body which was almost flowing out of the expensive skimpiness of the glamorous evening dress she'd been pictured wearing.

'No.' She made the denial both mentally and verbally. 'Disappointed. Before we married we made certain commitments. One of which, if I remember correctly, promised complete discretion in the possible area of extra-marital affairs. This—' she flicked the newsprint again '—can't, by any stretch of the imagination, be called discreet.'

'No.' His frown was sudden and ferocious as he agreed. 'I apologise.' He tossed the paper aside, rocking back on his heels, the whippy muscles of his long, lean body held together with a tension that had to be down to the unpalatable fact of discovery, Claire decided with weary cynicism as she set about collecting his discarded jacket and tie, settling into mundane domesticity rather than meet his eyes. Eyes that stalked her every movement, as the ripple of awareness down her spine attested.

'Apology accepted,' she stated, her fingers curling

into the soft mohair and silk fabric of his jacket. The warmth of it. His warmth. It made her voice shiver unaccountably as she tacked on quickly, 'I suggest we forget it.' Then she took herself in hand. She was nervous, that was all. And why shouldn't she be? She had turned the tables, fending off his questions, his disbelief, with the printed evidence of his own misdemeanours. But that didn't mean he wouldn't turn back to his own attack.

'Can I get you something to eat? To drink?' It was too late to go out to a restaurant and she'd had her own sparse supper hours ago. There was little food in the apartment. She hadn't expected him. He unfailingly let her know where he would be, and when, so that she could be there for him, getting everything organised, oiling the wheels of his busy life. This evening's deviation, colluding with that piece in the Press, his eavesdropping on that private phone conversation, had thrown her.

His lack of response forced her to turn, and she masked her reluctance with the lie, 'You look tired.'

He didn't, of course. He never did. Restless, energetic, he was never happier than when he was on the move, making things happen. At the age of thirty-seven and looking ten years younger, he was a millionaire several times over, his fortune made from asset-stripping—buying up large, moribund companies all over the world, splitting them into smaller, leaner, profitable components, selling some of them off as soon as they were viable but keeping the pick of the bunch, personally overseeing every last one of them.

He had the energy, dynamism and enthusiasm of ten ordinary mortals and the enviable ability to switch off immediately.

As he was doing now. He was utterly relaxed as he sprawled out on one of the two matching sofas which flanked the hearth—the genuine Adam surround setting off a state-of-the-art coal-effect gas fire.

'I ate on the plane, but I could use a drink.' Relaxing, his eyes closed, he looked completely composed, but there was a tightness in his voice that made her drag her lower lip between her teeth. Was he still thinking about that phone call, turning it over in his mind? Hadn't the photographic evidence of his own indiscretions thrown him off the scent?

Time to attack again, perhaps, before he started asking questions, demanding answers she wasn't ready to give him.

Unusually, her fingers were shaking as she poured two fingers of the single malt he preferred into a glass and added just the right amount of bottled spring water. Her composure—one of the things he frankly admired about her—had been leaching away over the last few days. She was going to have to take herself in hand, think things through to find a logical, inevitable conclusion and act on it. That was something else she was good at. Usually.

And would be again. Starting as of now.

She hovered above him, patiently getting her breathing under control. His thick dark lashes lay heavily on those high, jutting cheekbones, softening them, and, like this, relaxed, the hard, arrogant line of his mouth was transformed into a thing of pure male beauty. Eminently kissable. Which, no doubt, the *principessa* had discovered, to her endless delight.

The lancing pain that sent her heart into spasm was an unwanted revelation. She hadn't believed herself capable of such a reaction. They had been married for almost two years and she had often wondered how many women he'd bedded. No one could doubt his virility—it shouted through every line of his lean, tough body, blazed in the depths of his knowing grey eyes. But he had promised discretion—they both had—and he had broken his word. Maybe pain was a shattered promise, she thought bleakly, her hand tightening around the glass.

Leaning forward, she touched the cool surface to his artlessly open palm and watched him snap to full alertness in the disconcerting way he had. His hand closed around the glass, deliberately trapping her fingers, and she felt the little colour she did have in her pale ivory skin wash out of her face.

He never touched her. He had always been almost painfully careful not to, not even accidentally. Not even when their coolly constructed 'perfect marriage' was on public display.

If she struggled to free her hand the whisky would go all over the place, and there was no room for such indignities in their relationship. Aquamarine eyes battled with incisive grey until she saw the sudden flare of hard mockery and lowered her lids and he transferred his glass to his other hand, releasing hers, asking grimly, 'Do you dislike being touched, *per se*, or is it only by me?'

'I don't think that question deserves a response, do you?' she uttered calmly, forcing herself to retreat with slow and careful dignity to the opposite sofa and not fly headlong from the room as every cell in her body urged her to do. But as she sank into the comfortably upholstered depths nothing on earth could prevent her snapping out acidly, 'I'm surprised you cut your Italian trip short. Wasn't the *principessa* as irresistible as she's made out to be?'

She was appalled at herself. They never quarreled. Never came near it. She didn't know what was happening. And when he announced, with languid grace, 'I couldn't possibly comment, my dear,' she wanted to hit him. Wanted it with an intensity that shook her to her soul.

'What's bugging you? I'd have marked you down as a woman who could handle a slice of unpleasant publicity with a sophisticated shrug of one superlatively elegant shoulder.' He took a reflective sip of his drink, his narrowed eyes never leaving her. 'We were pictured leaving the opera. If you'd been there— you were invited, remember—it wouldn't have happened. And you would have enjoyed it. *La Traviata*. Juanita del Sorro sang Violetta. She was quite superb.'

'I'm quite sure she was.' Only by forcing herself to respond could she stop her teeth from audibly grinding together. Was he saying his public lapse from grace was all her fault? How dared he?

And of course he had expected her to be in Rome with him. Although he did a fair amount of business there they didn't own an apartment in the city for her to turn into a home on the hoof. They always used the same small, privately run hotel near the Piazza Venezia where she acted—as was her part of the bargain—as PR officer, private secretary, mistress of the wardrobe, companion and sounding board. Everything she had been happy to be for the past two years.

The visit to Rome had been scheduled for months and she'd been looking forward to another all too brief trip to her favourite city until that phone call from the UK. Thankfully Jake had been out, so she'd had the Manhattan apartment to herself. If he'd been in she wouldn't have been able to avoid his inevitable questions. She would have had to tell him the truth. And although she knew she owed it to him, that honesty within their relationship had been something they'd both decided on, right from the start, she knew she couldn't face it, not quite yet.

And when he'd turned up, all fired up with the successful completion of yet another brilliant business deal, she'd dealt with the pressing emergency and had come up with a believable excuse for backing out of the Rome trip.

'It's the first time I've ever let you down, Jake, but would you mind if I skipped Rome? Say if you do. But suddenly I feel tired.' She'd felt drainingly guilty at his swift look of concern and had had to force herself to add, 'I could spend an extra, quiet day here, fly back to England and have the London apartment ready for when you get home from Rome.'

She had needed a few days' grace, time to face up to the consequences of telling him the truth and what would be the inevitable ending of their marriage. But he'd returned two days ahead of schedule, and she didn't know why, but she still hadn't worked up enough courage to tell him. Just thinking about it made her ask now, suddenly in deadly earnest, 'Jake—you and the *principessa*—is it serious?'

It had been part of the bargain, the let-out clause. If either of them, at any time during their paper marriage, met someone, felt serious enough about them to want a real marriage, then the other wouldn't stand in their way. There would be an annulment, followed, if Jake was the one who wanted out, by a healthy financial settlement. If she invoked the clause she would forfeit the settlement, but she could live with that now. She wouldn't give the lack of the kind of lifestyle she'd enjoyed during her marriage a second thought.

'Of course not.' He sounded as if he was on the point of yawning. And, moments later, did. He stood up, stretching, the fabric of his shirt pulled tight against his strong, lean torso. 'I'm for bed. I'm surprised you weren't tucked up hours ago, considering how desperately tired you were supposed to be.'

She ignored that, the acid tone, everything. She didn't know why she felt so buoyant, as if she'd won a reprieve, when she should be feeling thwarted. If he'd told her he'd fallen in love, at last, found a woman he genuinely wanted to spend the rest of his life with—for all the right and natural reasons—then that would have created a way out for her.

She didn't understand herself. She managed a cool goodnight and took herself off to her own peaceful room, and decided she was being dog-in-the-manger about it. She didn't want him to walk out on her. That was what it boiled down to. If their marriage ended— and it had to, of course—then she needed to be the one to do it. A matter of pride, perhaps?

She fell asleep not liking herself very much but feeling strangely comforted.

However, any feelings of comfort, undeserved or otherwise, flew straight out of the window the very next morning.

Jake, as always, was up before her, his energy making her feel tired. Breakfast was prepared—eggs and fruit and coffee.

'All I could find. The cupboard is bare. Not to worry.' He flashed her the sudden white grin that had the mega-watt power to make unwary females quake at the knees. 'I've been making phone calls. Eat—' he gestured to the table in the immaculate high-tech kitchen '—before the eggs get cold, and I'll tell you what I've arranged.'

In this mood, he made her feel as if she was in the middle of a whirlwind. Not a morning person herself, she'd taught herself how to handle his restless energy by simply letting it wash over her head until she'd dragged herself together sufficiently to cope with it. She would watch him with sleep-drugged eyes, rarely taking in much of what he said. But this morning he shocked her into full and definitely unpleasant wakefulness as he told her, 'As I said, I've made a couple of calls. As soon as we've eaten we'll drive up and visit with Liz and Sal. I know you speak to your mother regularly—' his eyes pinned her to her seat '—but she's looking forward to seeing you. Us. And tomorrow we'll go on from there to Litherton. I'll leave you in Emma's capable hands until I join you for Christmas. She'll see you get all the rest you need. And feed you up. You've lost weight recently.' His dark brows rose, as if inviting her to explain why, and she suddenly felt desperately conscious of her body, even though it was adequately concealed by her heavy peacock-blue satin robe.

She put down her fork, her throat clogging up. He wasn't stupid—far from it. He knew something was going on. He'd walked in on that phone call and didn't believe her swift assertion that she'd been talking to her mother. So he was going ahead, making sure he found out—or forced her to tell him.

There was no doubt about his genuine wish to visit Liz, see that she was comfortable, had everything she needed, find out from Sally Harding, her mother's companion, if the elderly lady was as well as she always assured them she was. For Jake had been wonderful with her mother. Liz had never been physically strong and the hard life she'd had meant that her health had suffered, and her future care and downright cosseting had been offered as part of Jake's side of the marriage bargain they'd made. It, and it alone, had been the factor that had made Claire agree to tie herself to what was, in fact, a purely business arrangement.

But there was more to the visit than that. He was suspicious, and had decided to manage and manipulate her. He'd try to get to the truth through Liz, and if he didn't—or not completely—he had made other contingency plans. Shut her away at Litherton Court, the Winter family home, where his younger sister, Emma, would keep an eye on her until he turned up for the usual family Christmas.

Christmas was two weeks away.

She straightened her spine, lifted troubled sea-blue eyes to his and said quietly, 'I have something to tell you.'

CHAPTER TWO

JAKE put his coffee-cup back on its saucer, the tiny click of the china sounding desperately loud in the hollow silence that had followed her statement, making her feel as if she was in a vacuum, the act of breathing impossible.

Her fingers twisting together nervously in her lap, she watched him go very still, the tension coming from him like a physical blow, making her helplessly nervous. Brimming with agitation, she lifted her eyes to his and saw an uncharacteristic look of wariness there, as if he, and not she, were the one who was trapped. And then it went, hard grey steel back in place, his mouth grim as he invited, 'So? Tell me.'

Aware that she'd been holding her breath, Claire dragged in air. What she had to tell him meant the beginning of the end of their relationship. A dreadful, draining reluctance took her by the throat but she managed thickly, 'Liz has news. She heard last week that an uncle had died and left her a fortune. It was totally unexpected. She hadn't seen him in years. He never married and ended up as a complete recluse. Liz was the only relative he had. I met him once but don't really remember him. I was seven.'

It had been shortly after her father had walked out on her mother and one bleak day Liz had dressed her in her best clothes and taken her to visit her great-uncle. A dreary journey entailing three separate bus rides, an even drearier welcome. Claire recalled only one thing about that meeting—the cynical way he had said, 'Just because your mother was my sister, don't come looking to me for hand-outs. It's not my fault your husband chose to run away with another woman. It's up to him to support his child, not me.'

They'd left at once. Her mother's mouth had trembled as they'd walked through the cold rain to the bus-stop and Claire had clasped her hand, transmitting her sturdy love, feeling the fragile bones beneath the scratchy, hand-knitted gloves. But later, during the tedious journey home, Liz had brightened and told her, 'You have to be sorry for him. He thought I was after his precious money when all I wanted was what was left of our family. He has no one but we have each other. That's worth far more than any amount of money. We're the lucky ones.'

'In the end he must have decided to will everything to his niece,' Claire told Jake reflectively. 'He wasn't the sort of man who would leave anything to charity, no matter how deserving.'

'I'm pleased for her,' Jake said warmly, but she saw the question deep in those unfathomable eyes of his before he voiced it. 'And that is all you have to tell me?'

His long, lean fingers were drumming silently on the table-top. Her lashes swooped down, hiding her confusion. The way he was looking at her made her feel guilty even though she had nothing to feel guilty about. And when he slid in, his voice coldly silky, 'You don't want to tell me about the lover you were speaking to when I disturbed you last night? Don't be shy about it; the eventuality was provided for in our agreement, with the accent being on discretion. I take it you are being discreet?' she bit out with brittle haste,

'Unlike you and that Italian!' Shocked by the stab of pain that prompted the outburst, she reined in her temper and stressed with stony-voiced patience, 'I was speaking to Liz—as I told you. She wanted to know if I'd given you her news yet.'

'Oh, of course!' he countered with heavy irony. 'It's always nice to hear good news—I fully understand her desperate urgency.'

'Don't be sarcastic!' She snapped to her feet, the breakfast he'd prepared for her barely touched. He didn't believe she'd been talking to her mother. He took lovers, so why shouldn't she? That was the way he would look at it. 'To Liz it is urgent. She wanted you to know so that you could stop the allowance you make her. Stop paying Sal's wages—she can well afford to do that herself now. It was all I could do to prevent her from insisting that she repay every last penny you spent on Lark Cottage.'

'I deeded Lark Cottage to her on our wedding-day,' Jake said grimly, and stood up too, turning and walking through to the living-room. Claire followed, her eyes puzzled. For a moment she thought she'd glimpsed a flicker of pain in his eyes, as if it hurt him to think of Liz throwing the generosity of the past two years back in his face.

He had his back to her, his fists bunched into the pockets of his trousers, staring down at the quiet street from one of the tall sash windows that graced the elegant room. And although her softly slippered feet could have made no sound on the thick carpet he clearly knew she was there because he muttered tightly, 'There's no question of Liz repaying the cost of the cottage. And as for the comfortable living allowance I make her—that was part of our marriage agreement. I have no intention of going back on it.'

Claire walked slowly towards him, noting how tightly the muscles on his impressive shoulders were clenched. The allowance he'd made Liz over the past two years had been far more than merely comfortable. He'd been generous with his time, too, making sure they visited the elderly lady whenever they were in England, keeping in close contact by phone when they were not, making time in his packed schedule for them to take Liz and Sally Harding to the Italian lakes for ten days each spring, sending her books he thought she'd like to read. Little things, granted—set against his immense wealth—but meaning so much, and going far beyond the letter of the agreement they'd made.

She couldn't bear him to think his generosity was being tossed back in his face. She couldn't bear him to be hurt.

Not stopping to analyse the depth of her feelings or the impulse that made her move quickly to place her body in front of him, reach out to touch his perfectly hewn features, she said gently, 'Liz would hate you to think she was ungrateful. It's the last thing she'd want. But her pride is all she's ever had, remember. And now she finds herself in a position to provide for herself she's walking on air. Don't try to deny her that.'

She wasn't conscious of the way her cool fingertips were softly stroking his temple, the palm of her hand gently laid against the hardly sculpted side of his face, until he turned his head, his eyes holding hers with lancing intensity as his lips moved erotically against the suddenly unbearably sensitised palm of her hand. She gave a small, shaky gasp as wildfire sensations seared through her body and saw his hooded eyes grow speculative. She snatched her hand away.

Touching hadn't been part of their contract. Non-consummation had been agreed on. She was too fastidious to contemplate sex without love and he wouldn't want a sexual relationship, with all its inherent emotional complications, to put their down-to-earth and mutually beneficial partnership in jeopardy.

Was that why he had gone out of his way to avoid any physical contact—even the most innocent? Had he known something she had never even suspected—that his slightest touch would send her up in flames?

Praying she wouldn't betray her humiliation with something as uncool as a blush, she stepped briskly back and squared her shoulders, summoned her normal, politely friendly tone and stated, 'If we're going on to Litherton from Lark Cottage then I'd better throw a few things in a bag. But I warn you, much as I like your sister, don't expect me to bury myself down there for the next two weeks. I'd be bored out of my skull.'

Not true. She and Jake had spent a wonderfully relaxing time at Litherton Court last Christmas, plus a gloriously lazy long weekend in the early autumn, but she wasn't going to admit that she would be miserable if she didn't see him for two whole weeks, because she wasn't ready to admit it to herself.

And despite having been the last to speak she had the distinctly edgy feeling, as she swept out of the room, that she hadn't had the last word.

Four hours later Liz said happily, 'Oh, it's lovely to see you!' and stood on tiptoe to plant a kiss on Jake's lean, hard cheek, smothered in the bulk of his sheepskin jacket as he hugged her, then turned to her daughter for her embrace. As Claire's arms went round the tiny frame she thought, She's not nearly as frail as she used to be, and felt tears of gratitude for all Jake had done sting behind her eyes and clog her throat.

'Come along in, out of the cold. As soon as we heard your car come round the corner of the lane Sal went to put the kettle on. And your rooms are ready, so go along up if you want to freshen up before we snack.'

As the door closed on the cold grey mist of the December afternoon Jake's height and breadth and alarmingly magnetic male presence filled the tiny, cheerful hall and Claire grabbed her suitcase, suddenly needing the quiet privacy of her room, space to breathe, away from that throat-grabbing presence. But Jake, shrugging out of his sheepskin, said, 'I want a private word with you, Liz, before we do a damn thing.'

'Does that dour tone tell me that Claire has at last got around to giving you my news?' Faded blue eyes twinkled up into commanding grey slits. 'I always think it's bad taste to get excited over a legacy. But in Uncle Arnold's case I think I can be excused. He never cared about anyone in the whole of his life and in the end no one cared about him.' Her mouth drooped at the corners as she added, 'Though I sent him a card each Christmas, keeping him up to date with whatever news there was, even after he…'

Her voice tailed away and Jake took her arm in a gentle but inescapable grip, urging her towards the door that led to the sitting-room, his voice firm as he told her, 'Stop trying to soften me up. You've got some serious explaining to do. What are families for, if not to help each other when possible? I hope you're not going to tell me you found what little help I gave a burden you're delighted to shrug off?'

Although his words were tough his voice was soft around the edges as he ushered Liz into the sitting-room. Claire sighed briefly and mounted the stairs. The question of his allowance was something they'd have to thrash out between them and she was deeply thankful that she'd been able to persuade her mother that her decision to reimburse Jake fully for the purchase price of Lark Cottage, and everything in it, would have been seen as gross ingratitude, and hurtful.

She was thankful, too, that she'd made Jake promise never, in any circumstances, to divulge that his care of her mother had been the only reason she'd agreed to marry him.

As she reached her room and closed herself in with the cottage pine antiques, the lemon-yellow and grey and cream fabrics which picked out the main colours of the sunny sprigged wallpaper and the thick scatter rugs on the oak-boarded floor, her mouth twisted wryly as she remembered how appalled Liz had been, the first time they'd visited, when she had explained that, being modern and sophisticated, she and Jake had decided on separate rooms.

But Liz would be even more appalled, and permanently so, if she knew that her daughter's marriage to the son-in-law she openly adored and respected was nothing but a business arrangement.

She hung her mulberry-coloured wool coat in the wardrobe, unpacked the few things she'd need for the two days Jake had said they would be spending here and allowed the tranquillity of the cottage, set as it was on the outskirts of a tiny Shropshire village, to soothe her unaccustomedly ruffled soul.

There really was nothing to get in a state about, she assured herself. She and Jake had agreed that their paper marriage would end when it was no longer useful. And as far as she was concerned its usefulness had ended with that legacy. And as for Jake, well, his unprecedented lack of discretion over the *principessa* affair had to signal that he wanted his freedom—even if he wasn't fully aware of it yet.

So their days were numbered, the last hours ticking away, and it truly didn't matter, did it? she asked herself as she sank down on the window-seat and gazed down on the garden that, even at this dead time of year, was her mother's pride and joy.

With a sense of inevitability, the tying up of loose ends, her mind slid back over the years, looking at everything that had happened, taking her to the point when she had agreed to marry Jake.

The foundations had been laid in her childhood. She barely remembered her father because he'd gone by the time her seventh birthday came around. Apparently, he had never wanted the responsibility of children and Liz had been thirty-eight when Claire was born. Liz had never been physically strong and after the birth she had had to give up her job working for a florist, pushing even more responsibility on to the man who hadn't wanted it in the first place.

So no, she wouldn't recognise her father now if she passed him in the street, but she could remember the build-up of tension as the weekends approached, when her father, a company rep, would be home. Recall how her mother had seemed frightened of him, of his sudden bursts of temper, his long sulks.

Once, long after he'd disappeared, and the eventual divorce, Claire had asked her mother why she had stayed with him as long as she had. Liz had looked blank, as if such a thought had never entered her head, and simply imparted that she'd made her marriage

vows in good faith and, having made them, wouldn't
be the one to break them. It was then Claire had realised that her father had taken a naïve, trusting, loving
soul and turned her into a doormat, and she had made
a private vow never to allow it to happen to her.

When her husband had walked out on them Liz had
had to find work to support them. She'd brought a
child into the world and loved her devotedly, and no
way was that child to be deprived of decent food and
respectable clothes. They'd moved to a small flat because Liz couldn't afford the rent on the house they
lived in, but somehow there had always been treats—
a coach trip to the coast each summer, a birthday
party to which all her friends were invited, a visit to
the local theatre for the Christmas pantomime.

All at the expense of her health, Claire had realised
years later.

Never strong, Liz had taken only part-time menial
work because while her daughter was at school she'd
insisted on being there when Claire came home. So
she had often been exploited, poorly paid, having no
qualifications which might have opened more lucra-
tive, less physically gruelling doors for her.

After gaining her secretarial qualifications and a
year's practical experience, Claire had joined a top-
quality agency because she could earn more that way,
insisted that Liz give up all her part-time jobs, and
had been filling in for Jake's personal secretary—the
one who went everywhere with him, and who was
recovering after an appendectomy—when Liz had had
a heart attack.

Claire had been out of her mind with worry. Just as she had begun earning enough to allow her mother to take life more easily, fate had dealt this blow.

Jake had been wonderful, far more sympathetic and supportive than her ephemeral position as a temp could have led her to expect. He had insisted on waiting with her through that dreadful night at the hospital when she hadn't expected her mother to survive the attack, metaphorically holding her hand and, somehow, drawing her whole life story out of her.

And later, when her mother's recovery had been assured—this time, so her consultant had warned— Jake had broken the news that his personal secretary had decided to call it a day. Her fiancé apparently took a dim view of the unsocial hours she was often called upon to work, the times—many of them— when she had to be out of the country, dancing attendance on her employer.

'I've a proposition to put to you,' he had told her. And now, without even having to try, she had total recall of every last inflexion of his voice, the way the pale afternoon winter sunlight had been streaming through the long sash windows of the London apartment, sheening his raven-wing hair, highlighting the taut, olive-toned skin on his jutting cheekbones, throwing those enigmatic grey eyes into deepest shadow.

He'd waved aside the bunch of faxed reports she'd just brought through from the study. 'Sit down, put that sharp brain of yours into receiving mode, and listen.'

She'd sat, the slight smile his choice of words had brought to flickering life quickly fading because she couldn't put her concern over Liz's future to the back of her mind as a good secretary should.

The excellent salary she was earning through the agency meant that her mother no longer had any pressing financial worries. On the other hand, working for the agency meant that she often had to travel to distant parts of the country, and that, in turn, meant there was no one to keep an eye on Liz, see that she ate properly, took the regular periods of rest that were so important to her long-term recovery.

And she wouldn't put it past her, as soon as she was back on her feet, to trundle out to find some kind of job. Liz had her pride, didn't want to be a burden, was inclined to mutter on about Claire being able to spend some of her hard-earned salary on herself instead of using it to support her parent in idleness.

'As I've told you, Anthea won't be coming back, which leaves me, again, without a permanent personal secretary,' Jake growled. 'They come weighed down with all the right qualifications and good intentions, and before you know it they find some lame excuse or other to quit.'

So a disgruntled fiancé, Anthea's love-life, was considered to be a lame excuse, was it? Controlling the upward twitch of her mouth, Claire pushed her own worries out of her mind and concentrated on his.

While she sat, composed and still, he paced the floor, displaying all that restless energy she had grown to admire, and marvel at. He smacked a fist into the open palm of his other hand and grated, 'They know what's required and receive a blinding salary to compensate for any minor inconveniences! And God knows, I'm not a monster to work for, am I, Claire?' He glared at her, his brows bunched, as if he couldn't believe anyone fortunate enough to work for him would ever willingly depart—for any reason under the sun—and she clamped her teeth tightly together to control the grin that threatened to break out and gave him back a soothing, if necessarily tight-lipped smile, a confirming shake of her head.

Not a monster, never that. Demanding, brilliant, restless, capable of long, sustained bursts of energy that left lesser mortals feeling drained and giddy, sometimes impossible and sometimes staggeringly, generously thoughtful and kind. But never a monster.

'Any suggestions?' He had come to a standstill, hovering over her, his hands now bunched into his trouser pockets.

Disregarding the bluntly aggressive tone, she lifted cool eyes to meet the piercing blaze of his and replied calmly, 'Hire someone who's not interested in a love-life. A widow-woman, say, well into her fifties.' She was trying very hard to keep a straight face. 'Or, better still, a man. A man with a family to support, who would be grateful for a spectacular salary and the opportunity to escape the kids from time to time.' A touch of bitterness there? she wondered. Memories of the way her own father had been?

'Would a man take charge of my laundry, cook the occasional meal, buy my socks?' he scorned. 'And would your putative widow-woman have the stamina to keep up with my schedules?'

His smile was tight, almost feral, as he swept her suggestions aside. Then, with one of the mood swings she had come to expect, he dropped on to the opposite sofa, swinging one immaculately trousered leg over the other, tipping his head on one side as he gave her a long, considering look, before saying with languid smoothness, 'Having wiped out the options, I want you to consider my proposition. Take the job; work for me. Permanently. And, to ensure you don't dredge up some flimsy excuse to terminate your employment, I will marry you.'

Marriage! Her stomach muscles shivered, then clenched. She had expected him to offer her a permanent position, had been reluctantly prepared to turn it down because if she was on the other side of the globe with him who would keep an eye on Liz—but marriage! That was the last thing she'd expected him to offer! Quite out of the question!

'And before you verbalise what's written on your face,' his voice came through the whirlpool of her thoughts, silky soft yet carrying the core of that iron will of his, 'listen, absorb and contemplate. Firstly,' he ticked off on a lean, long forefinger, 'the marriage will not be consummated. To the outside world it will appear the perfect match, but privately you will function as my personal secretary. No more, no less. Your salary will be paid in the form of an allowance—and you won't find me ungenerous. Secondly, you will enjoy the financial security, the luxury, my wife would naturally expect. In return, I will have the loyalty and continuity of service I need.'

'This is crazy!' Ignoring the fluttery sensations that invaded her insides, Claire fixed him with a cool, sea-blue stare. 'I won't pretend I wouldn't jump at the job offer if it didn't mean leaving Liz to her own devices, but you don't need to tie yourself down to that extent, surely? When you find someone suitable you could insist on a watertight contract.'

'In which a clever lawyer could find any number of leaks!' He shook his head, leaning forward a little, his superbly hewn features softening with an obvious need to understand. 'We get along well together and I can't fault your work—the past few weeks have demonstrated that. And during that night when you feared you would lose Liz—and I'll come to her in a moment—you were open enough to tell me of her disastrous marriage, confide that her experience, plus the way you'd seen quite a high proportion of your friends' marriages go down the drain, had put you off ever making that commitment yourself. So tell me, where do you find the problem in my proposed business agreement?'

'You,' she said with stark honesty. Then wondered why her mouth had gone dry. Avoiding his eyes, she flicked her tongue over her lips and made herself elaborate, 'Who you are, what you are.' She didn't need to go further, tell him what he already had to know—that with his looks, all that sexy charisma, his wealth and staggering power he could have the pick of any woman he fancied. Instead she said primly, 'I can't believe you're a stranger to the opposite sex. And I can't believe the day won't dawn when you'll fall in love and want a real marriage, a family to enjoy the empire you've created. And when that day does arrive I'll be the first to go, with nothing but the dubious honour of being the first, and discarded, Mrs Jake Winter.'

Hearing the rising note of bitterness in her voice and not having any way of understanding it, she slumped back against the soft cushions and waited to hear how he'd get out of that. And she went into a state of shock, or something very like it, when he simply turned the power of his wide white smile on her, explaining lightly, 'I won't even try to pretend I'm a stranger to your sex. However, much as I enjoy female company I know myself well enough to avoid making any long-term emotional commitments. To make a marriage happy, secure and stable you have to work at it. I wouldn't find the time. My business gives me all the challenge I can handle. It's as addictive and demanding as playing chess at the highest level—I'm not looking for anything more. I could handle a paper marriage—I've neither the time nor the inclination to work at a proper one. Inevitably I'd get bored and restless. And, as I've experienced, paid secretaries and housekeepers can be a pain. I need someone who will be emotionally undemanding, always there when needed, wherever I happen to be. I hate hotel life as a general rule, so have my own apartments in most of the major capitals around the world, and I need someone there to organise some kind of home life as well as business breakfasts, lunches or dinners, put on her secretary hat when needed and, as I mentioned—' his grin was sapping all her strength '—buy my socks. Or whatever. And as far as I'm concerned, unless and until I make a family of my own—which, at this moment in time, I can't see myself ever contemplating—any children my sister and her husband might have would become my heirs. And I suppose there should be an opt-out clause,' he clipped, his change of tone suddenly making her see how seriously he was taking this plethora of alarming nonsense. 'In the unlikely event of my deciding I wanted to be free to remarry, you would receive a substantial settlement in money and property. If you wanted out, for the same reason, then I wouldn't stand in your way. You would, however, forfeit the settlement.'

The smile he gave her was chilling, sending shivers riding down the length of her spine, and, shifting uneasily against the cushions, she was about to decline his offer politely when he forestalled her, knocking the breath out of her lungs as he added, 'About Liz. As an added and, in my opinion—having spoken at length to her consultant—necessary inducement, I guarantee to keep her in comfort for the rest of her life. In a house of her own and your choosing, with a resident companion—medically trained—to keep an eye on her health and wellbeing, keep her company, do all the little jobs around the place she shouldn't be allowed to tackle. Think about it, Claire. Think carefully, and give me your answer in the morning.'

He stood up, terminating the crazy interview, and Claire, her legs feeling unbelievably unsteady, tottered off to the study, finishing up there and driving home in a daze, not able to bring herself to say goodnight to him because everything inside her head had gone on hold.

It was the promise he had made regarding Liz's future that tipped the balance. True, the actual job he was offering was a challenge that was difficult to resist, and she could live with the marriage part of it. She would look at it as a strange type of job description, the utter sterility of the relationship a secret between Jake and herself. But it was the thought that her mother would at last be able to relax, live a life of comfort and ease, having a cosy home of her own and the lush country garden she had always dreamed of—with the added bonus that wherever Claire found herself she would know that Liz had someone close at hand to keep her from being lonely, watch that she didn't overtire herself, make her go for regular checkups—that brought Claire to Jake's London apartment, an acceptance of his offer of marriage firmly lodged in her head.

Jake received her acceptance with a calm, 'Thank you. You won't regret it,' but persuading Liz to accept his charity was a different matter.

She had met Jake, of course and, although bemused by the suddenness of it, was delighted by the prospect of the marriage. Her darling girl had fallen in love with a man who would care for her, provide handsomely for her, for the rest of her life. What mother could ask for more? But living on charity was something else altogether.

Not until Jake was brought in to fight Claire's corner were matters resolved. He simply told her, 'In three weeks' time I am marrying your daughter. That makes you, like it or not, part of my family. And what type of man—especially one who has more money than he can count—leaves a valued member of his family to mooch around in a mediocre flat in an unlovely London backstreet?'

And so Lark Cottage was found, furnished with every comfort and convenience, Sally Harding, an ex-nurse, forthright but kind, employed, everything—even their paper marriage—running smoothly until now. Until her mother's legacy had set her free.

An impatient rapping on the bedroom door had Claire dragging her eyes from the window-pane. The winter darkness had descended. She'd been looking at nothing. Blinking, she watched Jake enter the room, his impressive height and sheer physical presence seeming to diminish everything in it. His features were expressionless, yet his eyes pierced her, his voice harsh as he said, 'Liz is presiding over the tea-table, staring with longing at the teapot. As is Sal. Might I suggest you join us and put them out of their misery?'

She rose slowly to her feet. She'd lost count of time. Eating her share of one of Sal's massive teas—three different types of dainty sandwiches, mountainous sponge cakes, slab cake, a wild selection of home-made biscuits—was not, at the moment, very appealing.

She sighed, and he heard it. His eyes narrowed. He made an 'after you' gesture as she reached the door and his tone when he spoke, silk cloaking iron, rasped on her strangely jangled nerves.

'Liz's delight in finding herself so unexpectedly and independently wealthy was so transparent, I hadn't the heart to insist that she continue to live off my allowance. However,' he added, his mouth straightening in a grim line, 'that doesn't give you an opt-out, grounds for terminating our agreement. Only one thing can do that, so don't you ever forget it.'

CHAPTER THREE

"ONLY one thing". The only opt-out Jake would accept was if one or other of them fell in love.

Claire fastened her seatbelt as Jake slid into the driver's seat. She didn't look at him, concentrated instead on waving goodbye to Liz and Sal, doing her best to look relaxed and cheerful.

For some reason the couple of days they'd spent at Lark Cottage had been a strain. Normally, it was no such thing. Claire valued any time she was able to spend with Liz, and her pretend marriage hadn't been a problem before because Jake had the ability to make everyone relax. When it suited him, that was. And it always suited him when he was around Liz.

So she couldn't put her edginess down to him, or only obliquely. The only reason she'd agreed to marry him had been to secure her mother's future welfare. But, for him, the fact that he'd no longer be supporting Liz didn't count. He'd made that abundantly clear. And what troubled her was the stupid, surging relief she'd felt when he'd spelt it out!

'Still adamant about not staying on at Litherton until I join you for Christmas?' Jake asked tautly as he smoothly negotiated the big car through the tangled network of narrow country lanes that would, in around twenty minutes, bring them to the Winter family home.

She shrugged, biting down on her lip, staring fixedly ahead. She was all churned up inside, her emotions warring. She didn't want to stay on at Litherton without him; she had already acknowledged that much. And when she'd believed that Liz's legacy would inevitably lead to the end of their marriage she had been—well, 'disconsolate' was the word she thought she was looking for.

It would be madness to allow herself to become dependent on his company. Sooner or later the marriage would end, and probably sooner, if his indiscreet relationship with the *principessa* was anything to go by.

Without being aware of it she had allowed herself to be drawn into the false security of dependency. It was time she did something about it. And so she told him with a lightness she was far from feeling, 'No, I've had second thoughts. Long walks in the fresh air, coming back to roaring log fires and Emma's marvellous cooking—just what I need.' And she cursed herself for feeling so miserable because she'd done the right thing, committed herself to two whole weeks without him. Which only went to show how uncomfortably real the danger was becoming.

She opened her eyes very wide at the look of frowning suspicion he darted her then closed them on a spasm of unadulterated pain when he returned his attention back to the road and told her, 'Good. I'm glad you've seen sense. There'd be no point in your

kicking around on your own in London. I'll be in
Rome, plunging into some rather exciting unfinished
business.'

The voluptuous *principessa*, of course. And did he
have to be so crude about it? Any other time he would
have wanted her there with him, arranging meetings,
sitting in on them wearing her secretarial hat, acting
as a sounding board for his involved thought-
processes as they shared a nightcap together back at
the hotel.

But not this time. And she didn't have to be a
mind-reader to know why.

Half reluctantly, she turned her head and allowed
her eyes to dwell briefly on his savagely handsome
profile. Was he aware that the rot had set in, that his
indiscretions were pointing the way to the final break-
up, that he had at last found a woman for whom he
was happy to throw caution out of the window?

She looked quickly away again, misery darkening
her eyes. In agreeing to stay on with his sister and
her husband she had done exactly the right thing. The
process of weaning herself away from him was about
to begin.

Litherton Court had been in the Winter family for
generations. The sturdy stone house, built in the reign
of Elizabeth Tudor, looked particularly lovely on this
bright, crisp morning, Claire thought as she emerged
from the copse, looking down on the house in its
smooth green hollow of land.

Sunlight glittered on the tiny panes set in elegant

mullions and made the pale building stone look warm
and mellow. Claire wondered, not for the first time,
how Jake could have turned his back on the property,
handing it and the vast estates over to Emma when
she'd married Frank.

But it was impossible to imagine the restless, dynamic Jake Winter settling down to run a country
estate, she acknowledged, pushing her hands deeper
into the pockets of her sheepskin coat. And that being
the case, what could be more natural than his handing
over his inheritance when Emma married? When he
had been twenty-five and already a force to be reck-
oned with in the business world, and Emma a sheltered eighteen, their parents had been killed in a motorway pile-up. The double blow had traumatised
them both, particularly Emma. It had taken her a long
time to get over it and Jake had become very protective of her. Until the advent of the *principessa* Claire
had believed that Emma was the only female under
sixty Jake had any tenderness or respect for. The way
women had always thrown themselves at him had
made him cynical. So did he know he was ready to
fall in love, ready to make a lasting, worthwhile commitment? An expert at second-guessing other people's
moves, correctly judging their motivations, had he
recognised his own slip for what it was—a willing-
ness, in the case of this one special woman, to give
the world at large advance notice of his intentions?

If it had been a slip then it had been a deliberate
one. No one could ever accuse him of being a man
who didn't know what he was doing. During the two

years of their marriage he must have had the occasional short-lived affair; he was too virilely male not to have done. But there had never been a breath of scandal, never a hint.

So this was different.

Her fine brows knotted together, she set her booted feet on the downward track, heading back towards the house. How many times during the five days since he had left for Rome had she worried away at the conjectures that kept rearing up inside her head? Was he with Lorella Giancotti now, at this very moment? Was he explaining about his paper marriage—something that had been their secret up until now? Making plans, promising to get an annulment very soon, asking her to marry him?

With a savage spurt of temper she kicked out at the loose stones in her path, sending them skittering. The decisions he made about his private life didn't matter, did they? She had entered into marriage for purely practical reasons, with her eyes wide open. In spite of his offhanded denials, she had always known that this was on the cards, accepted that he would fall in love one day and ask her for an annulment. So why did she feel as if her whole world was falling apart?

Because the breakdown of their marriage would mean the end of her job, she answered herself staunchly as she unlatched the gate in the high stone wall that surrounded the gardens proper, keeping them separate from the rest of the estate.

Relief poured through her like a flood of sweet warm water and she whistled cheerfully for the two young Labradors and the pensioned-off sheepdog who had accompanied her on her morning walk, smiling as they bounded towards her. She had heard Emma say that she could never have too many dogs and they seemed to be all over the house, curled up in armchairs and sofas, heaps of them on the rug in front of the Aga, basking in the warmth. And because Frank was devoted to his prettily plump wife he tolerated them cheerfully.

Ushering the dogs through the gate, she closed it securely behind her, feeling light-hearted for the first time in days.

She loved her job, thrived on the challenges and hassles, the praise Jake gave so generously, the companionship that inevitably built up when you worked so closely with someone you admired and respected. But she certainly couldn't keep it after they separated. It would look very odd to the rest of the world if she were to continue to work for her ex-husband after he remarried.

So the prospect of losing her job had to be responsible for the bleak mood she'd been in ever since she'd seen that photograph and realised the implications behind his first ever indiscretion. And before that, even, beginning when Liz had told her about that legacy and she'd thought—wrongly, as it happened—that Jake would terminate their agreement because the conditions were no longer being met and he, above anything, was an honourable man.

And the relief that she had worked it all out must have shown on her face because when she walked into the big, cosy kitchen Emma, heating milk on the Aga to add to the mid-morning coffee, turned and said, 'What's happened to cheer you up? You've been looking like a wet Sunday since Jake left. I said you were missing the brute but Frank thought you were sickening for something.'

Claire didn't like to think she was so transparent, but she hid her unease with a smiling shrug and offered, 'Fresh air and exercise does wonders! It's a beautiful morning and you don't feel the cold if you keep moving. The dogs enjoyed it, too.'

Thankfully, the mention of dogs deflected her, as it had been meant to do. Emma petted and crooned over the dogs which had just returned, sitting at her feet, pink tongues lolling. Claire rescued the milk.

She and Emma had taken an instant liking to each other the first time they'd met. Jake had insisted she spend that first Christmas here. They'd just got 'engaged'—one of the shortest on record—and he'd brought her down to meet the only family he had. And last Christmas they'd been here as a married couple, he giving the same reason she had for their preference for separate rooms, and they would be here together again this year. For the very last time, she expected.

Jake always spent the festive season at Litherton, and was openly impatient for Emma to provide him with nieces and nephews for him to spoil and play with. But Emma was in no hurry to oblige. She had her dogs and her husband, not to mention the absorbing business of running the big estate like clockwork, with the occasional input from Frank, who was Jake's personal accountant, handling his impressively massive portfolio.

Claire deeply regretted being unable to let her sister-in-law get really close. Emma was open and bright and bubbly and would have liked nothing better than to have long heart-to-heart chats with her brother's wife, but Claire, recognising the dangers in that, put on an act of reserve and refused to be drawn. No one but she and Jake knew what a sham their marriage was. They both wanted to keep it that way.

'There's just the two of us today,' Emma remarked as Claire finished making the coffee. 'Frank's spending the day with Liz. He'd have asked you along too, but they'll be spending the time talking investments. Boring!' She pretended an exaggerated yawn and Claire's mouth twisted in a wry smile. One of the first things Jake had done after they'd arrived at Litherton was to tell Frank of Liz's newly acquired wealth.

'At the moment it's swilling around in her bank account. I want you to go and see her. You can do better than that for her.' His tone had implied 'or else', and that was typical of the type of man he was. Claire pushed him quickly out of her mind and the wall-mounted phone rang.

She was already—more or less successfully— thinking of her marriage in the past tense so when she realised Emma was talking to Jake the shock made her stomach curl up in a ball and turn to ice. And they were obviously talking about her, because Emma was saying, 'No. Only to do some Christmas shopping. She borrowed one of the cars and took off for the day.'

Claire watched the puzzled frown gather between her sister-in-law's eyes and just knew he was checking up on her. He was still suspicious about the phone call he'd interrupted, and that made her coldly angry because who was he to poke and pry into her affairs when his was splashed all over the papers? He would want their marriage to end when the time was right for him. He wouldn't want her jumping the gun, painting him in the guise of a cuckolded husband!

'Of course I didn't go with her,' Emma was saying, running out of patience. 'I always get mine done early, you know that. No. No— Look, she's right here; ask her yourself.'

She handed Claire the receiver with an upward hunch of her shoulders and Claire managed coolly, 'Ask me what?'

The tiny ensuing silence was electrifying and, for no reason that she could fathom, her heart began to beat like a drum gone out of control; then cold anger took over as he told her without an atom of shame, 'Just checking up on how my wife spends her time. Get all your shopping done, did you? Or perhaps you forgot something vital? Find you have to spend yet another day in town?'

If theirs had been a normal marriage she would have thought he was harbouring deep suspicions, half believing she was seeing someone else, was blisteringly jealous. As it was, she knew he was simply anxious not to be made to look a fool.

She hated it when they were like this together. Up until his return from Rome they had got along fine, becoming really close companions. Squashing the impulse to reassure him, because getting back on to a best friends footing again would only make the inevitable break-up much more difficult, she gushed, 'Now however did you guess? Such a bore! Was there anything else you wanted to check up on, or can I go? My coffee's getting cold.'

'No, you may not go.' The tone of his voice set all the nerves in her body on edge. It was the tone she had heard him use when dealing out reprimands to underlings who had earned his displeasure. He had never used it to her before. And now that clipped, arrogant voice was telling her, 'I'm buying a property in Haveling. The agent will deliver the keys to you in the morning. As soon as he does, I want you to drive over there and wait for me. I should arrive around lunchtime. Got that?'

She answered, 'Yes,' but was talking to silence. Her face went red. He'd put the phone down, just like that! How dared he treat her as if she were a mere employee he'd suddenly lost patience with?

But an employee was all she was, all she had ever been, she reminded herself with a swift return to rationality, and maybe the brisk arrogance he'd used on her for the very first time was his way of easing them apart, phasing out the strange but special relationship they'd had.

'What was that all about?' Emma wanted to know. 'I've never heard him so snappy—someone been giving him a bad time?' She was cutting fruit cake and suddenly looked deadly serious. 'You? Before he left he asked me to keep an eye on you,' she went on slowly, as if thinking things out and not liking the conclusions she was reaching. 'He said he was worried about you. You'd got overtired, I must make sure you had plenty of rest and didn't go racketing round on your own. But just then he sounded on edge, as if there was a lot more to it than that. Is there?'

'Of course not. What more could there be?' Claire sat down at the table, tried to look relaxed as she cupped her hands round her coffee-mug. Emma wasn't stupid. Jake must have been unguarded enough to allow his sister to deduce that he hadn't been merely checking up on his wife's wellbeing. Her fingers tightened around the mug. It wasn't like Jake to be unguarded. He was the most controlled person she knew.

Falling in love with the *principessa* had obviously knocked him for six. But Emma mustn't know there was something wrong. Give her the slightest hint and she'd worry away at it until you gave her the truth out of sheer exasperation!

'He's buying a property in Haveling, or so he said,' Claire offered as a red herring. It was nothing unusual. Two months ago he had purchased a tract of land and a decaying plantation house in the Caribbean and was currently in the process of transforming it into a mind-bogglingly exclusive hotel. 'The agent's delivering the key tomorrow, Jake's returning from Rome and I'm to meet him there.'

'Haveling! Oh, it's one of the prettiest villages you could hope to see, and only a dozen or so miles from here! I've told him and told him it's time he had a proper base—the London flat's magnificent, of course, but it hardly counts—not if you're thinking of putting roots down at last and starting a family. It would be wonderful, wouldn't it? We'd be practically neighbours, and you could see Liz much more regularly, couldn't you?'

As a diversion, it had worked wonderfully, and Emma wasn't to know how far she was from reality. Grinning, caught up in the fantasy of her own manufacturing, she put a slice of cake on a plate and slid it over the table.

Claire shook her head, declining. The thought of eating anything made her feel ill. Emma had painted a rose-coloured picture but to Claire it was black. She caught herself wishing it could be true, and slapped that treacherous notion right on the head, hating herself for being so impossibly stupid.

'Now, let me think…' Emma ruminated over a mouthful of cake. 'It's a while since I went through Haveling. There's a handful of gorgeous cottages, but they'd be much too small. A Georgian place that used to be a rectory at the back of the church—that's a possibility—and a lovely Queen Anne house, a bit away from the village proper—lots of ground, lovely gardens. Harnage Place, I think it's called. Now that would be perfect. I can't wait until the agent gets here and we can find out for sure. You should have asked

Jake to be more specific. Never mind— Oh, isn't it exciting?'

Claire stopped listening. It was far too painful. There could be any number of reasons why Jake had decided to buy a property in this area. A hotel conversion, conference centre, health farm—any number of possibilities. But the one that made the most sense was the one that Emma had mooted.

Jake had fallen in love, wanted to tie his *principessa* to him for the rest of his life, wanted her to be the mother of his children, needed, at last, a settled home. It didn't bear thinking about, so she wouldn't, and she gave all her attention to those of the dogs who had sniffed out the presence of cake, breaking her own unwanted slice into equal pieces, taking endless care to make sure it was fairly distributed.

And Emma had been right on both counts, she decided dully as she drew her borrowed car up on a broad sweep of paving slabs at twelve the next morning. Harnage Place was the house Jake was buying, and yes, it would make a perfect family home. It was spacious enough to house half a dozen children and, from the outside at least, extremely beautiful. But not large enough to make it a profitable commercial proposition.

Her heart dropped sickeningly. This was just one more clue to what was going on. But she didn't need clues, did she? The moment she'd seen that picture in the paper she'd known. It had been like a window opening on to her future.

Her legs feeling like lead, she let herself out of the car and the cold grey wind cut through her, making her shudder and drag the collar of her woollen coat higher around her ears. Rows of windows watched her blindly from the tall, elegantly graceful façade of the house, and she ignored them, squaring her shoulders and marching straight up to the main door.

It was a job, that was all, she reminded herself, perhaps one of the very last duties she would be called on to perform. She was paid very handsomely to iron out life's little wrinkles for him. Being here to open the house up would save him having to make a detour to pick the keys up himself. Jake didn't believe in wasting time or effort. Both were too highly prized to be squandered. And that was the only reason she was here.

With a sinking sensation she slotted the key into the lock. She hoped, with a sense of deep desolation, that she would find every interior aspect of Harnage Place quite repellent. She didn't want to have to like anything about Jake's future home—the home he would make with his *principessa*.

It was ironic, truly ironic, she thought grimly as she pushed open the door, because today was her second wedding anniversary.

CHAPTER FOUR

CLAIRE fully expected the empty house to be cold and dank, with cobwebs and dust and damp patches on the walls. But it was none of these things. Not even empty—not completely.

The parquet floor of the beautifully proportioned hall gleamed with polish, as did the delicately carved, richly dark banisters which curved up to the first floor. And the walls, not only in the hallway but in the room on the right that she poked her nose into, had been recently colour-washed in sophisticated shades that contrasted superbly with the deep, white-painted skirting-boards and architraves.

'Goodness!' she breathed out loud, knotting her brows. It was pleasantly warm, too. She undid the buttons of her winter-weight wool coat. The vendors must have left the central heating on. The place could only have been on the market for a very short time; it didn't feel lifeless as houses often did when their owners decamped, taking everything with them. This place felt vitally alive, yet tranquil too, and not all the furniture had gone because there were one or two pieces in this room, lovely antiques that looked as if they had been created especially for this particular house.

She wandered slowly back into the hall, still puzzled. How long had Harnage Place been on the market? Jake had been out of the country a great deal just recently, so how had he heard of it? And if he'd been negotiating for it for any length of time she would have known. For the last two years he hadn't made a move, finalised a deal, without discussing it fully with her.

Had he acquired it since meeting the *principessa*? Deliberately kept the negotiations secret? Had he asked her, Claire, to be here today because he was ready to tell her their paper marriage was over, and why?

I can't bear it, she thought tumultuously, her stomach churning sickeningly. But she knew she had to, and when she heard the arrival of a car, the deep silence after the engine had been cut, she knew she wasn't ready to hear what he had to tell her and she dragged the edges of her coat around her as she began to shiver all over.

Somehow, with the motivation of near desperation, she pulled herself together as she heard the unmistakable clunk of a car door closing, heard his quick, firm footsteps on the stone slabs, the steps leading up to the door.

Everything was going to be fine, she reassured herself sternly. No worries. She would find no problem getting another job, even though it wouldn't be as stimulating as this one. She had qualifications galore and, with Jake, the type of high-level work experience any other would-be personal secretary would give her eye-teeth for, not to mention every last one of her molars.

But the moment the door swung open she knew her job had nothing to do with it. He was wearing the continentally styled black micro coat she had personally picked out for him when they'd been in Italy last year, his dark hair slightly ruffled and spangled with the fine drizzle that was falling outside, his stunningly handsome features wiped clean of expression, and she knew she would miss him like some vital part of her own self, that when they parted something inside her would die.

For the timeless seconds while they faced each other wordlessly, she knew that despite the controlled, unspeaking features he was brimming over with restless mental excitement. It was there in the slightly flaring nostrils of his slim, acquiline nose, the heightened glitter of his silver-grey eyes.

Those eyes held hers with an intensity that was like a physical blow, sucking the breath out of her lungs, making her flesh quiver. Gazing helplessly into those glittering, mesmeric depths, she wondered how long she had loved him, when, precisely, the process of falling in love had begun for her. And why, in the name of sanity, it had taken her until this one fragment of time to admit that knowledge into her consciousness. It had jumped at her out of the dark, knocking her senseless.

Why did it have to hit her now? Why now, when everything pointed to his desire to marry the woman he loved?

The need to hide her internal torment turned her face to stone and when he asked, 'Like it?' she looked away from the gleam of suppressed excitement deep in those silver eyes and answered stiltedly,

'I haven't investigated further than one of the rooms, but yes, it seems to be a desirable property.'

If he noted the aura of distance she was deliberately projecting he didn't comment. Perhaps he was too enmeshed in his own private anticipations to notice anything about her, she thought as he closed the door behind him, shrugged out of his coat and tossed it haphazardly over the newel-post of the banisters as if marking the house with his ownership.

'Good,' he remarked, apropos of nothing, she decided. She wished now she'd insisted that the estate agent accompany her. She didn't want to be alone with him, not now. It hurt too much. And she had suggested it, but the elderly man who had delivered the keys had looked astonished, waving the suggestion aside, looking at her as if he thought she was two bricks short of a load.

'You're thinking of buying it?' she asked in the same cool voice. She was building a wall between them. It was necessary. But she hated it, mourned the old days of innocence when she had looked on him as her best friend, and he pushed his hands into his trouser pockets, rocking back slightly on his heels, one brow arched as he tipped his dark head on one side.

'Bought it. Signed and sealed six weeks ago. The electricians, plumbers and decorators moved out a few days ago. The key they used was left in the safe-keeping of the agent who delivered it to you this morning.' He slanted her a droll look. 'Amazing what a loud voice and a blank cheque can do, isn't it?'

Six weeks ago they'd flown in from Hong Kong. Just for a day or two, he'd said, for a breather. She'd lunched with old friends, catching up on their news, gone shopping. He, so he'd said, had relaxed at the London apartment, 'messing about', as he put it, which meant, she knew, recharging his batteries, listening to taped opera, wallowing sensually in the pure beauty of sound. But in reality he'd been seeing solicitors, signing deeds, engaging tradesmen—no doubt the best in their individual fields because he wasn't the type to settle for less than excellence.

Devious. Never, to her knowledge, had he kept anything from her in the past. The hurt was almost impossible to contain.

His affair with Lorella Giancetti must have been going on for far longer than she'd realised. There had always been times, towards the end of their stay in any particular country, when she would be expected to go on ahead of him to their next port of call, especially if they were planning on staying in one of the apartments he owned. To get it ready, aired and functioning, set up meetings.

He would have used that time to be with his lover. The *principessa*, and his plans for her, could have been the only reason why he'd kept the transaction secret.

'Why?' she asked tightly, not wanting to hear the

answer, and he gave her a crooked grin, shrugging loosely.

'To live in, of course. After years of rolling it's time I gathered moss. And where better? I was fascinated by this house when I was a boy. I did a lot of riding in the area and was drawn to the place like a magnet. When I was around fourteen I made up my mind to live here one day. I handed Litherton over to Emma when she married, as you know—and I don't regret that. So when I first began to think of settling someplace I thought instinctively of this house. I made the owners an offer they couldn't refuse.' He glanced at his watch. 'Come; let's take a look around.'

He was almost bristling with pent-up energy, she noted, the lump in her throat growing larger by the minute. She could feel the enthusiasm vibrating through his tall, lean body.

She shivered, swallowing hard. A tour of the house was impossible. Out. She couldn't smile and make pleasant noises while they walked through the rooms that would be his and his lady's, imagining them eating, relaxing, laughing, making love...

She took a deep breath and pushed out, 'I'd rather not. And shouldn't Lorella Giancetti be the first to see it? You bought this house for her, didn't you? You want to marry her, settle down; don't try to deny it.'

There, it was out. Now he would have to stop pretending that all was as it ever was. He would have to tell the truth. The prospect made her shake inside.

And pushing herself to the point of bringing it all out into the open had exhausted her.

'What do you mean she should be the first?' His look of astonishment confused her. She closed her eyes on a wave of disbelief and heard him tell her, laughter just below the surface of his dark voice now, 'If you can see the *principessa* living in the depths of the English countryside you've a better imagination than I have. She's strictly a city bird.'

She could hear him getting closer and her eyes winged open, wide and deeply blue. His voice was so warm, his eyes crinkling at the corners. He looked enormously pleased with himself.

'I have no intention of marrying La Giancetti. I am married to you, remember? I'm not about to invoke the opt-out clause—you're far too valuable an asset. Shall we begin?'

Just like that! She stared at him blankly. Did he really mean what he'd said—that he had no intention of ending their agreement because she was too valuable to him? So he wouldn't be marrying his voluptuous Italian princess—she would have to make do with being his pampered, indulged, sated mistress! And she, Claire, would have to turn a blind eye and be a good little drudge! Not that she'd ever considered her job in that light—

She gave herself an impatient mental shake. Drudgery or joy, what did it matter? It had to end; that was all she knew. She couldn't go on as before, not loving him the way she did…not with La Giancetti a sensual threat, forever in the background…

She ignored the invitation to accompany him on a tour of the house, standing her ground, telling him, her voice very tight, 'Might I suggest you use a little more discretion if you don't want rumours about the possible break-up of our perfect marriage—' she invested the words with scorn '—on the front page of every newspaper in the country? I'm sure your recently reported outing with that woman wasn't the first, and won't be the last. But do try to keep yourselves out of the limelight in future.' Hopefully, that constraint might make him think twice about wanting to have his cake and eat it, the restrictions on conducting a wild affair with the luscious Lorella too irksome for him.

Just saying the words, bringing them out into the open, made Claire's stomach churn with nausea, but her pale skin flared with vivid colour when he said softly, very close to her now, 'I do believe you're jealous.'

'Don't be absurd!' The words of denial flew off her tongue like arrows, instinctive, defensive words that she reinforced by adding, with a hastily gathered calm, 'We both knew something like this was bound to happen, sooner or later. Why else would we have agreed on the opt-out for just such a contingency? If you've had affairs before, no one's known about them, least of all me. You're either slipping, in this case, or serious.'

She turned and tramped away, down the hall, her back rigid. She was probably heading for the kitchen regions. She neither knew nor cared. If he intended to settle here, put down roots, delegate more perhaps, he would need a permanent housekeeper. A place like this couldn't be left to its own devices as were the apartments he had scattered around the globe. And she wouldn't be around to do the honours.

Somehow she was going to have to make him agree to end their relationship, which had now become untenable—at least as far as she was concerned—without exacting too many penalties.

But he was a man of honour; he kept his word and expected others to do the same. His wrath, as she had witnessed once when a business associate had tried to pull a fast one, was terrible, his retribution swift and sure and quite, quite deadly.

If she just upped and left him, sought an annulment, he could make sure she never worked again. At least not in the field she was qualified for. He made a good friend and a bad enemy.

'You're going in the wrong direction.' The touch of his hand on her shoulder made her jump out of her skin. He turned her round, using two hands now. She was facing him and felt brittle, as if she would shatter into a million pieces, because he was near to her, touching her, and touching each other was an unwritten taboo. Or had been in the past. He seemed increasingly inclined to break it, which was treachery—in the circumstances.

Her soft mouth trembled and the small gleam of amusement in his eyes disappeared—his eyes were kind now, his voice softer than she had ever heard it, as if he understood what she was going through, as if he wanted to ease her pain.

But he couldn't, she thought wildly. He couldn't know how she felt about him—she had only recently known herself! And he hadn't even tried to deny that he was having an affair with that woman!

'Loosen up, Claire,' he murmured, the silver discs of his eyes softened by the lowered thickness of black-as-night lashes. 'Why so tense? Tell me what's wrong.' His hold on her tightened, the tips of his fingers sending shafts of electrical excitement deep into the most secret parts of her body.

She gasped, desperately trying to ignore the sweet, insidious sensation, curling her tongue round her lips to moisten them because this was her opportunity, the best she would probably get, and she managed at last, thickly, 'I must warn you—all the plans you're making for the future—this house.' She knew her words were fractured and disjointed, and that wasn't at all like her. He probably thought she was going simple. But there wasn't much she could do about it. She dragged in another breath, aware now of her skittering heartbeat, and added, less decisively than she would have liked, 'I want to call it a day, Jake. Our agreement, I mean. I— It worked well, it suited us both. But not any more.'

The sudden sensation of utter silence, the cold, empty absence of any sound, was horrible. And even more awful was the aching void inside her when his touch lightened, his hands falling away, the stark sharpness of his tone ripping through her when, at last, he asked, 'Why? It suits me fine; what's happened to make you want out?'

What could she say? That she loved him? That she couldn't continue living with him as his wife—and yet not his wife at all—in such circumstances? That the arrangement which was a smooth convenience for him was now, because she loved him, nothing but a nightmare for her, a nightmare that would intensify with every moment they were together?

'I'm bored; I need a new challenge.' She tried to invest the tiny shrug she gave with a touch of insouciance, but didn't know whether she'd been successful, didn't know anything; how could she when he'd turned the situation on its head, looking relieved—of all things?

She'd fully expected disbelief, scorn, a display of pricked pride. After all, who could have the temerity to be bored in The Presence, dynamic as it was? What she hadn't expected and couldn't handle was the sudden wicked gleam in his eyes, the upward quirk of his deeply sensual lower lip, the way he said, 'Is that all?' as if what she'd said were totally irrelevant. 'I think I can remedy the boredom,' he told her, his voice a soft drawl, sending shivers down her spine. 'And if it's new challenges you want, I'll think of something.' He placed a hand in the small of her back, urging her to move, but she resisted stubbornly.

The last thing she wanted from him was a challenge. Working as closely with him as she had, she'd coped with enough of those to last a lifetime, handled everything with what he had been generous enough to term grace and intelligence. But that had been then and this was now, and everything was different.

Perhaps he was joking. She hadn't the courage to look up at him and find out. But she knew he wasn't taking her seriously and her voice was blank, underlining her resolve not to take defeat so easily, as she told him, 'I mean it, Jake. I need to move on. Nothing stays the same forever.'

She risked a glance at him then, going cold when she saw the intent assessment in his eyes. She knew that look only too well. He was using his mind like a computer, sifting through every known fact, making projections, finding a path that would lead to the truth.

He didn't want to lose her 'valuable services'; the thought of having to rely on possibly fickle hired help again would make him blisteringly angry. But did he really think she would be content to leave things as they were indefinitely, acting as his secretary, sounding board and nanny, as well as housekeeper and cook when they were at one of the apartments?

She had never led him to believe that things would stay as they were until she was in her dotage. He had been made fully aware that she'd agreed to his preposterous proposal because of Liz. Her mother's consultant had warned that she wouldn't make old bones, but that with care and cosseting, freedom from anxiety, the next and probably fatal attack could be delayed.

So no, she had never said it would be forever.

'Is that a fact?' His eyes were cold and uncompromising. 'You calmly tell me you need to move on and cite boredom as your excuse.' His mouth twisted in a cruel parody of a smile. 'You'll forgive me, my dear, if I think you're lying. Shall we put it to the test?'

His dark voice was heavily laced with irony and she shuddered, not knowing how to answer. Of course she'd been lying. She'd never been bored for a moment during the past two years. She didn't know how he intended to disprove her statement, wasn't going to ask, and didn't intend hanging around to find out.

'I have to go.' An ostentatious look at her wristwatch and the way she busily re-buttoned her coat gave her remark credibility, she hoped, and although she was prepared for his snapped out 'Where to?' she found the probing intensity of those silver eyes totally unnerving.

'Back to Litherton,' she managed to get out without faltering too much. 'Emma will wonder where I've got to.'

She wouldn't; of course she wouldn't. And Jake picked that up with smooth scorn, telling her, 'Are you going to make a habit of lying? Emma is fully aware of where you are and whom you're with, as you very well know.' He cupped his hand firmly around her elbow. 'Stop behaving badly. We're wasting time. I've got something I want you to see. Humour me.'

The touch of his hand, the closeness of his body as he herded her through the house, made insignificant crumbs of her resolve. Their relationship had undergone a remarkable sea change ever since he'd returned from Rome and she'd waved that newspaper under his nose. He'd never been angry with her, or scornful, or frogmarched her anywhere. Theirs had been a relationship of equals, made comfortable and pleasant by friendship and courtesy.

She no longer felt equal; she felt dominated. Jake Winter in masterful mood, uncaring of her wishes, was difficult to take. But she wasn't fighting him, because she knew she wouldn't win, and besides, she thought, swallowing around the lump in her throat, no harm could come of humouring him, as he had demanded. Their time together was marked, each passing second bringing them closer to the end, whether he liked it or not.

She was breathless, dangerously close to tears as he whisked her through the library, the empty shelves protected by elegant mahogany and gleaming glass, his long, loping stride relentless until they faced a panelled door at the very far end. Here he paused, one hand on the painted porcelain knob, the other sliding away from her elbow to take her hand, lacing their fingers together. Shock-waves of sensation crashed through her as her fingers gripped his convulsively, powerless to let go because the feel of her flesh and bone cleaving to his, the scalding of skin against skin, was a craving, a drug that could so easily become an addiction.

Pushing a half-crazed whimper back into her throat, she steeled herself to drag her hand from his. She must not betray the way she felt, this longing to be his, the desperate need to stay with him always, loving and loved.

But he forestalled her too long delayed attempt to remove her hand, his voice deep and soft and tinged with triumph as he challenged, 'Tell me this bores you and I'll call you a liar. For the third time in under an hour,' and pushed open the door, leading her into paradise.

CHAPTER FIVE

IT WAS like stepping into another world. Perennial summer in the bitterly cold depths of December. It took Claire's breath away. All she could do, for several long moments, was stare around her, her soft lips slightly parted, her eyes very wide.

The Victorian conservatory was immense, the huge glass dome arching high above catching the pale winter light, magnifying it, layer upon layer, until it was a shimmering opalescent glow, filtering down through the rich, jungly growth that was like wave after wave of a scented, exotic sea.

'I'm speechless!' She turned to him, her eyes glowing, her sudden smile wide and beautiful, the pain of loving him momentarily knocked out of her mind by the unexpected loveliness of this sumptuous, scented, exotic and quite perfect place—until he answered her smile with the brilliance of his own and the pain returned, battering her, slashing her with the points of a thousand knives. Holding herself together somehow, she untangled her fingers from his and turned away, praying the hurting wouldn't get worse, get so bad that she wouldn't be able to hide it from him.

'It affected me that way too, the first time I saw it all those years ago,' he told her as she walked further in, her heels tapping on the black and white tessellated floor. 'I'd tethered the horse at the edge of the orchard, out of sight of the house, and made my way down here. As I told you, the house fascinated me, but I hadn't known of the conservatory until I saw it glittering in the sunlight. One of the doors was open and I looked in, careful not to be seen—the then owners, an ancient man and his sister, were reputed to be extremely well-connected but half crazy. They didn't like people and lived for their plant collections. That was the moment I promised myself I'd own the house one day.'

'I can understand that.' She was in control again, determined to think about what she was seeing, exclude everything else, enjoy and appreciate, because tomorrow, all her tomorrows, would be bleak and dreary. He wouldn't be part of them so how could the future be anything other than a series of months and years to be plodded through, gradually, and probably slowly, learning to exist without him?

'Do you know the names of all these plants?' she asked stiltedly, for something to say. She could recognise the obvious—the orchids, lilies, camellias and sweet-scented jasmine—but the majority were exotic strangers to her. 'And, more importantly, do you know how to look after them?'

'No, but I know a man who does.'

She heard the laughter in his voice as he walked beside her and she bent to run her fingers gently over the feathery arching leaves of a miniature date palm, turning her head away to hide the ache that must show in her eyes as he explained, 'The couple I bought the house from—he inherited it from his uncle, the old man who lived here with his sister when I was a boy—knew nothing about the plant collection and cared even less. They employed a gardener to look after it full time, and I kept him on—along with the two men who look after the grounds and a couple of part-time cleaners who come up from the village each day.'

He had everything organised—had she expected anything less?—but he was going to discover that he couldn't have everything his own way, no matter how minutely he planned. He couldn't make her stay with him, not the way things were, the way things had changed.

But she wasn't going to think of that, not now. She stepped past him, moving round a stand of orange trees planted in white-painted square wooden tubs, and stared with wide-eyed wonder at the sudden revelation of a wide expanse of quiet water, the edges thickly planted, graceful statuary half hidden by lush, jungly growth and reflected in the still surface, large golden carp moving serenely in the clear depths, flicking laconic tails.

'Unbelievable!' she breathed.

'Boredom gone?' he drawled, and she flicked him a quick, warm smile, forgiving the little dig because she had earned it.

'You know how to spring a surprise,' she granted. 'This place is utterly fabulous, like a fairy-tale! It's so beautiful, calm and—'

Her powers of description failed her, the sensory

delights of sight and scent taking over, and he ran a soft finger down the curve of her cheek and supplied, 'Sensuous is the word you're looking for. The air in here is thick with sensuousness.' His fingers hovered at the corner of her mouth and she looked up at him, her eyes drowning in his, her lips parting.

She couldn't help it, this instinctive betrayal of all she had meant to hide, and his head dipped, as if he was about to kiss her, and her pulses began to race because their relationship wasn't physical and he had never shown the slightest desire to have it any other way. She would have picked it up if he had, but if things had changed for him, as they had for her...

But he didn't kiss her; of course he didn't. Why should he, when he had the Italian woman to gratify that kind of need?

'You look like a child in wonderland. Gratifying,' he said, sounding smug. 'Let me take your coat. You must be sweltering.'

So the danger, that moment of utter confusion, was past, and she allowed him to help her out of her coat because she couldn't think what else to do and couldn't find anything to say. She had wanted him to kiss her so much it hurt. She could only pray that he hadn't been aware of it.

Jake draped her coat over his arm and glanced at his watch. It wasn't the first time he'd done that and she guessed he had an appointment lined up—lunch perhaps, or maybe a flight to catch later in the day. Back to Rome—or was the Italian woman here in England, maybe at the London apartment, eagerly waiting his arrival? She wasn't going to ask because she didn't want to know. Ignorance was less painful than the truth.

Even without her coat she was still too warm and she resisted the impulse to undo the buttons of her suit jacket, remembering just in time that she was wearing nothing but a serviceable, no-nonsense bra beneath it. Without thinking she had chosen to wear the Romeo Gigli softly structured deep olive suit in preference to the jeans and sweaters she'd lived in while staying with Emma.

Because she knew he liked it? Because he admired the elegance she had learned to acquire during her time with him? Had she, unconsciously, been dressing for the man in her life all this time—in love with him and not knowing it?

She was learning truths about herself and was having difficulty coping with them, and although she knew she should insist on leaving right now, and drive back to Litherton to work out how she could force him to agree to end their arrangement, she found herself mindlessly tagging along without a trace of resistance when he took her hand and led her to the opposite side of the indoor lake.

Unlike her, he was casually dressed, wearing soft black chinos and a cream-coloured heavy silk shirt which enriched the olive tones of his skin. He looked magnificently sexy, overwhelmingly, potently male, and the touch of his hand was like dynamite, creating frantic explosions of sensation all over her body.

He was lethal, she thought, subsiding weakly on to

the padded seat of one of the Edwardian cast-iron chairs set around a decadently ornate matching table. Quite lethal and a threat to the entire female sex.

'Time for lunch,' he said, his gaze tangling with hers, his smile hungry, as if she were on the menu, and that made her feel distinctly nervous. But his blunt statement knocked her theories about a pressing appointment right on the head and she said dourly, trying to douse down the ridiculous sense of relief which, with the jumpy, jangly nervous state she was in, was making her feel utterly confused,

'Brought a packet of jam butties, did you?' And she didn't have to wait for a response to her feeble joke because two white-coated waiters suddenly appeared, gliding out of the tropical growth, one with a trolley, the other with a tray of champagne on ice and two glasses.

'I think I can do better than that,' he murmured, smiling blandly as the champagne was poured into the carved-crystal flutes, the Russian caviare in its bowl of crushed ice placed on the table, with the succulent wedges of lemon and the blinis that went with it. And only when the two waiters had discreetly moved away could Claire find her voice at all.

'Don't tell me you inherited those two from the previous owner. Do they live here all the time? Where have they been hiding?' She knew she was babbling but couldn't help it. She felt as if she had stepped inside a dream, where anything could happen, and probably would.

Jake, heaping the black caviare on to a corner of a

hot buckwheat pancake, told her, 'They and the chef have been in the kitchen for an hour or so. They were hired to give us lunch. No mystery. Their instructions were to serve the food exactly one hour after my arrival.'

So that was why he had been checking up on the time. But, 'Why?' she found herself asking. Her smooth brow wrinkled. Why go to so much trouble? Was this lavish gesture his way of celebrating his acquisition of the house he had coveted since boyhood? Must be, she told herself, taking nervous sips of the deliciously cold champagne. It was a pity it had come on such an inappropriate day, the day when she had made up her mind, quite firmly, at last—to ask him to agree to end their marriage.

'Why not?' Grey eyes sparkled like moonlight on a silver sea. 'But if you're getting prosaic in your old age and need a cut-and-dried reason for celebrating, isn't the date sufficient? It's our second anniversary after all. Or had you forgotten?'

Claire winced. He was unconscious of the irony, of course, but that didn't prevent her feeling as if he had stabbed her in the heart. She clutched at her glass again, the surface cool and dewed with condensation, and sipped, just a little, and then a little more, trying to ease the aching dryness of her throat.

'I hadn't forgotten,' she husked out at last. 'It's simply that ours is not that kind of marriage, and you know it.'

'Who better?' he responded drily. And then, leaning back a little, he watched her in silence, his hooded, enigmatic eyes sliding over her classically lovely features, the stylish wings of her silky dark hair lying smoothly against the clear whiteness of her skin.

She looked down quickly, aware that her fingers were shaking as she tore a blini into tiny pieces, aware for the first time of the soft whirring of the classic colonial bronze-bladed fans that stirred the air high above, suspended beneath the soaringly splendid, multi-faceted glass dome.

If she met the challenge of his eyes she knew she would see resentment in the way he was looking at her. He couldn't enjoy having his personal life controlled by his ingrained beliefs that hired help, no matter how handsomely paid and fulsomely recommended, was not reliable, knowing that the one person who could be utterly relied upon to iron out all life's wrinkles for him was the one person who stopped him openly enjoying his passionate affair with the *principessa*, perhaps even marrying her, giving her his children.

So of course he must resent her.

Longing for the waiters to return, collect the debris and break the taut silence, she went very still as his voice, lowered to a sultry whisper, sent her nerves and pulses skittering.

'But that could change, couldn't it, my dear? As you pointed out yourself, nothing stays the same forever. Our arrangement has worked perfectly. Would you enjoy meeting the challenge of a change within it?'

Going into a blind panic, she looked back at what

she had said. So was he suggesting that their relationship should change, their marriage become a real one—with all that implied? If he had suggested it months ago, before she'd known about his affair with the Italian woman—which he had definitely not denied—would she have jumped at the opportunity? She knew without the shadow of a doubt that she would have done. She'd been falling in love with him for ages, putting her happiness at being with him down to the stimulation of the work she did for him, her enjoyment of his clever, restless, lavish personality.

He expected a response, she knew that, but speech was beyond her. Her tongue felt like a lump of wood and she was sure her throat muscles had gone into spasm, and she had never been so pleased to see anyone in her life when the two waiters appeared silently along the path that meandered through the semitropical plantings. One cleared the debris while the other set out half a dozen small bowls of different salads and served a herby mêlée of mixed mushrooms casseroled in red wine, and to Claire's utter yet wary relief Jake made no more mention of making any change to their relationship, and even the wariness evaporated as the meal progressed through a light-as-air cold raspberry soufflé to savoury Angels On Horseback, with limitless champagne and his unrivalled ability to put her at ease.

He bewitched her, there was no other word for it, she thought muzzily, snatching greedily at this one, and possibly last, interlude of happiness as he captivated her with the rapier-sharp wit she had come to treasure over the time she had been with him, and with the ability he had to laugh at himself, which she had always found so endearing, making him, despite his great power, wealth and terrifying drive, seem more human and lovable than anyone she had ever met. Lovable…

It all came down to that in the end, didn't it? She held his eyes, her own shimmering. At this moment it was something she simply accepted. She could do no other. She was beyond fighting love; he had intoxicated her—more than the wine or the exotic, perfumed surroundings. And when he rose to his feet and held out his hand, she took it, rising fluidly, bonelessly as he instructed one of the waiters, 'We'll have coffee on the loungers and then you might as well call it a day. We can look after ourselves from now on.'

Speak for yourself, she whispered inside her head. She couldn't vouch for herself. She had wandered into a dream, where logic, responsibility and control over what happened didn't exist. She could no more look after herself than fly! And the waiter, his young face bland—as if he and his colleagues cooked and served long, sybaritic lunches for two in huge glass domes every day of the week—silently departed. And Jake led her to a secluded terrace, arboured by vines which in the summertime she guessed would be thick with heavy clusters of grapes, to an intimate arrangement of padded loungers and low tables, just right for relaxing.

She needed no invitation to sit; her legs felt decidedly wobbly, which was down to the unusual intake of vintage champagne with lunch, she decided blithely. Perched on the edge of one of the loungers, she watched while he poured the coffee. His movements, as always, were deft and economical. She could watch him for hours, no problem—he was visual poetry—but she tried self-protectively to make her face go blank and unrevealing as he looked sideways at her, suddenly, taking her unawares, catching the unfocused, dreamily loving look on her face during that tiny unguarded moment before she'd frantically tried to rearrange her expression.

Had he recognised the look on her face, translated it correctly? she wondered, horrified. It seemed so, the way he was watching her now with narrowed, calculating eyes. She felt as if he'd stolen from her, like a thief, taking her innermost, private thoughts without her permission. She shivered slightly, suppressing the sensation of spiritual violation, then saw the hard silver glitter of his eyes soften to gentle misty grey and heard him tell her, 'You look as if you've got a train to catch. Relax. Didn't the champagne work after all?' he queried softly, shaking his head, teasing her as he eased her back against the slightly tilted, padded back of the lounger. 'You were uptight when I arrived, your beautiful head full of nonsense, but I'll be damned if we leave here before I've got you to unwind.'

The trouble was, the champagne had worked *too* well; it alone had to be responsible for the way she sank back against the comfortable upholstery without even the sniff of resistance. And did he really think she was beautiful? In the same class as the *principessa*? Of course not, how could he? she answered herself, lowering her eyelids to hide the sudden, silly surge of tears. He'd accused her of talking nonsense, so he had to be referring to the way she'd told him she was bored, needed a new challenge, wanted to end their arrangement.

And, as far as he was concerned, that was what it was. Nonsense. Something to be categorically dismissed because it didn't suit him. He wanted to have his cake and eat it.

But for the life of her she couldn't dredge all that up again, not right now; she felt too muzzy, boneless and weak. And he was sitting at the foot of the lounger and slowly, one by one, he was removing her shoes, his lean fingers curling round her high, arching insteps, stroking so softly, so sensually, and all at once she didn't have the wit or the will to do anything about it. Like telling him to back off, leave her alone because touching each other was a no-no.

Her eyelids fluttered. The sensation was indescribably erotic and she knew she really should put a stop to it, especially when one of his hands slid stealthily along the calf of one leg, sliding beneath her knees, ruffling the hem of her skirt, then higher, inexorably higher, until his fingers found what they had been seeking and he drew down the tiny zip at the side of her skirt.

'Better? More comfy?' He had moved slightly. Now his hipbone was nudging hers. And just as she had been powerless to stop him removing her shoes, loosening the waistband of her tight-fitting skirt, she also appeared to have lost the power of speech. No answering words would come. But 'Better', 'More comfy'—that was crazy!

She was burning with a heat that came from deep inside her, freaking out on it, and she made a tiny moaning sound in her throat that could have meant anything and actually welcomed the release when his cool fingertips brushed her skin as he began to undo the buttons of her jacket.

The near-tropical temperature made the wearing of a fine woollen suit sheer and sudden purgatory, the touch of the costly, soft fabric against her unbearably sensitised skin quite unendurable. And her head drifted back, like a broken flower on the slender stalk of her neck, as he part lifted her, easing the beautiful jacket away, allowing it to drop to the floor as if it were a rag.

Slowly, very slowly, he eased her back against the padding, and even with her eyes closed she knew he was looking at her body. She could feel it, sense it, knew it because of her responses, because of the way her tummy muscles tightened, the spiralling heat that suddenly and violently formed deep inside her, the way her breasts surged and pushed against the cotton of her prosaically ordinary bra.

And she knew she should be feeling shy, or something. But didn't. It was Jake who was undressing her so that was all right. More than all right. It was won-

derful, a release from the frustration that had been
building for ages without her being aware of it.

Fighting up out of the layers and clouds of delicious languor that had been keeping her drugged and
supine, a piece of meat he could play with at will,
she decided she just had to join in and peeped at him
through the fringing veil of her black lashes.

His awesomely honed and beautiful features were
dewed with tiny beads of sweat, darkening and highlighting his olive skin tones, and that added to the
magic, the male mystery of him, and his jaw muscles
were taut, tightly contracted, as if he was trying to
hide something. She didn't know what and didn't
think she cared, and wriggled a little to allow him
better access because his long fingers were dealing
with the formidable back fastening of her sturdy white
bra.

And even the grim practicality of that garment
couldn't embarrass her. Although she had always
spent lavishly on what she wore, to please him and
fit the image he wanted her to project, some puritan-
ical streak in her nature had ensured that she cut
sternly back on the things that didn't show, buying
plain, serviceable undergarments and nightwear, and,
although he had never actually seen her wearing the
stuff before, you couldn't travel the world with a man,
share the same homes, without his being aware of
what went into the laundry.

She felt the sudden release of the fastening and
chuckled irrepressibly. He had wanted her to lighten
up, and she had, irredeemably so, it seemed. She was

so light she was buoyant, floating on air, and the slow-burning intensity of his eyes, the way he was looking at her—as if she were the most desirable woman in the world—the slight, responsive indentation of his very male mouth did nothing to bring her back down to earth. She didn't think her feet would ever touch the ground again.

And then her arms took on a glorious life of their own, reaching up and wrapping themselves around his neck, her fingers buried in the thick dark hair at his nape, and she watched his eyes change, saw the turbulent darkness alternating between the silver gleam of satisfaction, and his voice was thick and soft, like melted honey as he said her name.

'Claire, my love…' Then his head came down and he took possession of her mouth and her whole body and soul turned to brilliant, soaring incandescent flame as she submitted to his demanding lips, and knowing this was right, so very right, that she was where she had been born to be, took what she knew to be her birthright, let him know how desperately she wanted him and made demands of her own, lips tasting and plundering, withdrawing and teasing, her body becoming softer, pliant and responsive, moving explicitly against his, clinging to him because she couldn't bear this to end.

Eventually, he broke away, only to hold her with savage possession, her head imprisoned against the strong arch of his shoulder, his hand stroking her hair as he murmured her name, over and over, his voice thick. Claire clung to him dizzily, knowing that they had embarked on a journey that could have only one ending, wildly exultant because of the inevitability of it.

Had he known, for two long years, the thing that she had never suspected until recently—that he had only to touch her to turn her into an insatiable wanton? Was that why he had kept an almost clinical distance between them physically, waiting until the time was right? Right for them both.

She could feel the heavy beat of his heart and her fingers walked unsteadily up his broad chest, undoing buttons, and she hadn't noticed before, but the short winter afternoon was dying and as it did so tiny lights sprang automatically to life, myriads of them, glowing, gleaming and glittering among, above and below the lush green foliage, the stands of tall, stately lilies, the rambling, exuberant tropical chaos, and she sighed blissfully as he laid her back on the lounger and, his hands unsteady, began peeling off her skirt.

No woman alive could hope for a more beautiful setting for her first journey into ecstasy with the man she loved. Ecstasy and beyond, she acknowledged feverishly as her flesh shuddered responsively beneath his seductive hands.

And the perfumed silence was broken by the music of his ragged breathing, her own gasps and tiny moans of heated pleasure an erotic counterpoint, and he told her thickly, his hands and his lips exploring her body with tormenting sensuality, 'I'm going to make this as long and as sweet and as memorable for you as I know how. So tell me what pleases you most—we have all the time in the world, remember. And when I've taken you to the limits and beyond, we'll wait just a little while and I'll take you there again…' And then he went still, as if turned to stone, and Claire, even in her delirium, heard it too. The intrusion of pattering feet, Emma's raised voice.

'Are you in here, you two? I've looked all over the house. Your cars are outside so you've got to be somewhere!'

CHAPTER SIX

CLAIRE did her best to empty her mind of the way Emma had walked in and interrupted them late yesterday afternoon—and just what she had interrupted.

But her mind had other ideas and vivid, nerve-shattering images kept gatecrashing, scalding reminders of the way she had felt—awash with the sensation of tarnished glory—as Jake had swung to his feet, rapidly rebuttoning his shirt, his muttered expletive low but blistering as he'd walked, soft-footed, away, to intercept his sister. She had been left to dress herself with fumbling fingers, aching with frustration, burning with the far greater pain of knowing that if it hadn't been for Emma's timely interruption she would have belonged to Jake, body and soul, mortgaging her future, emotionally tying herself to him forever, knowing her love would never be returned, always wondering whom he was with when he was away.

Pausing for breath now, she leant against one of Litherton's impressive gateposts. She didn't want to have to face him, to begin the deception. But she had been out for three hours, ever since first light, marching across fields and down green lanes, scrambling through thickets and fording streams, and exhaustion and common sense told her she had to go back. She couldn't hide forever.

Last night it had been easy, relatively so. She'd been feeling sick with anguish when Jake had come back with the voluble Emma, actually shaking with it, barely able to dredge up a smile when her sister-in-law had hugged her, bubbling over with excitement.

'He has actually bought it, he tells me! Oh, I did so hope it was on the cards—we'll be neighbours, practically! You don't mind me coming along and poking my big nose in, do you? Only I couldn't stay home wondering a minute longer! And isn't this the most gorgeous conservatory ever? If it were mine I'd live in it, never mind the house!'

And she'd insisted on being shown all over, right down to the last broom cupboard, and Jake had done the honours, and if his sister's inconvenient curiosity had left him feeling frustrated he hadn't shown it. And as for the way she'd felt herself as she'd tagged along, not really registering the lovely rooms, well, 'empty' would be an apt description—drained of self-respect, empty of hope, the foolish hope that he might have fallen in love with her, as she had with him.

If she hadn't been bewitched by the magic of his hands, his lips, his eyes, if the flame of her own de-sires hadn't burned out her ability to reason, she would have read his intentions correctly, been able to handle him—and her own needs. But she had been bewitched and her ability to think clearly had been a long while returning, but by the time they'd got back to Litherton, in separate cars, she'd known what she had to do, only she hadn't known how to do it.

The plea of a headache—no fabrication—had guaranteed her an early night. Emma had said, 'What about supper? I've made lemon chicken—Frank's favourite. If you can't face that, how about some hot milk and biscuits? I'll bring it up to you. I must say you do look pale and peaky. Let's hope you're not coming down with flu—I hear it's running round the village like nobody's business.'

Declining, Claire had edged out of the door, making her escape while Jake was still in the hall, talking to Frank, who had just returned from his professional visit with Liz. Slipping through the kitchen and up the back staircase, she'd turned the key in her bedroom lock, deciding that if anyone came up—Emma with her hot milk, or Jake to get down to unfinished business—she would pretend to be deeply asleep.

And this morning she'd slipped out before anyone was around and not even the dogs had clamoured to go with her. They'd probably thought she was crazy; it was barely light outside, and the deep sofas and armchairs, soft rugs and the background central heating were far more appealing than the grim dawn light of a bleak December day.

Crazy or not, the long solitary walk had cleared Claire's mind of emotional debris. She had worked out what she had to do and she had to stick with her decision because although the alternative was dangerously appealing it was unthinkable.

Staying with him, allowing their marriage to become a real one in every detail but the honouring of the vow to forsake all others, would inevitably become the ultimate in degradation and pain.

She wasn't about to commit emotional suicide.

Her head high, her stride long, she headed back to the house, to be greeted by the usual sea of dogs and Emma's relieved nagging.

'Where do you think you've been? You must have been out for hours! Are you feeling better? You don't look quite so washed out. And Jake's been looking all over—he's not long got back. If I know him, he's already rounding up a search party.'

'Why? Because I went out for a walk?' She smiled as she unlaced her walking boots, but one finely arched brow rose ironically. A flurry of anxiety might come naturally to a loving husband, but Jake only wanted to keep tabs on his possession. He had invested a great deal of money in her, one way or another, and he meant to keep her valuable services. While Liz had been dependent on his allowance he'd had no fears that his smart little helper would hand in her notice—and the paper marriage had acted as a kind of cement, ensuring that she grew accustomed to the glamour and luxury of their shared lifestyle.

But Liz was no longer dependent and the first murmurings of discontent from his smart little helper had set wheels turning in his devious, tricky mind. He'd bed her and bind her; making love to her now and then wouldn't be too much of a hardship—she wasn't hideous.

'No, of course not,' Emma chided good-humouredly. 'Last night you looked on the point of collapse and this morning you'd vanished into thin air. Jake took you breakfast in bed and there was nothing there. Anyway, go and put him out of his misery. There was a phone call for him and he took it in the study. He said if you showed up while he was busy you were to go to him immediately.'

Claire went; she had no option. But she didn't go willingly. She and Jake had never had a formal employer-employee relationship, not even when she'd been working as his temp, standing in for yet another personal assistant who'd found the going too hectic. Theirs had always been a relationship of partners, as if one couldn't function on all cylinders without the back-up of the other. And today, for the very first time, she felt as if she was a very junior dogsbody being summoned to appear before the chairman of the board.

Emma's study, one of a warren of rooms at the rear of the house, was its usual clutter of box files, books on estate management, forestry and stock rearing leaning drunkenly against each other on the shelves, paperwork littering every inch of the big oak table that served as a desk.

Claire closed the door quietly behind her, psyching herself up. Jake was still using the phone, his broad black leather-clad back to her as he faced the window overlooking the paddocks. Whoever he was talking to was obviously not flavour of the month, judging by the terse, bitingly arrogant tone, the barely leashed impatience as he edgily paced the length of the desk, never moving away from the window.

Was he anxious, watching to see if she returned from that direction? Was he still wearing the leather jacket because he'd meant to set out again, searching for her, but had been delayed by this call? Was it possible that he might worry about her? Care?

She swallowed convulsively. She would not think along those lines. Then she made him aware of her presence, speaking out with cool clarity, 'Emma said you wanted to see me,' and was braced and ready to face whatever strategy he meant to employ. Even if he mentioned what had happened yesterday she was sure she could handle it, yet she couldn't prevent an inner shudder as, after one tiny, frozen second, he swung round on the balls of his feet, snapped, 'See to it. Now!' into the receiver before slamming it down, adding, in the same savage breath, 'Where the hell do you think you've been?'

Grey eyes had darkened to charcoal beneath the black, frowning bar of his brows, the strong jaw ominously clenched. He looked, she decided coolly, as if he would like to strangle her on the spot. An impression strengthened by his wrathful, 'I've spent most of the morning scouring the countryside looking for you!'

His anger was in stark contrast to the mood of the previous day. Then he had been the essential male predator, intent on seduction. But she couldn't think about that, not if she wanted to stay cool and collected, so she turned her back on him, idly tidying the bookshelves, her tone nice and light, with just a tiny undertone of sarcasm, exactly what she had in mind, as she told him, 'Somehow I didn't think I had to get your permission to go for a walk. How silly of me!'

'No, not silly,' he said in a voice as cold as ice. 'Bloody thoughtless. Or do you enjoy worrying the socks off me?'

Of course she didn't, she thought despairingly. How could she, when she loved him more than life? She had been too bound up with her own dark problems to give a thought to the way he might react to her disappearance. And never, in her wildest imaginings, would she have expected him to worry.

Recognising that her hard-won sense of detachment was rapidly splintering in the face of his concern, she gave the merest sketch of a shrug, said, 'There's no need to snarl. Since I've been staying here I've got into the habit of taking long early morning walks. I imagined Emma would have told you,' and swept to the door, knowing she had handled what could have degenerated into a fraught situation with coolness and dignity. But then the self-congratulatory bubble burst around her head as he intercepted her swiftly, taking her arm, swinging her round into close contact with the hard length of his body.

Too close a contact, she thought as her flesh relished the secret pleasure, her whole body taut with trembling expectancy as the heat in the pit of her stomach turned into ravaging flames.

'Don't ever think of walking out on me again.' He

gave her a tiny shake. His voice was dark but that achingly attractive wry half-smile shook her soul, held her motionless, in thrall to the magic of him, held her where she knew she should not be. 'I over-reacted. I'm sorry. But you looked like death last night. I believed Emma when she said she thought you were coming down with flu. When I brought you a hot drink and some aspirin you didn't answer when I knocked on the door, so I thought sleep the best preventative medicine. I've been imagining all kinds of horrors since I discovered your room empty at eight-thirty this morning. Am I forgiven for snarling?'

How could she answer him when her throat was clogged with pain? He had cared; he had been anx-ious for her wellbeing. How could she have forgotten the compassion he was capable of, when it had been he who had been with her all through that long and dreadful night when she'd feared Liz wouldn't pull through, comforting and supporting her, holding her together?

But remembering was counter-productive; she had too many reasons for loving him, and she wasn't go-ing to add to the burden. Making a supreme effort, she tried to pluck his fingers away but his grip tight-ened, his voice low and rough as he told her, 'We have to talk. About what happened between us yes-terday, about the future, our relationship.'

He pulled her closer, holding her in the gentle, se-ductive prison of his strong arms, and she yearned to melt into him. When she was with him now every-thing in her was programmed to be warm and pliant and feminine, but the instinct for self-preservation was fighting on her side, enabling her to make her body go rigid in the circle of his arms, to say distantly, 'There's not a lot to talk about, is there?'

'Only your crazy idea that we split up,' he countered softly. 'We make a good team. The best. Why spoil it?' His voice was a honeyed tease but there was nothing teasing about the masterful way his strong, lean hand cradled her head, pulling it against the proud breadth of his chest. He had her and he meant to hold her, she recognised fuzzily as she inhaled the heady scent of soft leather and warm, vital male.

She made a small, distressed sound in the back of her throat, protesting against the way her body burned to wriggle even closer to his, and he brushed her neck with his lips and she felt giddy, delirious, hearing his softly teasing voice through a swirling mist.

'We'll go over to the house, get Emma to pack a picnic lunch—and promise not to come near! We have furnishings to acquire, and although I already have one of the best teams available on the job I want your input on our future home. But, more importantly, we need the privacy to talk. I want to make our marriage a real one. Yesterday proved how good we'd be together. If Emma's damned curiosity hadn't got the better of her we'd have been man and wife in every sense of the word by now.'

Did he think she didn't know that? His words made her go cold. Everything he appeared to be promising was cruelly tempting. But he'd said no word of love, said nothing that could be construed as such. And she had never allowed herself to hope he would. All the same, the forlorn realisation gave her a wicked stab of grief.

He knew, only too well, how he affected her; those clever eyes had watched her go up in flames of desire beneath his roving hands and demanding lips, become a wanton, willing, eager slave to his magnificent male dominance. He believed he only had to take her into his bed to bind her more closely and permanently than their agreement—albeit made with honour and integrity on both sides—could ever have done.

And he was right; of course he was. Devastatingly right. But somehow she had to make him believe he was wrong. It was going to be the hardest thing she had ever had to do.

She pulled away from him, using her hands as levers, and forced herself to tell him, 'Sounds a cosy offer, but I'm afraid I'm going to have to pass.'

And she turned her head quickly, not willing to let him see the haunted look in her eyes, and flinched when he said grimly, 'I've never known you to lie before, but recently you seem to be doing an awful lot of it. Are you honestly asking me to believe you weren't more than willing to consummate our marriage? Don't forget how well I know you. You're highly intelligent, loyal, fastidious and sexually unaware—or were, until I took you in my arms. Are you trying to tell me it meant nothing?'

'I was drunk,' she said thickly, and felt her face go bright with colour. 'I'm sorry—it shouldn't have hap-

pened. I shouldn't have let you believe— Oh, hell!'
She began to pace the small room, wrapping her arms
around her body. She felt cold inside, as if she would
never be warm again, as if her blood had stopped
flowing and had turned to ice, frozen by the dreadful
thing she was doing. She was denying her love, her
need, her plain old-fashioned adoration. She was lying. She would never find another man to match him.
'The champagne, the lunch, the atmosphere in that
place—it made me behave stupidly,' she flung at him.

There was a frighteningly hard glitter in his silver
eyes and she wished she hadn't risked that defiant
glance in his direction, and turned her attention to the
window, not seeing anything, muttering, hating the
way her voice emerged so sullenly, 'I did mean it
when I said I wanted to move on.'

'Just like that?' he asked with humiliating distaste
and she shook her head wretchedly. Oh, no, it hadn't
been a spur-of-the-moment, selfish whim. Just a matter of her own emotional survival.

But she couldn't tell him that; she could only pull
her former character—the serene and unflappable,
morally sound part of herself that he knew so well—
out of the corner it had been hiding in, and deny, 'No,
not just like that. Give me some credit. As I explained, I need to move on, but I'll certainly carry on
as usual, doing my job, until you find a replacement—
provided you find him or her within a reasonable
amount of time,' she added, not trusting him not to
pretend that every applicant he saw was a waste of
space.

'And what's Liz going to make of it?' he wanted to know, his voice dry. He flung himself down on the office chair, his endless legs stretched out in front of him. 'She thinks we're the perfect couple, beloved by the gods. What sort of state is she going to get herself in when you tell her the marriage is over?'

'She'll be upset,' Claire said tightly. She wasn't going to let him get to her with emotional blackmail. She'd square it with Liz, perhaps even tell her the truth—that her marriage to Jake Winter had been a matter of convenience, for both of them. But circumstances had changed, again for both of them. She would be horrified, probably, but she'd get over it. 'She's an essentially sensible lady,' she told him. 'She wouldn't expect me to stay married forever to a man I don't love.'

He gave her a hard look. 'If I double the amount paid into your account each month, would that make any difference?' And at the impatient shake of her head he got to his feet. 'No, I thought not. I don't understand what's going on here,' he brooded. 'But I'm working on it.' He walked to the door then turned, his face impassive. 'You mentioned a reasonable amount of time for finding a replacement. Exactly how long will it be before you walk out?'

She wanted to tell him, Until this time tomorrow, but couldn't do that to him. The sooner the arrangement was terminated, the better from her point of view. Every second that passed made her die a little more inside, but she told him stiltedly, 'Two months should give you ample time. But I'd appreciate it if you could make it sooner.' She watched him dip his dark head in acknowledgement, his features blank, as if he no longer cared, had washed his hands of her and consigned her to the past.

Then he disappeared.

Wondering how she'd find the energy to leave the study and make like a house guest, Claire tried to look as if her world wasn't falling apart when Emma breezed in through the door.

'Good. I can call my office my own again.' She shuffled through the papers scattered all over her desk. 'I don't know why I'm expected to fill in endless forms and stuff. Still, needs must— Look, sweetie, Frank's home for lunch. Pop a pizza in the oven, would you? And there's salad stuff in the fridge. Half an hour suit? That husband of yours drove off like a bat out of hell. I bet he forgot to buy your Christmas pressie! Otherwise you'd both be lounging around in that gorgeous conservatory—I know I would, given half a chance. And when are you going to start measuring for curtains and stuff?'

Claire forced a smile and closed the door on the happy burblings. If she told Emma she wouldn't be sharing Harnage Place with Jake, that in two months' time, at most, their marriage would be over, her sister-in-law wouldn't believe her ears. She would leave Jake to drop that particular bombshell, she would have a tough enough time of it when she came to shatter all Liz's fond illusions.

In the meantime she knew she had to act as if everything was right in her corner of the world, and made herself look enthusiastic when, lunch over, Emma suggested the two of them set off in the Land Rover and cut holly and ivy for decorating the house, and outwardly, at least, didn't bat an eyelid when Jake phoned from Heathrow just before supper with the blankly imparted news that he was catching a flight to Rome and would be back some time on Christmas Eve.

'He'll have to get rid of those itchy feet when you've moved into that gorgeous house,' Emma grumbled as the three of them sat over supper. 'I mean, you can't own a place like that and leave it empty for nine-tenths of the year. You'll have to put your foot down, Claire. It isn't as if he needs to keep hopping around the world. He could delegate a lot more than he does, couldn't he, Frank?'

Claire never heard his reply through the dull roar in her ears which came from the battle with a threatened crying jag that was going on inside her head. She somehow managed to get through the rest of the evening until it was time to say her goodnights and seek the privacy and solitude of her room.

But the threatened tears had all dried up, solidified into a hard, painful knot behind her breastbone, and she stood at the window, looking out into the dark night with empty eyes.

She had done and said what she had decided on, put her foot on the road that would lead to their separation. She had begun to deceive him because it was the only option open to her. And the utterly heartbreaking aspect of it was his acceptance. He'd offered and she'd refused. As far as he was concerned that was the end of it. He could do no more, and would do no more.

Had she secretly hoped he would use the shattering charm he could call on at will, use that powerful sexual magnetism, to make her stay where he wanted her to be? She knew, in the aching depths of her heart, that she had. No matter how degrading the inevitable outcome, she had secretly wanted him to persuade her.

But after his initial offer he had accepted her lies when she'd laid the blame for her behaviour on the sparkling wine. Accepted it, it now seemed, with indifference. Had cut his losses and gone to find consolation and pleasure in the arms of his *principessa*.

CHAPTER SEVEN

NEVER before had Claire been so thankful to see the back of the Christmas season. Liz and Sally Harding joined them, of course, staying until the new year had been well and truly welcomed in, and the constant strain of having to pretend that she was enjoying herself, that she and Jake were a doting couple, had left her feeling a wreck.

As he had promised, Jake had appeared late on Christmas Eve, looking utterly exhausted, earning himself dark mutterings from Emma about never knowing when to call a halt, working himself into an early grave for no good reason that she could see.

Claire had never seen him look like that, totally drained, weariness scoring lines on his harshly crafted face that hadn't been there before, making his features austere, an unreachable quality leaching the light out of his eyes. He'd looked as if will-power alone was responsible for keeping him upright and she'd almost voiced her own sharp and sudden concern, but had remembered in time precisely why he would be looking this way.

The *principessa* must have given him an ecstatic welcome—and then some. He'd probably had no sleep at all over the past few days. And maybe the sexy Italian woman had been giving him a hard time, too, demanding that he spend more time with her, send his unloved wife packing, marry her to give her the legal entitlement to the physical and financial favours that at the moment were only granted when it suited him.

Lorella Giancetti obviously didn't know the brute as well as she imagined she did. She probably thought she could bring him to heel. Claire, for a time, had believed that, too, that he had at last found the one woman he could put before all else. Until events had shown otherwise. Jake had said himself, when he had proposed their sterile marriage arrangement, that he couldn't be bothered with long-term emotional commitments, that making a proper marriage work would take time, and he was too involved with his various business enterprises to give that precious commodity to a permanent relationship.

He wanted the best of all possible worlds. The freedom to enjoy affairs as long as his interest was caught, and a presentable 'wife' in the background to run the more tiresome aspects of his life with grace and efficiency, like a good little woman; and if he had to bed the good little woman from time to time, to keep her sweet and willing, then so be it.

So Claire had flattened all that sharp, instinctive concern, making herself give him a cool little smile, fixing him a drink, just the way he liked it, asking, 'How was Rome? Did everything go to your complete satisfaction?' knowing that he and she were the only people in the room who knew what she meant. But she'd been unprepared for his blank stare, the slight deepening of the frown-lines between his weary eyes. And then, shaming her, because he'd known what she was driving at, he'd flashed her a gratified smile.

'Superbly satisfying, thank you. You are looking at a completely fulfilled male animal.'

'Looking at a complete wreck, you mean!' Emma had snorted, not catching the double meanings because why should she? She thought they were a devoted couple. And her remark had given Claire the opportunity to fade into the background, smothering her rage, her impotent jealousy.

The bastard had offered to consummate their marriage—had had the gall to pretend he actually wanted it. But he'd met her refusal with indifference and walked away. How right she'd been to think with her head instead of her wayward heart—not to mention her wretched hormones!

'And not to be wondered at—' Jake had ruffled his sister's hair '—given all I've been through the last few days. And nights. Which reminds me...' He'd pushed himself to his feet. 'If you'll all excuse me, I'll go catch up on some sleep.'

The following morning he'd been his usual energetic, vital self. Eight solid hours of uninterrupted sleep had worked a miracle, Claire had thought sourly, doing her best to keep her mind off why he'd got himself into such an exhausted state, finding her own energy and good humour slipping through her fingers as each day of the holiday dragged past, the effort of acting the part of a happy wife becoming more and more intolerable, harder to sustain.

But now, settled back into the London apartment, away from the eyes of her unsuspecting parent and in-laws, she must steel herself to begin her campaign. It couldn't be put off any longer. It wouldn't be pleasant and it wouldn't be fun, but it had to be done or she would be destroyed.

As it was, each day brought a deepening sorrow, a greater awareness of loss, a larger sense of separation from the man she knew she would always love.

It was past time she did something about it, she thought, clipping the concise set of notes she'd made to one of the endless projection reports he'd been calling in from each and every one of his enterprises, handing them to her for her comments.

Loving, and knowing she would never be loved in return, had plunged her into a limbo of misery, robbing her of the ability to make things happen. Maybe if he had tried to make love to her again, or renewed his verbal offer to make their marriage a real one, she might have dragged herself together enough to do something about it. But, as had happened during most of their time together, he had carefully avoided even the most casual touch.

Straightening her shoulders, she looked across the room which functioned as an office. He was, as usual, engrossed in one of the earlier reports, occasionally scribbling furiously in the margin of the notes she had attached. His itchy feet hadn't been in evidence since they'd returned from Litherton. Neither of them had left the apartment, the woman who came in three times a week from the domestic agency they used being delegated to bring in essential foodstuffs.

She stood up, smoothing her slender dark grey alpaca skirt over her hips, then carried the latest report to his desk. A slight movement of his lips was the only acknowledgement she got as she dropped it on the relevant pile. He had withdrawn into solid hard work, allowing neither of them time to draw breath, only remembering she was human when they took a break for mealtimes, or called a halt at the end of the day when he decided it was time for sleep.

But she was used to it. She'd worked through several of these marathon stints during her time with him and knew that just when she was about to drop from mental exhaustion he would push his swivel chair away from his desk, cross his arms behind his head, give her that devastating grin and announce, 'Right, that's sorted. Time to play.' And he would whisk her out to the theatre and supper, to dinner and a nightclub, to an island retreat, which he just happened to have heard about, for a few sun-soaked days, bringing as much restless energy to his chosen method of relaxing as he did to his work.

This time, though, she wouldn't allow that to happen. Circumstances had changed, and she with them—of necessity—and so she interrupted his chain of concentration, her voice clipped and expressionless as she told him, 'It's time I advertised my position. I'll sift through any applicants we get and compile a short list for you to interview.'

'Don't bother. I'll see to it.' He didn't look up from

the paperwork, just slashed an underlining pen beneath part of the text, tossed the report aside and dragged the next one from the pile.

'That won't be necessary,' she stated firmly, letting him know she was in control in that department. If he was left to his own devious devices, the advertisement would never be placed. He was probably right when he believed that very few people would put up with his eccentric work habits!

And he probably believed that if a replacement wasn't chosen within the time she had stipulated he could work on her sympathies, her loyalty, the two years they had shared and persuade her to stay on... and on...

'I know exactly how to word the job description, what qualifications are needed, how to stress the importance of the right attitude to your far from normal working hours,' she added tartly. 'I do know what you want.'

'Do you? I wonder!' Grey eyes impaled her, the lancing silver gleam almost her undoing. 'In fact, I'm quite sure you don't, but that's something I'm prepared to work on.' He dipped his dark head again, intent on his paperwork, informing her, almost offhandedly, 'Put the problem of your replacement out of your head and concentrate on the job in hand. I already have someone in mind. I make plans for each and every contingency—you, of all people, should know that.'

That pushed all her hard-won control out of sight. Clamping her jaws together, she stared at the back of his head. She very much wanted to hit him. So he had already found a replacement, had he? He must have conducted that particular search at the speed of light! Had he proposed a paper marriage—with lots of lovely financial embellishments—to some other poor idiot? The arrangement to take effect just as soon as he'd rid himself of the present incumbent?

'Stop grinding your teeth,' he said, sounding just slightly bored. 'It could develop into an irritating habit. And don't slam the door on your way out.'

Had he always been able to second-guess her reactions, read the way her mind worked? she asked herself stormily as she stalked out of the room and found herself slamming the door behind her with a crash which reverberated around the sumptuous apartment. And was it her imagination, or did she really hear a deep masculine chuckle from behind the smooth wood panels?

Telling herself she didn't care either way, she walked away, and only realised she was standing in the centre of the kitchen when Mrs Fellows, from the agency, busily cleaning the inside of the windows, imparted, 'I put the fish and the eggs in the fridge, and the fruit's on the dresser. Give me a list if there's anything you want me to bring on Friday when I'm in next.'

'No, nothing, thanks.' Claire managed a smile and hauled her brain together. 'I've one or two personal bits and pieces to get; I can pick up any provisions we need at the same time.'

Whether Jake liked it or not, he was going to have

to learn that she wasn't a mindlessly willing append-
age, bound to his side by a length of convenient, invisible, unbreakable string.

Besides, the personal bits and pieces were a vital
part of the plan she'd formulated. And maybe if she
dug her heels in and became really uncooperative he
would get his act together and install her replacement—whoever that might be—with all possible
speed.

Deciding to find out over lunch who the replacement was, and when he or she could be expected to
put in an appearance, Claire glanced at her watch and
broke eggs into a bowl for an omelette. Lunch would
be a good hour earlier than normal, thanks to the way
she had stormed out of the office in a temper, and if
he objected to the timing he could do without.

But he didn't, and he didn't give her time to raise
the subject of her replacement, talking business all
through the light meal, but informally, as always,
bouncing ideas off her, really listening to what she
had to say, so much his usual irrepressively incisive,
dry and clever self that she wanted to cry. She loved
him so much, loved every single damn thing about
him.

And the pity and the pain of it was, she had to
leave him.

'...let the Caribbean thing drop. I'll off-load it, and
if I make a loss it can't be helped. Get a fax through
to the architect—Richardson—Gerald Richardson,
isn't it?'

'Jethro,' she supplied automatically. 'He won't like

being pulled off the job.' She'd been with Jake when they'd wandered, with the infectiously enthusiastic young architect, around the neglected plantation house on the wooded spur that overlooked one of the loveliest tropical beaches she had ever seen.

'He might not like it, but he'll be well-paid,' Jake replied, his ruthlessness tempered by his well-honed business acumen. 'And as I'll recommend his excellent services to the buyer when we find one, he need shed no tears.'

'I'd have thought you'd have wanted to hang on to the property,' she objected as she left the table to fetch the coffee. 'It has enormous potential.'

'I don't touch anything that hasn't,' he replied cuttingly, helping himself from the fruit bowl. 'As you must know. But in this case I don't think the eventual rewards will be worth the hard work and hassle, the time I'd have to put into the project.'

Quickly, she poured his coffee, noting dispassionately the unsteadiness of her hand. That last statement of his said it all, confirmed everything she had thought. He had viewed his offer to make their marriage a real one as a way to combat her alleged boredom, her need to move on. And perhaps he had cynically decided that that was what she'd been angling for all along. But he'd backed off at her first refusal. The eventual rewards—ensuring that she stayed safely put, more bound to him than ever—hadn't been worth the trouble of trying to persuade her.

He couldn't have known how little persuasion she would have needed. A kiss or two and she would have been lost to reason, to everything, jeopardising her future happiness and peace of mind for passionate love of him.

No, he hadn't known, and probably hadn't cared too much either. He was an expert at cutting his losses, putting them behind him and getting on with his brilliant life. So he'd given a mental shrug and walked away, leaving immediately for Rome and that woman, and was now acting as if nothing had changed, waiting to see if she would carry out her threat to leave him and throw away all the financial benefits that came with their arrangement.

And if she did walk out, well, he could live with that. He'd already found a possible replacement.

'I'll go and put a message to Jethro Richardson together,' she told him tightly. 'I don't want coffee.' Her pale features set, she left him and went to the office. He could be a callous bastard. She didn't know why she was stupid enough to love him. The true state of his feelings for her—total indifference—should make her radiant with relief for her lucky escape— not like a cold, wet Sunday, she told herself tartly, hovering over the phone, waiting until she heard him approach the door. And when he walked through she dropped the receiver back on its rest, her pale ivory skin stained with the feverish flush of a guilt that was in no way contrived because she was hating what she was having to do.

But he had brought it on himself.

'Who were you phoning?' The tone of voice was almost offhand, but the sharp, bright query in those silver eyes gave him away. There was more than idle curiosity there, and that was what she wanted.

'Oh, no one,' she answered, her voice bright and just a little too shrill. 'Wrong number.'

'Really? I didn't hear it ring.' As he would have done if it had—there were extensions in almost every room in the apartment. She could tell by the sudden slitting of his eyes that he knew she was lying.

Claire turned away quickly, shrugging, and he rewarded her duplicity by snapping rapid-fire dictation at her all afternoon until her head, wrist and eyes were aching and she was driven to interrupt, 'Does my replacement know what a slave-driver you can be? And when does she start? It is a she, I take it? A mere male couldn't be expected to cook your meals and choose your clothes and sort your laundry!'

Which got her precisely nowhere because he merely gave her a look which told her he hadn't listened to a single word and carried on dictating. And from what she could gather from the content he had digested the mountain of reports they'd been working on all week, decided which of his varied enterprises he would keep on, which he would off-load—no doubt at huge profits—and as it would appear that he would be off-loading the majority she sourly deduced that her replacement would have a much easier time of it than she had ever had!

And she was beginning to have serious doubts about her plan of action. When she'd first told him she wanted out he had as good as dismissed the idea. He'd gone out of his way to tell her that Liz's new-found financial independence didn't negate their original agreement. But it now seemed that he had accepted it. He'd gone to the trouble to find her replacement, so that meant she didn't have to go ahead with her plan to invoke the opt-out clause, she thought wearily.

He called a halt for supper at eleven. Eleven hours since they'd had that omelette. When he was in furious-work mode he never seemed to remember to eat or take even a short breather. Claire had gone beyond hunger now and, bleary-eyed and aching with fatigue, grilled the fish for him, put a potato in the microwave and prepared a salad which was far below her usual high standard.

He was punishing her, not only for her temerity in telling him she wanted their agreement to end, but for that lie about the phone call. Even when he was working flat out, driving himself beyond the capabilities of any other mortal, he had always insisted she take a break, waving her away when she suggested that he do the same.

He wandered through to the kitchen, which was where he preferred to eat, just as she put his solitary meal on the table.

'You're not joining me?'

'Not hungry,' she answered listlessly, wondering how he could look as fresh as a daisy while she felt like a four-week-old lettuce. He gave her a narrow-eyed, disapproving glare and she asked, because if she didn't her stupid, over-tired brain would worry away at it all night and deny her weary body the sleep it craved, 'You told me you'd already found my replacement. Will you want me to show her the ropes? When does she start?'

'I have absolutely no idea.' He grinned at her, his eyes full of wickedness. Then he sat at the table, piling salad on to his plate, boning his sole with his usual expertise and beginning to eat with every sign of enjoyment. 'Let's forget about your replacement, shall we?' he suggested infuriatingly, his eyes caressing her stiff little face. 'You know you don't want to leave me.' He made an expansive gesture with one hand. 'So why don't you sit and we can talk about it?'

She had opened a bottle of light, crisp Moselle. It was on the table, with one glass. He poured some of the wine and edged it over the table.

'If you're too wound up to eat, drink a little wine to help you relax. Then we'll talk this thing through like two sensible people,' he purred, the glint in his eyes telling her what she already knew. In this mood he was doubly dangerous.

'No,' she got out in a strangled voice. When he looked like that, spoke like that—as if they were closer than lovers, dearer than friends—he could persuade her, and any other female in existence, to anything. 'I'm too tired to think straight. I'm going to bed.'

And too angry to argue coherently, score logical points. Running away from a battle wasn't her style, but she needed all her wits about her—and then some—to outwit Jake The Devious, The

Machiavellian. She would need a very clear head indeed. Ragged rage wouldn't win this particular battle, she fumed as she dragged her plain cotton nightshirt over her head.

He had lied. He hadn't found a replacement at all. His airy 'I have absolutely no idea' said it all. In his arrogance he was still sublimely confident that he could persuade her to stay on—when he got round to putting his mind to it.

She was going to have to stick to her original plan. Make him believe she had fallen in love with someone else. Invoke the opt-out clause in their agreement. Not even he could argue with that!

CHAPTER EIGHT

SPANGLES of snow glittered on the soft dark silk of her hair and her cheeks were flushed a delicate pink from the cold east wind as she entered the apartment, the black carriers with their classy gilt logo dangling from her kid-gloved fingers.

It was very quiet in here, the understated luxury doing nothing to soothe her taut nerves. Too quiet. A hushed stillness that boded no good at all. Claire dragged in a long, deep breath, slid open the mirrored doors of the wardrobe and hung up her coat, fingering the slim gold chain around her neck, undoing the top button of her sleek scarlet suit jacket, and reflecting that her deception was costing an arm and a leg, and not only financially. Deceiving Jake was making her hate herself.

But there really was no other way. If she had come straight out with it, cold, and told him she had fallen in love, wanted to end their agreement because she was going to marry the man in question and live happily ever after, he would have immediately wanted to know who the man was, where they had met, demanded to meet the guy to satisfy himself that he would make her a fit second husband because, as she knew very well, he had a strong sense of duty.

This way, sowing seeds of suspicion, letting him

figure out for himself exactly what was going on, was the best, the only way. Even if it did leave a spectacularly nasty taste in her mouth.

His suspicious reaction to her phone call to Liz, all those weeks ago, had given her the idea. And she'd been working on it ever since they'd come back to the apartment, over six weeks ago now. The phone calls she'd made sure he interrupted, the new, ultra-feminine clothes she'd splurged out on, the sultry perfume, the excuses she'd made to pop out for an hour or two...

And it was working; she knew it was. The evidence of that was all there in the way she would sometimes look up and see him watching her, catch the hard, speculative look in his eyes, note the grim line of his mouth.

Not that she'd given him anything concrete to base his suspicions on up until now, just hints, a change in her behaviour patterns. Like the way she'd put on a sulky act when she'd had to accompany him to Hong Kong on business a couple of weeks ago, the untypical and total lack of interest she'd shown in the way he was selling off the majority of his interests, backing out of her role of hostess when, as today, for instance, he'd asked her to set up a working lunch with a couple of bankers, his UK company lawyer and an overseas buyer for Harlow's, manufacturers of high-quality glassware.

Harlow's had been the first ailing company he'd bought out, pruning and streamlining it, making it a highly profitable and prestigious world leader. And because it had been his first venture he had always had a special affection for the company and why he was off-loading it now was a mystery to her.

As were other things. It wasn't like him to liquidise so many of his assets in one fell swoop. If he went on like this he'd have nothing to do but sit on his millions and grow fat. And bored.

Unless, of course, he was planning on spending far more time with his *principessa*. But that didn't make a whole load of sense because, apart from the occasions when she'd deliberately absented herself for a few hours, he hadn't been out of her sight since he'd returned from Rome on Christmas Eve. There'd been no contact between the two, as far as she knew. And if the Italian woman was content to wait in the wings until he'd settled his affairs, she, Claire, was the Emperor of China.

From the photograph she had seen, Lorella Giancetti looked wayward and spoiled, far more capable of petulance than patience.

She dragged in a shuddering breath, feeling wretched. His plans wouldn't affect her, of course. But they were keeping secrets from each other, for the first time in two years, and it hurt more than she would ever have believed possible.

Still clutching her carriers, she headed for the office. From the silence in the apartment, the absence of strange overcoats in the wardrobe, she knew the business lunch was long over. Knew, with a sensation of deep inner dread, that Jake would be furious, and rightly so.

And his face, when he turned from the window where he had been watching the quiet London square, told her how right she'd been to anticipate his fury.

A shudder wrenched through her slender body but she suppressed it, unwilling to let him know how deeply everything about him could affect her, and deliberately opened her eyes very wide, in a painfully achieved parody of innocence, when he rasped, 'So you finally decided to float back. I'm beginning to find your excuses of exhaustion more than a little tiresome. I made my own notes; you'll find them on my desk. It's your problem if you can't make sense of them.'

The grimly savage line of his mouth tore at her heart. She wanted to fling herself into his arms, tell him she was sorry, sorry for everything, confess that she hated having to act this way. The temptation, for a moment, was almost more than she could cope with. But resist she must; the other was unthinkable; it would negate everything she had been forcing herself to do.

'Oh, don't be such a grouch!' She made herself smile but wasn't quite able to meet his eyes now. 'I offered to get the agency to send round a secretary to sub for me, but you refused point blank, remember? And I engaged the best caterers I could lay my hands on, so the lunch, at least, must have been a success. And if I'd sat in on it my head would have exploded.' She wandered over to her own desk, doing her best to look relaxed. 'You've worked my socks off these past few weeks; you know you have. So is it any wonder I need a few hours' leisure now and then? I'm just about fit to drop.'

'From where I'm standing, you don't look it.' A threat was threaded through the hard, dark irony of his voice. Claire gulped. What could he possibly threaten her with? Nothing. She sat down behind her desk, airily tossing the carriers to the floor where they proved the distraction she desperately needed as the exotic contents spilled out, as she had intended they should.

Slinky, slithery wisps of silk and satin and cobwebby lace. Seductive underwear fit for a siren. As far different from her normal sensible choices as it was possible to get. Keeping her eyes on the little pile of froth and frivolity, she heard him cross the room, saw one well-polished leather toe-cap touch an ice-blue satin teddy, and felt her face go very red as he asked with frozen venom, 'Blossoming out, Claire? Who's the lucky beneficiary—or shouldn't I ask?'

So the suspicions she'd so carefully planted in his mind had taken root, blossoming into certainty. Everything was working out better than she'd expected.

She didn't know why she suddenly wanted to cry. But she did.

Swallowing hard, she scrambled from her chair, on to her knees, and began thrusting the tell-tale garments back into the bags, and the ring suspended on the fine gold chain around her neck swung freely from the neckline of her jacket, as she had planned that it should at some time during the afternoon.

With a flare of hectic colour that she knew must look like guilt, she tried to push it back into hiding, but he was too quick for her, bending and grasping her upper arms, dragging her to her feet, one lean, steel-fingered hand snapping the chain from her neck, holding it out, the showy paste ring dangling, glittering with a faked brightness that suddenly seemed obscene.

Enclosed in a prison of raw emotion, he held her eyes with his own, with a savagery as harsh as the vice of his single hand. And his words came slowly, precisely enunciated, utterly damning in the silence that was broken only by her fluttering heartbeats. 'Who gave you this?'

His eyes bemused, confused her, held her. Black with emotion. She might have called it pain, if she hadn't known better. Anger she could understand. He wouldn't want to be seen as a cuckold in the eyes of the world. But there was more than that, she would swear to it. But what? She felt disorientated, her breathing ragged, pulses beating frantically in her throat...

'Tell me, Claire.'

His hand gave her arm a little shake while the dreadful ring swayed hypnotically from the fingers of his other hand, and she scrabbled around in her mind, dredging up the lie she had thought of for just this scenario, and croaked, trying to sound bright and flippant and failing dismally, 'It belongs to Liz. She asked me to get it altered. It's too big.'

He dropped her arm immediately, stepping back

from her, dropping the ring on the broken chain on to her desk. The heat of intense emotion dissipated, coldness creeping round her. He didn't believe it. He hadn't been meant to believe it. Liz wouldn't be seen dead wearing such a gaudy, graceless thing. He knew his mother-in-law very well, certainly well enough to know that her tastes wouldn't run to such cheap ostentation.

She watched him walk to the door, picking up his discarded grey suit jacket on the way, hooking it over his shoulder. The blank look in his eyes made her want to throw back her head and howl. She loved him more than life itself, yet she was building a sordid barrier of deceit between them, one that would never be breached, something that would push all the warm and stimulating companionship that had once been the hallmark of their relationship right into the background where it would wither and die and be completely forgotten, by him, at least.

Soon now, very soon, she would tell him she had met someone she wanted to marry, to share the rest of her life with. He wouldn't be able to argue with that—she had carefully planted all the false evidence—and he would have to let her go.

The prospect of never being able to see him again, talk to him, share her life with him, filled her with dread. But there really was no sensible or sane alternative.

'If you're not too exhausted…' he paused at the door, his eyes pinning her to her seat '…you can type up my notes, get the relevant letters written and off.

And if you'd wanted a ring, my dear wife—' his mouth tilted cruelly '—you only had to ask. I'd have given you the real thing, not a piece of tat.'

The real thing, she echoed inside her head as he closed the door decisively behind him. He might have given her diamonds instead of paste, but only because he wouldn't touch anything that wasn't the best. But when it came to affairs of the heart he wouldn't recognise the real thing if it bit him.

Their marriage, such as it was, had been a sham from the start. A living lie. And, even when he had tried to persuade her to make it a real one, that had been another kind of sham, a cruel decision to take advantage of her weakness. And, had she gone along with it, it would have degenerated into a living hell. So no, he wouldn't recognise the real thing, a truly loving relationship, if one walked right up to him and took his hand and introduced itself!

Feeling as if her heart was being wrenched in two, she dropped the showy ring into the top drawer of her desk, retrieved his notes and spent the rest of the afternoon at the keyboard, trying to decipher his impatient scrawl. And she couldn't believe her eyes when he strolled into the room just as she was finally finishing up.

He looked serene; that was the only way she could describe it to herself. She couldn't understand it and it made her feel confused.

'I've put the notes on the computer and the letters on your desk for your signature,' she informed him stiltedly, blinking at the warmth of his smile. It was as if the sour altercation of a few hours ago had never happened, she thought, hating the way a simple smile could take her breath away.

'Good girl,' he approved. 'That takes care of just about everything.' His mouth twitched, making her poor, stupid heart judder all over again. 'I've made supper, as a reward.'

A reward for what? For doing what she was handsomely paid to do? And Jake make supper? Unheard of! No one could come less domesticated than him. He appreciated good food, but only if it was exquisitely prepared and put in front of him, just as he always insisted on wearing the best but relied on someone else—her, as it happened—to look after his wardrobe. Left to his own devices he would appear in jeans and a dinner-jacket and two odd shoes because his clever mind was too bound up with his huge business empire to have much time for anything else.

So this was a peace-offering? she wondered warily, following him from the room. She could face his culinary attempts with equanimity; she was perfectly willing to settle for what would probably turn out to be a hunk of bread and a lump of cheese—but this forgiving attitude, this let's-pretend-it-never-happened scene gave her considerable cause for alarm.

She neither wanted nor needed his forgiveness. Good grief, if he'd decided to overlook what he would surely class as a sneaky affair, return to the status quo and turn a blind eye if she upped and went at totally inconvenient times, returning drenched with unfamiliar perfume, all flushed and flustered, that would mean that all her carefully laid clues had been a total waste of time. Not to mention all the misery she'd given herself all through the deception.

And the wariness increased, almost making her cut and run when she realised that, far from supping at the kitchen table on whatever cold scraps he'd dragged out of the fridge, he'd pulled out all the stops. The elegant dining-room was lit by the twin glittering chandeliers, the inlaid oval table set with the exquisite china and cutlery that was only ever used on the occasions when they entertained in style.

'My, my, you have gone to town!' She'd hoped to sound vaguely amused, condescending, but had to admit privately that her voice could have belonged to a sore-throated frog. And no one could have faulted the meal he'd produced, simple but perfect, the spaghetti cooked just as she liked it, the sauce rich and aromatic, the side-salads a creative masterpiece.

'I aim to impress,' he told her softly, serving her lavishly before serving himself and pouring the Chianti Classico, and she felt her eyes go bleak because impress her he certainly had, but she didn't know why he'd bothered, things being as they were, and she wasn't going to ask because the answer might frighten her silly.

'Both Lungarotti's banker and mine were more than satisfied with the arrangements for the Italian buy-out,' he told her, expertly winding spaghetti round his silver fork. 'You would have liked him, had you met him. He's what I'd call a creative corporation man, with the rare bonus of a great sense of humour, style and wit. Harlow's will be in safe hands.'

Claire concentrated on her plate. Despite having skipped lunch she wasn't hungry. It was difficult to swallow. As difficult as his strange change of mood. She had fully expected him to be righteously wrathful at the way she'd let him down over today's important meeting, bunking off, only telling him of her intention, the arrangements she'd made with the caterers a scant hour before his guests were due to arrive.

And let him down for what? A clandestine meeting with a lover during which she'd been presented with that awful ring, followed by a quick flip around one of the most expensive boutiques in the city to stock up on frillies to add spice to her affair.

So why wasn't he still stingingly angry? Why was he discussing his complicated business affairs with her, giving her information that would have set the stock market on its ears? Because he still trusted her implicitly, believed her sneaky love-affair—though annoying because it was the first he had found her out in—would soon fizzle out, leaving her more than content to stay put, despite her stated contrary intentions, because those he obviously regarded as hot air.

Over the two years she had been with him she had become adept at reading his mind, congratulating herself that she was probably the only person who could. But now he confused her, troubled her, and if eating the food he'd prepared was a very private problem, then trying to figure out what he was up to while, at the same time, endeavouring to make intelligent comments was another.

'That was delicious,' she told him when she judged she'd eaten just about enough to be polite. 'You've been keeping secrets from me. I had no idea you were such an excellent cook.'

'I am?' He seemed mildly astonished as he leaned forward and replenished her glass. Claire flicked her eyes away. The taupe silk shirt he was wearing above classical, narrow-fitting dark grey trousers highlighted the superb configuration of the sleek muscularity of his chest and shoulders. 'I can't remember when I last cooked anything remotely resembling a meal. I recall helping my mother make cheese straws when I was about six.' A dark brow lilted upwards, his mouth wry. 'After all, it's merely a matter of common sense. I decided to feed you for a change, and when I decide to do something I approach it with enthusiasm and do it properly.'

His words disclaimed his new-found ability with herbs and sun-dried tomatoes and rich olive oil but his eyes were telling her something else.

She buried her nose in her wine glass, hoping to hide her sudden, unwelcome and totally unsophisticated flush. She knew all about his enthusiasm, his total dedication to whatever he had in hand. Harmless enough as a comment on his particular, vital personality, yet wicked because his eyes were telling her he remembered—and was making sure she remembered, too—the enthusiasm and expertise he'd brought into play when he'd decided, on that never-to-be-forgotten occasion, to make love to her.

It was something she refused to think about. She couldn't afford to remember how nearly he'd persuaded her to consummate their marriage, how easily…

So maybe now was the right time to invoke the opt-out clause, tell him she'd fallen in love? That, at least, wouldn't be a lie because she had. With him. And the bald statement would at least put a stop to this awful forgive-and-forget magnanimity of his. It was dangerous; it made her melt with love for him, made her feel so guilty, mean and besmirched…

But the moment was gone, the painful resolve to verbalise the lie she had merely, up until now, told through her actions melted away, she weakly yielding because, after all, the telling was utterly distasteful, and she dismissed it without any real regret at all, just for now, as he began to gather the used dishes and plates, telling her, 'Our estimable home help can deal with this lot tomorrow. I've got a few phone calls to make so why don't you get off to bed? Perhaps a really early night might help with that exhaustion you're plagued with,' he ended on a sardonic drawl that made her cringe inside and meekly do as he had suggested because her lies had rebounded on her and she really did feel exhausted in body and mind, unable to cope with the strain, unable to think on her feet and come up with answers.

It probably served her right, she thought drearily as she crawled into bed. And the only thing she could do to end the present misery was to steel herself to tell the final lie first thing in the morning, demand that he release her, allow her to walk out of his life, and try, somehow, to come to terms with the fact that the man she loved would never love her, never see her as anything more than a useful right hand, the perfect cover for his uncommitted affairs.

Try, if she could, to get over him.

CHAPTER NINE

'Move it, small sloth! Drink your tea—it's a great day out there. Sun's shining, snow's gone. Did you know you snore? I learn something new each day—ain't life fascinating?'

'I do not snore!' Claire argued sleepily, pulling the duvet over her head and settling more neatly into the nice warm nest of her cosy bed. And how would he know, anyway? He was making it up. And how any normal person could be expected to cope with his early morning vitality was beyond her, but she'd been working on it for the past couple of years, and was probably getting there, because she didn't even scowl when he tweaked the covering away from her head, just gazed up at him blearily as he repeated,

'Drink your tea.'

Since when had he started to bring her a wake-up cup of tea in the morning? she wondered fuzzily. Since never. With the tiny part of her mind that was just beginning to show some signs of intelligence from the middle of the fogs of sleep, she registered that he was casually dressed in black cord trousers topped by a chunky Aran sweater, looking more vividly alive than anyone had a right to be before ten in the morning at the earliest.

'Go away,' she grumbled good-humouredly. 'Go dig a hole in the road and bury a bus, use up some of that dreadful energy out of my sight.' Making a determined attempt to wriggle further down the bed, she gasped as she felt his hands on her arms, hauling her up against the pillows. And the touch of his strong warm hands on her naked skin was all that was necessary to bring everything back, all the awfulness of what was happening.

She bit hard on her lower lip and her fingers gripped the cup and saucer he placed in her hands. Just for a few moments, before she'd come properly awake, she'd forgotten. It had been wonderful. Imagining she'd been back in the safety of their old harmonious and mentally stimulating relationship—before she'd spoiled everything by falling in love with him—had been blissful, a balm to her troubled soul and a comfort to her poor aching heart.

'Thank you,' she said stiffly, meaning for the tea. 'I'll get up just as soon as I've had this.' Because she expected him to observe the proprieties and leave, agitation made her a nervous wreck as he did no such thing, sitting casually on the side of the bed, watching her from those inscrutable silver eyes.

Was he comparing her plain cotton sleeveless nightshirt with the frothy bits of nonsense she'd made sure he saw in all their glory yesterday afternoon? Was he wondering how she would look in that wicked black silk nightdress, for instance, all perfumed and melting as she waited for her lover in some sleazy hotel room, where such clandestine assignations were made?

'Get dressed in something comfortable and pack a load of warm gear,' he instructed, astounding her. She had expected some reference to her recent behaviour, his own deductions, perhaps even a little speech, telling her that he would turn a blind eye to her affair, provided she was sensible about it and, above all, discreet. She had not expected instructions on what she would wear today. And why should she pack? They weren't going anywhere.

But apparently they were. She finished the last of her tea in a painful gulp as he imparted, quite at ease, not looking for ructions, 'We'll be spending the next two weeks or so in a cottage in Wales. Tucked away in the mountains of Dyfed.' He rolled the word around his mouth as if savouring the sound of it and Claire thought wildly, That's impossible.

She snapped defensively, 'You're not expecting me to spend a couple of weeks on a mountain at this time of year, are you?'

And he picked that up immediately, of course he did, doing her character an unknowing injustice as he questioned, 'Why? Too uncivilised for you?' His hard eyes mocked her. 'You've grown immensely in sophistication and, hopefully, maturity over the past two years. But don't forget there are other things in life besides the jet-setting, push-button life of luxury you've got used to.' He eased one long, lean, formidably strong black-clad leg over the other, but the would-be casual movement didn't hide the inner tension that encroached on his beautifully hewn features. 'Or is there another, stronger reason than a fastidious dislike for roughing it?'

Now was the right time, the absolutely perfect time, for coming out with the speech she'd rehearsed so often in her head. The other man, the love of her life… But she floundered, the words jumbling up in her brain like a tangle of mangled knitting, making no sense at all, taking no recognisable shape. Mutely, she shook her head to try and clear it and the moment was lost and he was telling her succinctly, 'I don't believe you, but we'll leave it for now. I have a project in mind and I need you there.' He added with a dangerous softness, 'You are still working with me, remember?'

That did it, she thought weakly, leaning back against the pillows as he walked from the room. He didn't know it, of course, but his whole attitude had the ability to touch her deeply. He had always insisted she work with him, not for him. And he still did. Even though he knew she was trying to squirm out of their agreement, and had to suspect the reason why, he still regarded the two of them as the close-knit working item of happier, better days.

She wondered, a little wildly, if there happened to be such a word as 'unwomaned'. Because if there was that was precisely what he did to her.

Two hours later, driving out of London in the brand-new four-wheel-drive vehicle that had been delivered to the apartment at ten that morning, Claire still felt disorientated, as if daylight reality had been invaded by strange, misty, shifting dreams where nothing was ever as it seemed.

The last couple of hours had been hectic. She'd packed for them both while Jake had been making long, complicated phone calls, telling Mrs Fellows, who had come in as usual, that she wouldn't be needed for a couple of weeks, finally coming across Jake in the kitchen stuffing the contents of the fridge and storage cupboards into carriers, which, with last night's successful venture into the culinary arts, added up to an interest in things domestic that she would never have expected from him in a million years.

'We're going to have to fend for ourselves,' he'd told her, a wicked gleam in his eyes. 'There'll be no delivery service where we're going, no Harrods food hall around the corner. It should be fun.'

'Really?' she'd answered dully. Two weeks with Jake in pioneer mode might just be more than she could take. Enthusiasm had lit his strong-boned, handsome face and the dark hair, the short, conventional style—the end result of exceptionally expert cutting—had been ruffled, making her fingers clench at her sides, aching to run through the soft, warm thickness of it. 'I don't understand why you're interested in an isolated cottage,' she'd followed on quickly because her thoughts were running in directions they had no business taking and that sensual, beautiful male mouth of his seemed on the verge of laughter—at her expense, no doubt. 'Recently you've been more interested in off-loading than acquiring.'

'Do you know, sweetheart—' he'd tipped his dark head consideringly on one side, that grin breaking out, blinding her '—you look gorgeously sultry when you try to be prissy? And I'm not acquiring, merely borrowing.'

'Why?' she'd asked stiltedly, doing her best to ignore the sweetly painful lurch inside her. She didn't know how she would handle it if he decided to amuse himself by flirting with her.

'Well, that's for me to know and you to find out. All I'm prepared to tell you is that it has important implications for the future.'

She'd almost drawled, Really? again, but had stopped herself just in time. As far as she was concerned the going-nowhere conversation was over. Taking one of the bulging carriers, she'd exited huffily, dumping it in the elegant foyer where the suitcases she'd packed were waiting. He was impossible, and she didn't know why she was going along with this latest madness, why she hadn't taken the heaven-sent opportunity to tell him the lie that would end everything.

But she knew why, she'd thought sadly as she'd waited while he activated the complex security systems and called down to the janitor's office to advise on the length of their probable absence. She knew perfectly well why she had let the opportunity go without any fight at all. She hated lying to him and she wasn't going to start lying to herself. She wasn't brave enough, or strong enough, to take the final, irreversible step on the road that would lead to a permanent separation. That was the shameful truth.

Since then she had retreated into her cool little shell, sitting mutely beside him as he handled the big vehicle with consummate ease through the snarl of mid-morning traffic. He wasn't to know how desperately she was trying to replace the backbone that seemed to have gone missing, and he wouldn't realise how that contained vitality of his, hitting her with violent shock-waves in the confined space, interfered so diabolically with her good intentions.

She hadn't been born weak, or been brought up to be that way. Quite the opposite, in fact. But here she was, meekly going along with him—his reasons for going at all not making sense—just because she needed and craved every last moment she was able to spend with him, hoarding them up against a barren future.

Loving him had made her a mental wreck. She should have left him weeks and weeks ago, the moment she'd realised she loved him. But all she'd done was plot and plan, prevaricate, make endless excuses for lingering, prolonging the sweet torment.

She despised and loathed herself.

'Sulking?' he asked, breaking the silence at last, and she shot a wary sideways glance at his clean profile. It told her absolutely nothing. He had accused her of doing just that on the Hong Kong trip, and she hadn't argued because she'd been putting on that act, letting him know she was far from happy at being away from London, leaving him to come up with the reason.

She gave a non-committal shrug, knowing his attention was on the road, that he wouldn't see it. Knowing, too, that he would sense it. He didn't miss a thing. He never had, which was one of the reasons why his high-flying career had been the success story of the decade.

'Just thinking,' she gave him the truth, leaving him to make what he liked of it—hopefully that she was devastated because he was enforcing a distance between her and her lover.

'Tell me,' he commanded lightly. 'I like to know what goes on inside your head.'

She wasn't going to rise to the provocation and ask him why. The seeds of suspicion she'd sown had grown into the sturdy plants of conviction, surely? Let him wonder; it would only help her sorry cause in the end. Bringing out the subject that popped straight into her mind, she said idly, 'I take it the house has been put on the back burner. Or is that yet another of the projects you've lost interest in?'

She couldn't help the sting of bitterness. He'd soon lost interest in her as a 'project', hadn't he? That particular inconstancy still had the power to hurt unbearably. The place hadn't been mentioned since they'd been back in London and she didn't know why. He had been so pleased with it, his newest acquisition—though 'pleased' was too tame a word to describe the deep, simmering satisfaction of that time. And in some strange, counter-productive way she had been piqued because he hadn't asked for her input, as he had said he would.

Could he see the inevitability of their separation, even though he was trying to deny it would happen? Was he already—maybe only unconsciously—beginning to shut her out of the private, personally important part of his life?

'Harnage?' The brief glance, the tight turn of his head, was at once intense and demanding. Then he returned his attention to the road. 'No way,' he disabused her. 'We're both going to be putting a considerable amount of time in on the house in the near future.'

He left it at that, as if that explained everything, leaving nothing left to be said, and Claire slumped deeper into her seat, foolishly, fiercely glad.

By the time they came to the end of the stony track and the sturdy vehicle was parked in front of a squat stone cottage that appeared to be halfway dug into the bleak mountainside, the day had lost all semblance of an early spring and had slid back into an unarguably wintry afternoon.

A shrill wind blew out of the immense, darkening sky and the vast, empty miles of mountain ranges were painted in shifting shades of silver and grey, and Claire huddled into her coat while Jake dug in his pockets for the door key. She sniped, 'Whoever you borrowed this place from has to be a masochist.' Because she couldn't let him know, could she, that being alone with him here, just the two of them, in this wild and splendid isolation, would test her to the limit of her endurance?

'You should see it in the summertime.' The quality of the light toned his skin to dusky olive. His teeth gleamed a white contrast. 'Martin Beck, the guy who owns it, was at school with me. We never completely lost touch.' He slotted the key into the lock and pushed open the heavy wooden door. 'He heads one of the busiest advertising agencies in London and whenever he feels he's in danger of losing his marbles he brings his family out here. He owes me a couple of favours and I called them in last night over the phone. He sent me the key by special messenger and we have the run of the place for as long as it takes.'

For as long as it takes for what? Claire thought dizzily, following him inside, her legs feeling like lead. She had believed she knew him as well as one person could ever know another, but his behaviour and his motives right now were frankly beyond her and, just as obviously, there were huge chunks of his past life she knew nothing about. Was never likely to now.

The stark realisation caused her unassuageable grief.

But she was going to have to live with it, wasn't she? she told herself derisively. That she was here at all was entirely her own fault. She'd had the chance to do something positive, tell him their marriage was over because she'd found another man, and walk right out. So she'd just have to grit her teeth and muddle along for as long as it took, she thought, echoing his own earlier phrase, still with no idea of what he'd meant, and blinked when he lit an oil-lamp and the room they were in flickered to life.

The stone walls had been washed in a soft apricot colour and the furniture was chintzy or pine, with warm-coloured rugs on the slate floor and enough accumulated chill to freeze the bones.

'Apparently we have a generator in a shed at the back,' Jake said, as if he couldn't wait to get his hands on it. 'Lamplight's romantic, but we need the power for the fridge and the hot-water supply. Why don't you fetch the stuff in from the car while I get it going and root around for the makings of a fire?' And he disappeared through a door at the far end of the room.

Claire wondered if his old schoolfriend had given him a detailed description of the layout over the phone and trudged outside again to do as she'd been told.

If playing Girl Friday to his unexpected Robinson was what it took, then she'd comply because simply by being here she had no option, but 'romantic' she could do without. She was under enough emotional pressure as it was, without him rabbiting on about the effects of lamplight.

By the time she'd deposited the suitcases in the living-room and stowed the foodstuffs they'd brought from the apartment into the quietly humming fridge in the huge, homey kitchen, Jake had built a fire, and as he was washing his hands in icy cold water at the deep stone sink Claire was wound up enough to forget that she'd decided not to ask, and wanted to know, 'Now what do we do? I still don't know why you wanted to come here.'

'We're here to relax,' he told her, his slow, burning smile turning her bones to water, making all her nerve-ends jump. 'Makes a change from tropical islands or tiny Spanish fishing villages.'

Claire turned quickly, walking stiffly into the other room. She had to remove herself from those clever, gleaming eyes. She would give herself away, let him see how much she loved him, how desperately she needed him. He couldn't know how cruel he was being.

Harsh tears choking her, she knelt in front of the youthful fire and poked at the barely burning coals savagely, for something to do, something to drain away just a little of the building tension. And Jake said behind her, his voice warm and slow, 'You'll put it out if you do that. Leave it.' He cupped his hands beneath her elbows, hauling her to her feet, his hands sliding down to her waist, pulling her against the steely strength of his body.

She stood rigidly still; it was the only way to maintain her shaky self-control. If she moved, against him, the sensation would be her undoing, her ruin. And she almost cried aloud when he said with a soft compassion that tore at her heart, 'Something's going badly wrong. It started when Liz received that legacy. And we're here to talk it out, put it right. But not yet.' His head dipped briefly, resting against her own, and she held her breath, terribly, terribly afraid that she would turn in his arms and bury her head against the warmth of his body, tell him everything, the truth, that she loved him, couldn't go on living with him, couldn't quite see how she would live without him... She bit down hard on her lip, tasting blood, and he lifted his head, released his hold on her and said lightly, 'We both need a few days to relax and unwind first. So why don't we go upstairs and see what sleeping accommodation's on offer before we settle down and make a meal?'

And three days later a kind of magic had eased away the last of the tension. They had fallen into a comfortable companionable routine, and Claire wasn't questioning it. While it lasted it was lovely, doubly precious to her because she knew it couldn't go on for very much longer. Sooner or later he would want to know what was wrong, and she would tell him that nasty looming black untruth. And that would be the end of it all.

After twenty-four hours she had stopped holding her breath every time he opened his mouth to speak, fearing that he would begin to question her. They talked all the time, the way it had always been, nothing contentious, nothing dangerous. They were comfortable, close, the spice of his dry wit making her crack with laughter, just like in the old lost days of her innocence. Before she had done the unforgivable and fallen in love with him.

They'd walked each morning, high in the tumbled

mountains, because the weather pattern remained the same, spring-like until mid-afternoon, then back to winter, and then the sturdy stone house, the warm fireside beckoned. But today was different. They'd been running low on provisions, so had spent the morning shopping together in the nearest small market town, and were now taking their walk in the afternoon.

'It looks like rain. We'd better make tracks before you freeze to death.'

Claire's eyes drifted to him helplessly. With the collar of his dark, oiled jacket turned up against the cold wind, his black head flung back on the strong, corded support of his neck, he looked like a wild pagan god, king of these recklessly rambling mountain ranges.

The cosy, companionable fireside, soft mellow lamplight, the lazy preparation of the evening meal with its attendant laughter-edged, friendly bickering was a pleasure to look forward to, lodged in her mind as something to be savoured, treasured. As was the here and now, together with him beneath the wild sky, a joy to be clung on to, not willingly relinquished, even for the pleasure in store, because each hour of each day marked the passing of time, marching closer and closer to the inevitable, the final break.

'If we climbed to the top of that spur,' she said dreamily, deliberately extending this particular fragment of time with him, 'would we be able to see the sea?'

He gave her a laughing glance. 'Don't even think it, goose-brain. I'm not hauling you up there to find out. Tell you what, though—' he caught her gloved hand in his, tugging her back along the narrow sheep track '—we could drive down to the coast in the morning. Would you like that?'

Her fingers clung tightly to his, as if they would never let go. She could allow herself this small rapture because he wouldn't think anything of it. The track was steep, the going rough, and if he thought about it at all he would put her eager compliance to the physical contact he'd initiated down to that indisputable fact.

'Maybe,' she answered, her breathing ragged. And he could put that evidence of the effect that touching him had on her down to the terrain, too. And maybe she'd veto that trip to the coast. Even out of season there would be locals about. Up here it was just the two of them and the wild birds; even the sheep had been taken down to more sheltered pasture.

Being here with him, like this, growing closer than even before, couldn't be so wrong. Leaving him, as she must, would cause her more pain and anguish than she had previously imagined possible. This sweet time of deepening friendship couldn't make it worse; nothing possibly could. And it would be something to remember, something infinitely precious, helping her to discount the dark things—how he'd offered to make her his wife in more than name, his lovemaking binding her more closely than any shackles, simply because she was, in his opinion, unbeatable at her job. How he'd made no attempt to deny his affair with the Italian *principessa*, and his confession that he had no inclination to form a lasting relationship with the woman—his meaning clear: that he would continue to take mistresses, as and when it pleased him.

So all that was something that this time with him would help her to push out of her mind, edit out of her memories of him. She didn't know that things were already changing, the accent shifting, not even when she hovered uncertainly on a slippery stone in the tumbling stream they were crossing and he held out his arms and commanded, 'Jump, sweetheart. Close your eyes and jump. I'll catch you.'

And she did. Unquestioningly. There was no doubt in her mind that he would fail to keep her safe, the only doubt creeping in when he caught her, holding her for a spellbinding moment in the strong haven of his arms before sliding her slowly, oh, so breathtakingly slowly, down the powerful length of his body.

But he couldn't possibly know how her flesh immediately burned with the tumultuous, leaping, ravaging flames of desire, how every nerve-ending responded wildly to his fierce masculinity, leaving her weak and vulnerable, open to him in every way there was. No, of course he couldn't. How could he?

Sternly, she made her clutching fingers release his arms and pushed herself away, hoping she didn't look as flushed and utterly wanton as she most certainly felt, babbling distractedly, 'Thanks. You saved me from getting a thorough soaking. I just know I was about to lose my balance and fall! I'll put your name down for the mountain-rescue team any time you like—' She only bit off the rest of the gushing, breathless nonsense when she saw the long, speculative look take control of his eyes and knew she was in danger of giving herself away.

In the end they both got a soaking because the skies opened while they were still half a mile away from

the cottage, and when they arrived back Jake, not
even slightly out of breath despite their last frantic
dash down the track, told her, 'Get straight into a hot
bath while I make the fire, and don't get out of it until
you're warm right through.' And he patted her bottom, as if helping her in the direction of the stairs.
As she went up them Claire wondered dizzily if that
playful pat hadn't been playful at all, if it had lingered
rather too long, the tap from the palm of his hand
turning into something else entirely as his long fingers
had curved, holding, exploring, relishing the softly
rounded, feminine shape of her.

Of course not, she assured herself firmly as she ran
her bath and began to strip off her sodden clothes.
She was letting her imagination run away from her.
An imagination already heightened beyond sanity by
the very close contact with the body she desired so
intensely way back at the stream.

Her brows knitted together as she struggled to get
out of her rain-soaked cord jeans, she recalled that for
the greater part of their time together he had carefully
avoided touching her at all. That had changed after
Liz had become financially independent, and Claire
knew why. And refused to think about it. He wasn't
about to make another pass at her. He had tried it
once, to no avail. He wouldn't be bothered to try
again. So she had to be crazy even to allow the idea
any room in her head. The casual touching meant
nothing; it was just part and parcel of their ever-
increasing closeness, a deepening friendship that
would be irretrievably shattered—for him, at least—
when she confirmed his suspicions.

As for herself, all she asked was the privilege of

keeping those few days as a precious memory, remembering him not as her boss or her paper husband, but as her best friend. She couldn't remember him as her lover; nothing, not even her need for him, could bring her to allow that to happen—even if he wanted it to, which he probably didn't—so she would settle for friendship.

Climbing into the hot, scented water, Claire lay back and made a determined effort to relax and empty her mind. And she succeeded so well that by the time she was dressed in an old pair of denim jeans, gone soft and pale with washing, and a raspberry-red lambswool sweater, and was walking downstairs to be welcomed by a blazing fire, she felt soft and boneless and remarkably tranquil.

Jake walked out of the room as she walked in. He didn't say a word, but his eyes were warm, as if he liked what he saw. To her deep amazement, she felt her breasts peak and harden, push against the warm, soft lambswool, even though he wasn't near, wasn't stroking her body with that long, burning, appreciative gaze.

As if in a dream, she walked slowly into the tiny hall where a three-quarter-length mirror hung on the wall. Over the past few days he would have been seeing her in a different light, too.

To suit her position as his wife she had spent freely of the huge allowance he made her, always appearing impeccably groomed, speakingly elegant. Even when he had whirled her away to relax in some impossibly exotic spot her casuals had borne top designer labels.

The jeans and anoraks she'd worn up here were relics of the days before she'd gone to work for him, dug out of forgotten suitcases, because, thrifty by nature and early upbringing, she had never been able to bring herself to throw anything away.

Almost unconsciously she stroked her hands down over her body. Her sleek, short hair still looked tousled, even after brushing, and the warm red of her sweater imparted a rosy glow to her pale, translucent skin, while the pert, rounded thrust of her breasts, lovingly moulded by the soft wool, belied the boyish slenderness of her hips and legs encased in the worn old denim.

Had his eyes been telling her the truth? Did he really like what he saw? He had always been satisfied with—no, frankly admired—the elegant style she had acquired for him. But perhaps he hadn't been seeing her as a real woman then. Only as an accessory, an adjunct to his high-powered lifestyle. Maybe, over these past few days, he'd been seeing her as a flesh-and-blood woman for the first time?

Dangerous thoughts. But she was bewitched, taken over by something beyond her control. She was not going to worry over anything right now. Not even dangerous thoughts, even more dangerous dreams. Everyone should be allowed to dream, just sometimes.

Idling back into the living-room, she noted the opened bottle of red wine, set to breathe on a low side-table, and took herself off into the kitchen to prepare a salad to go with the steak they'd decided to have for supper. She was chopping walnuts and celery when she felt warm hands at either side of her tiny waist and leaned back instinctively into his hard male body, then turned in his arms, because she couldn't help herself. And she breathed in the freshly bathed smell of him, and something else that was essentially, simply Jake, letting her hands rest against the soft cotton of the loose black shirt he was wearing now, feeling his heartbeat, feeling the raw contraction of his muscles as he said softly, 'It's too early to eat. Come with me.'

And she went. Too foolish, bewitched and bemused to do anything else.

CHAPTER TEN

THE lamp had been lit, adding its gentle glow to the flickering firelight. Jake turned to face her, his eyes dark and unreadable, and slowly he raised his long-boned, hard hands to cup her face and she just stood there, immobile, as if she had wandered into a dream, couldn't move, couldn't speak, could only love him, want him...

His thick, midnight-dark lashes drifted down, hiding his expression as his gaze rested on her mouth. Her lips parted weakly on a silent gasp as her whole body ignited, trembled, swayed and burned with fever in that wicked conflagration; he was going to kiss her and that mustn't happen.

And it didn't. He said, 'Time to talk, sweetheart,' the words spoken so gently that it hurt, tore at her heart and broke it. The moment had come. The awful, inevitable, black moment. Not of truth, but of lies. And once they were told there would be no going back, not ever.

But she couldn't go back to the way things had been. That avenue had definitely closed when she had fallen in love. There were two ways open to her, the one unthinkable, the other deplorable. Choices to be made. And she had made hers.

Her breath came on a long, fractured sigh and his hands slid down, his arms going round her, holding

her with a tenderness that made her want to cry. A
sob built up, cramping her lungs, and his hold on her
tightened, as if he knew what was happening, and his
dark voice whispered softly over her, 'There's no
problem too big to be solved.' One of his hands traced
the line of her spine and she shivered convulsively,
fighting the fatal desire to melt bonelessly against him
and allow fate and her love for him to take over. 'You
don't have to say a thing, sweetheart. Simply relax
and let me sort it.'

And he could so easily, with his hands, his lips, his
fantastic male body. And then she would be his, for
all eternity, with no peace of mind, ever, the deepest
human need forever ungratified because he didn't
love her.

The sob burst then, aridly, painfully. Desperately
she tried to fight the traitor inside herself, pulling out
of the sweet prison of his arms, but he scooped her
up as if she weighed no more than a child, settling
her on his knee as he sank down into one of the armchairs.

Weakly, only for a moment, she told herself, she
allowed her head to rest against the wide span of his
shoulder. Just gathering her resources, she assured
herself frantically. Just one more minute and she
would have got herself together, would ask him what
he thought he was doing. Unhand me, you villain!
she could hear herself saying, and she shook with
hysteria.

Jake picked up on the deepening tension and mur-
mured against the top of her glossy dark head,
'There's nothing to get uptight about, believe me.
You've been seeing another man—no, please don't

try to deny it, sweetheart,' he injected warningly as she went rigidly still against him. 'You left too many clues around—which is one consolation, I suppose, because if you'd had several lovers, one after the other, you'd have learned how not to spread evidence all over the place. And there were dozens of clues. Right from the time I came home early from Rome and found you deep in an animated phone conversation. You said you'd been talking to Liz. But the guilt on your face said that wasn't the truth. Then the sudden crazy desire to end our fantastic working relationship for no better reason than you were restless and bored. Oh, yes, sweetheart, the clues were endless. I won't go on to give you chapter and verse.'

The breath she hadn't known she'd been holding came out of her lungs in a whoosh. She could hear the steady, controlled rhythm of his heartbeats. Hers were racketing around like the drumbeats of a lunatic. Add to that chilling little fact the total absence of anger—never mind jealousy—and it pointed unmistakably to what she already knew. His complete lack of emotional involvement where she was concerned.

The only thing he loved about her was her ability to organise his hectic life to his complete satisfaction. Something, he'd often told her, no other employee had been able to do.

'I won't pretend I like the situation,' he told her now, making her twist her lower lip between her teeth, feverishly wondering if she could have been wrong and her supposed affair might wrest some declaration of personal, hurting involvement from him. But not so, she decided defeatedly, that small, silly whisper of hope denied her as he went on, 'But I do understand, and you mustn't feel guilty, because the greater blame is mine.'

She whimpered inaudibly into the soft fabric of his shirt, the heat of his body burning her up. She closed her eyes. He had left her nothing to do, nothing to say. All she had to do was confirm his deductions.

It had all been far too easy. She'd imagined a dreadful scene, his anger cold and cutting as he ordered her to keep well away from her lover until their marriage was legally over. How he would hate the gossip columnists to dip their pens in vitriol and titter about his straying wife in the Press, making him look a laughing-stock, people talking and smirking about him behind their hands.

Yet that didn't seem to have occurred to him, or perhaps he'd decided he was big enough to rise above it. Whatever, it was difficult to think clearly when one of his hands was stroking her hair so gently, soothing her as if he wanted to take all her troubles on his own broad shoulders...

'You'd made it clear, before I suggested our current arrangement, that the commitment of marriage held no appeal. Fine and dandy. We were two of a kind— although for different reasons. I didn't think it out properly,' he confided tersely, the first hint of tension coming through as he shifted beneath her, his arms tightening round her. 'You have all a normal woman's physical needs and you're much too beautiful to have any trouble at all finding a man panting to assuage them. The way things were between us, it was bound to happen—'

'Was it really?' Stung to long-overdue fury, she found the strength to push away from him, to sit bolt upright though still shackled by the steely, indomitable strength of his arms. He was bringing it down to the level of basic biology, talking as if she were a bitch on heat. He insulted her! 'The way it was "bound to happen" between you and the Italian woman?' she spat, her eyes glittering, her high cheekbones slashed with heated colour. 'Her and how many others? Or have you lost count?'

'Ah!' The utterly infuriating gleam of sinful satisfaction in those silver eyes made her want to slap him for the decadence it implied. Was he simply thinking of that voluptuous Latin body, or gloating, relishing all the others, those in the past and those still to come? 'La Giancetti. I wondered when you might get around to mentioning her.'

His mouth softened, appallingly sensual, and Claire stared at him wildly. Hating him. Hating him for making her love him. Her small fists beat at him in a frenzy as she struggled to get free, and she gasped in outrage as one of his arms tightened around her hips, the other binding her shoulders, his voice thick as he commanded, 'Quit wriggling, woman, or I won't be responsible. We still have some talking to do. I'm trying to stay calm but I can't answer for myself—'

Was he implying that she was responsible for this—this unlooked-for arrangement of bodies? Claire snorted, her little face pinched, not a hint of sophistication left now, just fury and hurt and a desperate need somehow to defend herself.

'So talk!' she huffed against the side of his neck, powerless to move when his arms held her prisoner. 'But let me go. I don't have to be jammed right up against you. I can sit on the other side of the room and still hear you. I'm not deaf, you know!'

But he appeared to be. He ignored her demands and if anything his hold on her tightened, his voice raw-edged as he rasped out unforgivably, 'You need a full, loving relationship. I understand that and blame myself for not having seen it long before now. I did offer, remember?' Pressed against his wide chest, she heard the disgust in his voice. 'But not with the finesse you deserve and obviously expect. So I'm asking you to let me try again—for old times' sake, if for no other reason, I think I deserve a second chance.' His voice lowered alarmingly, sweet, soft, dark honey. 'I promise to make you forget him, whoever he is.'

Just as if she were a woman with an itch to be scratched and didn't care who offered the relief! The ball of tight fury inside Claire almost exploded. Never a word of need from him—the driven need that took her by the throat and shook her senseless every time she looked at him. Never a word of love.

But what else had she expected? He wanted her to stay within the bounds of their agreement, that was all. And if her hormones were playing up, well, he could understand that—after all, his obviously did, and he took great delight in placating them behind her back. She had never felt so insulted and degraded in the whole of her life!

The coil of tension inside her exploded in a rush of fury and she beat at his chest with her fists again, this time using every last atom of her strength to push away, and he let her go, but only so far, trapping her, his hands clamping on her hips, keeping her on his lap, an impotent bundle of rage.

'What the hell do you think I am?' Her words lashed him with disgust, her eyes narrowed scornfully on his face, her hands itching to slap him for that slow, soft smile.

'A beautiful, intelligent, utterly desirable woman.' His eyes glowed into hers, the planes of his face golden in the lamplight, softened and sensual in the dancing strokes of radiance from the flickering fire, and all her love came surging back—she couldn't stop it—and when his hands rotated gently against the swell of her hips she burst into tears because it was all too much.

He looked appalled. 'Don't cry. I never want to have to see you cry!' He shifted in the chair, holding her against his body, his big hands soothing, stroking the line of her spine, his voice gentle, oh, so gentle, murmuring, 'Leave it all to me. I'll make it better, I promise.' As if she were a child with a tiny problem that could be eased out of the way with adult common sense.

But she wasn't a child, she was a woman. And the woman in her cried out desperately for the man she loved, and, far from soothing, his stroking hands were driving her wild. Her hands clutched at his shoulders as the storm of her weeping abated, and she burrowed her tear-wet face against the rough triangle of naked skin at the base of his throat as he whispered, 'Better, sweetheart?' and captured her hands in his, dragging her upright again.

She was too boneless now, and soft, to make the effort to scramble off his lap, and she blinked the last of the tears away, seeing the brilliant silver glitter of his eyes, the near-violent expansion of his chest as he dragged breath raggedly into his lungs.

'Here—you might need this. I know I do.' His voice sounded slurred as he reached out to the low side-table and poured wine into the two waiting glasses. He handed one of them to her; her shaking fingers clutched it as if it were a lifeline and she drained half the contents as if she were dying of thirst.

Gently, he took the glass from her and put it on the table beside his untouched one and she said shakily, because the wine and her need for him had rushed straight to her head, 'I thought…I thought you said you wanted a drink.'

'Not like that.' He eased himself forward. His head was above hers now. It dipped towards her, his lips against hers as he whispered, 'Like this.' The tip of his tongue lapped her soft, wine-wet mouth. 'This is all the intoxication I can handle.'

The throaty words were a soft seduction, his sensual laving of her mouth creating a tumultuous explosion of sensation inside her that went far beyond the teasing, voluptuous tasting of her lips, and at her deep, shuddering response his hands began a slow, glorious shaping of her body, sliding from her hips to her shoulders and tenderly back again.

The slow, lingering caresses set her body on fire, eating away at her will-power, eroding the functions of her mind, and her hands curled round his wide shoulders, holding him to her, and the teasing stopped as his mouth opened in a kiss that was almost barbaric in its intensity, reaching deep into her soul, making her body melt bonelessly into his as his restless hands slid beneath the hem of her sweater, moving urgently against the soft, warm silk of her skin, enticing quivers of sexual tension wherever he touched until she was shaking with ecstasy, with the promise of still more to come.

When he lifted his head her lips felt swollen and bruised, branded by his possession, and she made a wild cry of protest in the back of her throat that changed to a guttural moan of pleasure as his hands curled round her breasts, his thumbs brushing back and forth over her aroused nipples.

'Sweetheart, you belong to me. I won't let you leave me.' His eyes were black now except for the sharp, bright, possessive gleam that exhilarated, enslaved her. Enraptured, she wanted to be his, only his, on any terms. For always. Trembling, she reached out her hands and placed them on either side of his beloved face, her heart bursting within her under the magic of his hands as she waited for him to tell her he couldn't live without her, that he loved her, would never let her go... And still his eyes held hers with an intensity that might have frightened her if the spell of her loving hadn't been so strong. Her thumbs stroked the deep clefts at either side of his mouth, all her love in her eyes as she held his pinioning gaze.

Briefly, his eyes closed and beneath her fingers she felt the clenching of his jaw. He swallowed hard and his hands slid down, balling into tight fists at the side of her hips. Bewildered, she felt a slight tremor rack its way through his body and her hands dropped down, on to his shoulders. He opened his eyes, and it might have been a trick of the light but she thought she saw a slicing glimmer of pain; but she knew it had all been in her fevered imagination when he whispered, 'We could make our marriage whole. What's happening to us now proves it.' Again he swallowed, his throat tightening, his voice low and hard as he told her, 'Sort out the other guy or I will. Don't tell me anything about him, I don't want to know—unless he gives you trouble. In that case, I'll make him wish he'd never been born.'

His mouth went tight. Brusquely, he put his hands on either side of her waist and set her on her feet, standing up himself, looming remotely above her. And even through the haze of tears she could appreciate the effort he was making to get back to normal, but was in too deep a state of shock to do or say a single thing as he said gently, 'Right now I want you desperately. But we'll both have to wait until you've done what you have to do. Write him a letter.' The wide, hard shoulders lifted grimly, but he was almost smiling as he added, 'You can't disguise how much you want me. And I'll make it better than good for you, I promise.' He brushed the back of his hand lightly over her rigid face. 'But for now I'll make supper and tomorrow we'll get things sorted.'

He went through into the kitchen as if nothing had happened, as if she hadn't seen a glimpse of heaven then had the door to paradise slammed in her face.

Shakily, she refilled her wine glass and sipped slowly, watching the fire go out. She was too drained of energy now to overcome her inertia and cross the room to do anything about it.

So nothing had changed. He still believed she was starved of sex, needed a man. Any man. So he had offered himself, like a stud, anything to keep her content and make her stay.

'You belong to me', he had said. 'I won't let you leave'. As far as he was concerned, possession was ten-tenths of the law. She suited him and he wasn't letting her go, no matter what it took. He would even overlook the trifling business of a lover in the background, so long as she gave him the push. And she, poor fool, had simply hung around, letting him take the seduction scene as far as he thought necessary, without putting himself to the trouble of going all the way, waiting to hear the words of love which would never come.

He didn't love her and never would and that made her hate him almost as much as she hated herself for being so stupid.

The smell of grilling steak made her feel ill. Dragging herself to the doorway, she told him woodenly, 'I don't feel like eating. I'm going to bed. See you in the morning.'

And she would, just to say goodbye.

She didn't sleep. She couldn't. And she didn't hear him go to his room, but then she wouldn't. Her mind was frozen, on hold. If she allowed herself to think, to feel, she would probably go to pieces, remembering the flickering instant of time when she had believed, truly believed, that he was about to confess his love for her. Or she might truly absorb the injustice he'd done her, the way he'd implied that all she needed to keep her sweet and under his thumb was a romp between the sheets now and again. And if she really let herself think about that insult she might find herself sticking a knife between his ribs as he slept.

So she didn't think at all. She packed methodically then sat on the edge of the bed, huddled beneath the duvet, watching the window until the coming of dawn obliterated the reflection of her small, pale face.

Moving slowly, like a very old woman, she brushed her teeth, ran her fingers through her hair, draped her anorak round her shoulders and carried her gear downstairs.

She could smell coffee, but Jake was nowhere around. The sound of splitting wood drew her outside. If the early morning air was cold, she didn't notice. Jake was at the log pile, the axe slashing with rhythmic violence through the air as he split the wood into more manageable sizes, and the same violence was stamped on to his taut features as he glanced up, aware of her presence. Then it slid away and he simply stood there, his breathing fast but his eyes gentling as he chided, 'Don't stand around getting cold, sweetheart. I've made coffee. Pour yourself a cup. I'll join you as soon as I've finished up here.'

Just as if everything were right as rain. Perfectly normal.

'I'm leaving.' Her voice sounded hollow. Her throat was dry. Fever raced through her blood, making her shake all over. She met his suddenly narrowed eyes, noted how white his knuckles were as his hand clenched around the heavy handle of the axe and made herself go on because she couldn't stop now. She had to go, and make him believe it. If she stayed her love would destroy her in the end.

'You were wrong about him,' she said thinly, feeling the wind cutting through her clothing now and shivering suddenly, uncontrollably. 'I want to be free to marry him. I love him quite desperately. Freedom, no recriminations. That was written into our original agreement for such a contingency. Remember?'

For a moment she thought he would come to her. Then he imposed the rigid control that he possessed in such great measure. Just stood there, watching her with hard, dark eyes. Saying nothing. Because he couldn't? What could he say to a statement like that?

'May I use your mobile to phone for a cab?' she persevered grimly, not wanting to ask him for anything. He had given her everything except the one thing she needed.

'You can't mean this.' The harsh words seemed dragged from him. 'After what happened only last night, the way you turned on for me—' The axe fell from his hand and she looked away, her stupid heart lurching.

But that said it all, didn't it just? she told herself bitterly. 'Turned on', as if he knew he could push the right buttons, make her do what he wanted her to do, be what he wanted her to be.

'Oh, that,' she dismissed, shrugging. 'Believe me, I'm not proud of myself. I've…I've been missing him dreadfully.' The stumble over her words only worked in her favour; he wasn't to know how much she hated the lies he was making her tell. 'We love each other and you haven't made it easy for us to be together.'

She refused to look at him, even when she heard the harsh drag of his breath. If she did she might not be able to prevent herself from flinging herself into his arms, weeping, telling him that none of this was true, that she loved him, only him, would stay with him always if only he would try to love her, just a little.

She walked back into the cottage, her spine very straight. He would never know how much this was costing her.

CHAPTER ELEVEN

OLYMPIA GORES-TAMLYN rose majestically from behind the highly polished, uncluttered mahogany desk and held out the telephone receiver as if it were something too unpleasant to mention.

'It's for you. Please be brief. And tell whoever it is not to contact you during working hours again. I thought you understood my ruling on that.'

Swallowing a very rude retort, Claire left her own small desk which, burdened by piles of heavy, dusty old books and an ancient thump-and-pray manual typewriter, threatened daily to disintegrate. It was cheap and flimsy, expressly chosen for those very qualities, she guessed, to remind her of her lowly station.

Time to think of moving on, she told herself as she traversed the acres of carpet. Olympia insisted it was a family heirloom, and perhaps it might have been a couple of hundred years ago, but now it was threadbare, with no discernible colour or pattern.

Applying for the position of the formidable old woman's secretary six months ago had seemed like a good idea at the time. Buried away in the Gores-Tamlyn family home—a bleak stone barracks of a place in deepest Northumberland—she had believed it would give her the time she needed to lick her wounds, get herself back together again, with no chance at all of being anywhere where she might accidentally bump into Jake.

But six months of being treated as if she were a servant of the most inferior variety, of typing out Olympia's deadly boring memoirs—which nobody in their right mind would want to read, let alone publish—and researching her family background—Olympia's maternal great-grandmother had been the youngest daughter of an impoverished duke—and the 'duke' bit was brought into every conceivable conversation—as well as organising her social calendar, which, in the time Claire had been here, had included nothing more exciting or demanding than making the arrangements for her to open the village flower show in a strange hat and giving an uninspired dinner party for five dreary people, was, Claire decided, more than enough.

Ignoring her elderly employer's haughty black eyes, Claire took the proffered receiver and that lady imparted icily, 'Grice should have my coffee ready. I shall take it in the drawing-room. When I've finished, I want you to wash my hair. Grice is getting much too rough-and-ready in her old age.'

It was a miracle that Mrs Grice, the mainstay of the mouldering old place, hadn't strangled the misery decades ago, Claire huffed to herself as she turned her back and said a puzzled hello into the mouthpiece.

She had explained to Liz and Sally about not contacting her before eight in the evening and no one else knew she was here. But it was Sally Harding and what she said sent a tide of ice tumbling down Claire's backbone.

'Can you come? I don't want to panic you, but it's Liz. She's asking for you.'

'She's ill,' Claire stated hoarsely. Of course she was; there could be no other explanation. That highly independent mother of hers wouldn't dream of asking her to drop everything for anything less than a dire emergency. 'Where is she? Which hospital?' she demanded.

Sal mumbled quickly, 'No, she's here. Lark Cottage.'

On the point of asking what was wrong, what the doctor had said, Claire changed her mind and clipped out quickly, 'I'll leave straight away. Tell Liz I'll be with you by early evening at the latest.' The sooner she got there, the sooner she could find out for herself what was wrong, weigh up the situation.

Liz couldn't be too desperately ill, she tried to console herself as she hurried out of the room. She hadn't been hospitalised and Sal was too sensible and forthright to allow her condition to be neglected.

Yet something must be deeply wrong if she had sent for her, she worried as she tapped briefly on the drawing-room door and walked straight in.

As always, the huge, heavily over-furnished room was chilly, despite it being a sweltering August day. And Olympia put down her coffee-cup and snapped, 'I'm not ready for you yet. Come back in half an hour and continue typing from this morning's dictation in the meantime.'

'I have to go,' Claire said. Her employer's haughty attitude no longer affected her. She had other, more worrying things to think about. 'The phone call was from my mother's companion. Liz—my mother—is asking for me. She's not strong, has already had one heart attack. It's not something I can ignore.'

Not waiting for a reaction, she walked swiftly to the door, then turned, tossing out, 'I don't know how long I'll be away. I'll let you know. But I think I should warn you I'll be handing in my notice when I return. I'll get in touch with the agency myself and ask them to find a replacement.'

Niggles of guilt were her uneasy companions during the long drive. Six months ago Liz had been visibly stunned when Claire had broken the news of the break-up of her marriage, even though she'd done her utmost to present it as gently as possible.

'You've always said he was the best son-in-law any woman could hope to have,' she'd said, and, recognising the note of abject apology in her voice, had tried to iron it out, affecting a lightness she was far from feeling as she'd followed up, 'And I'm not expecting you to cross him off your Christmas card list, only to understand that it wasn't working out, for either of us. Our separation is for the best, believe me.'

It had been hard, so desperately hard, to pretend her heart wasn't breaking, to ignore the tears in Liz's eyes as she'd come out with what Claire had braced herself to hear—that all marriages went through stale patches, that all couples argued, that goodwill and patience on both sides could work wonders…on and on until Claire had had to bite her lip to stop herself from screaming, from demanding to know how Liz could be so sage on a subject she knew nothing about. Her own marriage had been a disastrous failure, after all. It was either that or fling herself, weeping her heart out, into her mother's arms, confessing that their marriage had never been a real one, that she had only agreed to be his wife because he'd promised to look after Liz financially, that she'd ended up loving him more than life and had had to leave to salvage her sanity.

And that Liz must never know. So Claire had extricated herself from a situation that had been growing more painful by the moment, going to the kitchen to brew a pot of tea, and the subject hadn't been raised again, only her mother's occasional heartfelt sigh, the way she opened her mouth as if to say something, then abruptly closed it again, showing that she was still brooding.

And two weeks later when she'd accepted the job with Olympia Gores-Tamlyn, through the agency she had been with until the time of her marriage, Liz had seemed resigned to the situation. But who knew how it had affected her? How much she had privately worried and fretted about her daughter's broken marriage?

Claire knew that Liz had seen her glittering marriage to 'the best man outside a saint' as a compensation for what she considered her own failure in that area. And maybe, she thought, chewing on the corner of her mouth, she should have thought less about her own untenable situation and more about Liz's peace of mind, gritted her teeth and stayed married to the man she loved, even though she had known he would never love her, just to keep Liz from fretting…

But what was done was done and couldn't be changed, she told herself roughly. Her marriage was over and she was doing her level best to forget him. And not succeeding. Every day brought a deepening of the pain, of the regret—not that she had learned to love so overwhelmingly, but that it had been the wrong man, a man who couldn't love her in return.

Maybe if she heard from his solicitor, through hers, that he had started divorce proceedings she might be able to face the reality of it all and begin to put her life together. But she hadn't heard a single thing from him, or of him, ever since he had wordlessly driven her back to the London apartment, delivered her to the doorstep, and immediately driven away...

It was early evening when she parked the car outside Lark Cottage. The garden was alive with late summer flowers but the house itself looked sombre, closed in on itself. No windows were open to catch a welcome breeze and the front door was firmly shut.

Claire had expected to find Sal on the doorstep or, at the very least, watching for her arrival from one of the windows.

A dread that Liz's condition had worsened since Sal had relayed that worrying message, making hospitalisation inevitable, clutched at Claire's heart as she hurried up the path. And it solidified into an awful certainty when she tried the front door and found it locked.

Scrabbling in her handbag for her keyring, Claire refused to think the worst. She had lost Jake; she couldn't bring herself to face up to the fact that she could lose her mother too.

Her voice strained, she called out as she walked through into the hall but no one answered and the silence was deafening. The beginnings of panic clawed round the edges of her mind and intensified spitefully, making her feel ill, when she spotted the

glaring white envelope propped up against the telephone on a small side-table.

She reached for it, her suddenly icy cold fingers
shaking as she ripped it open. But at least she would
learn what was happening. Knowing she was already
on her way, Sal would have scrawled a message for
her. Claire could hardly bear to read it.

But she sagged with relief when her mother's neat
handwriting practically leapt off the page. Whatever
had happened, she couldn't have been feeling too ill
to set pen to paper. The relief turned to outrage as
she quickly scanned the contents.

Darlings,
I do hope my message didn't give you too much
cause for concern. Try to forgive me, if it did. And
I do want to see you, both of you, but must forgo
the pleasure this time. First and foremost I want
you to see each other, and talk, properly talk until
you've ironed things out. We've left plenty of food
in the fridge, and Jake, dear, you'll find a particularly good champagne there too. You see, I'm so
sure you'll find celebrations in order! In the meantime, Sally and I will be relaxing in comfort in a
marvellous hotel in Bath. And keeping our fingers
firmly crossed!

The sneaky old besom! Claire balled the sheet of
paper and hurled it in a corner, angry tears clogging
her throat and stinging her eyes. Had Liz no feelings
at all? Couldn't she have guessed how racked with
anxiety she, Claire, would be? How could she do that
to her own daughter? Didn't she know she and Jake

had nothing to talk about, that being forced to meet him again would give her nothing but heartache and pain?

Her instinct was to get right out of there, jump in her car, drive to Bath and comb the hotels until she located her devious, manipulative parent and blast her into orbit with a few well-chosen words! But her knees gave way and she groped for the chair by the telephone table, sagging down on it, relief that her mother was fit and well overriding everything else, making her feel exhausted after all that anxiety.

And of course Liz couldn't know how even the thought of seeing Jake again made her feel as if she was coming unstitched. Liz believed their marriage had been the love match of the decade, that love conquered all, that forcing them into each other's company would be as good as waving a magic wand.

Claire groaned hollowly. She had to get out of here, and fast. Even now Jake would be on his way, summoned, no doubt, by the same misleading message.

But she couldn't leave him to face the same anxiety she'd experienced when she'd found the house locked and empty. She wouldn't put him through that, and, forcing herself to her feet, she retrieved the crumpled sheet of paper and smoothed it out. She would pin it to the outside of the door, together with a brief apology for her mother's antics. He would be justifiably angry but he had always been fond of Liz and, like herself, he would be relieved that the elderly lady wasn't fighting for her life in some hospital bed.

Hurrying to the desk in the sitting-room where Liz kept her writing materials, Claire extracted a sheet of paper—and froze. She had been too occupied by her thoughts to hear a car in the lane outside, but the sound that had penetrated her consciousness was definitely the opening and closing of the front door.

She was too late, had lingered too long, she thought, her stomach lurching sickeningly as she heard Jake call out, just as she had done a scant half an hour ago.

She bit her lip. Much as she would have liked to be able to crouch down behind the sofa and hide, she knew such craven behaviour was out of the question. She had to face him, face the man she loved more than her life, and see the cold contempt in his eyes. That was her punishment for giving her love where it wasn't wanted.

He called out again, his voice sharper this time, betraying his anxiety, and she stiffened her spine, pulled in a deep breath and walked out into the hall.

'I'm here, Jake.'

He'd had his back to her and when he turned her heart squeezed with shock. He looked older, harder, as if they had last seen each other six years ago, instead of six months. And the cold, ungiving expression on his starkly hewn features, the immaculate pale grey suit he wore put a more effective distance between them than all the miles in the world. He gave her no greeting, asking immediately, his tone curt, 'I had a message from Sally Harding. It sounded urgent. Where is Liz?'

Claire swallowed thickly. He was letting her know that as far as he was concerned she no longer existed. But she hadn't expected anything else, had she? Silently, she castigated her mother all over again for putting her into this painful and embarrassing situa-

tion and, because it had to be done, she held out the
letter. It would do all the explaining for her. No need
for her to say a single word. He would read it and
walk out. She expected no comment.

Despising herself for the forbidden painful pleasure
it gave her, she allowed her eyes to dwell on the
honed, hard features as he read the words Liz had
written, and apart from an obvious tightening of his
tough jaw the import made no impression. She deeply
envied his control. Or maybe control didn't come into
it. Maybe he had so successfully wiped her out of his
life that the crazy schemes of an old lady to bring
them together again couldn't even raise a flicker of
annoyance for the way she had interrupted his day,
wasted a few hours of his precious time.

'So you didn't tell her the truth?' he drawled
coldly, dropping the letter down by the phone, and
Claire's pulses leapt with shock. She'd convinced herself that he would simply walk away. He wouldn't
want a post-mortem. She had said everything that
needed saying when she'd told him about the other
man.

'How could I?' she asked jerkily, instinctively
wrapping her arms around her slender body. 'Her own
marriage was so awful. She thought ours was wonderful. How could I disillusion her and tell her the
truth—that it had never been anything other than a
cold-blooded commercial arrangement?'

'I meant the truth about the ending of it,' he countered dismissively. 'The other man. The man you
couldn't live without. I'm surprised you haven't done
anything about it. I take it you still want to marry
him?'

His tone of indifference was frightening. She was shaking inside, and what could she say? Tell him more lies? She simply couldn't. She shrugged helplessly but he didn't let it go, his cruelty uncompromising as he clipped out, 'But you don't need to go through a wedding ceremony to have all the fun, do you? I had ample evidence of that during the final weeks of our—' his hesitation was minute '—arrangement. Is that why you look so drawn? Why you've lost weight? Doesn't he let you get any sleep at all?'

Stung, she retorted savagely, 'Pot calling the kettle black? I don't suppose you've changed your habits and missed out on your fun! Still keeping the *principessa* in a darkened cupboard, are you? Or have you grown bored and moved on to some other glitzy bimbo?'

For six long, hateful months her image had been just about the last thing that had entered her head. But his deliberately unkind comments on her appearance made her suddenly aware of her body beneath the severely styled saxe-blue lightweight linen suit she'd been wearing when that worrying message from Liz had come through. Once elegantly slender, she was now gaunt, and she could well imagine how the months of unremitting heartache had taken their toll, making her look drawn and exhausted.

Her blistering come-back drew a flash of silver anger from those narrowed eyes but then he shrugged those impressively wide shoulders and pushed his hands in the pockets of his narrow-fitting trousers.

'It's too late to rake over the past,' he told her bleakly. 'And it's too damned hot to fight. I could use a drink. I dropped everything, walked out of a meet-

ing, when I received Sal's cryptic message. Shall I
make it, or will you?'

He was moving towards her, heading for the tiny
kitchen. She retreated backwards as he advanced, the
coward in her making her want to put as much distance between them as possible.

Scurrying to one of the cupboards, she bent down
to fish out the coffee-maker and swayed dizzily, stum-
bling, putting a hand out against the work surface to
stop herself from falling, and his big, impatient hands
were on her shoulders in a split-second, pushing her
on to a chair, withdrawing with insulting rapidity—
as if he couldn't bear to touch her at all—as he instructed brusquely, 'Sit down before you fall down.
I'll make coffee; you look all in.'

And whose fault was that? she wondered numbly,
watching with dazed eyes as he flung open windows
to let in the welcome, fresher evening air, then dealt
with the filter machine. She loved him so much and
loving him had forced her to leave him, and his attitude told her quite plainly that he held in her contempt, that her present frailty was regarded as a nuisance, enough to draw a couple of scathing
comments, and that was all.

Perspiration was beading her forehead yet she shivered convulsively as Jake put a mug of steaming coffee on the table in front of her. He gave her a narrow-
eyed stare then turned to the fridge. Within moments
he had assembled the makings of a meal—a golden-
brown cold roast chicken, a salad Sal must have prepared before they left.

He shrugged out of his suit jacket and draped it
over the back of a chair, rolling up the sleeves of his

crisp white shirt, and she looked away quickly, the very sight of the hair-roughened, olive tones of his skin making every pulse beat cry out with longing.

She would swallow some of her coffee, make an excuse and leave. She couldn't take much more of this torture. She reached for her mug and watched him carving the chicken, putting two finely cut slices of white meat on a plate and sliding it towards her.

Shaking her head, she pushed the plate away with a shaky forefinger, took a mouthful of coffee and heard the clatter as he flung down the knife in exasperation.

'You have to eat, dammit!'

Raising her eyes to him, she tried to tell him she wasn't hungry, but the words wouldn't come. She was too churned up inside to force anything down. His mouth was a hard, compressed line and she shook her head again in sheer perplexity. Why should he care whether she ate or not? As far as he was concerned she was beneath contempt.

'What are you trying to do to yourself?' he asked bitterly. 'Or, perhaps more to the point, what is he doing to you?'

She frowned, not understanding, and then she remembered her fictional lover and felt herself go impotently scarlet. She had got herself caught up in the web of deceit she had woven and there was no way out.

He turned brooding eyes on her, his voice tight as he lashed out, 'The bastard's hurt you, hasn't he? And don't lie; it's written all over you. You should have stayed with me. I would never have let you down. I loved you, dammit!'

He turned and stalked across the room, his back firmly to her as he stared from one of the windows. She watched him, frowning. She had misheard him, misunderstood him. She couldn't allow herself that much hope. But, to be absolutely sure, she asked him to repeat himself, and his shoulders went rigid, the tense line of his shoulders telling how hard he was fighting to keep in control as he said cynically, 'That I loved you? Why? Does hearing me say it give you a kick?'

Her heart gave a terrifying leap and she put a hand to her breast to steady it, her voice shaky, still not quite able to believe what she was hearing as she reminded him, 'You were having an affair with that Italian woman—still are, as far as I know—so how could—?'

'La Giancetti? Hilarious, isn't it?' he cut in, turning, his mouth curving in a humourless smile. 'Your obvious jealousy when you pointed out that press photograph gave me my first real hope. She's the complete extrovert, incorrigibly high-spirited. When that picture was taken she was telling me how much she'd enjoyed the opera. The man in the background is her father. I'd opened business negotiations with him and his senior partner, Lungarotti, regarding the sale of Harlow's, and we'd all attended the opera together. You would have been there too if you hadn't cried off.'

He turned back to the window and his voice was so low that she had to strain to hear it. 'But you had cried off. While we were in the States you told me you were too exhausted to face the trip to Rome. I could see the strain on your face. And it hit me like a bombshell. I loved you. It had been coming on since I'd first set eyes on you and I'd been too stupid to see what was happening. It was then I decided to cut down drastically on my holdings. The life we led, the pace I set, was wearing you out. I was going to take things easily, try to make you fall in love with me, and when I saw you were jealous of Lorella I thought I stood a chance. So I said nothing to deny the rumour; I even turned the knife a little. You're highly intelligent; I knew it wouldn't be long before you worked out why you were jealous, admitted you cared for me, even if only a little. I set about buying a home for us—Harnage, if you remember.' His mouth twisted. 'And suggested we make our marriage a real one, set out to prove I could make you want me physically. What I didn't bargain for was the other man. Not at first.

'When I cut short my stay in Rome,' he told her bleakly, 'getting back to London as quickly as I could because I was worried about you, and found you on the phone, calling someone "darling" and saying you'd meet up soon, that I was still away, and no, you hadn't broken the news to me yet, I was deeply suspicious, agonisingly jealous, but told myself I was being paranoid—the reaction of a man deeply in love for the first time in his life, unsure of himself for the first time in his life.'

'Oh, Jake…' Claire pushed herself unsteadily to her feet, her huge eyes swimming with tears. He had loved her all this time, and she hadn't known it. The lies, the deceit, had all been for nothing, hurting them both. She still couldn't quite believe this was happening. She needed to go to him, to fall in his arms and confess how much she loved him, but he stopped her in her tracks, his voice brutal as he bit out, 'Don't! I can do without your pity. I lost out to that bastard but I can live with it. It's not the end of the world, so you can save your pretty speeches. I don't need them.'

Her fist went to her mouth to push back a sob of sheer wretchedness. Her darling didn't understand. He had talked of loving her, but it had all been in the past tense. He was an expert at cutting his losses. And now he looked as if he loathed her, she realised weakly. But he would never understand unless she explained, so she said thickly, 'Jake, I lied. There never was another man. I made him up.' Her voice wobbled dangerously. She was shaking all over. He looked as if he would like to kill her. 'The interrupted phone calls, my unexplained absences, the frilly knickers—everything. All lies. To make you believe there was another man. I knew it was the only way to make you release me from that agreement. I had to get away, I—'

'Was I so obnoxious to you?' he interrupted savagely. 'If what you say is true, then that has to be the case.' He reached for his jacket, his eyes like grey stones, flat and lifeless. 'As soon as Liz became financially independent you couldn't wait to get away from my distasteful presence, so you lied, played tricks, hurt me beyond bearing, all the while laughing at my attempts to prove I could be a good husband— one who was even prepared to forgive and forget your little fling!' He shrugged into his jacket, not looking at her. 'I wonder why it took me so many years to realise what a fool I am? But don't let it worry you;

I'm a survivor.' He walked to the door. Turned and faced her for a bleak, final second. 'I'll get things moving on the divorce. I don't want you bearing my name. As far as I'm concerned, you're dead history.'

And he walked away.

CHAPTER TWELVE

SHOCK paralysed Claire for long blank moments. Wide eyes stared at the space where he had been. And then a surge of white-hot anger flooded her bloodstream and sent her racing out of the cottage, down the twilit path.

How dared he? Who the heck did he think he was? How dared he treat her like a worm, not fit to carry the Winter family name?

He'd said he'd once loved her. He couldn't have done. He wouldn't be able to treat her this way if he had! She had opened her heart to him, poured out her soul, confessed to those shameful lies, and all she had gained in recompense had been contempt and scorn.

She would see him in hell before she allowed him to walk out on her this way!

His car was parked behind hers in the lane. He was unlocking it, not hurrying. He didn't seem desperate to get away. He had the set, arrogant features of a man who had just emerged from a distasteful episode, determinedly unscathed, had put it firmly behind him, not allowing himself a single regret, and was ready to get on with his life, in his own time, on his own terms.

At that moment she hated him. Hated him with a violence she had never believed herself capable of. She bounced out of the gate like a whirlwind, snatching his arm, her fingers digging into the hard flesh and bone beneath the immaculate suiting.

'Don't walk away from me like that!' she spat. 'Don't treat me like dirt!'

He barely moved, his features unyielding as his shuttered eyes dropped from her furious ashen face to the pale fingers that were gripping his arm. Disdainfully, he dislodged them, one by one, insulting her with his total lack of involvement on any level whatsoever. And when the last gripping finger had been prised away he dropped her hand with cool contempt, and without a split-second's thought she brought it up, stinging through the air, all her weight behind her as she slapped his arrogant face.

The ringing retort was followed by an utter, deadly silence, the blistering glitter of his eyes penetrating the dusky evening light. Claire held her breath, appalled by what she'd done, stunned and overwhelmed by it. She had never used physical violence against anyone in her entire life.

And then everything inside her broke at once and she covered her stricken face with her hands, distraught sobs tearing at her chest, racking her too slender frame. She didn't think her heart was capable of containing so much abject misery without exploding, shattering into a million pieces.

When she felt his hands on her shoulders she made an instinctive, desperate attempt to get away, to crawl back into the cottage and weep until there were no tears left in the universe and then, and only then, begin the long painful process of putting herself back together again.

But the pressure of his hands increased, defeating

her, and she hung her head with beaten shame, fighting against the loss of control, the tears that were pouring down her face.

'Don't cry,' he muttered harshly. 'I told you before, I can't bear to see you cry.'

'I can't help it,' she howled. 'You hate me. I can't take that. I didn't mean to hit you. I was hitting your contempt. I might deserve it, but I'm not strong enough to take it.'

'Claire…' His arms wrapped round her. 'I don't hate you, and I probably deserved that slap.' He sounded weary, as if something had got through all his impeccable defences, defeated him, too. And his iron control was getting thin round the edges; she could feel his big body trembling against hers.

Blinking away the tears, she put her hands flat against the wide span of his shoulders and tried to push him away. Whatever else she deserved, it wasn't the torturing agony of being held so closely against him, and his arms fell away immediately, as if he deeply regretted the quixotic impulse that had made him try to comfort her.

'I was too harsh,' he said flatly. 'I apologise. I found the idea of you deliberately setting out to lie to me, deceive me, abhorrent. The honesty, the closeness we'd had had been something infinitely precious.' He stepped away, putting more distance between them. 'If you'd told me the truth, explained that you couldn't bear to breathe the same air, to be in the same room, let alone share my name, I would have let you go immediately. There would have been no need to go to such lengths, believe me. I may be impossible, but I'm not a monster.'

He turned back to his car and somewhere in the warm, dark night an owl hooted—a poignant, mournful sound that tore at Claire's aching heart—and she said thickly, 'You're a fool! It wasn't like that! I lied because I could see no other way out. Are you too stupid to understand? I was in love with you, you big ape! And married to your work—not you. And I thought you'd got a mistress—you never once denied it. And even when you suggested we make our marriage a real one I knew it was only because you wanted to make sure I stayed on, running around after you as usual. You were devious and tricky. Even when I'd told you I wanted our arrangement to end and offered to advertise my position, you said you'd already found a replacement—just to torment me. You had no intention of losing my invaluable services. So I had to resort to deception. There was no other way. I couldn't stay with you, loving you, knowing you didn't love me, thinking about your mistresses—and—well, everything,' she finished lamely, sniffing, belatedly wishing a final spurt of rage hadn't led her into that tirade.

Because he still had his back to her. He hadn't moved a muscle. He was bored. He had believed himself in love with her, once. Just for a little while. But her lies had killed all that. The reasons behind them didn't matter. His own integrity wouldn't let him love a liar.

Her shoulders slumping, she walked silently back to the cottage, closing the door behind her and leaning against it wearily. She had fouled up, and how. Ruined her future and tainted her past.

Spent and drained, she pushed herself away from

the support of the door just as it opened behind her. He had come back to torment her, she decided dully, too emotionally exhausted to do anything other than hold herself rigid, trying to contain her grief. Torment her with the cold comfort of his pity. His deeply ingrained sense of duty must have forced him to make sure she was all right. Make sure you eat something, he would tell her. You're too upset to drive, so stay here tonight. It was too much to ask her to bear, she thought wildly. She didn't want his pity, his disinterested concern!

But he simply spoke her name, with a soft warmth that lapped her body with delight, and, not knowing whether she was dreaming or not, making things up because she wanted them to be true, she melted against him when he pulled her into his arms.

'For an intelligent woman you can be impossibly stupid,' he murmured against her hair. 'Of course there wasn't a replacement; how could there have been? You're irreplaceable, my darling. I was so sure, at the time, that I could persuade you to stay, persuade you with love to stay with me, be my true wife. Why do you think I kept the negotiations for Harnage Place such a secret? I wanted to surprise you, overwhelm you—it was to be my second wedding anniversary gift to you. And why do you think we were going through all those reports so minutely, selling great chunks of my holdings, if not because I wanted to off-load the bulk of my business responsibilities, giving me time to put down roots with you?'

'Oh, Jake!' She wrapped her arms around his neck, lifting her face to his, drowning in his steadfast eyes.

'You haven't stopped loving me, have you? Tell me you haven't!'

Her arms tightened. She was holding on for dear life. Even if this was a dream, she had no intention of letting it go. And her heart soared as he answered her thickly, 'Never for a single moment. I've lived in hell these past six months. Missing you with every breath I took, aching for you, thinking of you with that other guy...'

'I'm sorry—I'm sorry—I'll never be able to say it often enough!' she cried. 'He never existed—loving you, how could I have looked at another man?'

He cupped her face with his hands. 'No more tears,' he said softly. 'I accept the lion's share of the blame. Even when all the evidence pointed to your having a lover I was too bloody arrogant to allow the possibility of losing you into my head.' He touched her lips gently with his and her body melted as she heard the deep passion in his voice. 'We had so much going for us, you and I. And I'd discovered, to my half-crazy joy, that when I touched you you went up like a torch. I could make you want me, so it followed that I could make you love me—or so I reasoned in my arrogance. I wouldn't lose you to any man. I should have told you how I felt, laid my soul bare and placed my heart at your feet—allowed you to make your own decisions.' His mouth quirked, disarming her. 'But humility had never been my strong point—'

'Past tense?' she injected, not believing it for a second. And he smiled down at her, his silver eyes soft with love.

'Deeply past,' he grinned. 'And to prove it I humbly ask if you will be my true wife, stay with me always, love me forever.'

'You know I will.' She sighed contentedly, snuggling up to him like a happy little cat. 'But aren't you forgetting something?'

His hands were stroking her back, his body hardening against hers, and his voice was thick as he said roughly, 'So remind me, witch.'

'Aren't you supposed to kiss the bride?' she murmured shakily, her whole body on fire, her mind spinning in orbit because his love had been all she had ever craved. And now she had it and it all seemed too impossibly beautiful to be true.

And then there was no room in her dizzy head for any thoughts at all as he covered her mouth and kissed her until she felt herself dissolve right into him, and she felt all his magnificent control begin to disappear as his body shook with the intensity of his desire. She knew now that when he'd called a halt that night in the mountain cottage he'd been giving her choices, refusing to seduce away her right to make her own decision.

'You'll never know how much I love you,' she murmured breathlessly against the possession of his mouth, and he assured her hoarsely,

'I will, my darling. You are about to show me.' And he lifted her into his arms, mounting the stairs, no trace left in him of that very short-lived humility as he told her, 'We are both going to show each other, beyond any shadow of doubt. And then—' he set her gently down on her feet in the room she had always used when staying here '—when we've got our breath back, my love, we'll talk about our wonderful future.'

Tenderly, he undressed her, his adoring eyes darkening as he stated, 'And feed you up. You need pampering and cosseting.' His hands stroked her too slender body, hardly touching, as if afraid she would break.

She trembled, her voice uncertain as she whispered, 'Please don't tell me you hate skinny women!' trying to turn it into a joke, then sighing with joy as he buried his head against her throbbing breasts and said raggedly, 'I love you so much—so very much. You are my life.'

Dawn was breaking and they were curled up against the pillows, each drowning in the eyes of the other, drowning in love, in the bright joy of finding each other, and Jake leaned forward and tenderly pushed her damp hair away from her forehead, his voice drowsy as he instructed, 'Stay right where you are. We need to build up our strength. That scheming mother of yours will have enough sense to stay away for another twenty-four hours, at least. I'll fix us some food and then we'll see if we can't lose our breath all over again.'

Her drowsy eyes revelled in his perfect, unashamed nakedness as he rolled off the bed and walked out of the room, and she held out loving arms to him when he walked back in, champagne and two glasses in one hand, a plate of thickly cut chicken sandwiches in the other, and as he slid in beside her she mentally composed the note she'd leave for Liz: We drank the champagne. Thank you.

'Later, wicked one!' He untwined her arms, plumping up the pillows and lifting her up against them.

'Now we eat. And talk.' He handed her a sandwich and bit into his own. 'I keep only a few enterprises going. Just enough to keep our hands in. And if you don't want to wear your PA hat, then throw it away. I'll hire that keen young family man you babbled about. After all—' his eyes smiled sinfully into hers '—you'll be around to buy my shirts. And there'll be so much more for us to do—furnishing Harnage exactly as we want it, playing with our children, playing with our conservatory—you did love it, didn't you, sweetheart?'

'Every inch,' she said truthfully, remembering how close they'd come to making love in that lush, exotic place, recalling how much pain they'd both had to go through before they'd each admitted their love.

But she wasn't going to think about that time and her eyes smiled into his as he handed her a glass of the foaming wine and sipped from his. 'To you, Mrs Winter, my dearest love. And while I remember…' He put his glass aside. 'Liz told me you were working, for a writer, some woman or other.'

'You knew where I was?' She wrinkled her nose at him and the bubbles. Liz had to have told him, and she'd promised faithfully—

'Not where. Only that you were working, and who for. Liz said she'd agreed not to tell me where you were, but told me she would, if I asked.'

But his pride, and his pain, hadn't let him ask. So Liz had taken matters into her own hands. Claire forgave her, utterly, whole-heartedly.

'You were living in, I believe?' And at her affirming nod he dictated, 'Then tomorrow we drive up and collect your things.'

'I'm supposed to work a month's notice,' she said sweetly, her eyes sparkling at him over the rim of her glass.

'Not allowed,' he said firmly, and she put her half-finished food and drink aside and slid into his waiting arms, sparing a tiny, flickering, pitying thought for the formidable Olympia Gores-Tamlyn.

In Jake Winter she would at last have met her match. More than her match.

'You'll break the news to her for me, won't you, my darling?'

And she drowned his murmur of assent with a series of tiny, teasing kisses that took them on the pathway to heaven again.

MILLS & BOON®

Makes any time special™

Mills & Boon publish 29 new titles every month. Select from...

Modern Romance™   Tender Romance™

Sensual Romance™

Medical Romance™   Historical Romance™

MAT2

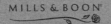

experience the fantasy...

Arabian Nights

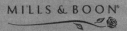

Modern Romance™

SEDUCED BY THE BOSS *by Sharon Kendrick*

Dan, Megan's boss, insisted she pretend to be his lover
to ward off a girl with an obsessive crush on him. But
after sharing a room—and a bed—they found it
impossible to stop their pretend romance when they
returned to work…

THE MISTRESS SCANDAL *by Kim Lawrence*

Ally is reminded of her night of intense passion with Gabe
every time she looks at her beautiful baby. Then a
coincidence reunites the lovers and Gabe is astonished to
discover that he's a father—and that he wants Ally back…

THE UNMARRIED FATHER *by Kathryn Ross*

Melissa had agreed to pose as Mac's partner to help
him secure a business contract. But after spending time
with him and his adorable baby daughter, Melissa
wished their deception could turn into reality…

A DARING DECEPTION *by Amanda Browning*

Rachel had been in love with Nathan for two years—
and was determined to change his misconception that
she was a gold-digger. Now the perfect opportunity:
they were to undertake a daring deception…and that
meant a weekend in each other's company!

On sale 4th August 2000

*Available at most branches of WH Smith, Tesco,
Martins, Borders, Easons, Volume One/James Thin
and most good paperback bookshops* 0007/01b

S H A R O N

Sala

He couldn't forget. She couldn't remember.

Frankie Legrand's last two years are lost in
the black hole of her memory.
But the answers are waiting in the shadows—
along with a dangerous man who wants her
for his own. But he's going to have to get
past an indomitable force:
Clay LeGrand's love for his wife.

Remember Me

MIRA® **Published 21st July 2000** M186

JASMINE CRESSWELL

THE INHERITANCE

A disk. A simple disk that named names…

That was Isabella Joubert's inheritance from her
father. And then her home was ransacked,
threats made and people started turning up
dead. Clearly, somebody wanted the disk
—badly enough to kill for it!

Published 21st July 2000

M187